All of Me Duet

Let Me Love You

USA TODAY BESTSELLING AUTHOR
SIOBHAN DAVIS

WWW.SIOBHANDAVIS.COM

Copyright © Siobhan Davis 2021. Siobhan Davis asserts the moral right to be identified as the author of this work. All rights reserved under International and Pan-American Copyright Conventions.

This is a work of fiction. Names, characters, places, incidents and dialogues are products of the author's imagination or are used fictitiously. Any resemblance to actual people, living or dead, or events is entirely coincidental.

This book is sold subject to the condition that it shall not, by way of trade or otherwise be lent, resold, hired out, or otherwise circulated without the prior written consent of the author. No part of this publication may be reproduced, transmitted, decompiled, or stored in or introduced into any information storage and retrieval system, in any form or by any means, whether electronic or mechanical, including photocopying, without the express written permission of the author.

Printed by Amazon
Paperback edition © May 2021

ISBN-13: 9798507852420

Editor: Kelly Hartigan (XterraWeb) editing.xterraweb.com
Cover design by Robin Harper https://wickedbydesigncovers.wixsite.com
Photographer: Sara Eirew
Cover Models: Lucas Bloms and Maeva Milijour
Formatting using Vellum

My heart and soul forever belong to two men.

It's an irrefutable truth that won't ever change.

Reeve is the air I breathe.

Dillon is the fire that consumes me.

How am I expected to live without a part of my heart?

GLOSSARY OF IRISH TERMS/SAYINGS

The explanation given is in the context of this book. Also includes pronunciations.

Aisling – female Irish name pronounced Ash-ling
Aoife – female Irish name pronounced E-fa
Bandied about - said
Bedside locker – nightstand
Beggars belief – is unbelievable
Bin – trashcan
Biscuits – cookies
Blanked – ignored
Boot - trunk
Chinwag – conversation
Clodagh – female Irish name pronounced Clo-Da
Cooker – stove
Crisps – chips
Emer – female Irish name pronounced E-mer
Feeling peckish – feeling hungry
Gob – mouth
He's a little nutter – he's a little crazy/wild
Hen's and stag's nights – bachelor and bachelorette parties

I was in bits – I was a hot mess
Knackered – tired/exhausted
Knickers – panties
Knocks me for six – knocks me for a loop
Leaving cert – state exams you take in the sixth year of secondary school (senior year of high school)
Letter box – mailbox
Made up for you – so happy for you
Paracetamol – acetaminophen
Permanent horn – permanent boner
Porky – lie
Press – cupboard
Pulling myself away from her is a wrench – pulling myself away from her is difficult
Solicitor – attorney/lawyer
Steady on – calm down/take it easy
Ten-dollar note – ten-dollar bill
Virgin One – a TV channel in Ireland
Wouldn't have lasted pissing time – wouldn't have lasted long

NOTE FROM THE AUTHOR

This book contains scenes which may upset some readers. If you have specific triggers you are concerned about, please email siobhan@siobhandavis.com

All of Me Duet playlist: https://bit.ly/3eu9gdo

There is a **glossary** at the start of this book you can refer to, which includes some explanations of Irish words/phrases and Irish/Gaelic pronunciations. We phrase some things differently, so if some of the Irish characters' dialogue seems a little odd, that is why!

DEDICATION

For Christina Santos, Jennifer Gibson, Ciara Turley, Bre Landers, Lauren Lesczynski, Aundi Marie, Brenda Parsons, Elizabeth Clinton, Amanda Marie, Megan Smith, Dana Lardner, Danielle Smoot, Sinead Davis, and Carolyne Belso.

PROLOGUE

Dillon – The night Vivien leaves Ireland

"YOU DISGUST ME." My sister's pretty face contorts into a scowl as she glares at me before shooting daggers at the gold digger situated in my lap. Aoife paws at my chest, her fingers creeping upward to my neck. Before Viv, Aoife's touch used to turn me on. Now, she makes my skin crawl because the touch is all wrong. Too desperate. Too harsh. Not the soft loving caresses from the only woman who matters. A woman who has just poured her heart out to me in front of everyone. A woman who just bled her truths at my feet.

But it's not enough.
She's still leaving.
To go back to *him*.

Anger glides up my throat, and a muscle clenches in my jaw, the same way it always does whenever I think of Reeve Lancaster.

"More than that, you disappoint me," Ash continues, shaking her head sadly. "I know you love her, Dil. You can deny it until you're blue in the face, and I won't believe you. You love *her*. She loves *you*." Leaning down, she puts her face all up in mine. "Fight for her, for fuck's sake."

I tried, and it didn't work. Even if I were to run outside and chase her, it won't change a damn thing. Viv is still getting on that plane to return to L.A.

To return to my *twin*.

I asked her to choose me, and she rejected me.

It's over, and the sooner my sister understands that, the better.

"It was a summer fling, and we both knew it had an end date." I shrug, bringing my beer to my lips. "The only one who doesn't seem to get that is you." I swallow a healthy mouthful of beer, hoping the alcohol will calm the violent emotional storm brewing inside me.

"I never took you for a coward, Dil, but that's exactly what you are."

Aoife drops a line of kisses on my neck, and my skin itches like I've stumbled upon a bed of nettles. I need my sister to fuck off so I can get rid of the parasite on my lap. My gaze lifts to my best friend in silent communication.

"Ash." Jamie reaches for my sister, but she swats his arm away.

"I'm going after Viv," she tells him, "because someone has to make sure she's okay." She sends one last scathing look in my direction before storming off.

Aoife giggles at Ash's retreating back. "You're well rid of that stuck-up American bitch," she says, pressing her ass down on my flaccid cock.

I shove her off my lap, needing her the fuck away from me. Ro rides to the rescue, grabbing Aoife around the waist before she hits the deck.

"What the hell, Dil?" Aoife plants her hands on her hips, pinning me with an angry stare.

"Fuck off." I don't look at her as I spit the words out,

bringing the bottle to my lips and draining the rest of my beer.

"I can tell you're in one of your moods, so I'll forgive you." She plonks down on my lap again.

"Are you fucking deaf as well as stupid?" I hiss, shoving her harder. This time, she lands unceremoniously on the ground, whimpering while fixing me with hurt eyes. "I don't want you. I've *never* wanted you. You were nothing more than a hole to fuck when I needed a release."

Ro helps Aoife to her feet, glaring at me. "Don't be an even bigger asshole. It's not fair to take this out on Aoife. You fucked this up. *You.* Not anyone else."

Jamie whispers in Aoife's ear, and she leaves, taking her three friends with her. "Ro." Jamie shakes his head. "Drop it."

"No, Jay. I won't drop it. He needs to get his head out of his ass and remember where his priorities lie."

Conor leans back in his chair, nodding in silent agreement.

"We have a real opportunity this time," Ro continues, "and he's not going to fuck it up for all of us."

An opportunity we wouldn't have if it wasn't for Viv. My brother seems to have forgotten that. "Don't hold back, bro. Say what you really think."

"You knew what you had with her was temporary, so stop acting like someone ran over your dog. You should apologize and end things amicably. Ash is right in that respect, but you have no right to be pissed at Viv for returning home when it was the plan all along."

He has no idea how close I came to giving it all up. How I was prepared to quit the band and stay by her side if she had told me she'd stay.

I love music. I love performing. I'm happy doing what we're doing, and it's enough for me because I don't want the nasty side of fame. I don't want my private life under a microscope, and not because the truth about my twin brother would most likely come out. Why can't the music be enough? We could make a comfortable living producing and streaming our own stuff. Playing local events. Building a loyal fanbase locally. But it won't be enough for Jamie and Ronan. Even Conor is champing at the bit at the prospect this A&R scout might want to sign us.

Going to America and making it big has never been my dream, but I'll do it for the guys, for my brother, because there is nothing holding me here now anyway.

"What is she doing here?" I slur a few hours later, spotting Aoife standing a few feet away, scowling in my direction.

"Ro invited her." Jamie flops down beside me on the sofa. He hands me a beer, and I drain the last dregs of the one in my hand before tossing it on the carpeted floor. "You know your brother is a bleeding heart. Apparently, she was crying in the toilets at Bruxelles, so he took pity on her."

"I hope he's planning to fuck her because I'm not ever going there again." I pop the cap on my beer, glugging a few mouthfuls.

"You should go after Viv. It's not too late," he says, glancing at the time on his mobile phone.

"Nah." I scrunch up my nose. "Ro is right. It was always leading to this point."

"I'm calling bullshit." Jamie scrubs a hand along his stubbly jawline. "There is no shame in admitting you're hurting. I know you love her. We all saw it happening."

It wasn't supposed to go down like this.

I was going to steal *her* heart.

She wasn't supposed to steal mine.

But steal it she did. The plan was to make her fall in love with me and then break her heart so badly he got a shell of the woman he loved back. My heart was never meant to get involved, but she reeled me in before I even realized what was happening. She made me feel things I have never felt before. Love. Hope. Possibility. She made me believe I was worthy. That things could be different, and for a little while there, I believed in a future where we were together.

Yet it wasn't real. She was always preparing to return to him.

Now, I'm the one left nursing a broken heart while she swans back to that selfish prick.

How does he do this? How does he always come out on top? I have never hated anyone as much as I hate Reeve Lancaster and his father. I hate them with a burning intensity that grows hotter and stronger with every passing day.

"What is that slut doing here?" Ash snaps, materializing in front of us an hour later. The party is in full swing now, and our small living room is bursting at the seams. Music thumps through the loudspeakers, almost drowning out the sound of conversation and laughter.

"Hello to you too, sister," I slur, swiping the joint out of Conor's fingers before he can lift it to his lips.

"I'm not talking to you," she hisses, pinning me with red-rimmed eyes as she crawls into Jamie's lap. Ash curls into a ball against her boyfriend, sniffling into his neck.

She has the saddest expression on her face, and pain presses down on my chest as the realization dawns. "She's gone."

"No thanks to you." Ash swipes at the dampness on her cheeks.

"It's nothing to do with me." I blow smoke circles into the air. "This was always the way it was meant to be."

She opens her mouth, and Jamie whispers something into her ear. A hushed conversation ensues, and they both glance at me as they debate something. Jamie kisses her, and a pang of longing for my girl hits me square in the face.

I force beer down my dry throat, needing to numb myself to all thoughts and emotions. Ash stares at me as she cuddles with her boyfriend, letting him comfort her, but her angry expression has been exchanged for something worse—pity. I pretend I don't notice, sitting there stewing in a mess of my own making, drinking and smoking to drown out my pain.

The rest of the night is a blur, and I don't budge from my position on the sofa, observing the party raging around me like an objective bystander. I'm vaguely conscious of Jamie and my brother carrying me up to my room at some point, and everything is a blank after that.

Muffled voices tickle my eardrums, attempting to lure me from sleep, but I ignore them. Drums are pounding a new beat in my skull, and my tongue feels like it's superglued to the roof of my mouth. Someone prods me in the leg, but I play comatose, knowing they'll go away if I continue playing dead.

"Aarghhh!" I bolt upright as ice-cold water drenches my upper torso, waking up every single cell and nerve ending in my body. "What the fuck?" I shout, shaking droplets of water all over my duvet as I push wet hair back off my face.

"Get up!" Ash says. "We need to talk, and I'm done waiting."

"Fuck off, Ash." I glare at her through blurry vision.

"You can't speak to Ash like that," Jamie says. "She's only trying to help."

I rub at my eyes, and my vision focuses. Jamie and Ash are standing in my bedroom, leaning against the wall, eyeballing me with an intensity that scares me. "I don't need any help," I mumble, pulling myself up against the headboard.

"Said the blind man as he was standing on the edge of the cliff," Ash deadpans, pushing off the wall and perching on the dry side of my bed. "I love you, Dillon, but you're a stupid fucker at the best of times."

I open my mouth to protest, but she clamps her hand over my lips. "Nope. You're going to sit there and shut up. I've got shit to say, and I'm saying it. Besides, your breath reeks, and I'm about to pass out from the fumes." She passes me a glass of water and two paracetamol. "Take those." She twists around, looking at Jamie. "Babe, can you make coffee? Lots and lots of strong black coffee. We need to sober him up fast."

Jamie nods, walking out of my room. His feet thud on the stairs as he heads down to the kitchen.

I knock back the painkillers because my head is pounding and pain rattles around my skull, reminding me I completely overdid it last night. "Spit it out," I tell my sister, needing to get this over and done with.

"I won't pretend to know the exact inner workings of your mind, nor am I asking you to tell me, but you're my brother, and I know you well enough to know part of what is going through that thick skull of yours." She grabs a towel from behind her, gently mopping the wetness on my face. "You love her. I know you do. Like I know it terrifies you to trust your heart to someone. I understand she hurt you, but she's hurting too. I should've knocked your heads together weeks ago and forced you to have a conversation about the future. You've both been skating around it instead of just talking."

"We did talk. I told her how I felt. I asked her to stay, and she said no."

"You sprung it on her at the last minute, Dil! You didn't even give her time to consider it before you stormed off all butthurt."

"She rejected me, Ash." I rub at the tightness spreading across my chest. "She was never going to choose me over him. She's been in love with him most of her life. A few months with me isn't going to change that fact."

"Dillon. Jesus." She crawls up beside me, wrapping her arms around my wet chest. "She broke up with him because he betrayed her. He let her down, and she might never be able to forget that. She came here to heal. She didn't plan to meet anyone let alone fall in love. But she did. She fell in love with *you*." She taps my chest, directly where my heart beats sluggishly. "You caught her off guard when you asked her," she continues. "She's confused, and her past is compounding the situation, but it doesn't mean she doesn't love you like crazy because I know she does." Ash grabs my face between her small, soft palms. "She told you she loves you in front of everyone last night. Didn't that mean anything?"

Of course, it did. That took huge guts, something Viv has in spades. I know I should have chased after her last night, but I was already drunk and hurting too much to think logically. All I wanted to do was hurt her, so she'd know what it feels like.

"It did, but it's too late now," I say, spotting the time on my mobile. It's already seven in the morning and her flight left at four. "She's already in the air. And I'm not sure her saying that changes anything."

"You won't know unless you fight for her." Ash scrambles off the bed as Jamie reappears, carrying a steaming mug of coffee. "Stay here. I've got something to show you." She disappears as my best friend hands me a coffee.

"What are you going to do?" he asks, lighting up a cigarette.

I shrug. "What can I do? She's gone now."

Ash returns, carrying a brand-spanking-new guitar case into the room.

"What's that?" Jamie inquires, walking around the bed.

"It's for Dil. From Viv."

I set my mug down on the bedside locker, taking the case from my sister's hands.

"Holy fuck." Jamie kneels on the floor as I remove the expensive Fender from the case. "Is that what I think it is?"

My fingers run along the curved edges of the guitar with reverence. "It's a sixtieth anniversary American vintage 1954 Stratocaster."

"That's good, right?" Ash asks.

I can barely nod over the lump in my throat. "Just under two thousand of these were manufactured back in 2014."

"They're collector's items," Jamie says, his eyes still out on stalks.

"I thought it was new." Ash shrugs, not understanding the significance of this gift.

"It basically is," I admit, knowing from looking at it that whoever she bought this off hasn't used the guitar.

"She engraved your initials," Jamie says, rubbing his thumb along the DOD etched into the glossy wood.

"Look at the strap," Ash prompts, and I hold it out, examining the custom-made Toxic Gods strap. My heart, swollen with so many emotions, slams against my rib cage. I can't believe Viv did this for me. We spoke about it one time. She knows my goal was to buy one of these at auction someday.

"Bro. She must really love you to leave you this after how you treated her last night." Jamie pulls a drag on his cigarette before Ash swipes it from his hand, stubbing it out.

Shame washes over me for the first time, and I'm embarrassed at how poorly I treated Viv at Bruxelles. I let my pain take control, hurting the girl who means everything to me.

"I wasn't with Aoife," I blurt, eyeballing my sister. "I just did that to hurt Viv."

"I know, dumbass. It was a shitty move, and you hurt my best friend." Her eyes turn glacial. "I don't know if I'll ever forgive you for that, even if you do make things right with her."

I set the guitar aside, too guilt-ridden to test it out right now. "I don't see how. She's gone, and I missed my chance to fix things."

Jamie and Ash trade conspiratorial looks. My sister grabs my mug, thrusting it into my hands. "Drink."

"What are you up to?"

"Do you love Vivien, Dillon? No bullshit. It's just us three here."

"I do. I love her so much."

"Then get on a fucking plane, and tell her that. Talk to her. Make her see she has options. That this doesn't have to be the end for you two." Ash's eyes blaze with determination. "I think she just needs to hear the words from your lips and she'll change her mind."

Ash isn't aware of everything. I wonder if she knew the

truth if she would still want me to chase after her best friend. Going after Viv is risky as fuck, and there are no guarantees. This could all end badly and cause a shitstorm of epic proportions. She could take his side when she discovers the truth. "What if she doesn't?"

"You won't know if you don't try, but you've got to hurry. Reeve is going to try to win her back, and she's vulnerable now." Ash extracts her phone from her jeans pocket. "There's a flight leaving for LAX in four hours. Say the word, and I'll book the ticket."

Of course, he's going to try to get her back. I've known that all along.

Reeve Lancaster always gets what he wants.

Except this time.

Fuck it.

I'm not a coward.

I'm not a quitter.

And Vivien is worth fighting for.

It's time to man up and claim my woman.

He is *not* taking her from me.

I will fight him to the bitter end because I love her. I love her more than life, and she's worth risking everything.

With my mind made up, I wish I could click my fingers and be in L.A. already. I don't know how much a plane ticket costs, but I have some measly savings, so I can probably just about afford it.

"Don't worry about the cost," Ash says, as if she's a mind reader. "I'll get it, and you can pay me back when you make it big. I haven't paid rent all year, so I've managed to save a lot. I'll book you a plane ticket and a hotel room. Just say the word." Her finger hovers over a button on her phone.

"How will I find her?"

Ash flashes me a triumphant grin. "I have her US mobile number. You can call her when you get there and arrange to meet."

Ripping the duvet off, I swing my legs out of the bed. "Book it. I'm grabbing a shower."

Ash squeals, and I hope I'm doing the right thing.

"Pack my shit," I tell Jamie, knowing time is of the essence. "Enough for a week."

"A week?" He lifts an eyebrow. "Don't forget the scout is coming to see us perform in ten days."

"I need some time to work through things with Viv, but I promise I'll be back in time for the event."

Navigating my way out of LAX and finding the shuttle bus to my hotel is challenging because the place is ginormous, but eventually I find myself on the right bus, nabbing a window seat at the back. Thank fuck, I managed to sleep off my hangover on the plane, so I'm not feeling too bad, despite the change in time zone, climate, and culture. My nose is pressed to the glass as we leave the airport, heading for downtown L.A.

Viv wasn't joking about the traffic, and it takes forever to reach my hotel. After checking in, I grab a quick shower, order some room service, and map out what I want to say to her.

I've got to lay it all on the line. That means coming clean about everything—Reeve, Simon, my initial plan, and how I ended up falling completely and utterly in love with her to the point I know she's the only woman who will ever own my heart. I know it might mean losing her for good, because she's going to be pissed, but I can't beg her to come back to Dublin with me if she isn't privy to all the facts.

It's a huge risk, because she'll want to run straight to Reeve with the truth, but she deserves to know he's been lying to her too. She deserves to know what kind of man she's been in love with all these years. I hope the fact I've come all this way will help. That she'll see how important she is to me and how sincere I am about never keeping secrets from her again.

I'm even willing to set aside my vengeance for her. If she agrees to be with me, I will drop all plans for revenge. Viv means more to me than getting even with my twin and my father. If she loves me as much as I love her and she agrees to spend her life with me, that is all I will ever need.

I know it's not black-and-white.

There's a lot of gray matter to trudge through, but she is all I want.

Nothing else matters except having her by my side, now and always.

Nerves fire at me and my palms are sweaty as I press dial on her number. Her voice mail automatically kicks in, confirming her phone is off. Maybe she's sleeping or it's out of charge.

Or she's already with him.

I rage at the devil on my shoulder, not needing his pessimistic comments right now. Viv wouldn't do that. Even though I was a total prick to her before she left, I know she loves me. She wouldn't run straight back into his arms because what we shared meant something to both of us.

I try a couple more times, but it's the same. Always sent to voice mail. Frustrated, I toss my phone on the bed, pacing the room as I contemplate leaving her a message. I decide against it. I'd rather speak to her in person so she can't duck out of meeting me.

I turn on the TV for something to do, instantly wishing I hadn't. All the color leaches from my face as I turn up the volume. Pain slices across my chest as the image of Reeve with Viv fills the screen. They are on an apartment balcony, and he's holding her in an intimate embrace, his chest to her back. The photo only shows from the waist up, but it's obvious they are naked. Reeve's arm is wrapped around Viv's bare breasts, and he's nuzzling into her neck, kissing her.

She's clinging to his arms, smiling like she hasn't a care in the world. Like she wasn't in my arms mere hours ago. Like she didn't just leave me behind in Ireland. She shows none of the emotion I saw in her eyes yesterday when she was telling me she loved me. I don't even look like a distant memory. I'm like a speck of dust that's there one minute and gone the next.

Pain eviscerates me on all sides, and I drop to my knees clutching my aching heart as tears sting the backs of my eyes.

The image changes to a live feed, and a reporter thrusts a mic into Reeve's face as he emerges from a high-rise building. "Reeve! Is it true you are back together with Vivien Mills?" a pretty blonde reporter asks, claiming his attention. "Is the photo from earlier today proof you are in love with your childhood sweetheart again?"

"I've always been in love with Viv," Reeve says, stopping to talk to her. He pins her with a wide disarming smile, and he's practically glowing. A swarm of reporters crowds around him, and camera flashes go off in his face. "I never stopped loving her, and I never will. She's the only woman for me." He stares pointedly at the camera, and I want to wipe the superior look off his smug face. "Nothing or no one will ever come between us again." He might as well be saying it directly to my face because I know this message is directed at me. "She's back in my arms, exactly where she belongs. Where she's going to stay."

I throw the remote at the screen, cracking the glass, as rage infiltrates my veins, replacing the blood flow. Anger unlike anything I've ever felt before races through me, and I tear through the room, ripping pictures off the walls, tossing the furniture around, destroying the curtains and bedding, and throwing anything that isn't pinned down at the walls and the windows. I can't see anything over the red layer tainting my vision and the angry tsunami sweeping through my insides, obliterating everything in its path.

I'm still in a monstrous rage when security enters my room and I'm hauled outside the hotel in handcuffs. I lose my shit in the back of the police car as they take me to the headquarters of the Los Angeles Police Department and throw me into a cell. Fury continues to pummel my insides even as the mad adrenaline rush leaves, and my exhausted body slumps against the bench. Vengeance returns, a million times stronger than before, and I know what needs to be done.

I am such a fool, and Viv has played me for a right idiot.

She never had any intention of staying with me. She waltzed straight back into his arms—into his bed—only hours after being with me. How could she do that? Did I mean so little to her that she could fuck me and then fuck him without any remorse or guilt? Because I saw zero regrets on her face in that picture. She was basking in his possessive adoration, like I no longer existed.

The walls around my heart harden along with my resolve.

Simon and Reeve are no longer the isolated entries on my shit list. I've now added Hollywood to the mix.

She will pay. They will all pay for treating me like I don't matter.

The seriousness of my situation hits home when I let my mind wander, and I realize how badly I've fucked up. It's quite likely I will be kicked out of the US and forbidden from ever returning. We can kiss our music dreams goodbye if that happens. I wouldn't care except it will devastate the guys. They are banking on things working out with this A&R guy, and I won't be the reason things fall apart. I need someone with clout in this town to make this go away, and I know just who to call. My mind churns ideas as I align both goals. It will take longer to achieve if I do this, but it's the only way.

Standing, I grip the cell bars, shaking them to get the attention of the woman behind the counter outside. "I want my phone call." I've watched enough US police dramas to know my rights.

Ten minutes later, I'm sitting in a small interview room while the surly cop rummages through my duffel bag. "This?" he asks, holding the wrinkled brown envelope in his hand.

"Yeah. See that number written on the top? That's the number I need." Thank fuck, I thought to stuff the old NDA into my bag before I left home. I've held on to it all these years because I knew there might come a day when I'd have to sign it. Some sixth sense told me to bring it with me, and now I know why. It's the leverage I need to get myself out of this mess and begin to put a new plan of revenge in place.

The cop picks up the handset and gives it to me. I punch in the private number, holding the phone to my ear as I wait for him to answer.

"Simon Lancaster," he drawls, arrogance dripping from his tone.

"I'll sign it on two conditions," I say, knowing he already knows who I am. "I want five million dollars, and I need your help to extract me from a situation."

CHAPTER 1
VIVIEN

A few days after the end of SITO

ROLLING UP MY YOGA MAT, I head into the changing room to get showered, hating how quickly I lose my inner Zen. Panic jumps up and slaps me in the face, and my mind races with so many scary thoughts. It's been the same since Dillon resurfaced in my life, turning my world upside down.

Thankfully, he didn't show up for Easton's birthday party, but it didn't stop me from fretting on the day, terrified he was going to make an appearance. I have barely managed to grab more than a few hours of sleep each night because I'm too stressed to switch off. My brain spins thoughts on a continuous loop until it feels like I'm going crazy.

I shower and dress as if on autopilot, my mind preoccupied to the point I don't see anything around me and I'm not aware of my movements. I'm exhausted in every possible way.

Standing in front of the mirror, I rest my hands on the edge of the sink as I examine my lackluster complexion. Whatever pregnancy glow I was sporting has evaporated in the days since the news broke that Dillon is my husband's twin. The thought he could be Easton's father is beyond anything I can comprehend.

How can I tell Reeve?

I know this will break his heart, but I can't hide it from him for much longer. Dillon warned me not to mention anything to my husband, making veiled threats to force me into toeing the line, but he can eat shit. He doesn't get to show up and start dictating what I do and what I say.

Audrey was as shocked as me when I told her everything. She can't believe Dillon seduced me in Ireland as part of some sick revenge pact, but I believe it because I saw the hatred in his eyes a few days ago. Dillon hates me, and he hates Reeve, and he's not going to stop until he's sucked all the joy from our lives.

How could I be so gullible to fall for his ruse? No wonder he didn't come to Dublin Airport. He must have been reading my letter and laughing his head off at how easily I fell under his spell. I feel like such an idiot. Especially considering Dillon owns part of my heart to this day. I desperately want to reclaim it because he doesn't deserve any part of me.

Including my son.

God.

Tears prick my eyes, and I hang my head, clutching the countertop as I barely hold it together. A sob escapes my mouth, and I'm grateful the other ladies have already left and I'm here alone. I wouldn't want anyone to witness this. I break down; letting days' worth of pent-up emotion leak from my eyes.

I've been walking on eggshells around Reeve, plastering fake smiles on my face in the hope he doesn't notice anything amiss, but I can't do it for much longer.

I'm trying to decide if I should fess up now or wait until I have the paternity test results. I know Reeve's first concern when I tell him the truth will be Easton. It would be nice to reassure him with the test results—assuming Reeve is revealed as his father. If it turns out Dillon is his biological father, waiting will be in vain. I'm also worried about the impact this will have on my marriage. Concealing this from Reeve is a massive abuse of his trust. I'm not sure he'll forgive me if I continue to keep this a secret from him.

My cell pings in my purse, forcing me to get a grip. I'm going to be late if I don't hurry. Drying my eyes, I apply some makeup to disguise my blotchy cheeks before running a comb through my hair. My quick blow-dry means my long brown hair falls in unstructured waves over my shoulders, but I have zero fucks to give right now. My pretty summer dress highlights my blossoming bump, and I run my hands over my swollen belly, drawing comfort from my unborn child.

I owe it to my daughter to pull myself together. All this stress can't be good for my baby, and Dillon only has the power to destroy me if I let him—which I won't.

Sliding my sunglasses over my eyes, I grab my purse and head out of the yoga studio to my car. I managed to ditch my bodyguard, but I could tell he was suspicious. Thank fuck, Reeve is at production meetings all day, or he would never have let me leave the house without Leon.

The hour-long drive to the medical laboratory just outside of Santa Clarita is anything but soothing. My nerves are shot to pieces by the time I pull into the parking lot of the small gray brick building. Dillon arranged the testing, but I insisted on being here because I don't trust him and I want to ask the doctor some questions.

Climbing out of my car on shaky legs, I draw a brave breath as I walk toward the entrance doors. As I make my approach, I spot Dillon waiting outside for me. He's leaning against the wall, looking at something on his cell, appearing at ease, as if he hasn't a care in the world.

He's got a ball cap and sunglasses on, shading his recognizable face. His usual black T-shirt stretches tight across his ripped upper torso, pulling taut along his toned biceps. Ripped navy jeans and black and white Nikes complete his understated look. Leather bands wrap around one wrist, and he's sporting a bunch of silver rings on his right hand.

Dillon was always effortlessly hot, and today is no exception. I hate how good he looks almost as much as I hate myself for noticing.

He looks up, as I step onto the sidewalk, coolly sliding his cell into the back pocket of his jeans. Although he's wearing shades, I feel the intensity of his gaze crawling over every inch of my skin, heating me from the inside out.

I come to a standstill in front of him, and we stare at one another in silence. A multitude of emotions blankets the air between us. I have so many muddled feelings when it comes to this man. Tightness spreads across my chest as we stare wordlessly at one another with all the what-ifs going unanswered.

"You have the samples?" he asks, in a gruff tone, after a few beats of tense silence.

A retort lies idle on my tongue as I nod. "Let's just do this." I want to get in and out as fast as possible.

Dillon holds the door open for me, and I enter the building first. I take a seat in the small waiting area while he talks to the receptionist. A tall thin man in a white lab coat comes to collect us, and we follow him in strained silence to his office.

My heart pounds behind my rib cage as I take a seat alongside Dillon in front of the doctor's desk. Removing my sunglasses, I knot my clammy hands on my lap, willing my frantically beating heart to slow down. The man's eyes widen as he looks at me before he hurriedly composes himself.

Clearing his throat, he hands an envelope to Dillon. "The NDA has been signed by me and all the laboratory staff though there really was no need. We are always discreet. The nature of our work commands it, and our stellar reputation rests upon it."

"I'm sure you can understand the need for extra precaution," Dillon smoothly replies, in that husky Irish tone I used to love so much, jerking his head in my direction.

"I can assure you both you have nothing to worry about. I am personally handling your case, instead of one of our geneticists, to ensure your confidentiality is protected." He shoots me a reassuring smile that does little to reassure me.

If Reeve were to discover the truth via the media, he would never forgive me.

It's just another reason why I need to talk to him sooner rather than later.

"As agreed, I will enter the samples under false names as an added safeguard," the doctor continues, his gaze bouncing between Dillon and me.

"Thank you." I remove the two sealed plastic bags from my purse, placing them on his desk. "The blue toothbrush is my husband's, and the smaller red one is my son's," I explain, almost choking on the words. "Are you sure these will be enough to extract a DNA sample?"

"The DNA in a person's blood, saliva, hair, or skin cells is exactly the same. Toothbrush samples are commonly used for forensic testing, and it's no better or more or less accurate than a cheek swab or providing a blood sample, provided there is enough DNA on the sample," he says, helping to alleviate some of my concerns.

Pulling on surgical gloves, he rounds the desk, standing in front of Dillon with a swab in his hand. Dillon opens his mouth without hesitation, and I watch with mounting trepidation as the doctor swabs the inside of his cheek. He then secures the swab in a sealed bag and writes labels that he attaches to the three samples.

"How long will it take to get the results?" Dillon asks, beating me to the punch.

"Approximately ten days to two weeks."

That is way too long. "Can't you expedite it? We can pay more," I offer.

"That is as fast as we can deliver the results. This is not a routine paternity test. In order to determine paternity in cases of identical twins, we need to examine more than just the standard markers. There is no way it can be rushed."

"And you're sure you can conclusively determine paternity with these samples?" I ask.

He nods. "We will examine the entire genome sequence which will isolate at least a single mutation in one of the twin's genetics that has been passed on from father to son. The test will confirm which twin fathered your son."

Warmth spreads to my cheeks at his words. What must he think of me? Not that that's even high on my list of worries at this point.

"We'll await your call." Dillon stands. "Thank you."

The doctor shakes both our hands before showing us back out to the reception area.

"I need to speak to you," I tell Dillon, not looking at him as we make our way outside. "We can talk in my car," I add, not waiting for him to reply, striding across the half-empty parking lot toward my SUV.

CHAPTER 2
VIVIEN

I SLIDE behind the wheel as Dillon climbs into the passenger seat. My SUV has tinted windows, so we're shielded from potential nosy bystanders. Cranking the AC to the max, I moisten my dry lips with my tongue before I turn to face him.

It's still such a shock seeing him with darker hair and blue eyes, so much like Reeve. I don't know if I'll ever get used to it. Yet he's uniquely Dillon too with that slight bump in his nose, the small scar over his eyebrow, his dimples, and the defining piercings and ink. He looks like my husband *and* like himself, and I can't wrap my head around it.

A familiar smirk curves the corners of his lips. "Did you want to talk or just ogle me?"

Snapping out of my trance, I scowl at him. His arrogance clearly hasn't faded with the passing of time. I'm trying to be mature about our situation. To not let my feelings toward him distract or derail me, but he makes it difficult. I'm so angry with him, and there's a whole lot of hurt and pain mixed in with fear and anxiety and the sheer helplessness of the circumstances.

My priority is Reeve and Easton, and doing right by them is my sole focus. I can't lose sight of that. "I need to tell Reeve, and it can't wait ten days. I'm telling him everything tonight." I cannot keep this from my husband any longer. Not without causing irreparable damage to our marriage. As much as I might want to wait for the results—in the hope they'll confirm Reeve is Easton's bio dad—I can't lie to him for that long. Every day that passes tears another fragment off my heart.

All humor drains from Dillon's face, and a muscle pops in his jaw. "No."

"You don't get to decide this." I grip the wheel tighter, as tension bleeds into the air.

He barks out a harsh laugh. "Yeah, I'm pretty sure I do."

"No, you don't!" I hiss, letting anger get the best of me. "My husband deserves to know the truth, no matter how painful that might be for all of us."

"Oh, Reeve *will* hear the truth." He puts his face all up in mine. "But he'll hear it from both of us when we have the results."

"You're crazy if you think I'll agree to that. I don't know why I even bother trying to reason with you. You don't care about anyone but yourself." I glare at him, while he swipes his finger along the screen on his phone. "Just go, Dillon. I have nothing more to say to you." That's not exactly true. There is something else playing on my mind I wanted to ask him about, but screw it. I don't have the mental capacity to deal with him right now.

"You will say nothing to Reeve, or I'll post these photos online." He shoves his cell in my face.

I gulp over the sudden lump in my throat as I scan the old photo. It's from the first night we slept together. Just after the Trinity Ball. I'm topless, wearing only a flimsy lace thong and silver stilettos. I remember that night as vividly as if it was yesterday. That he's attempting to use one of the most special nights of my life against me hurts so much. Anger comingles with sadness as I lift my head and stare at him. "Why are you doing this? Why are you twisting all the good memories I have of us? Of you?"

"Those memories are as fake as the man you call your husband."

"You're wrong. On both counts."

He barks out a bitter laugh. "How can you be so gullible?!" He snaps his fingers in my face. "Wake the fuck up, Hollywood. Your husband has been lying to you for years, but you don't give a damn."

He made the same accusation a few days ago, and it's the other thing I wanted to ask him. "What is it you think you know about my husband? Hmm? Last I checked, I was the one who grew up with Reeve. I'm the one who knows him inside and out. Not you!"

"He's known the truth for years!" he roars, his nostrils flaring. "That charade he put on the other day was all an act. How can you not see him for who he truly is?"

"I know who Reeve is! I was there when he found out about you, and he's not acting!"

"Why do you think Simon Lancaster looked me up at seventeen?"

My brow puckers in confusion. "We already discussed this. Simon was protecting his own ass."

"Wrong." Dillon removes his ball cap, dragging a hand through his hair as he sighs. "Reeve knew about me, Viv. He's the one who sent Simon to buy my silence."

I shake my head. "That is ridiculous! I would know if Reeve knew about you, and he didn't! He was overjoyed when he discovered he had a twin, and he couldn't wait to meet you. Those are not the actions of a man who knew." I slap a hand over my chest. "Reeve would have traded a limb for a sibling growing up. He had such a lonely existence. If he knew you were out there somewhere, he would have looked for you." I turn pleading eyes on him. "You don't know him like I do. He would've moved heaven and earth to find you if he'd known."

Dillon's jaw flexes. "He knew, Viv. Reeve was the one who shunned me. He's the one who believed I murdered our mother."

"Oh my God." I throw my hands in the air. "Can you just stop and listen to yourself right now? That makes no sense. Reeve was only a baby when his father made the decision to give you up for adoption. How the fuck was Reeve the one who shunned you?"

"I'm not denying Simon put those notions in Reeve's head, but he went along with it! Simon told Reeve when he was twelve. He told him he would find me if Reeve wanted to reunite with his brother, and Reeve told him no."

I rub my pounding temples. "That never happened. Simon lied. He said whatever he needed to say to keep you away, and boy, did he do a number on you." I shake my head again as a veil of sadness shrouds me. "C'mon, Dil. You've got to hear how this sounds."

"Your blind faith in him beggars belief."

"If you won't believe me, then tell Reeve. Look him directly in the eye and tell him what happened when you were seventeen. We all just need to sit down and work this out."

He shoots me a scathing look. "You'd like to package this into a pretty box so your perfect life isn't disturbed, but that's not how this is going down." Determination splays across his face. "I've paid the price for long enough. Now it's Reeve's turn."

I wonder if Dillon requires psychiatric care, because he genuinely sounds insane. Maybe I should reach out to Ash. This behavior is not normal.

I make one last attempt at getting through to him. Tentatively, I reach out, touching his arm. Delicious tremors dance across my skin, reminding me what we once shared is still lying dormant, waiting to be woken from slumber. "Please, Dil. Let's just go to my house and talk to Reeve. Let's get everything out on the table and sort through all the lies."

He wrenches his arm back, glaring at me. "No. I told you we're doing this my way. You won't breathe a word to him. You'll do as you're told, or I'll release the photo."

"Go ahead. Post it and see if I care. You can't even see my

face. No one will know it's me." I'm not bluffing. It will take more than that to force me into doing his bidding.

"Reeve will." He swipes his finger across the screen, moving to the next pic, showing me the photo of us I sent to Reeve all those years ago. While Dillon's face isn't visible in this one—he's hiding against my shoulder—you can see the ink on his back and his arms, and my features are unmistakable. "I'm guessing this image is imprinted in his brain the same way the image of you and him on that balcony is imprinted on mine."

Wait? What? "Why would—"

"If you need more convincing, I think these photos will seal the deal." He thrusts his cell at me, swiping in quick succession, revealing a host of photos I didn't know existed. They are all of me, taken without my knowledge or consent. Some are of me in bed asleep, and others are pictures of me laughing or goofing around, either by myself or with Ash. There are even a few where I'm reading or sketching designs on the couch in my old apartment, so lost in a book I didn't realize my boyfriend was stealing sneaky pics.

Why the hell did he hang on to these photos? Did they serve as a way to reconnect with me when the pain and loss got too much, like my photos were for me? Or has he been plotting to use them as part of his revenge plan for years?

"Say one word to him now, without me, and I'll share all of these online along with the truth of our relationship and who Reeve is to me." He shrugs, repocketing his cell as I stare at him in shock. "I'm sure everyone will be able to join the dots from there."

"You unimaginable bastard." I rub my hands over my bump as I contemplate various ways to murder Dillon O'Donoghue. "You had no right to take those pictures without my permission!"

"You were my girlfriend. I had every right, and we both know it."

"Why, Dillon? Why are you doing this?" I know he has

issues, and I get that, to a point. What I don't understand is why he's hell-bent on taking it out on Reeve and me.

"We will tell Reeve together because I want to see his face the moment he realizes he's lost everything to me."

He is delusional if he truly believes that. "Even if Easton is your biological child, Reeve is still his father." I work hard to keep my voice controlled and calm, running my hands back and forth across my bump. "Reeve is his father in all the ways that matter, and that will never change. And he will never lose me. I would never leave him for your selfish, manipulative ass!"

"You won't be the one to make that call. Do you think he'll still trust you when he finds out the truth?"

"I know my husband, and I've done nothing wrong. I didn't know he was a twin when I got pregnant. I did the right thing and waited to prove paternity." I *did* lie to him about that, and Reeve will be pissed when he finds out, but I did it to protect him. Once he gets over the initial shock, he'll come around. I'm more concerned about concealing the truth of what I know now from him. "And he knew about you. I just didn't tell him your name or that you were in Collateral Damage. Reeve never asked because you were a part of my past he didn't want to know about."

"I will sue you for joint custody," he adds, drilling me with a dark look. "He'll have to watch me develop a bond with *my son*. He'll have to live with me there for every birthday, every Christmas, every family occasion. I might not be an expert on relationships, but even I know that kind of situation isn't conducive to a happy marriage. I will make it my life's mission to inject myself into every aspect of your lives. To make you as miserable as sin. It's nothing less than you both deserve."

CHAPTER 3

VIVIEN

"THAT'S NOT how it works! You would never get joint custody! You don't even live here full-time, and your reputation would work against you."

Why is he so vindictive?

So determined to ruin Reeve and me?

I just can't wrap my head around this. It's blatantly obvious Simon manipulated both his sons. They should be working together to undo everything he did; instead Dillon is planning to destroy his brother. His *twin*! As angry as I am with him, I'm also hurting for him too because he clearly still struggles to accept and embrace love. He's choosing to hate Reeve, instead of trying to forge a relationship with his brother, and I won't forgive him if he continues on this path.

He smirks that annoying smirk I used to hate to love, and I want to slap him. "When I'm not touring, I spend more time at my L.A. house than my Dublin one. I've hardly drank since February, and I've already begun the naturalization application. My US citizenship is a given. I was born here to US parents. It's only a matter of cutting through some red tape." His eyes drill into mine. "My lawyers are every bit as experienced as yours and Reeve's. If I go for joint custody, I'll get it."

I know he will, but it will most likely take time. Years maybe. Even then, any access he is granted to Easton will be gradual and supervised by the courts. It's not as black-and-white as he seems to think it is. "That doesn't mean you'll be entitled to encroach on our family time. If you are Easton's dad, we won't stop you from developing a relationship with him or from seeing him, but that doesn't automatically give you a free pass to participate in family occasions and events. Your relationship with him will be separate from ours."

I won't let Dillon come between me and Reeve or my family. I can't stop him from getting to know Easton if it turns out he is his father—nor would I want to—but he doesn't get to inject himself into our lives purely to fulfill his vengeance agenda. "This is all hypothetical anyway until we get the test results and way too premature."

"I'm not going to argue with you over this. You say nothing to Reeve until I say the time is right."

His arrogant tone pisses me off, and I'm not letting him boss me around. "Fuck you, Dillon. You don't dictate what I tell my husband."

"I'll post right now," he threatens, extracting his cell again, his finger hovering over the keypad. "You won't even have time to call him before he discovers the whole sordid truth online. And how do you think his fans will react to this news? Hmm. How do you think *my* fans will react? They will come after you with the full extent of their disgust, and the hatred you endured in the past will pale in comparison to this." He waggles his brows, and I want to punch him in his handsome face.

I know exactly how this would play out in the media. I'll be the villain in this tale, while Reeve and Dillon will come out smelling like roses. I'll be branded a cheater and a whore, and it'll give further ammunition to that element of Reeve's fanbase who have never thought I'm good enough for him. Dillon's fans will think I've done wrong by him and lash me for it.

There is no scenario where I come out of this well.

However, I don't care about that. The fans and trolls can throw shade at *me* all they want, but I can't tolerate the idea of anything or anyone hurting Easton. While he is young, he's not immune to the impact of social media on our lives. If Dillon is his father, we will need to work out how and when to tell him. I don't want this getting out in the media and forcing our hand before any of us are ready.

Easton is the reason I need to keep this private. He is the only way Dillon can force my hand now. "If you do this, you will hurt Easton. He's either your son or your nephew. Would you really do that to him?"

He schools his features into a neutral line, and he looks so cold and clinical when he says, "Easton is a child. He won't be privy to what's being said online and in the media. I can make it disappear fast, after I've achieved my goal."

My stomach sours, and I wonder if I ever knew Dillon at all. "You're a despicable person and not worthy of being a father to my child."

Dillon reaches across the console, gripping my chin in a tight hold. "You know nothing about me or what I'm capable of as a father."

"I know any man who would try so hard to destroy a child's mother's happiness is not a good father. Trying to ruin Reeve, the only man Easton has ever called Daddy, is not the actions of a good person."

Dillon releases my face, his hands dropping to his lap. "You continue to act like you're both blameless. I'm not the only villain here. Reeve is as fucking manipulative as his father, and that doesn't make him a very good role model either."

"You're so wrong."

He harrumphs, shaking his head. "He manipulated you the second you got off the plane that day."

"You're delusional." I'm genuinely contemplating calling Ash because Dillon has serious issues.

"You're fucking naïve." He jabs his finger in the air. "Who

do you think arranged that photo of you two on the balcony?" His brows lift as he pins me with a challenging look.

I burst out laughing. "You cannot seriously be suggesting Reeve was behind that? After everything we'd endured at the hands of the media at that time? Come on, Dillon. Don't be ridiculous."

"God. He really has pulled the wool over your eyes, hasn't he?" Dillon tugs on his eyebrow ring before leaning into my face. "I saw the little statement he gave to reporters later that day. His message was clearly directed at me."

"His message was for Saffron! He was warning her to stay away from us. Besides, you didn't give a shit about me. Sending me home in tears was all part of your plan, so why the fuck do you even care?"

"I never said I did." A mask of indifference cloaks his face again. "I'm merely pointing out Reeve isn't so squeaky-clean himself. Be careful before you throw stones at me."

I deliberately ignore that comment, because we're starting to go around in circles. "Believe whatever you want, Dillon." I huff out a sigh. "It doesn't change the fact I'm not keeping this from Reeve."

"You don't have a choice." He eases back in his seat. "I tell you what. I'll sweeten the deal. I'll cancel lunch with my *beloved twin* on Saturday, and I'll stay away from him until we have the results."

That would help because I'm petrified of Reeve spending time alone with Dillon. For two reasons. One, I'm scared what Dillon will say, but it seems like he won't blab anything until he knows if he's Easton's father or not. Two, I hate the thought of Reeve growing close to a guy who's pretending to like him while plotting to destroy his life behind his back.

Letting Dillon reveal the truth to the world, in such a cruel way, would devastate my husband and hurt my son. The last thing we need is the entire world speculating over Easton's paternity before it's confirmed.

I hate I'm letting my ex blackmail me, but I don't see how

I have any option. Dillon is determined to keep this from Reeve until it suits him to deliver the worst possible blow.

Maybe he is calling my bluff and I should challenge him on it, but I'm not sure that's a risk I want to take. Would he really do this knowing he could be hurting his own flesh and blood? Is he saying this to force me into toeing the line, or is he callous enough to do it without losing sleep? The Dillon I once knew could be deliberately cruel with his words and his actions, lashing out in anger, yet deep down, I always knew he didn't mean it. It was a defense mechanism to protect himself. But he's no longer the same man I knew, so I can't rely on my past experience to guide me now.

I could lie. I could tell Dillon I agree and still come clean to Reeve, but I know if I fess up Reeve won't be able to resist going after Dillon and Dillon will then release everything to the press and our lives will become a media circus. We would have no choice but to tell Easton, and he's too young to have this thrust upon him, without building up to it.

If Dillon *is* Easton's bio dad, I will need time to introduce that information to my son in a way that doesn't upset him too much. He will have to get to know Dillon as an uncle first, and when the time is right, he can be told the truth that he has two dads.

I can't let Dillon force my hand with Easton, so I have no option but to agree to his evil plan.

Even if I know it means Reeve may never forgive me for keeping all of this from him.

CHAPTER 4
VIVIEN

"YOU MISSED DINNER," Reeve says, entering my home office, carrying a tray.

"Sorry." I lift my head from my laptop, offering him a guilt-ridden half-smile. "I know I've been working a lot, but I really need to finish this script before I can consider going on maternity leave," I semi-lie.

"I'm worried about you." Setting the tray on my desk, he moves behind me. His hands land on my shoulders, and he slowly massages my tense muscles. "You're working too much, and you've been so quiet this past week. Are you sure something isn't troubling you?"

"I'm just trying to get organized so I can stop working in a couple of weeks."

"You're only twenty-nine weeks. You can space your workload out more evenly and still finish up in plenty of time before Lainey arrives."

"I want to spend ample quality time with Easton and you before our daughter makes her grand entrance." That's not exactly a lie. I just have added motivation for finishing work early now. Even if the test confirms Reeve is Easton's father, I still have to tell my husband about Dillon and everything that has gone on since he showed up here twelve days ago. Reeve is going to be upset with either outcome, and I want to focus my sole attention on my family.

Plus, working around the clock helps to keep me distracted from the impending paternity results.

And it helps me to avoid Reeve.

A pang of guilt and remorse wallops me in the face. I hate I've been avoiding my husband, but I'm terrified he'll see the fear on my face and coax the truth from me. Dillon texts me a picture every day, and it's all I need to be reminded of what's at stake. He doesn't need threatening words. Sending those photos of me from the past works like a charm. I can't bear the thought of Reeve discovering the truth from the internet. He deserves to hear it from my lips.

Every night, I have been praying the results confirm Reeve is Easton's father. Dillon loses all power with that outcome, and I can tell my husband everything without his twin's gloating face in the room. So what if Dillon releases the pictures of me after the fact? All it confirms is I was in a relationship with him while Reeve and I were broken up. It was before I knew they were twins. Yes, some of the photos are intimate and show me semi-naked. That isn't something I want out there in the world, but it's a small price to pay to protect Reeve and Easton now.

"You're so tense, babe." Reeve digs his fingers into the corded knots in my upper back. "Please call it a night. You can eat that while I run you a bath. Then maybe we could watch a movie together in bed." Leaning down, he presses a kiss to my cheek. "Let me take care of you. I need it as much as you do."

A fresh wave of guilt washes over me. Reeve is upset Dillon seems to be withdrawing. He canceled their planned lunch meeting, and he has been reluctant to set a new date, citing crazy work schedules, but Reeve is no idiot, and he senses there is more to it. My husband is bitterly disappointed by his twin's apparent apathy toward him, and I'm partly responsible. "Okay." I clasp his hand, bringing it to my lips.

"That sounds nice." I kiss his fingers. "I love you, Reeve," I whisper with tears clouding my eyes. "I love you so much."

"Hey." Reeve drops to his knees in front of me, taking my hands in his. "I love you too." He tilts his head to one side, examining my face. "I wish you'd tell me what's wrong." Concern is etched upon his gorgeous face, and I feel like the worst wife on the planet. I'm clearly not a good actress either if Reeve suspects I'm hiding something from him.

Panic claws its way up my throat, and I stuff my tears back down inside, forcing a smile. "Don't mind me. It's just pregnancy hormones."

Reeve leans in, dotting kisses all over my bump through my dress. "Hey, little Lainey. How's Daddy's girl? Give Mommy a big cuddle, and no kicking tonight. She needs to relax."

As if on cue, our daughter delivers a mighty kick, causing my stomach to visibly move. Reeve runs his fingers over the protruding lump, his eyes lighting up at the sight of it. "Lainey is going to be a troublemaker, I think." His gaze jumps to mine as he rubs my bump. "I can't wait to meet her."

Placing my hands over his, I lean down and kiss him. "Only eleven more weeks."

"We should bring E with us to the ultrasound on Wednesday. Let him see his baby sister." I nod because it's a great idea. "Maybe we could take him to the zoo after and then grab a bite to eat?" His hopeful eyes lock on mine, and I can't say no.

"That sounds like a perfect plan."

Reeve straightens up, kissing me softly before placing a fork in my hand. "You eat, and I'll go run your bath."

"Mommy, Mommy!" Easton tries to jump out of Reeve's arms. "I see her leg! I see my sister's leg!" He points at the screen where Lainey is wiggling her legs.

"That's right, buddy." Reeve hugs Easton closer, his eyes turning glassy. "That's your baby sister."

"I love her." Easton's lopsided smile melts my heart. "I can't wait for her to come out of Mom's tummy so I can hug her. I'll even let her play with my Hot Wheels and my monster truck."

My heart swells to bursting point. This kid slays me every day. "That's really sweet, E. Your sister is so lucky to have you as her big brother." Reeve and I exchange a look loaded with emotion. I reach out for his hand, needing to touch him, needing to believe we are going to get through this, even if Easton turns out to be Dillon's.

Reeve sets Easton down in the chair, taking my hand and pecking my lips, uncaring the doctor and nurse are in the room. "I love you," he whispers against my mouth. "You are amazing." He slides his arm around my back as the nurse wipes the goop from my exposed stomach.

The doctor smiles at us as she switches off the machine. "I bet she'll be every bit as adorable as her big brother." She pats my hand. "Everything looks great, Vivien. You're on track for a healthy, normal delivery."

"You might tell her to stop working so hard," Reeve says, arching a brow in my direction.

"I'm sure Vivien has it all under control," the doctor replies with a smile. "Try not to worry, and whatever you can do to alleviate her workload will be appreciated, I'm sure."

"Reeve takes good care of me," I assure her. "He just worries too much."

"Why can't my sister come out now?" Easton huffs as Reeve straps him into his booster seat in the back of my SUV.

"She's still growing and developing," Reeve calmly explains. "Lainey will come out when she's good and ready."

"Brody says his sister was all covered in green slime when

she came out of his mommy's belly. Will my sister be covered in green slime too?" His cute button nose scrunches up, and I suppress a giggle.

"Nope." Reeve ruffles his hair, fighting laughter as well. "Your sister will be perfect when you meet her. Just like you were when you were born."

Seeming satisfied with that answer, Easton turns on his iPad, losing himself in cartoons.

"Green slime." Reeve chuckles as he gets behind the wheel. "What the hell are kids talking about these days?"

We spend a wonderful few hours at the Los Angeles Zoo despite the irritating paparazzi following us around at the start. Reeve sent Leon to complain to security, and the paps were told to leave. Some people stop to ask Reeve for autographs, while other families shoot curious looks our way, but most leave us to enjoy our family outing in peace.

This isn't our first time here, but Easton is as excited as every other trip. The Rainforest of the Americas is still his favorite exhibit, and he races across the wooden bridge toward the two-story Amazonian stilt house, hollering and screaming with sheer excitement. From the upper level, we see the eagles' habitat and the otters messing around in the lake below. From the lower level, we get up close and personal with piranhas, stingray, and other aquatic species. The monkeys and jaguars are Easton's favorites, and I snap plenty of pics of Reeve posing with our son beside the enclosures.

"That was awesome," E proclaims, holding my hand and Reeve's as we leave the zoo. "Next time, can we bring my sister?"

"We sure can, buddy." Reeve crouches down. "Want to climb onto my shoulders?"

Easton doesn't need any further invitation, scrambling onto his dad's shoulders without hesitation. My heart aches behind my chest cavity as I watch E perched on top of Reeve with his legs dangling over his dad's shoulders. Reeve loops my arm through his, and we walk toward the parking lot, flanked by Leon and a second bodyguard. The paparazzi snap photos of us as we head toward our car, but I do my best to ignore them and the painful ache spreading across my chest. This is probably the last time we will enjoy an outing as a family before the truth is revealed.

I know my husband. I know he'll be devastated if Easton isn't his, but it won't change who he is to Easton or how much our son means to him. Reeve will still be my husband, and Easton's father, even if Dillon is thrust upon our lives.

"Penny for your thoughts?" Reeve whispers, tucking strands of hair behind my ears as we wait for the waitress to bring our drinks.

"Did you imagine this?" I blurt, turning my head to face him. "All those years ago when we were kids. Did you think we'd end up here?"

"Yes," he admits with zero hesitation. "I often dreamed of this. Marrying you. Having a family and a successful career. It's all I've ever wanted." He kisses me, and I'm glad we're tucked into a private booth, away from prying eyes, in our favorite Italian restaurant. "I'm glad we're giving Easton a sibling." He flashes me a cheeky grin, waggling his brows. "The first of many."

"Define many," I say, watching Easton out of the corner of my eye. The waitress gave him crayons and some paper, and he's coloring to his heart's content. Our bodyguards are seated at a table next to us, keeping an eye on everything.

"Three. Four. Five. An entire football team." Reeve shrugs, and my jaw trails the ground. His arm slides around my shoulders as he chuckles. "Don't look so alarmed. You know you're in the driver's seat."

I thread my fingers through his brown hair. "It's a joint decision, but I'm not sure this body is up for another four or five pregnancies." Though, in this moment, I would give

Reeve anything his heart desired if it helped to lessen the blow of what's coming.

"You can withstand more than you realize. We both can. I think we've already proven that." It's not like Reeve to directly, or indirectly, refer to our past, so I'm surprised he's gone there. "Viv." He clasps my face in his palms. "You know I love you completely and utterly with no limitations or boundaries. You know there is nothing you could say or do that would ever change that. Right?"

My heart jackhammers against my rib cage, and my pulse vibrates in my neck. Are his words coincidental, or does he know something? "I know that. And I love you the same way. You have given me everything, Reeve, and I have never regretted my decision to marry you. I love what we've created together, this wonderful life we share, and I would do anything to protect our family. I hope you know that." It's slightly risky saying this, but I need to get those words out.

"I know." He kisses me, and I'm surprised at the intensity of his kiss as his mouth works against mine. When he breaks our lip-lock, he rests his forehead against mine. "You're my world, Vivien. Nothing matters more to me than you, Easton, and Lainey."

Unspoken words hover in the air between us, and I'm grateful when the waitress arrives with our food. If Reeve had asked me again what was wrong, I think this time I would've told him.

I hope I get the results in a couple of days so I can finally talk to my husband and tell him what's been going on.

Reeve's cell rings in the car on our way home, but he quickly silences the incoming call, switching off his phone so as not to disturb our sleeping son.

When we get home, Reeve carries Easton to his bedroom, leaving me to undress him and tuck him into bed.

After settling E, I pad into our master suite carrying my shoes and stifling a yawn.

"Do you want me to run you a bath?" Reeve asks, buttoning up a new shirt.

I shake my head. "Going someplace?" I inquire, dropping my shoes on the floor.

"I need to head out to meet Edwin. He wants to discuss potential options for announcing the new baby."

"And he needs to do that at eight on a Wednesday night?" My brows climb to my hairline. "We have weeks until our daughter is born."

"You know my publicist. He's organized in the extreme. He has a few potential magazine offers."

I reach around my back, my fingers struggling to touch the zipper. "I hate that we have to do this." And I'm not sure we'll want to commit to anything with the impending bomb I could be dropping.

"Here, let me." Reeve tucks his shirt into his pants, striding toward me. Brushing my hair aside, he presses a kiss to my shoulder before lowering my zipper. "I know it's a pain, but it's better if we control the situation. Giving official interviews and exclusive photos keeps the fans happy and ensures we're not giving the paps the ultimate scoop. I feel safer knowing we're managing them instead of the other way around."

I know if we feed the media regularly, we can manage them, to an extent, so what Reeve is saying makes sense. If we share exclusive news, in a manner that's controlled by us, it leaves less of a window of opportunity for the gossipmongers to make up shit too. It's hard to create bullshit when you're confronted with the evidence of the love we share and our joy at expanding our family.

Except this time is different. For reasons my husband isn't aware of yet.

More guilt darkens my soul.

"What time will you be home?" I ask, stepping out of my dress.

Reeve's hands gravitate toward my bare belly. "I won't be too late." Bending down, he kisses my stomach before straightening up and lifting his lips to my mouth. His kiss is as urgent as earlier, and when he slides his tongue into my mouth, devouring me with possessive need, I don't protest, meeting him thrust for thrust.

Reeve unclasps my bra, tugging it away before cupping my fuller breasts as he continues to worship my lips. I groan into his mouth, and heat pools in my core. "Fuck it." He trails a line of kisses along my jawline, down my neck, and onto my chest. "He can wait a while longer." His mouth closes over my nipple, and I arch into him, whimpering as a jolt of desire ripples through my body. Reeve backs me up to the bed, and I fall flat on the mattress, automatically spreading my legs.

Reeve rips my panties down my legs before shucking out of his clothes. When his hot mouth lands on my pussy, I almost explode on the spot. He fucks me with his tongue and his fingers, and it doesn't take long for me to reach a sensual peak. Reeve knows my pregnant body, inside and out, so it's no surprise.

We crawl up the bed, and I press a reverential kiss against the ink on his chest. My fingers trace gently over the heart with my name. Just underneath it, to the left, is a smaller heart with the initials EL. Reeve has already stated he'll be adding LL as soon as our daughter makes her arrival. If we end up having as many kids as he wants, he's going to run out of space to ink their initials. "I love you," I whisper, kissing his lips quickly as he helps reposition me on my side.

"Right back at ya, Mrs. Lancaster," he whispers, as he carefully eases into me from behind. "I love you more than words can say." He dots soft kisses along my back as he moves his cock in and out of my pussy, while cradling my belly, and it feels so damn good. Warm breath tickles my skin as he presses his mouth to my ear. "Can you come again?"

I giggle, angling my head back as he picks up his pace, thrusting into me more urgently. I peck his lips. "Don't you know your wife?" I quirk a brow, offering him a teasing grin.

Reeve stares deeply into my eyes, tenderly kissing my lips

as his hand moves to my clit. "Ready?" He rubs two fingers against my sensitive bundle of nerves as he slams in and out of me with greater need.

So many emotions swirl inside me as I nod, clinging to my husband, drinking everything in. The feel of him flush against my hot skin. The comfort of his body wrapped around mine. The pleasurable sensations he invokes in my body as he pivots his hips, driving deeper and deeper inside me. The almost pained expression on his gorgeous face as he stares at me while stroking my clit, bringing me to new heights. I shatter around his cock, my inner walls tightening and pulsing, and he throws back his head, grunting my name as he deposits his seed inside me.

Sighing in contentment, I melt into the bed, holding my husband to me in the aftermath of our lovemaking, never wanting to let him go. I nap in his arms, blinking my eyes open when he tucks me carefully under the covers. "Love you," I murmur, reaching for him. I cup his face, and he plants a kiss on my palm.

"Rest, my love."

I drift in and out of sleep while Reeve gets dressed. "Sleep, sweetheart. I'll be back later." He kisses me sweetly, and I smile at him before my heavy eyelids shutter. I'm descending into heavenly darkness when his mouth brushes my ear. "It's all been for you, Viv," he whispers. "Everything I've done was for you. Please let it not have been in vain."

CHAPTER 5

VIVIEN

STRETCHING my arm across the bed, I frown when my hand finds nothing but cold sheets. Rubbing the sleep from my eyes, I haul myself upright, glancing at the time on my cell. It's four a.m., and Reeve isn't in bed. Trying not to panic, I swipe through my call log, but there are no messages or missed calls from my husband. He has never not come home before, and he said he wouldn't be late. If something popped up, he would have contacted me, knowing I'd worry. Acid crawls up my throat as panic twists my stomach into knots.

What if something has happened to him?

I press his number on my cell, biting the inside of my mouth as I listen to it ring. *Pick up, Reeve! Goddamn it!* I try a few more times, before climbing awkwardly out of bed, working hard to stop my growing hysteria from reaching coronary-inducing proportions.

Grabbing my silk robe, I tie it around my balloon-sized belly as I slip my feet into my slippers. I keep dialing his number as I head out of our bedroom, wondering what to do. Fear raises goose bumps on my arms and lifts all the tiny hairs on the back of my neck. *Please let nothing have happened to my husband.*

I'm just about to end the call and call Reeve's publicist when I hear the sound of a phone ringing coming from one of our guest bedrooms. Another familiar sound tickles my eardrums as I approach the room, and a layer of stress instantly flitters off my shoulders.

The door is ajar, and I push it open, almost collapsing in relief when I discover Reeve, fully clothed, facedown, sprawled across the top of the bed, snoring like a freight train.

Whisky fumes tickle my nostrils as I softly step into the room. Edwin and Reeve obviously indulged in a few drinks after their meeting, and it's just like my husband to sleep it off in one of our spare bedrooms rather than risk disturbing me.

He knows my sleep has been erratic lately. He's always so thoughtful, and as I stand staring at his sleeping form, I'm almost overwhelmed with the love I feel for this man. Powerful emotion sweeps over me as I contemplate losing him. I pray he'll be able to forgive me for all my sins and we emerge on the other side stronger and more united. I've got to believe that, or I'd be an even bigger basket case.

He looks much younger in sleep, but his features aren't at peace. An almost pained look contorts his handsome face, even in slumber. Seeing him vulnerable like this hurts because I know the next few weeks are going to be hard for him. Reeve already senses something is wrong, but it's still going to come as a big shock.

Kneeling on the carpet beside the bed, I carefully brush strands of hair back off his face, pressing a gentle kiss to his brow. Tears prick my eyes as I peer at him with a heavy heart. He's in a deep sleep. Not even budging when I set another kiss on his cheek. Breathing softly, I stand and walk out of the room, quietly closing the door behind me.

Easton wakes me a few hours later, jumping on our bed, full of boundless energy. "Mommy! Wake up! Can we go swimming? Puh-lease." I pry my eyes open, smiling when I see he is wearing his swim shorts back to front.

"Sure, sweetie. Just give me a few minutes to get ready." I

ruffle his hair before pointing at my face. "And I need kisses. Lots of kisses to help me get out of bed."

Easton peppers my face with a slew of sloppy kisses, and I wrap my arms around him, holding him close. "I'm gonna kiss my little sister too. Just like Daddy does," he adds, pulling the comforter back and gently kissing my tummy through my silk nightdress. I thread my fingers through his hair, offering up silent thanks for my precious son. Even on dark days, he always brightens my world.

Ten minutes later, we are walking hand in hand along the hallway, ready for swimming. I check on Reeve, making Easton promise not to make a sound. It's early, and he needs more sleep. If the alcohol fumes still wafting around the room are any indication, he'll have one hell of a hangover today.

Easton and I take a swim in our indoor pool, and we have fun messing around until hunger attacks us both, and we get out to grab breakfast. We are both wearing bathrobes and flip-flops when we land in our large kitchen where Charlotte—our live-in housekeeper—is busy making pancakes. "A little bird told me someone was swimming," she says, leaning down to kiss Easton on the cheek. "I hope you're hungry."

"I'm always hungry for pancakes," E says, climbing onto a chair beside me at the kitchen table. "Especially if you have strawberries and chocolate." He rubs his tummy, his eyes popping wide as Charlotte slides a plate with two pancakes, chocolate, and strawberries in front of him. "Yummy. Thanks, Lotty." He blows her a kiss, making my heart melt.

Charlotte smiles affectionately at E before turning to me. "I can make you an omelet, or would you like some fresh fruit and yogurt this morning?"

I pour fresh orange juice into a glass for Easton. "Fruit and yogurt would be perfect though I expect Reeve will need something more substantial." My lips twitch.

"Oh. Mr. Lancaster has already eaten and left for the day. He said to tell you he'd be home in time to pick you up for the charity event."

I frown. "Reeve's already gone?" Prickles of apprehension tickle the back of my neck. Reeve never leaves without kissing me and Easton goodbye. He would only do this if he was deliberately avoiding me.

Something has happened, and I need to find out what.

I spend most of the day pacing the floor in my office, panicking as all my calls go straight to Reeve's voice mail. After lunch, I finally hear from him, but his text is brief, telling me he's in meetings with Margaret and Edwin all day and he'll talk to me later. His words do little to reassure me.

Later that evening, Carole and her hairdresser wife are just leaving, after helping me to get ready for tonight's event, when I receive another text from my husband, informing me he's running late and Leon will drive me to the hotel. Now I know for sure Reeve is avoiding me, and I almost empty the contents of my stomach all over my bedroom floor.

Does he know?

Has he somehow found out?

Wrapping my arms around myself, I fight tears as there's a knock on the door.

"Vivien?" Leon's deep voice booms through the door. "There was a delivery for you."

"I'm coming." I force myself to my feet and walk across my bedroom, opening the door. "Thank you." I slap a fake smile on my face as I take the envelope from him, hoping he doesn't notice how badly my hands are shaking.

"You don't look so hot. Are you feeling okay?" he asks, tilting his head to the side as he examines my face.

"I'm fine," I lie. "Just trying to psych myself up for tonight. It's hard to wear heels and a constant smile for hours when I'm carrying a giant watermelon in my tummy." I run my hands over my swollen stomach, and where it's normally soothing, right now, nothing could quell the storm rising to catastrophic proportions inside me.

"I'll have Charlotte send up some water and a snack. Why don't you rest up until we have to go?" He glances at the watch strapped to his wrist. "It's still early. We don't need to leave for an hour."

An hour to compose myself—when this envelope might contain news that will upend my world—is nowhere near long enough, but Leon is being sweet, and I don't want to worry him. "Thanks, Leon. I'll do that."

I close my door and pad in my bare feet to my dresser, sitting down in front of my mirror, staring at my reflection with mounting horror. I hold the envelope in my trembling hands, terrified to open it. This will either help soften the blow or make it ten million times worse. I'm tempted to shove it in a drawer to deal with tomorrow, but the knowledge Dillon has received a similar envelope means I need to look at it now. I know Dillon will, and I won't remain in the dark and give him additional power over me.

But I can't do this alone, so I grab my cell and call my bestie, praying she answers. Audrey is the only person who knows exactly what's going down because I needed someone to help keep me sane.

"Hey, babe." Audrey sounds breathless when she picks up.

"Where are you?"

"At the train station," she pants. "I'm out of breath because I just jogged up several flights of stairs and still missed the damn train."

"I got the results," I blurt.

"Shit. Give me a sec to find somewhere more private to talk."

I nibble on my lips and my foot taps on the floor as I wait for her to move to a quieter spot.

"Okay. I'm good now. Talk to me."

"I haven't opened the envelope. I've just been staring at it, feeling like I'm going to throw up."

"Rip the Band-Aid off, Viv. At least this way, you will know what you're dealing with."

"I'm so scared, Rey," I whisper, as I cut the top of the envelope with my silver letter opener. "I don't want anything to change. I don't want Reeve to leave me. I don't want to ruin Easton's life."

"Breathe, Viv. Please just breathe. God, I wish I was there with you."

"Me too," I admit, pulling the report out of the envelope with trembling fingers.

"It's going to be okay. Reeve won't leave you. He will be upset and angry for a while, but he loves you and Easton too much to walk away. And look at it this way; if Dillon is Easton's father, he gets two dads. That won't ruin his life. He might be confused for a while after he finds out, but you will love him and reassure him, and he'll be okay. He's an awesome little boy. He'll be fine."

"Thank you." I swallow over the thick lump in my throat. "I needed to hear that."

"I know you did, babe. You've got to remember this isn't your fault. You didn't know they were twins."

I place my phone on speaker, setting it down on my dresser as I unfold the letter. Tears blur my vision as I read, plopping onto the page with finality. Sobs burst from my chest as the floodgates open.

"Viv? What does it say?" Audrey asks as I cry.

"I…it's…I," I splutter, unable to form words over the messy ball of emotion clogging the back of my throat. Audrey waits me out, reminding me she's here for me. I stare at my tearstained face in the mirror. My makeup is ruined, but that's the least of my concerns. Grabbing a tissue, I dab at the dampness on my cheeks and try to rein in my emotions. "Oh God, Audrey," I rasp as a fresh layer of pain presses down on my chest.

"You're going to be okay, Viv. Take deep breaths. In and out. You need to calm down."

I do as she suggests, and gradually, I am composed enough to confirm what I've suspected since the twin truth was revealed. "Reeve isn't Easton's father. Dillon is."

CHAPTER 6
VIVIEN

MY HAND SHAKES as I lift my glass of sparkling water to my lips, keeping the false smile plastered on my face like I've done all night, from the moment I set foot in the hotel. The paternity results are only one of my concerns though. Reeve has barely spoken to me since I arrived. While it's been difficult to get alone time—because Reeve is the guest speaker this year, and he's in high demand—there have been a few moments at the table during dinner when we had time to ourselves, and my husband ignored me, eating his dinner instead of talking to me.

I've suspected all day that something happened last night, but I'm one hundred percent confident now Reeve is avoiding me because he's discovered at least part of the truth. It's the only explanation for the cold-shoulder treatment I'm receiving.

I wish I could drink alcohol because I could really use some vodka right now.

Reeve avoids eye contact with me as he delivers an emotional speech, from the podium at the top of the room, discussing the many ways the charity supports disadvantaged children and those removed from their homes due to neglect and abuse. Genuine tears pool in his eyes as he flicks through slides showing the various facilities the charity is building to offer an alternative home to some of these kids. Strong Together is a cause we are both passionate about, and we always attend the annual fundraising gala to throw our weight behind such a worthy cause.

Tonight is the first time I'm wishing we were anywhere but here.

I need to talk to Reeve.

Especially as Dillon is blowing up my cell, only adding to my stress. The sooner we get home, the better. I've decided I'm telling my husband everything tonight. I can't hold off for Dillon's showdown because it's clear Reeve already knows something.

It's time to come clean.

Now Dillon has the proof he is Easton's father, I very much doubt he will broadcast the news over social media. It's still a risk, but it's one I have no choice but to take. My husband can hardly look at me, and the only thing worse than the truth is fragments of the truth. In this moment, I have no clue what he believes, and that's a truly scary prospect.

After posing with Reeve and the charity directors for photos, I manage to grab him to one side for a few seconds. "Can we make our excuses and leave?" I whisper.

"Eager to get home or eager to get away from me?" he asks in a sneering tone I don't much care for.

"We need to talk, and this can't wait."

"You're right," he snaps. "It can't."

I rub my hands over my belly, fighting tears as Reeve levels me with an angry look I haven't seen in a long, long time. His eyes bore into mine, and he drops the invisible mask he's wearing for a second, showcasing his devastation for the entire room to see. Thank fuck, no one is paying us any attention right now.

A half hour later, we finally make our goodbyes and leave the room, hand in hand. The instant we are out in the hallway, Reeve drops my hand like it's on fire. Pain stabs holes in my heart as I hurry after my husband, half running to keep up with his long-legged strides.

Rain is plummeting from the sky in a heavy downpour that is most unusual for May. Reeve bristles with anger as we stand under the shelter of the awning while the valet retrieves our car. The porter opens an umbrella as our sleek black and gold Maserati draws up to the curb. Reeve slides his arm around my back, holding me in close as we walk carefully on slippery steps toward our car. At this proximity, I feel his entire body trembling, and my mouth turns dry.

This is bad. Really fucking bad, and I'm terrified I'm going to lose him.

Reeve directs me to the passenger side, and I turn to him as he opens the door. "You've been drinking. I'll drive."

He shakes his head, his jaw pulling taut. "I only had a few, and I'm not drunk."

"But it's raining and—"

"You really don't want to push me right now, Vivien." His eyes burn with conflicting emotions as he stares at me. "Do you honestly think I would drive if I wasn't fit to drive? Do you think I'd put your life and our unborn child's life at risk by driving if I wasn't in full control of my faculties?"

Swallowing thickly, I shake my head.

"Then get in the damn car, Viv."

I'm a quivering mess as I climb into my seat, buckling my seat belt with trembling fingers while I attempt to control my errant tear ducts.

Reeve tips the valet before sliding behind the wheel. Beads of rain cling to his hair and the shoulders of his black tuxedo jacket as he straps himself in. He doesn't speak or look at me as he starts the engine and glides out onto the semi-busy street.

Reeve avoids the highway, choosing to travel home on less busy roads. I stare out the window, wrapping my arms around myself as I cry invisible tears. Turmoil has been my constant companion since I got the results, and the pain in my heart is so intense I wonder if this is what it feels like when you are on the verge of a heart attack.

Reeve says nothing, quietly seething, until we're on a quieter stretch of open road, and then he rounds on me. "Is there nothing you want to say to me?"

Slowly, I turn to face him, flinching at the angry look on his face. "I think we should wait until we get home to talk."

His grip tightens on the wheel, and his nostrils flare. Rain pelts against the windscreen, and the wipers are working overtime to keep it clear. "Are you fucking him?" He takes his eyes off the road for a second to stare at me. "Are you fucking my *twin*?" he hisses, his tone elevating a few notches.

Oh God. He knows who Dillon is, which means he must know what we once meant to one another. "What? No! Of course, I'm not! Why would you say that?"

"Where did you disappear to when you gave Leon the slip last week?"

Shit. I bite down hard on my lower lip. "I can explain, but not like this, and you should slow down. The rain isn't showing any signs of stopping."

"Just answer the goddamn question, Vivien!" He slams his hands down on the wheel, and I jump.

"I was with Dillon, but it's not what you're thinking. I haven't been with him. I would never cheat on you, Reeve. Never. You've got to believe me!"

"I waited for you to tell me. It's been almost two weeks, and you said nothing!" he shouts as all his pent-up anger flies free.

"You've known all along? Why the hell didn't *you* say something?"

"Because I needed to hear it from my wife! I needed to know the trust I've placed in you all these years wasn't for nothing. I needed to know we are a solid team."

"We are, Reeve." I reach for his arm, but he shucks me off, sending splintering pain ricocheting throughout me. "How did you find out?" I ask, hastily swiping at the tears rolling down my face. This is all going to shit, and it's my fault for making the wrong call. I should've risked it and spoken to Reeve the instant I returned home from the laboratory.

"Your reaction the day he showed up at our house tipped me off, and I saw the way he was looking at you. His reaction to Easton's birthday was a major trigger."

My brows knit together in confusion.

"He said he thought E's birthday was in June," Reeve clarifies.

Maybe my brain is foggy because I'm so stressed, but I'm still not getting the point.

"We hadn't exchanged names in advance. Our identities were supposed to be hidden. I can understand how he might have recognized me, but knowing our son's birthday was reported as being in June, not May, was a major flag. I knew for sure something was amiss. Then I remembered that photo you sent me when you were in Ireland, and I recalled seeing a guy with the same kind of hair behind you in the hallway at the Oscars. Things started slotting into place. I was praying I was wrong. That it was just a coincidence your ex had bright blond hair and my twin used to." Our tires squelch as we race along wet back roads. "Until last night when I met with the owner of the private security firm I'd hired to watch you in Ireland."

"What the what?" I shout, my eyes popping wide. "What do you mean?" I splutter. The fact he went to a stranger instead of asking me—his wife—speaks volumes. But that's secondary to the main issue.

Reeve pins me with sharp blue eyes. "Did you really think I'd let the love of my life wander around Ireland without someone protecting her from harm? In case you've forgotten, you'd been viciously assaulted a couple of months previously, and I wasn't taking any chances."

"You had someone spying on me the entire time?" Disbelief lies heavy on my tongue, even as I recall the guy Dillon spotted hanging around outside my apartment one time. Dillon was sure he'd seen him outside Whelans too. Back then, I'd assumed it was paparazzi, but when nothing appeared in the media about me and the guy never reappeared, I forgot all about it.

"Not spying. *Protecting*. I hired a guy in L.A., and he found a reputable local firm in Dublin. They had guys watching you twenty-four-seven to ensure you were safe."

"That is… I can't believe you did that." Shock splays across my face. "What did they tell you? Have you known who Dillon is all along?"

"If I knew who he was, I would've thrown the motherfucking asshole out of my house the second I laid eyes on him!" Reeve yells, his voice cracking. When he looks at me, tears fill his eyes. "Back then, I knew there was a guy before you told me because the security firm sent me weekly reports."

I clamp a hand over my chest, rubbing at the sudden tightness. "That is such a massive invasion of my privacy. I can't believe you did that, Reeve. I asked you for space!"

"And I fucking gave it to you!" he shouts. "Every week when I got the reports, I wanted to hop on a plane and bring you back home. It took colossal willpower to stay away, but I did it because you asked me to. It almost killed me, Viv. I legit felt like my heart was breaking on a daily basis. I knew you were with him, and I risked losing you permanently. The only thing I could do was try to make amends and hope to fuck you were still mine when you came back. *If* you came back."

His chest heaves, and the car swerves a little when he places his head down on the wheel.

"You need to slow down," I caution again. "Please, Reeve." Tentatively, I touch his arm. "Why don't you pull over and I'll drive?"

"That day in Mexico was the day I found out about him," he continues, ignoring my pleas. "There were photos, but I refused to look at them. I knew my heart couldn't bear to see that, so I never saw any photographic proof." A tear leaks from the corner of his eye as he glances at me. "They were left out of my reports because I couldn't tolerate seeing you with him. I got trashed that day to numb my pain." A bitter laugh bursts from his mouth. "My twin was fucking shit up for me even then. This is all his fault. I found out about him, got drunk and high, and ended up screwing that psycho bitch."

CHAPTER 7
VIVIEN

VITRIOL SPILLS from Reeve's lips and pours from his eyes, and it's so unlike him. He's starting to sound as twisted up and angry as his brother. And just like Dillon, he's blaming his twin when it was others who were responsible. Simon set everything in motion. And Saffron manipulated Reeve in Mexico to aid her agenda.

Will this cycle of blame and hostility ever end?

"I saw the photos last night. They confirmed my suspicions about everything." He shakes his head, and the look of disappointment etched across his face is crystal clear. "You let him fuck you against a cross at the top of a hill in the middle of the night? And in the sea when others were around?"

Disgust replaces disappointment on his handsome face, and it makes me mad. It's not like Reeve is a prude or the type of guy fixated on vanilla sex. We're adventurous in our own way. Yes, we have never fucked in a public place, but that's only because it's too damn risky given his celebrity status. I don't like his judgy, hypocritical attitude one little bit. "You don't get to judge me, Reeve. I was with my boyfriend, and everything was consensual. At least my photos didn't end up splashed all over the tabloids and social media. You were spared that humiliation." That's a low blow for me, but I'm riled up now and seething at the sickening invasion of my privacy.

"Do I even know you?" he continues, narrowing his eyes, and I see red. He has no right to look down his nose at me. Certainly not after all this time. "Do you have any idea what it did to me seeing that?"

It's just like Reeve to try to turn this back around on me when he's the one in the wrong. "Well, maybe you shouldn't have invaded my privacy in such a revolting manner! Do *you* have any idea how it feels to know someone was watching me with *my boyfriend*? Capturing our most intimate moments on film?" Anger mushrooms inside me until it explodes. "Those photos should never have been taken! And they sure as fuck shouldn't be sitting in some pervy PI's office like a ticking time bomb." I'm enraged and horrified and feeling a ton of other emotions.

"I didn't know they'd done that because I didn't ask for it, and I never looked at the photos. After I got you back, I didn't give them a second thought." He pulls a thick white envelope from the glove compartment, tossing it into my lap. "There you go. That's all of them. Carson already got signed declarations from the US and Irish security firms confirming no other copies are in existence in physical or digital format."

I swivel on my seat, the leather squelching with the motion. "Did you arrange that photo of us on the balcony the day I came home?"

A muscle pops in his jaw, but he says nothing.

"Answer me, Reeve. We might as well bring all the skeletons out of the closet."

He looks at me with pleading eyes. "I was so scared I'd lost you. You were really upset. I knew you were in love with him. Possibly more than with me, and I wasn't risking losing you forever." Fierce determination glistens in his eyes. "I'd gotten friendly with a photographer. He'd suggested we could have a mutually beneficial arrangement. I called him that day and set it up."

Oh God. Dillon was right. My head drops back against the headrest, and I close my eyes as if that will ward off the incoming fresh wave of pain. Tears fall from my eyes, almost in sync with the drip-drip of the rain as it pelts our car. "You seduced me on purpose so the photographer would get the money shot and you'd use it to drive Dillon away."

"Don't rewrite history, Viv." I open my eyes, noticing his fingers digging into the wheel. "I seduced you because I fucking love you and I missed you. I wanted to feel close to you again. Staking my claim, and warning that prick off, was secondary." He casts a quick glance at me as he rounds the next bend. "You're mine, Viv, and that's never going to change."

I'm dumbstruck, and my brain is clouded with so many emotions. Did Reeve want me back for the right reasons, or am I a possession he was determined to win from his competition? Has Dillon been right about everything? I don't even know what is real anymore. All I do know is Reeve has been lying to me. And I've been lying to him. Which is worse? Are they even comparable? Can I call him out on his shit when I've been concealing big things from him these past two weeks? Are we both as bad as each other?

I can't make sense of the warring thoughts churning through my jumbled brain. "I always thought you stopped to talk to the reporters that day to send a message to Saffron. To let her know we were back together and to not try anything. I never stopped to consider you were sending Dillon a message too. I was so fucking naïve."

"Two birds. One stone." He shrugs, like it's no biggie, and I lose the tenuous hold on my emotions.

"Don't act so freaking flippant! You lied to me! Manipulated me! How often have you done that in our marriage, Reeve? What else don't I know?"

"Oh no, Viv. You don't get to throw that shit at me." The

car accelerates as an angry red flush creeps up his neck and onto his face. "You've done exactly the same! You should've confessed the second we stepped foot in our living room that day. You should've told me immediately who Dillon was. Instead, you sat there and let him try to make a fool out of me."

"I wanted to tell you," I cry. "I was planning to, but he blackmailed me into keeping quiet."

"He what?" Reeve roars, and I cover my ears at the bellowing sound.

"He took photos of me, when we were together, without my permission. He threatened to post them online along with the truth that he was your twin and that E…" I break down, sobbing into my hands.

"He has no intention of developing a relationship with me. He's here for you. You and…my son," he croaks.

I lift my face, staring at Reeve through blurry eyes. "We are yours, Reeve. He can't take us from you."

"If you didn't meet with him to fuck him, there is only one other reason you would." His chest heaves, and silent tears stream down his face. "You did a paternity test. Didn't you?"

I nod, swiping at the hot tears coursing over my cheeks. "He insisted on it. I wanted to tell you, but he blackmailed me into keeping silent. Then I thought maybe it was for the best to wait until we had the test results, but…" I sob into my hands, unable to keep my emotions in check.

"No, Viv. Please, God, no. Don't say what I think you're going to say."

His choked tone is killing me, along with the intense pain pressing down on my chest, making it difficult to breathe. "I'm sorry, Reeve. I'm so sorry. I didn't know you were twins! I kept my distance when I first returned from Ireland because I wasn't sure you were the father. I'm sorry I lied about that, but I was trying to protect you. I was so happy when Easton was born and the test confirmed he was yours." My cries bounce off the insides of the car.

"I knew you lied," he says, and I jerk my head up, my tears faltering.

"What?"

"You told me you'd been sleeping with him. I'm not an idiot. Of course, I knew there was a chance the baby wasn't mine. I knew you were refusing to commit to me, to accept my proposal, because you wanted to make sure. I don't hold that against you, Viv. I respect you for trying to do the right thing by me and your baby. It's why I never said anything, and if you're beating yourself up over that, don't."

"Oh, Reeve," I choke out, in between sobs, placing my hand on his.

He clears his throat and looks at me. Pain is written all over his face, and my heart is breaking. "Please tell me Easton is my flesh and blood? Please tell me he's *my son*. I love that little boy with everything I am. Please don't say he's his. I can't lose him."

I can scarcely speak over the lump in my throat. "Pull over, please," I croak. We're not that far from home now, but I can't tell him this while we're driving.

"No, Viv. Just say it. I can't bear it a minute longer!"

Tears leak from my eyes of their own volition. "You are still Easton's dad, Reeve. In all the ways that matter, he is still your son."

"Vivien," he rasps in a strangled voice. "Is he my biological child or Dillon's?"

Strained tension bleeds in the air, and the only sound is the whoosh-whoosh of the wipers and the pitter-patter of rain as it continues tumbling from the dark night sky. "He's Dillon's," I whisper, my lower lip wobbling.

"No!" Reeve's anguished cries fill the small space, almost smothering me. "No. He can't be. He's *my* son! He's mine. *You're* mine. He can't have you!" Tears cling to his lashes and his cheeks as he stares at me with the same lost, vulnerable expression I used to see on his face as a kid when his dad did something hurtful.

"I'm sorry, Reeve. I'm so sorry." I scrub at my eyes, smoothing a hand across the tight pain in my chest. "But he's still your son. You're still his father, and I'm still your wife. That won't change."

"You can't tell me this doesn't change things, Viv, because it does," he yells.

The car jerks forward as he accidentally presses down on the accelerator. Slamming his palms down on the horn, he pushes it repeatedly in a scary display of frustrated anger and anguished hopelessness. The horn blares along the dark, desolate stretch of road. Plush homes shielded behind high walls and gates are too far back to complain about the ruckus. Tall, old oak trees line the other side of the road behind flimsy fencing. Some are leaning at precarious angles; their branches battered by the brutal rain dumping from the heavens.

"Calm down, Reeve. Please. You're going too fast."

"Don't fucking tell me to calm down!" His eyes look wild as he fixes them on me. "I have sacrificed so much for you! For our family. And he's going to try and take it all from me!" Scrunching his fist, he slams it into the dashboard over and over.

Sacrifice? What sacrifice? "What the hell does that mean?"

"My heart is breaking, Viv." He stares at me with tears pouring down his face. "I don't want him near my son. I don't want to have to explain this to Easton. I can't lose him. I can't lose you. I won't. I—"

"Watch out!" I scream as a car pulls out onto the road from a small side road. Visibility is poor, and they haven't seen us.

Reeve reacts fast, swerving and accelerating to outrun the car, but it clips the rear end of our Maserati, sending us into a tailspin on the slippery road. I scream as Reeve struggles to regain control of the car, both of us bouncing up and down in our seats.

It all happens so fast.

Reeve yanks on the wheel, and my head whips forward

and then back with the motion as the car jerks violently to the left. A distressed sound rips from my husband's lips as our car darts forward, breaking through the rickety fence bordering the left-hand side of the road. Pieces of wood fly all over our car as we bounce forward. Reeve wrestles with the wheel, trying to regain control. I'm screaming, but it's as if someone else is making these high-pitched screeching noises.

The next few seconds happen as if in slow motion. Reeve curses before unlocking his seat belt and throwing his body across me. His arms band firmly around my upper torso as he clings to me. I want to shout at him to strap himself back in. To not be a martyr. But I can't get the words out of my mouth. I can't stop screaming. Adrenaline shoots through my veins as liquid terror plays havoc with my insides.

Metal scrapes loudly, piercing my ear drums, and I'm jostled forward with force as we plow into a tree. My terrified eyes startle in extreme shock and gut-wrenching panic as a looming darkness descends over our car. The tree lands horizontally on top of us with an earth-shattering thud. The roof buckles, pressing down on us, flattening the space in the car and crushing Reeve. Fear for my husband is my last conscious thought as my head slams into the side of the window and my world is plunged into pitch-black darkness.

CHAPTER 8
VIVIEN

"MISS? CAN YOU HEAR ME?" an unfamiliar voice asks as I slowly come to. Pain rattles around my skull, pounding, like someone is hammering on my head from the inside. I'm hot. Too hot. And there's a dead weight pressing me into the seat, gluing my ballgown to my back. Slowly, I blink my eyes open, wishing instantly I could close them again.

It all comes back to me in horrifying technicolor, and I cry out. The air is cloying and thick as it wraps around me. My eyes scan the confined space with mounting trepidation. "Reeve," I croak, lifting my hand, tentatively touching the back of my husband's head. I scream as thick blood coats my fingers. "Honey," I sob, shaking Reeve's frozen shoulder. "Wake up! Please, Reeve, I need you." Tears stream down my face as I stare at my husband's prone body. He's trapped between the dented roof and me, and the fallen tree ensures he can't move even if he was presently conscious. I don't have the strength to lift his head, to see his face, and I'm terrified to attempt to dislodge either one of us.

"Miss?" The voice speaks close to my ear, and I startle as the sound of blaring sirens echoes in the near distance. "Are you okay?"

LET ME LOVE YOU

I wince as I angle my head back, peering at the gray-haired stranger poking his head through the windowless back door. "Help," I croak. "My husband needs help." My eyes pop wide with shock as warmth pools under my butt, and I know what's happening. "My baby." I pin panicked eyes on the man. "Something is wrong. Please help us." All the lights are out in the car, so I can't see the blood spreading under my ass, but I feel it.

"Help is on the way. They should be here soon. I'm so sorry." I stare at him blankly with tears pouring down my face. "I was driving the other car. I didn't see you. It was dark and—"

He hangs his head, but I don't have time to concern myself with him. I'm too busy worrying about my baby and Reeve. Placing one hand on my bump and the other on top of Reeve's head, I pray like I've never prayed before.

Sobs rip through the eerily still night air as I barely cling to my sanity. "Reeve, please wake up. Please, baby. Don't leave me!" I cry. "You can't leave me. Not like this. Not when we were so angry with one another. Please, God," I scream, tilting my head up, brushing my forehead against the battered roof of our car. "Please don't take my husband and my daughter! Haven't you done enough already?"

The sirens draw closer, and I will them to hurry up.

I watch in a numbed haze as the firemen work to remove the fallen tree and lift the roof so they can reach us. Large lights shine down on the car as they work, illuminating the carnage. Physical and emotional pain ravages my body as I survey the wreckage I'm trapped in. There is blood everywhere, and Reeve still hasn't moved. I'm terrified and barely clinging to sanity. I whisper apologies to my husband as I run my bloody fingers through his hair. I beg him to wake up. I plead with him to hold on. I silently beg my little Lainey to fight. My head pounds, and my vision blurs in and out, but I refuse to close my eyes. I fight to remain conscious for my husband and my unborn child.

A paramedic asks me questions through my open window, but I can't answer her. I only have enough energy to focus on my family. Fear has a vise grip on my heart, squeezing and tightening until it feels like I can't breathe. My breath oozes out in wheezy, panicked spurts, and I'm struggling to get enough air into my lungs. An oxygen mask is carefully placed around my nose and chin just as the roof is finally lifted off.

A fireman wrenches the driver side door away, leaning in to press his fingers against Reeve's neck. He avoids eye contact with me while holding his fingers against Reeve's pulse point. Looking over his shoulder, he shakes his head at the male paramedic waiting behind him. He turns back around, and his sympathetic eyes lock on mine. An anguished sob escapes my mouth. "No!" I scream. "No! Don't say it! Don't you dare tell me that!" Hysteria bubbles up my throat, and I tighten my fingers in Reeve's hair, crying as I silently plead with the universe.

It's a mistake.

It's got to be.

Reeve would never leave me.

He's promised me so many times.

"Mrs. Lancaster," the kind paramedic lady says. She told me her name, but I can't remember it. "I'm so very sorry for your loss. There is nothing we can do for your husband now. We need to focus on you and your baby."

"Reeve." I hold on to him, clinging to his shoulders, crying with the worst, most unimaginable pain sitting on my chest. "You can't leave me. I love you too much! I can't go on without you. Please, wake up. Baby, please." It physically feels like my heart is rupturing behind my rib cage. Wracking sobs heave from my chest, and I want to die too.

"It's time, Mrs. Lancaster," the paramedic says, squeezing

my arm in a show of support. "You need to let my colleagues remove your husband from the car."

"No," I sob. "Don't take him from me." Tears coat my face in a steady stream, and fluid leaks out of my nose.

"You need to let go, sweetheart." A male paramedic gently pries my hands from Reeve as they pull him from the car and lay him on a stretcher. A blue sheet is placed over him, covering him from head to foot. My tears crawl to a stop, and I'm in a daze as I'm lifted out of the car and placed on a stretcher on the ground while the paramedics check me out.

"Mrs. Lancaster?" Kara—that's her name—says. "Can you feel the baby moving?"

I shake my head, running my hands over my bump. Warm liquid gushes down my legs. "She's not kicking," I whisper, closing my eyes. If I lose my daughter too, I won't survive this.

"We're going to airlift you to the hospital," she explains, pointing to a chopper in the middle of the field behind us. I hadn't even heard it land. I look up, spotting other helicopters in the sky. "Your baby is in fetal distress, and you're hemorrhaging badly. We need to get you to the delivery room."

Nausea swims up my throat, and I feel disoriented. My eyelids grow heavy. "Stay with me, Vivien," Kara says, her voice sounding distant. "We're losing her!" she shouts as I'm lifted off the ground, and that's the last thing I'm conscious of before I pass out.

CHAPTER 9
DILLON

"TURN ON THE TV," Ash shouts, barging into the recording studio on the grounds of my L.A. pad, with tears streaming down her face. "Hurry the fuck up, Jay!" she yells at her fiancé, impatient with his slow reaction. "Stick CNN on now!"

"What's going on?" I ask, immediately alarmed.

"Dillon," she sobs, throwing herself at me.

Goose bumps sprout on my arms, and my mouth is suddenly dry. Keeping one arm around my sobbing sister, I remove my guitar, setting the Fender aside. Ro shoots me a quizzical look, as Jamie flicks through the channels. Conor is sprawled across the leather couch, smoking a joint, oblivious to the tension in the air.

"This is bad, Dil," Ash whispers, wrapping both her arms around my body as the screen loads. "So, so, bad."

All the blood drains from my face as I read the headline flashing across the screen.

REEVE LANCASTER AND PREGNANT WIFE IN LATE-NIGHT CAR ACCIDENT

My heart throbs painfully behind my chest cavity, and I

hold my sister tight as the reporter speaks from the scene of the crash. Yellow police tape cordons off the road, and I watch with mounting horror as the shattered remains of a black and gold Maserati are hauled onto the back of a tow truck. Crowds of reporters, photographers, and innocent bystanders surround the cordoned-off area, holding up umbrellas to ward off the heavy rain that continues to fall.

"What can you tell us, Claudine?" the anchor in the studio asks the reporter.

"All we know at this time is that Reeve Lancaster and his pregnant wife, Vivien, were returning from a charity event when their car was hit by another vehicle. According to a local resident, who witnessed it from his bedroom window, Reeve lost control of the car and they crashed into a tree. The couple was trapped in their vehicle until firemen from a nearby station cut them free. Unofficial reports say Reeve was confirmed dead at the scene while a severely injured Vivien was airlifted to the hospital."

I tune out after that, shucking out of my sister's hold as I grab my jacket and keys. Panic slaps me in the face, and bile churns in my gut. "I need to go to her." I toss a look at Ash over my shoulder as my fingers curl around the door handle. "Find out which hospital they're at, and call me on the way."

"Like fucking hell I will." Ash stomps forward. "I'm coming with you."

"Will they even let you near her?" Ro asks, standing from his seat at his drum kit. "It's not like any of us have had any contact with her since she left Dublin."

Guilt swirls in my veins. I've been keeping so much from everyone, and it's all about to come out in the worst possible way. But I can't think about that now. All I can think about is getting to the hospital to see Vivien. "They'll let me in." I have no clue if they will, but I'll use the brother-in-law card if I have to.

"We're coming with you." Jamie slides his arms in his brown leather jacket.

"Conor can stay here and lock up," Ro says, stalking toward me. Conor grunts, barely aware of this conversation. Jamie grabs my car keys from my hand. "I'll drive. You sit in the back with Ash."

We race outside, climbing into my Land Rover. "I need to tell you something," I say after Ash has made a few calls and confirmed which hospital they have taken Viv to. Ro eyes me through the mirror as Jamie takes the next exit onto the highway. "I've seen Viv recently."

"What the fuck, Dil?" Ash fixes me with an incredulous expression. She jerks her head back suddenly, her eyes narrowing in suspicion. "Please don't tell me you're having an affair with her behind Reeve's back?"

"Jesus. Of course not." Vivien would be the last person to cheat on her husband, and my sister knows how I feel about the subject. I shake my head. "It's nothing like that."

"Then what is it like? And why are we only hearing this now?"

I wet my dry lips and exhale heavily before admitting the truth. "Reeve Lancaster is my twin brother."

Ash gawks at me. Jamie's mouth hangs open, and Ro's expression conveys shock. Silence descends for about three point five seconds before my brother, my sister, and my best friend all explode, talking over one another, as they fight to get the first word in.

"I fucking knew it!" Ash thumps me repeatedly in the arm. "You fucking laughed when I said you looked uncannily like Reeve after you removed the contacts and returned to your natural roots."

"Jesus Christ." Ro glares at me from the front passenger seat. "You knew all along, didn't you? I remember your reaction to Viv that night we first met her. You knew who she was, and you said nothing!"

I nod, and Ash thumps me again. "Stop fucking hitting me. I know you've got a shit ton of questions, and I promise I'll answer them, but not now." My throat clogs with emotion.

I take a shuddering breath, clamping my hand over my mouth as the seriousness of the situation hits me full force. "If anything happens to her—" I croak, horrified when tears stab my eyes. "She's got to make it. She's got to pull through." I cannot imagine a world without Vivien in it. It doesn't matter that we've been separated for so long. She still means everything to me.

Ash's pretty features soften. "Oh, Dil. It's still her, isn't it? Even after everything."

I nod, locking eyes with Jamie as he indicates to turn right. My best friend is the only one who knows I've been pining for her all these years. He knows she's the love of my life and how badly I wish I could change the events of our last few days together.

But Jamie doesn't know the rest of it. I purposely didn't tell anyone so they weren't accomplices. Shame crashes over me as I think of the stress I've put Vivien under these past couple of weeks. If my actions have caused this, in any way, I will never forgive myself.

"Does he know?" Ro asks. "Does Reeve know you're twins?"

"Yes," I say through gritted teeth. My feelings toward my twin are a clusterfuck of epic proportions. I hate him. He represents everything that was denied to me, and he has everything I want, but I have never wished him dead. I wouldn't wish that on anyone, no matter how much I despised them.

"The reporter said he died," Ash whispers, clutching my arm. "If it's true, it will devastate Viv."

"Let's not second-guess anything until we get to the hospital and find out what's going on," Jamie supplies.

"I have a son," I blurt, my gaze bouncing between my siblings and my best mate. "Easton. Vivien's son. He's mine. I only found out earlier tonight."

"What. The. Actual. Fuck?" My brother's shell-shocked expression drills a hole in my skull. His face pales. "I can't believe you've kept all this from us." Hurt and some indecipherable emotion glimmer in his eyes, and I feel like a total shithead.

Jamie glances back at me, his eyes showcasing his disbelief.

"Keep your eyes on the bleeding road, Jay." Ro glares at our bandmate and soon-to-be brother-in-law. "We don't want a second accident tonight."

The weather is still shite, but the rain isn't as heavy as it was earlier, showing signs it might be stopping soon.

"That's why Viv blanked me after she returned to L.A.," Ash muses, staring off into space. "She got pregnant and didn't know if the baby was yours or Reeve's." My sister is as sharp as ever.

I nod again, rubbing the back of my neck. None of it seems to matter now. What good was me loving her and her loving him if they both end up dead? Pain pierces me through the heart at that thought, and I bury my head in my hands, struggling to keep my composure. Viv can't die believing I hate her when the truth is the complete opposite.

Ash stares at me, as if she's looking through me, and there is nothing as scary as a quiet Aisling O'Donoghue. "I'm so fucking mad at you, Dillon," she says, a few beats later, as Jamie turns off the road toward the entrance to the hospital. "How could you keep all of this a secret?"

"I had my reasons, and I was planning on telling you. I was waiting for the paternity results."

"When did you find out Reeve was your twin, and did you deliberately target Viv?" she asks, working hard to keep anger from her tone.

"Our bio dad found me when I was seventeen. He offered me a million bucks to sign an NDA so I wouldn't come forward and ruin Reeve's movie career." Ash sucks in a sharp gasp, and I know she'll make the connection with the timing. "As for Viv, it was a pure coincidence she showed up in Dublin. I did go after her with an agenda, at first, but she got to me, and by the end, I was crazy in love with her." I peer deep into my sister's eyes. "You know that. You've seen what losing her has done to me."

Ash quietly nods, reaching out to squeeze my hand.

"You didn't win that money in the US lottery, did you?" Jamie inquires.

Shit. I really don't want to get into this now, so I give them an abbreviated version. "I renegotiated with that asshole Simon Lancaster when I found myself in a tricky situation after I chased Viv to America. I signed his damn NDA and pocketed the five mil, using it to fund our relocation to L.A."

"Fucking hell." Ro drags his hands through his messy brown hair. "I feel like I don't know you at all." He shakes his head. "I'm your brother. We're your family, and you didn't say a fucking word to any of us!"

"I'm sorry." It's pretty pathetic, but it's all I've got right now.

"Do Ma and Da know?" Ash asks.

"No. I didn't say anything to them either," I admit as we turn left into the hospital entrance. I poke my head through the gap between the front seats, watching the commotion up ahead. Thank God, my car has dark tinted windows and no one can see in.

Hordes of photographers swarm the front of the hospital, and several policemen are herding them behind a barricade. "I hate those fucking bloodsucking leeches." I crack my knuckles, wishing I could be let loose on them. With the amount of turmoil swirling in my veins, I reckon I could easily take a bunch of those dickheads out.

"Take that turn to the left up ahead," Ash instructs Jamie. "My contact said there's a side door we can enter. He has arranged for someone to meet us there."

Thank fuck for my sister and her connections. She's a kickass manager, and I know we wouldn't have achieved half of our success without her stellar management skills.

Jamie drops the three of us off before leaving to park my car.

As arranged, some PR jerk in a charcoal suit is waiting for us inside the door. He asks some loaded questions, and it's pretty clear we won't be getting near Vivien unless we have a justifiable reason. Reluctantly, I confess I'm her brother-in-law. The dude looks suspicious until Ash pulls up a picture of Reeve on her mobile phone, shoving it in his face. He looks between me and the photo, scrubbing his smooth jawline. After a few beats, he nods, mumbling a feeble apology, spouting shit about procedure and policy as we follow behind him.

Ash keeps him occupied with mindless chatter as we make our way through the hospital, doing our best to avoid drawing attention by keeping our heads down and our mouths shut. The last thing Vivien needs is the press sniffing around and uncovering the full extent of our sordid tale.

Mr. PR Prick Face takes us up in the elevator, escorting us to a private waiting room. Confirming someone will be along to talk to us in due course, he leaves. I'm grateful no one else is here so I can pace the floor, like a crazy person, without judgment.

"Sit the fuck down, Dil. You're making me even more nervous," Ash says, tapping away on her phone as Jamie slips into the room a few minutes later.

"It's a total shitshow outside and even more news vans are arriving," he explains as he slides onto the seat beside my sister, slinging his arm around her shoulders.

"Reeve's a big deal in Hollywood. What did you expect?" Ro says, arching a brow.

"Can't they ever show some respect?" Jamie shakes his head.

"We've lived here long enough to know they respect fuck all." I lean my head back against the wall, exhaling heavily. "When the fuck is someone coming to talk to us?" I snap, rubbing a tense spot between my brows.

"I'll see if I can find anything out." Ash stands. She drags her lower lip between her teeth as she contemplates me.

"Spit it out," I say, knowing she's got something on her mind.

"I regret it," she softly says. "I regret rejecting her when she reached out to me. I shouldn't have blocked her number. I let it go on for too long."

"Don't tell me. Tell her."

"I will." Fierce determination swims in her eyes as she stalks toward me. My sister is still the same pint-sized terror she's always been. "She's going to be okay. Vivien is tough as nails, and she's a fighter." She wraps her petite frame around me, and my arms automatically encircle her small body. I squeeze my eyes shut to contain the tears I long to spill. "If Reeve is gone, she's going to need you and me. Easton will too."

I know she'll have her parents and Audrey. I've seen photos of them online, so I know they are still friends. But Ash isn't wrong. She will need me, and I'm Easton's father. I want to be there for my son and his mother. Whether Vivien will let me help is another matter entirely, and I can't say I'd blame her. I've been a prick to her since I reappeared in her life, filling her head with the idea that I don't care about her anymore. God knows I have tried to forget about her over the years. But she has burrowed her way into my heart and my head, and I've never been able to get her out.

I can hardly breathe over the lump wedged in my throat. I've scarcely had time to let the news about Easton sink in.

I was elated earlier when I got the results. I assumed if I got confirmation he was mine that I'd be thrilled knowing how much the news would hurt Reeve and harm their marriage. But as I stared at that piece of paper, I didn't feel any of those things. All I was feeling was overwhelming joy I had made a precious little human with the only woman who has ever owned my heart. His adorable little face swam before my eyes, and my heart was overflowing with instant love and an almost insurmountable need to get to know him.

My son.

A little part of me, and a little part of Viv.

Now, everything has been turned upside down. I have no idea how things will pan out. I don't know if Vivien has survived or what's happened to her unborn baby or my…twin.

As Ash slips out of the room with Jamie, I sit down and pray for the first time in years.

CHAPTER 10
DILLON

"ALL WE COULD FIND out is that Viv is in surgery. They won't tell us anything else until her parents arrive," Ash says as she and Jamie reenter the waiting room. "They are en route from Texas and should be here within the hour." Ash clears her throat. "I spoke to Audrey."

"How did you get in contact with her?"

"We swapped numbers in Dublin. She's still using the same one. She's at the airport in Boston with her husband. Alex is Reeve's best friend." Ash flops down on the chair beside her fiancé, resting her head on his shoulder. "It seems Viv told her about you. She knows Easton is your son, but she's pretty sure Mr. and Mrs. Mills have no idea. She suggests you keep your gob shut for now."

"I'm not a fucking imbecile." I drag my hands through my hair, and I could kill for a beer or a smoke. "Viv is the priority right now." I have wondered who is taking care of Easton, but I'm guessing one of the staff they have at the house looks after him when they go out.

"You don't seem concerned about your twin," Ro says. "Why is that?"

"I can't get into all that now."

"I've often wondered if Viv and I would ever find a way to reconnect. I never imagined it would be under these circumstances," Ash says. "I should've spoken to her at the Oscars."

"Hon. Don't beat yourself up. There's no point wondering about all the what-ifs. You're here now. *We're* here now. That's what matters." Jamie kisses her on the lips, and she clings to him.

I turn around and face the window. Sometimes, it's hard to be around my best mate and my sister. They are so into one another, and it reminds me of everything I've lost. I rest my forehead on the glass, looking down at the chaos outside. The rain has petered out now, unlike the crowds, which appear to have trebled in size.

Time ticks by so slowly, and every minute feels like an hour. I can't sit still. I can't stop my mind from churning. Rehashing all the mistakes I've made, wondering if I'll ever get the opportunity to put them right. I'm thinking of everything and anything but the possibility Viv might not survive this because I cannot contemplate that scenario.

If I don't think it, it won't be true.

I jerk my head up when the door opens an hour later, and Vivien's parents enter the room. Lauren looks distraught. Her eyes are bloodshot, and her skin is puffy from crying. Jonathon holds her in his arms, and he's trying to put a brave face on it, but I can see the pain swimming in his eyes. Lauren frowns, her eyes creasing in confusion as she looks around the room. "Aisling?" She fixes her gaze on my sister as Ash stands. "What are you doing here?" she blurts.

"We came as soon as we saw the news. We couldn't not be here for Viv." Tears pool in my sister's eyes as Lauren pulls her in for a hug, sobbing. Jonathon's chest heaves, and he looks down at his feet.

Ronan and Jamie shoot me anxious looks.

"I'm glad you're here," Lauren says in a raspy voice that tells of copious shed tears. "Viv will be happy to see you. She misses you, you know."

"I miss her too." Ash glances up at Viv's mum. "Did they tell you what's going on? They won't tell us anything other than Viv is in surgery."

"They are sending someone in shortly," Jonathon says. "If they don't, I'll be screaming bloody murder."

Lauren eases out of Ash's embrace, approaching Jamie and Ro. "I'm Lauren, Vivien's mom. And this is my husband, Jonathon." She glances back at her husband, and he tips his head at my brother and friend.

"I'm Jamie, and this is Ronan."

"I wish we were meeting under better circumstances, but thank you for being here. I know it will mean a lot to my daughter."

Lauren moves back to the comfort of her husband's arms, and her eyes connect with mine. Her brow creases. "Who are you?" she asks, exchanging a puzzled look with her husband.

I clear my throat, shoving my hands in the pockets of my jeans. "I'm Dillon O'Donoghue. I'm Ash and Ronan's brother."

"You're Viv's ex-boyfriend!" Lauren steps away from her husband, walking toward me. "I saw pictures of you," she adds, scrutinizing my face. "But you didn't look like this." Jonathon steps up behind her, circling his arms around her waist as he regards me with suspicion. "You look like—" She clamps a hand over her mouth, sucking in a sharp gasp.

"He looks like Reeve," her husband says, rubbing his hand up and down her arm. "What is going on here?"

Lauren's hand drops to her side. "Oh my God. It's you! You're Reeve's twin!"

I nod. "I am. Viv didn't tell you we met two weeks ago?" I remember she was close to her parents. Her mum especially, and I know Reeve is like their prodigal son. I assumed they would've told them.

"What the hell is going on?" Lauren glares at me. "We knew you existed because we spoke to Reeve after he discovered he had a twin, but we left for location then." Lauren glances briefly at her husband before her eyes drill into mine. "Neither of them said a word on the phone, but I sensed something was troubling my daughter. She seemed distracted. Stressed."

She fixes me with a scary look, and her hands clench into fists at her sides. Honestly, she looks like she's seconds away from punching me. "I'm beginning to understand why. I don't believe in coincidence. You didn't want to meet us in Dublin on purpose. You were afraid we would recognize you." She hits the nail on the head, not that I'm confirming anything right now. I have zero desire to leave this hospital in a body bag, and with the way Viv's parents are glaring at me, it's a distinct possibility. "You knew who she was. You knew about Reeve. What sort of sick game were you playing?"

Viv's dad straightens up, regarding me with blatant hostility. "I'd like to know the answer to that question too," he says as the door opens and a man in blue scrubs enters the room.

"Mr. and Mrs. Mills. I'm Dr. Dwyer, and this is Officer Lawson. He's investigating the accident," he adds, stepping aside to let a tall man into the room. He has a head of thick black hair and a slight paunch, and he's wearing a wrinkled black suit. The cop's eyes widen when he gets a load of Jamie, Ro, and me, but he quickly composes himself. The doctor shuts the door, and tense anticipation bleeds into the air.

At least Viv's parents have forgotten about me.

For now.

My heart is ping-ponging around my chest, and I think I might throw up. Ash walks to me, looping her arm through mine. Her lower lip wobbles, and she's as white as a sheet. I know she's every bit as terrified as me.

"Is our daughter out of surgery? Is she okay?" Lauren asks in a shaky voice.

"Vivien is in recovery, and she'll be moved to a private room shortly. You can see her then. She lost a lot of blood, and we also discovered some internal bleeding. We found the source, repaired the damaged blood vessel, and cleaned out the pooled blood. She has a few bruised ribs, a concussion, and a sprained wrist, but she will make a full recovery. She needs rest and time to heal."

Relief floods my system, and I wrap my arms around my sister, squeezing my eyes shut as I press a kiss to her head.

"Thank God," Jonathon sobs, losing control of his emotions.

"What about the baby?" Ash asks.

The doctor's features soften, and Jamie is up on his feet, striding toward us with purpose.

"We delivered the baby by C-section, but she was stillborn. She was deprived of oxygen for too long, and we didn't get to her fast enough. I'm so sorry for your loss."

Ash bursts into tears, and I release her into Jamie's care. This will bring back traumatic memories for them.

"Oh no, Jon." Lauren buries her face in her husband's shirt, sobbing her heart out.

Pain slices across my chest. If Viv has lost Reeve too, I don't know if she'll be able to come back from this. "What about my brother?" I ask. "Where is Reeve?"

The cop clears his throat, clasping his hands in front of his body. "Mr. Lancaster was pronounced dead at the scene," he confirms, his features solemn.

I blink profusely, unable to process what he's just said or understand how I'm feeling.

"Oh my God. No!" Lauren wails, and her legs almost go out from under her. Her husband keeps her upright, even though I can tell he's struggling with the news too. "Not Reeve too! Not our son! She'll never get over this, Jon."

Lauren's tearstained face almost undoes me. Ro gets up, walking to my side, offering me quiet comfort.

"Why is this happening?" she cries. "Why is God doing this to us?"

Ash is full-on crying too, and Jamie is doing his best to console her.

"What happened?" Jonathon asks the officer while holding his devastated wife. "How did our son-in-law die?"

"It appears Reeve unbuckled his belt and threw himself across Vivien to shield her and the baby before the tree toppled on their car. He took the brunt of the injury. The paramedics at the scene said your daughter would most likely have died if he hadn't protected her."

Every ugly thought I've ever had about my twin, and every ugly word I've ever spoken about him, comes back to haunt me. I know his actions tonight don't exonerate his sins, but it's possible Viv was right.

That I didn't know the real Reeve.

And now I never will.

He sacrificed his life to save her and his unborn child, and that speaks volumes about the kind of man he was.

I hang my head as shame and a myriad of different emotions clouds my brain.

"I can't process this," Lauren says, clinging to her husband's tear-soaked shirt. "Please tell me this is a nightmare and I'm going to wake up and Reeve will still be alive and Vivien will still be carrying little Lainey."

Jonathon's shoulders heave as he wraps his arms around his wife, and it's clear he can't form words.

"I know you need time to grieve," the cop says, "but I just wanted to let you know we have taken the other driver in for questioning, and we're conducting a full investigation. He has openly confessed to not seeing their car and clipping the back of their vehicle, which ultimately caused the accident."

"Can we discuss this another time?" I say through gritted teeth. "I know you're only doing your job, but they are in no state to hear this."

"Of course." He hands me his card and gives one to Jonathon too. "I'll be in touch, but if you need anything else, feel free to call me." He retrieves a bloodstained large white envelope from inside his jacket, handing it to me. "These were found in the car. They are not evidence, but I didn't want to leave them where they might fall into the wrong hands." His dark brown eyes drill into mine. "I believe they are safest left in your care."

I nod, too numb to say anything. The officer leaves the room, nodding respectfully at Mr. and Mrs. Mills as they speak in hushed tones with the doctor.

"What is it?" Ro asks, staring at the envelope in my hands, ever the nosy bastard.

I open the top and pull out a bunch of photos, skimming through them with an aching heart. They are all of me and Vivien from Ireland, and they bring back so many happy memories. I peek into the envelope, spotting tons more. There must be hundreds of photos.

I wish the officer hadn't left yet so I could thank him for being a decent fucking human. This gives me faith there are at least a few good people left in the world. He would have made a fortune selling these, and it would've ruined Viv's reputation and clued the world's media in to our story. I shudder even thinking about it.

I slam my hand over the next photo before Ro can see, grinding my teeth to the molars as rage crawls up my throat. What the actual fuck? This photo was taken the night I took Viv up Bray Head and fucked her against the cross. Was someone spying on us? Automatically, my mind pivots to Reeve. Without proof, I just know he's behind this, and my wrath returns with a vengeance.

Forcibly dialing my anger down, I return the photos to the envelope and wrap it inside my jacket on the chair beside Jamie. Whatever this means, it will have to wait. There are more pressing matters like getting in to see Viv.

Ro and I sit down as Jamie comforts Ash, and Lauren and Jonathon cling to one another. Eerie silence fills the room, only interrupted by anguished cries. I'm on the verge of losing it when a nurse walks into the room, explaining Vivien is awake and ready to see her parents.

"I'm coming too," I say, standing.

"No, you're not." Lauren gives me a serious case of evil eye. "You are probably the last person my daughter wants to see."

"Please." I walk toward them, shielding nothing from my face. "Please let me go with you. I need to see her."

"We will ask her if she wants to see you," Jonathon offers, leading his wife to the door. "It will be Viv's choice."

CHAPTER 11
DILLON

I WAIT until they have left before rushing after them. "Dillon!" Ash hisses. "I know you're anxious, but they are right. Just wait for them to come back."

"They don't want me anywhere near her, Ash, and I need to see her. I need to see with my own eyes that she's okay."

"Let him go," Ro says. "He needs this."

I slip out of the room, spotting the nurse and Viv's parents up ahead. Keeping a few steps back, I trail them to the ICU, cursing when the door shuts after them and I can't get in without a nurse or the security code. I spend ten minutes arguing with the nurse behind the ICU reception desk, but she won't let me in. Nothing works as a bribe, and I'm forced to give up when she threatens to call security and have me thrown out.

Slumping, I make my way back to the waiting room, with my tail tucked between my legs. I pace the floor like a lunatic while my siblings throw question after question at me. I get it. There is lots they don't know. We have hours to kill, and they want answers. But I can't get into it all now. They are going to hate me for what I've done and call me a selfish prick, but I can't handle that now. Ro falls asleep, lying on his side across a few chairs, his soft snores rippling through the room. But Ash doesn't sleep, and she continues asking me shit I can't even think about, let alone answer.

"Enough, Ash!" I roar when I can't take it anymore.

"Watch your fucking tone," Jamie snaps, instantly defending his woman.

"I know you need answers, and I will give them to you. But not now." I grab fistfuls of my hair, hating I cut it, vowing to let it grow out again. "I'm hanging on by a thread here, Ash." I fix her with pleading eyes. "Viv means everything to me. She's everything." I thump my closed fist over my heart. "I love her," I croak. "And I've made such a mess of things. I need to speak to her. To tell her I lied. To see she's okay with my own two eyes. I need to fix the mess I've made. I—" Air whooshes out of my mouth as my legs give out, and I sink to the floor, cradling my head in my hands.

"It's okay." Ash sits on the floor beside me. "I'm sorry for pushing. I know you'll tell us when you're ready." She rubs her hand up and down my back. Strained silence fills the space between us. "You shouldn't expect much from her, Dil. She's bound to be in shock, and pain, and you can't lay anything heavy on her. You don't want to make things worse."

It's good advice. Advice I know I should take. But I'm itching to take all my cruel words back. "I said some horrible shit to her recently. I need her to know I didn't mean it," I explain.

"She won't hear it now," Ash softly supplies. "She's too consumed in grief. I know I was when we lost our baby," she adds, looking at Jamie with glassy eyes. She presses a kiss to my head, breathing deeply. "Viv has been dealt a double blow. I get you needing to see her, to know she's okay, but that is all you should do. Let her grieve, Dillon, and when things have settled, you can talk to her."

The hours roll by, and early sunlight bathes the room in hazy yellow hues. Ash is asleep with her head in Jamie's lap, and Ro is still out for the count, but Jamie and I haven't slept a wink. We don't talk though. He's too hung up worrying about Ash. Concerned this situation is dredging up their own loss, and worrying what it will do to her, no less. I'm too busy beating myself up for mistakes I've made that go back years. If only I had chased after her that night in Bruxelles. I should have gone after her when she told me she loved me and asked her one final time to stay. I didn't fight hard enough for her, and by the time I'd pulled my head out of my ass, it was too late.

The door creaks as it opens, and a tired Mr. and Mrs. Mills enter the room. Ash is instantly awake, rubbing sleep from her eyes as she sits up. "How is she?"

"She's in a lot of pain. Physical and emotional. She slept mostly," Lauren explains, ignoring me and focusing on my sister. "When she was awake, she was groggy and not very lucid." Lauren leans her head against her husband's shoulder, and he cradles her to his side. "I don't think she has fully grasped what has happened."

"You shouldn't be here," Jonathon Mills says, eyeballing me like he wishes he could slice my head off my shoulders. "I don't know what has happened between you, but my daughter doesn't need any additional stress."

"Leave or we'll arrange to have you escorted off the premises," Lauren adds.

"I just want to make sure she's okay. I'm not going to cause any trouble. The last thing I want to do is hurt her or add to her stress," I say, rising to my feet. I hold my shoulders back. "I love your daughter, and I have always regretted letting her go. She means everything to me."

"I don't trust a word that comes out of your mouth," Lauren replies. "And Vivien is in no fit state to make any decisions. If you care for her, like you say you do, you will leave. When Vivien is strong enough, she can decide if she wants to see you or not."

I want to tell them it's not that cut-and-dried. I want to tell them I'm Easton's father. But I won't add to their grief. Now isn't the time and my needs are bottom of the list of priorities. I don't want to leave without seeing Vivien, but I don't want to fall out with her parents either. I can always come back later, when they are not here, and sneak in to see her. "Okay. I'll go."

"I would like to see her," Ash says. "Is it okay if I stay?"

Lauren looks undecided.

"Stay," Jonathon says. "Audrey and Alex will be here shortly. Talk to Audrey. See what she thinks. If she says it's okay, it's fine by us." Lauren closes her eyes, and she looks like she can barely stand any longer. "I'm going to take Lauren to the house to freshen up. We want to be there when our grandson wakes."

"Maybe we should swap numbers," Ash says. "That way we can keep each other informed if there are any developments."

They exchange numbers as I rouse Ro. "Come on," I tell him. "We're leaving." I hug my sister. "Keep me posted too, please."

"I will. I promise."

I jerk my head at Jamie, dragging my brother to his feet. Wetting my lips, I eyeball Viv's parents. "I'm very sorry for any distress I may have caused you or your daughter. I just wanted to be here for her. I know I have made mistakes in the past, and I can only imagine what you must be thinking, but Viv is the love of my life. There has never been anyone but her. I know she's devastated and traumatized right now, and I would never add to that. I will give her space, but you should know I'm going nowhere. I let her walk away from me once, and I've regretted it every day since. Being apart from her all these years has killed me, and it's a mistake I won't be making again."

After a trip to the bathroom and the hospital cafeteria, Ro and I make our way outside, using the side entrance, keeping our heads down. There's a big ruckus out the front of the hospital, where the fans and reporters are, and I'm guessing the Millses have stepped outside. At least it means no one is focused on us, and we make a quick dash across the parking lot, finding my Land Rover exactly where Jamie said it would be.

I'm behind the wheel, ready to pull out of the space, when Ash calls me. "Have you left yet?" she asks.

"I'm still in the parking lot."

"Come back inside. Lauren and Jon have gone. Audrey and Alex are with Viv now. She's been moved to a private room, and I know where. You can take a glimpse at her, but that's all, Dillon. No talking to her, and you can't let her see you. That's the dealio. Take it or leave it."

"I'll take it. Thanks, Ash." I couldn't love my sister more in this moment. I know she's mad at me, and she's going to be even madder when I tell her everything, but she's still going to bat for me.

"Stay here," I tell Ro, handing him the keys. "I won't be long." He lowers his seat, to take another nap, while I grab a hoodie from the back seat. Yanking the hood up, I climb out of my car and head back inside the hospital.

Ash is waiting for me as soon as I step out of the lift. "Good call with the hoodie," she murmurs, dragging me down the corridor. "Security just found a reporter on this floor, snooping around."

"We need to get protection up here for Viv," I say.

"I've already messaged her parents asking if they want me to organize that. It seems Reeve has his own team of bodyguards. They are sending a couple over, which means you have to do this fast. Audrey will be pissed when she sees you, Dil, so just take a quick look at Viv and then go."

Jamie nods at his fiancée as we pass by. He's crouched over the nurses' desk, distracting the burly-looking blonde behind the counter, so we can sneak past.

Ash slams to a halt at a closed white door. "This one," she whispers, pointing.

Without stopping to second-guess myself, I open the door

and step inside Viv's darkened room. She is semi-propped up in the elevated bed, her tangled hair resting on a bunch of pillows. A large purple bruise on her cheekbone matches one on her right temple. A white bandage is strapped around her wrist, and she's hooked up to a drip and another machine. Lighting is low, and the blinds are closed, to help with her concussion, I'm guessing. She looks battered and bruised and lost, but at least she's alive.

"What the hell, Ash?" Audrey says from her place beside the bed. She is stroking Viv's hand, and exhaustion is clearly evident on her face.

A tall guy with sandy-blond hair and red-rimmed brown eyes growls at me from the other side of Viv's bed. This must be Alex. Audrey's husband and Reeve's best friend. Hostility rolls off him in waves as he stands. "Get the fuck out of here before I make you."

Viv winces, slowly turning her head in my direction.

"Alex," Audrey murmurs, shaking her head.

A cry bursts from Vivien's lips, and her tortured hazel eyes fill with tears. She tries to sit more upright in the bed, clutching her stomach, in obvious pain, at the sudden movement.

"You need to stay still, babe," Audrey says. "You'll rip your stitches."

"Reeve!" Viv cries, staring at me with bloodshot eyes. "Tell them to bring Lainey back. They took our baby!" Her hands move to her deflated stomach. "I can't feel her, Reeve. She's not kicking." Her eyes stretch wide as she looks up at me.

Horrified shock splays across Audrey's face as she stares between us. "Come sing to her, like you usually do," Viv adds, shoving the covers down and running her hands over her much smaller bump. "C'mon, Reeve. She'll wake up when she hears you singing. You have such a gorgeous voice."

I am rooted to the spot in horror. I shouldn't have come here. This is only making things worse. I want to leave, but I'm afraid to leave now. I don't know what I should do. I look at Audrey, beseeching her to tell me what to do. Silent tears are streaming down her face. She turns to face her husband, pleading with her eyes for him to do something. But he's as shell-shocked as we are.

This is tearing strips off my heart. I don't know how to handle it. I don't want to do or say anything to set her off. She's clearly traumatized and probably still drugged up and disoriented.

"Reeve, please." She stretches her arms out. "I need you," she wails, as tears trek down her face.

I move toward her as if on autopilot, hoping my instincts will guide me. Alex has moved over beside his wife, cradling her in his arms as she cries her eyes out. They watch me, and it only adds to the responsibility I'm feeling. Cautiously, I sit on the edge of Viv's bed, struggling to hold my own emotion inside. All I want to do is hold her and tell her I still love her. That I never stopped.

But I know I can't.

She grabs my left hand. The one I don't wear rings on. "Where's your wedding ring?" she asks, her voice rising. "Where is your ring, Reeve?" She stares into my face, and her eyes pop wide. She drops my hand as if it's poisonous. "You're not Reeve!" she croaks in a hoarse voice. "You're not him. You're not my husband." She pummels her fists against my chest, but there is no strength in her motion. "Go away! I don't want you! I want Reeve! Reeve!" she rasps, her fragile voice bouncing off the walls. "Reeve! Where are you? I need you."

I don't even realize I'm crying until tears drip off my chin, sloping down my neck and onto my chest. My heart is breaking in a combination of pain for her and for me. I know she's having a breakdown, but she will never want me. It will always be him.

"Vivien. It's Audrey." Audrey has pulled herself together. Bending over her best friend, she brushes hair back off her face as Alex glares at me like he wants to murder me with his bare hands. "You need to calm down. Please, babe. Just take deep breaths."

"I want Reeve! I want my husband. God can't take him too!" She swings tormented eyes on me. "This is all your fault! He knew! Reeve knew I was lying to him! He knew about Easton. He was so mad. So upset. He wouldn't slow down! I told him to slow down! He wouldn't listen. He didn't listen." The words spill from her mouth in a torrent of anguish and pain while her eyes dart wildly around the room. More words gush from her mouth, in a stream of nonsensical statements, and I'm seriously worried about her mental state. Viv's sobs echo through the clinical room, and each one strips another layer off my heart.

Her eyes connect with mine again, and there is no warmth in her gaze. "My husband died thinking I betrayed him because you blackmailed me into keeping quiet! He thought I was fucking you!" she croaks, rubbing a hand over her chest. "I hate you!" She beats me with her fists again, but she's so weak they hardly register. A part of me wishes she was strong enough to inflict real physical pain because it's the least I deserve.

"I hate you so much, Dillon!" She slaps my face, but I barely feel it. I let her attempt to hit and punch me as Alex presses the button to call the nurse. Audrey has her hand over her mouth, sobbing as she watches her friend self-destruct. "You ruined my life," Viv sobs, collapsing against her pillow as all the fight leaves her. A line of red stains her blue hospital gown across the middle. "You have taken everything from me, but you can't have E." She fixes me with dark eyes. "You don't deserve him. Reeve is his dad. Reeve will always be his dad. You'll have to cut my heart out of my chest before I let you take him."

"Dil." Ash quietly tugs on my sleeve, pulling me away from the bed. I had forgotten she was even here. "Let's go."

"Keep him away from me, Ash!" Viv shouts. "He did this! He did this to me!"

A nurse rushes into the room, and I watch helplessly as Viv is sedated while Ash tries to drag me away. My sister is a feisty, determined little thing, but she's no match for my height and my weight. Silent tears leak from my eyes as I watch Viv's eyelids close.

"Get him out of here," Audrey says, ignoring me and looking at Ash. "Get him out of this hospital. I don't want him anywhere near Vivien or my godson."

Jamie enters the room, and together, he and Ash drag me away. I stumble along the hallway, heartbroken and full of self-loathing. Shucking my sister and my best friend off me, I slump to the ground in the hallway, bringing my knees to my chest as I let it all out. I don't care that others are a witness to this. My chest heaves and my shoulders shake as I cry. Pain pummels me from every angle, and I wish I'd been driving. I wish I was the one lying on a cold table in a morgue. I wish I could rewind the years and do so many things differently.

Ash kneels, bundling me in her arms. "It will be okay, Dil. She didn't mean it. She's traumatized and grieving."

"I fucked up, Ash." I lift my eyes to her, hardly able to see her through my tears. "I fucked up real bad. Viv is right. This *is* my fault, and she's never going to forgive me. She will never get over losing her husband and her baby, and she will always blame me."

CHAPTER 12

VIVIEN

"ARE you sure you want to do this now?" Mom asks, stalling at the door to my bedroom.

"I can't keep putting it off. He's confused. Every time he asks for his daddy, I fall apart."

My parents have been keeping Easton sheltered at the house since the accident. They told him Mommy and Daddy were away for a few days, purposely keeping the details vague. Mom knew I would want to tell E myself, but I was so out of it when I returned home, and I've been unable to do much more than sleep and cry. My parents deflected his questions, and I know how hard that has been on them. They don't want to lie to their grandson, and I can't continue to keep him in the dark. Easton needs to know, and that responsibility falls to me. I've been trying to pluck up the courage to tell him for the last twenty-four hours.

How do you tell a five-year-old that his daddy is dead and the little sister he was so excited to meet died in my womb the same night?

How am I expected to go on when it feels like I died that night too?

Thank God for my parents. They have been caring for

Easton, and it brought me comfort to know he was well looked after when I wasn't here to do it and after I came home when I was incapable of doing much of anything.

It's been four days since I was discharged from the hospital and six days since I lost Reeve and Lainey, but it already feels like an eternity. Tears pump out of my eyes as that thought lands in my mind, and Mom rushes across the floor to hold me in her arms. "Darling, I wish I could take your pain away."

"The pain helps me to remember, and I never want to forget."

"Sweetheart." Mom strokes my hair. "You will never forget them. Don't cling to the pain because you won't heal unless you try to let it go."

"I'll never heal, Mom. I'll never get over losing them. I miss Reeve so much already." Heaving sobs wrack my chest, and I'm crying into her shoulder, clinging to her, wishing I could wake up and discover it's all been a bad dream. Pain races across my chest, infiltrating my bloodstream, invading every part of my body.

Physically, I'm still suffering after the accident, but that's the kind of pain I can tolerate. The strong pain meds the hospital prescribed help a lot. I wish there was a pill I could pop to numb the ever-present emotional pain.

"I know, honey. I know how much you will miss him. He's been such a huge part of your life, but he wouldn't want this for you. He wouldn't want to see you like this. He died saving you."

Mom's tears mix with my own as they have done so often in the past few days. Reeve was more than just a son-in-law to my parents. He was a son to them, from the instant he was born, except in name. "I know it's too soon. You need to process these emotions. We all do," she adds, sniffling. "But you need to find the strength to live because that is the best way you can honor Reeve. And that little boy needs his mommy, now more than ever."

I want to be there for Easton, but I've been so distraught

these last few days that I haven't been able to support him. That ends now. My son needs me, and I need him. He is all I have left. I dry my tears with the sleeves of my silk robe. "I won't fail Easton. I will fight to go on. For him."

She kisses my temple. "That's my girl. But make sure you do it for you too, Vivien. You deserve to continue to live your life to the fullest. It won't happen yet, or anytime soon, but you are not alone. We are all here for you, and we will be with you every step of the way."

That's not exactly true. My parents will have to return to the movie set soon. Oh, I know them. I know they are both trying to extricate themselves from the production. But there is no way that can happen. They can't lose the director and the leading lady. They can't reshoot a movie that's halfway through filming, and every day the movie is on hold costs hundreds of thousands of dollars. They will have to return after the funeral, and I'll just have to learn to cope by myself.

It's a scary proposition. One I'm not sure I can manage, but my son needs me to be strong, and I'm determined to at least try. "Can you get Easton now? I'm okay." As long as I try to keep thoughts of Reeve and Lainey from my mind for the few minutes it takes to break my little son's heart.

It feels like I've lied to him and betrayed him. E was there every day with Reeve, singing and talking to my belly, and I am letting him down in the worst way imaginable. He was so excited to meet his sister, and he's going to be so upset. My lower lip wobbles, and tears threaten, but I manage to hold it together.

"Mommy." Easton races across my bedroom, flinging himself into my arms.

"Careful, sweetheart," my mom says. "Remember we told you Mommy wasn't feeling well? Well, she has some pains in her tummy, and we need to be gentle with her."

"What about my little sister?" Easton asks, looking worried. "Does she have pains too?"

Gulping over the messy ball of emotion in my throat, I

breathe deeply as I pat the space beside me on the bed. "Come sit here. I need a cuddle."

Easton snuggles into my side, and I wrap my arms around him, closing my eyes as I brush my nose against his hair. The sweet strawberry smell from his shampoo provides comfort as does the feel of him in my arms. I hold him a little tighter, careful not to crush him. I wish I could put him on my lap, but I already ripped my stitches out once, and I've been warned not to do any lifting or holding for another few weeks. "Honey, I need to tell you some sad news," I start, working hard to keep the tremble from my voice. "You remember when we talked about Holy God and the angels and heaven?"

I'm not overly religious. Neither was Reeve.

His handsome face swims in front of my eyes, and I long to return to three weeks ago and do everything differently. If I had, we wouldn't be here now. Reeve wouldn't have been angry at me that night. He wouldn't have been drinking so much because he thought I was having an affair behind his back with his long-lost twin. We would have made it home in one piece, and I wouldn't be sitting here now about to crush my son's heart into itty-bitty pieces. Pain stabs me through the heart, and I briefly squeeze my eyes shut.

"Yes," Easton says, sounding confused and scared.

That snaps me out of my head. I open my eyes and place a kiss on his cheek. "Daddy and I were in a car accident. I was in the hospital getting better, but Daddy and Lainey have gone to heaven to be with God and the angels."

Inwardly, I'm screaming as the words leave my mouth. Right now, I hate God as much as I hate Dillon O'Donoghue.

Easton blinks, staring at me in confusion. "Why would Daddy go to heaven instead of coming home? Why didn't he get better in the hospital like you?"

Pain crawls up my throat, and I can barely force the words out this time. "If Daddy could've made the decision, he would have come home with me." I pause, emitting a few sobs. Mom makes a move, but I shake my head, needing to do this myself, even if I am making a mess of it.

"I don't understand," E says as tears roll down his cheeks.

I hold him closer, dotting kisses on the top of his head. "Neither do I, baby. But sometimes things happen, and we don't ever know why. This is one of those times. God needed Daddy and Lainey, and at least they are together. I bet they're up in heaven cuddling right now, just like we are."

"I don't want my daddy to go to heaven!" Easton bursts out crying. "I want him to come home and play with me on the slide!" he wails, burying his little face in my chest. I can scarcely see through my blurry vision, but I see enough to know Mom is crying too.

Will this ever get any better?

Will this pain ever go away?

"I know, honey. I wish for that too, but it's not going to happen." I hate to do this to him, but I can't leave him with false hope either. "Daddy is your guardian angel now. He's going to be watching over both of us from heaven."

"I want him watching over me from here," Easton sobs into my chest, and I don't know what else to say to make him understand. As I hold my heartbroken boy in my arms, I vow to do everything to help him get through this, even if it means papering over the cracks in my own heart to do it.

CHAPTER 13
VIVIEN

"YOU NEED TO EAT," Audrey says, zipping up my black dress from behind. "You look so thin."

"I know," I deadpan. I know a body needs food to sustain it. That I'll perish if I don't fuel my body, but I can't eat. Even the thought of food makes me ill. You can't tell I was ever pregnant now, and that only adds to my sadness. I'm barely surviving despite my silent promises to myself to do better for Easton's sake.

My son is struggling. He doesn't understand why his daddy hasn't come home. He's convinced himself Reeve is away on a movie set, and the only way I know to get through to him is to bring him to the funeral with me today.

Alex and Audrey have been a lifeline for me in the same way my parents have. They too have put their lives on hold to be here for us. I've wanted to keep Easton at home, away from prying eyes, and our best friends have been helping to keep him occupied while Mom tries to glue me back together. Dad is dealing with practical matters, like arranging the funeral, sorting out legal shit, and dealing with the police.

I told Officer Lawson I didn't want to press charges against the man driving the other car. It was a horrible night.

Visibility was terrible, and it was an accident. Faulty airbags didn't help, and toxicology reports taken during Reeve's postmortem confirmed he was over the legal limit. He should never have been driving. I should have forced him into the passenger seat and insisted I drive. I should have refused to get in the car until he agreed.

Round and round my mind churns, going over all the what-ifs.

"Are you sure you want Easton to attend the funeral?" Audrey asks as she runs some serum through my wavy hair. I've been like a zombie as my bestie got me in the shower, dried and styled my hair, and applied makeup to my pale face. She even helped me to bind my breasts, which are engorged and rock hard thanks to my milk coming in. Every time I touch them and they hurt, I'm reminded of my loss all over again.

"I asked him, and he said he wants to go."

She looks at me like I've truly lost my mind, and I get it. I know I said some mad shit in the aftermath of the accident when I woke in the hospital. Mistaking *him* for my husband being the worst of it. I turn around to face my friend. "I know he is young. Probably too young to make that decision, but I don't want him to turn around to me in the future and blame me for not letting him attend his father's and his little sister's funeral." I'm expecting tears to form, like usual, but my eyes are suspiciously dry.

Perhaps I have worn out my tear ducts.

"I know this will be horrible. I'm dreading it so I can only imagine how Easton is feeling, but it might help in a warped way. Maybe if he sees the coffin and he has a chance to say goodbye, it might sink in." I know I'm hoping it will for me because most days I still wake up believing it's just a bad dream. Until reality sets in, and I'm devastated as if I'm hearing the news for the first time.

Audrey reels me into her arms. "I can't believe we are

here. I still can't believe this has happened." She holds me tighter, sobbing. "It's not fair."

"I know." I sound devoid of life as I smooth a hand up and down her back. This past week has taken everything from me. Especially the last few days; hosting visitors who came to pay their respects. It almost felt like a test. Like God is continuing to push and push, to stretch me to my limits, to see how far he can go before I completely break. It's left me emotionally drained, and feeling completely unprepared for today.

"Ash called me," she says, easing back. "I don't want there to be any surprises, so you should know she'll be there with her family. With him."

I gulp painfully. "I don't know why he insists on being there. He made no secret of the fact he hated Reeve. It's too late now to care."

"I get the impression he's there for you and Easton."

Anger boils in my blood, and I grind my teeth to the molars. "He better stay the hell away from my son!" A red haze coats my retinas. "You tell Ash to keep him away from me and my son."

"That message has already been relayed. She assures me he won't approach you. That he just wants to pay his respects."

I snort. "A likely story."

"I can talk to your dad and Leon. We can refuse him entry to the church."

I shake my head. "I don't want to make a scene. Especially not in front of the media." Reporters and paparazzi are stalking us since the accident. They are all desperate to get photos of me and Easton. Desperate to hear what happened that night.

I hate them as much as I ever have.

Reeve's publicist, Edwin, dropped by the house to pay his respects. He suggested I talk to him when I'm feeling up to it. He says it's better to talk to the press in an arranged interview and he can make them go away, but I doubt I will ever be strong enough to do that.

"What are you going to do about him? From what Ash has said, he's not going to drop it."

"I don't expect him to, but I can't think about that right now. I just need to get through today." I know I need to tell my parents. They deserve to know the truth. Easton does too, and I won't lie to him about his parentage. But there is no way I'm mentioning anything to him yet. He needs time to grieve for Reeve. Only then will I even contemplate how to tell him who Dillon is to him. I know I won't be able to hold Dillon off that long. That we need to talk. But I can't talk to him yet.

Ash and I spoke when she came to visit me in the hospital. It was a brief conversation, and I was in and out of consciousness a lot of the time. I'm touched she came and that she wants to meet up. I think I'd like that too, but I need to survive today first. Easton is my sole priority and the focus of all my energy. I don't have room or the strength for anything else.

Easton clings to my side as we sit in the front pew of the church staring at the coffin. I asked for our daughter to be buried in her daddy's arms. While my faith in God is seriously tested right now, I take comfort in knowing wherever they are they are together. I know my husband is caring for our little girl in the same loving, adoring way he cared for me and E.

The church is packed as are the roads outside. Thousands upon thousands of mourners line the streets of L.A., coming out to pay their respects to Reeve.

The outpouring of love for my husband has been incredible. Fan posts occupy most every social media platform, and Margaret Andre and the woman who runs Reeve's fan club have had to hire additional temporary staff to cope with the influx of cards and gifts. A lot of it is for me. Some is for Easton too. Mom is handling all of that, sorting through it and boxing it up in case I want to look at it sometime in the future.

The minister says nice things about Reeve, but neither of us were practicing Catholics, so he's talking through his ass. It's only when Mom gets up to speak that we're hearing about the real Reeve from someone who knew him.

"Thank you all for coming," Mom says, her voice projecting to the back of the church.

She looks beautiful with her hair pulled off her face in an elegant chignon. She's wearing a black hat with a short black lace veil. I hold a confused Easton tighter, ignoring the sharp pain in my ribs from the motion. "I know my daughter would be up here, saying these words, if she could, but it's been an extremely difficult time for her. For Easton and for all of us." Mom's eyes fill up, and I wonder if she'll be able to do this. My dad gets out of his seat, walking to stand beside her. She leans against him, drawing strength from his presence.

"Reeve is beloved by many people the world over. People who have loved his movies and followed his career from those early days. But those of us who are here today knew the man, not just the actor. Jon and I were privileged to watch Reeve grow up. He was an integral part of our lives from the moment he was born. In all the ways that matter, he was our son, and we will miss him dearly." Her sobs echo through the microphone, bouncing off the walls of the eerily quiet church. A few cries and sobs surround me, but still, I don't cry. I press kisses into Easton's hair, clinging to him for dear life.

"Reeve loved Vivien from the time he was a little boy," Mom continues in a wobbly voice. "Jon and I would watch them playing together, and we always knew they were destined to be together. Reeve worshiped Vivien with an intensity that is rare for someone so young. No matter what he chose to pursue, whether it was acting or our daughter, Reeve did it to the fullest of his ability because he had the biggest heart and so much love to give. Watching him grow from a young boy into a man and later into a father was one of the most rewarding experiences of my life. Reeve adored our grandson, and he was the most amazing father to Easton."

"Mommy." Easton tugs on my sleeve. "Why is Grandma talking about me?"

I lower my head. "She's telling everyone how much Daddy loved you."

"He was so happy to welcome the new baby, singing every night to Lainey and making plans as only an excited father could do," Mom continues.

"Mommy." Easton pulls my head down to his face. "Is Daddy in there?" he asks, pointing at the coffin.

"He is. And Lainey is there with him so they can be together." I kiss his cheek as I see realization dawn on his handsome face.

"Reeve's last selfless act on this Earth said everything about who he was as a man, a husband, and a father. He didn't hesitate to protect Vivien and their unborn child, sacrificing his life so our daughter could live. We can never thank him for that." Her cries ring out around the church, and a chorus of tears surround us. "Or for all the joy he brought to our lives. His legacy will live on through Easton," she adds, and a lump forms in my throat.

I should've told my parents before the funeral there is no piece of Reeve left living on this planet. That hurts so much because my husband wanted tons of kids and the kind of family he was deprived of as a child. That he should die without that destroys me. All that remains are my memories and our cherished mementos and his legacy on the screen. He didn't leave any flesh and blood behind except for a twin brother who hated him and never wanted him in his life.

I hate that for Reeve and for myself. If God had to be cruel to take my husband, couldn't he have given me his daughter so I could love her for the both of us?

"I want my daddy!" Easton screams, breaking me out of my inner monologue. I watch in horror, like I'm floating overhead, as he wrestles out of my arms and races toward the coffin. He places his hands on the side of the coffin as heartbreaking cries trickle through the congregation. "Wake up, Daddy! Please!" he sobs, and I know I should go to him, but I'm frozen in place.

Running footsteps echo along the tile floor behind me. Alex stands, striding toward Easton and gently pulling him into his arms. Easton wraps his arms and legs around his Uncle Alex, crying into his shoulder. "I've got this," Alex says, in a clipped tone, looking over Easton's shoulder.

I glance around, spotting Dillon standing just behind me, staring at Alex with Easton. Pain ravages his face as he looks at his son, and I'm guessing he wishes he was the one comforting him. But Dillon is a stranger to Easton. They only met one time, and he is not who Easton needs right now.

I rise, walking to Dillon's side. "Please don't make a scene. Not here," I whisper in his ear.

"That's not—" Dillon drags a hand through his hair. "I just want to help."

"Then leave." I eyeball him, even though it almost kills me. Seeing Reeve's eyes on Dillon's face upsets me even more now. "If you want to help, that's the best way."

Tormented eyes peer deep into mine as rumblings from the crowd remind me that we have an audience. "I'm so sorry for your loss," he says in a choked voice. "More than you could ever know."

CHAPTER 14

VIVIEN

THE GRAVEYARD PROVES to be my breaking point, and I fall apart, collapsing against Dad as the casket is lowered into the ground. The finality breaks my heart all over again, and my tortured cries almost drown out the minister's words.

Reeve is gone, and he's never coming back. I will never again see his handsome face or melt into a puddle of goo when he fixes that flirtatious smile on me. The taste of his lips is lost to me forever, as is the protective strength of his arms. Waking up tangled between his legs with the comforting sound of his heartbeat against my ear will exist now only in my memories. Never again will I feel him moving inside me, coaxing pleasure from my body.

Sharp pain pierces my chest walls, embedding deep, and I want to die. I want to crawl into that casket with my husband and my daughter and never wake.

How could God take my husband and my baby? How much pain can one person endure in their life? Our daughter was the purest, most innocent treasure. A precious gift, cruelly snatched from us before she ever got to live. Our little girl never got to take her first breath. I will never get to hold her in my arms or to smell that gorgeous newborn smell. I won't get to feel her tiny fingers curling around mine or hear her desperate cries when she's hungry or unsettled or just craving a hug.

All of that has been denied to me.

Dad carries me back to the car when it's clear my legs are malfunctioning, and I sob into his shoulder, clinging to him as Mom rocks a sobbing Easton in her arms.

I manage to compose myself, just before we get back to the house, enough to hold Easton. He is hurting too, and I feel guilty for my thoughts back at the graveside. I need to be here for my son. He needs me, now more than ever, and I can't be selfish. Not even in my thoughts. We cling to one another, and I hold him close, telling him how much I love him and dotting kisses into his hair. I know my son is the only way I will survive this pain. I need to find the strength to go on for this little boy.

I take Easton to his room to get changed while Mom talks to Charlotte about last-minute arrangements. We're expecting guests to arrive any minute. "How are you feeling?" I ask E as I help him out of his little black suit.

"Sad. I'm really sad, Mommy."

I wrap my arms around him, hugging him tight. I understand exactly what he means. Before, sad was just a word, but now it's a state of being. It consumes every cell, overtakes every other emotion, and my bones feel weighted down with the feeling. It's as if this is the only way I know how to exist. Covered in this blanket of sadness until there is nothing else.

"Me too, honey. But we won't always be sad," I add, forcing a soft smile on my face as I ease back, brushing my fingers along his cheeks. I hope I'm not lying to him. I want to —no, *need* to—believe in this truth. "Daddy wouldn't want that for us. He would want us to try to be happy again."

"I miss him so much." Tears stab his eyes, and I hug him again.

"We will always miss him, but I have something that might help. Put your shorts and T-shirt on while I get it."

I return to Easton's bedroom a few minutes later, carrying

a few items. E is wearing his clothes, and he's slipping into his sneakers. "Sit up here beside me," I say, resting on the edge of his bed. I prop the framed photo of Reeve on his nightstand, ignoring the piercing pain in my heart. "Daddy is always going to be watching over you, and I thought you might like to say goodnight to him every night." Easton sniffles, snuggling into my side. "Anytime you want to talk to him, to tell him about something exciting that happened in school or maybe finding more bugs, you can talk to his picture, and he'll hear it in heaven."

"He will?" He lifts his head, his wide eyes staring at me with so much trust and hope.

I nod, hoping I won't be struck down. I hand him one of Reeve's watches. "This one was your daddy's favorite. It's a golf watch. I bought it for him when he turned seventeen. I think he would want you to have it." Easton slides it on over his wrist, trying to tie it. "It's too big for you to wear now, but maybe you could keep it in your drawer for when you're older."

"Yeah. For when I play golf too."

"Exactly." I smile as he opens his drawer, very carefully placing the watch inside.

"And this was one of Daddy's favorite T-shirts. I bought it for him when I was in Greece one summer. Maybe you might like to sleep in it or keep it for when you fit into it. The choice is yours."

Easton brings it to his nose. "It smells like my daddy."

Tears pool in my eyes. "Yeah, buddy. It does." I threw a hissy fit when Mom permitted Charlotte to change my bedsheets. I hadn't planned on ever changing them. Not as long as Reeve's smell was still embedded in the fibers. Now, I've resorted to sleeping in his shirts so I can still smell him.

I haven't sorted any of his things yet, and it's on my long list of things I'm dreading.

I hand Easton the last item. Going into the nursery to retrieve it had almost undone me again. "I think your little sister would like you to have this," I whisper, giving him the fluffy pink stuffed rabbit. "You will always be Lainey's big brother, and when you feel sad about her, maybe you can cuddle her bunny rabbit or sleep with it," I suggest.

"I'm glad Daddy is looking after my sister. I don't feel as sad knowing Daddy is with Lainey."

I gulp painfully, fighting more tears. "Me too, buddy."

"Is the funeral over now, Mommy?" he inquires, scrunching his cute nose as he hugs the stuffed animal close to his chest.

I thread my fingers through his hair. "Lots of people are going to be here in a little while. But I figured you'd much rather play outside, so Nash is coming over with his mom, and you can play in the playground with him. Angela will be there too." I think today has been taxing enough for my child. "Grandpa organized pizza for later, and you can eat it in the treehouse, if you like."

"Yay!" Easton puts Reeve's shirt under his pillow before throwing himself at me. My breasts, my ribs, and my stomach protest the enthusiastic hug, but I will never complain. "Thanks, Mommy. I love you."

"I love you too, little munchkin. So, so much." I pepper his face with kisses as Angela appears in the doorway.

"Hey, pipsqueak! Guess who just arrived downstairs?"

"Nash!" Easton bounces off the bed, almost tumbling in his impatience to get to his friend.

Angela laughs, ruffling his hair. I stand, and her expression softens as I approach. "It was a beautiful service, and your mom's eulogy was perfect." She squeezes my arm.

"It was."

"I'll take good care of Easton. Don't worry about him."

"Thank you." I blow E a kiss. "Have fun and be good for Angela."

"I will, Mom. Bye." He races off toward the stairs with Angela hot on his heels.

I find Mom and Dad downstairs in the formal living room,

greeting the first guests. They offer condolences, and I thank them for coming as I eye the bar with longing.

Charlotte hired a catering company today, along with waitresses and bartenders.

"I need to talk to you both," I tell my parents, jerking my head toward the door. If I don't grab them now, we won't get to speak, and I know Dillon's family will be here because Mom mentioned she spoke to Cath outside the church and invited them. I'm sure she didn't want to invite Dillon but she was too polite to upset his mother.

Funerals are a lot like weddings in that regard. You're forced to put up with guests you wouldn't ordinarily invite, except it's the done thing.

My parents follow me into my office, and Dad closes the door. I'm sorry I didn't grab a vodka cranberry for this conversation. "I have something you both need to know. Something I should've told you sooner, but, honestly, I've been trying to forget it." I sit on one of the leather couches, knotting my hands in my lap.

"Whatever it is," Mom says, dropping onto the couch beside me. "We'll deal with it together."

Dad squeezes my shoulder, before sitting on the couch across from us. "We've got you. Now and always, princess."

Tears prick my eyes. "I know you do. I can't thank you enough for everything you've done." I look at my father, and he seems to have aged so much in the past week. "I know you think you haven't helped much, Dad, but taking care of the funeral arrangements, and pushing the reading of the will back with Carson, and handling stuff with Margaret and Edwin means so much to me. I could not have coped with any of that."

"We hate to see you in so much pain," Dad says. "Whatever we can do to help make it better, we will."

"Love you, Daddy."

Dad gets up, leaning down to give me a gentle hug.

"You're our whole world, Vivien. You and Easton will always be our priority."

"Love you too, Mom," I say when Dad has moved back to his seat. "I could not have gotten through this week without you, and I know how hard it's been on you as well. I know how much you both loved Reeve. How much you were both looking forward to meeting Lainey." A lone tear treks down my face.

Mom cradles me in her arms. "It's going to be okay, sweetheart. We will all get through this together."

"I need to talk to you about Dillon."

Mom nods. "I didn't want to push you, but we need to know what's going on."

I tell them. I tell them everything. Giving them a summary of how it went down since Dillon showed up here that fateful day, explaining the things he told me and ending with the confirmation Dillon is Easton's father.

"Oh my God. Vivien." Mom clamps a hand over her mouth as tears stream down her face. "And Reeve knew this before he died?"

Tears leak out of my eyes. "Yes. My husband died angry with me for lying to him and with the knowledge the son he worshiped wasn't his flesh and blood," I croak. "I hate myself so much."

"Don't," Alex says, entering the room with his wife. Audrey is carrying a tray of drinks.

"We thought you might need these, and we wanted to let you know the O'Donoghues just arrived," Audrey says. I had told my bestie I was telling my parents everything right now.

"Don't hate yourself, Viv." Alex perches on the arm of the couch. "It's not your fault."

"It is no one's fault," Audrey says, shooting her husband a warning look. "It was a tragic accident, and pointing the finger of blame *anywhere* won't help." She sets the tray with drinks down on the coffee table.

Alex scrubs a hand along his stubbly jawline. "I can't

believe we're here. I can't believe he's gone. I'm going to miss Reeve so fucking much." His eyes turn glassy, and I squeeze his hand.

"He loved you like a brother. I hope you know that."

Alex nods, rubbing at his eyes, before grabbing a bottle of beer. "I heard what you said in the hospital that morning and just now, and you're wrong, Viv. Reeve loved the shit out of you. You were always it for him. Yes, I'm sure he was angry and hurt at the things he discovered, but he didn't die believing those things of you. His love for you drove his actions that night. He died protecting you and Lainey. Trust me when I say Reeve would not have wanted it any other way and he would not want you blaming yourself."

Mom clenches her hands into fists. "As much as I'd like to point the finger of blame in Dillon's direction, Audrey is right. It was a tragic accident, compounded by several things. That doesn't mean Dillon is off the hook though. He has a lot to answer for. His scheming contributed."

"I always believed Easton was conceived in love, but Dillon never loved me. I was a means of exacting revenge. That was all. I was such a fool." I loved him for years, feeling horrible guilt for harboring longing for my ex when I was blissfully happy with my husband. Discovering that Dillon played me the whole time makes me sick to my stomach.

"I wouldn't be too sure about that," Dad says, and I arch a brow. "Dillon was at the hospital with Ash and Jamie and Ronan, for hours, in the waiting room. You probably don't remember this, darling," he adds, facing Mom, "but he gave quite a heartfelt speech before we asked him to leave." Earnest hazel eyes meet mine. "He said he loved you. That he regretted letting you go and you were his everything."

Alex harrumphs. "Yeah, his actions these past few weeks really showed that," he sneers.

"I'm not defending the man," Dad continues, "but I think he should be given an opportunity to explain himself before everyone throws shade. I believe he was sincere at the hospital, and let's not forget the part Simon played in all of this."

"I have never wanted to dig up a body to whale on it more in my life," Mom says, and it helps to ease some of the tension.

Giggles bubble up my throat, and I don't fight them, setting them free. It's too funny hearing Mom say such things. "I say we dig him up, piss on his bones, then pour acid over him, and watch him disintegrate into nothing but ash that flitters away in the wind," I add, accepting a vodka cranberry from my bestie.

"Creative." Audrey kisses my cheek. "And a little bloodthirsty. I approve." She leans into Alex, and he slides his arm around her.

I look away, unable to bear witness to their love, which makes me feel like a bitter bitch. It's funny. I remember feeling a lot like this when I first fled to Ireland after Reeve had broken my heart. I thought every loving couple, every PDA, was going to kill me until Dillon helped me to heal. It might not have been real on his end, but at least he gave me that much.

"How could Simon keep so much from us? From me?" Dad shakes his head. "I thought we were friends, but I never knew the man. Not really."

"Come on, Jon. The friendship was tentative, at best, after Felicia died. He pulled away from us, and all the respect I'd had for him evaporated with his neglectful treatment of his son. Then to find out he'd given Reeve's twin away." Sadness ghosts over her face. "Look at what he set in motion. All the pain his actions have caused. Dillon was wrong to direct that anger at Reeve, but I can fully understand his feelings toward Simon. What Simon did to him was unforgivable."

Silence descends for a few minutes. "It doesn't change anything though," I say in between sips of my vodka. "And I'm the one left to pick up the pieces." I glance out the window, spotting Easton and his best friend Nash playing in the playground.

"The wrong twin died," Alex says, a muscle popping in his jaw. "Reeve was innocent in all of this, but Dillon knew what he was doing. If anyone had to die, it should've been him."

"Thanks for that," a familiar husky voice says, and I whip my head around, spotting Dillon and Ash standing in the doorway with the rest of their family in the hallway outside. "Don't hold back on my account," he adds, striding into the room.

CHAPTER 15
VIVIEN

"ALEX!" Audrey hisses, elbowing him in the ribs. "You should apologize."

"I'm not apologizing for speaking my mind," her husband says, glaring at Dillon as the O'Donoghues file into the room. They aren't all here. It's just Ash, Jamie, Ro, Cath, and Eugene. I know the rest of the family is here somewhere, because Mom confirmed they were at the funeral. Ciarán, Shane, their wives, and kids, too. The only people missing are Ronan's girlfriend and their baby daughter. I don't know if they purposely stayed away, for my benefit, or some other reason. I'm touched everyone else came, but I'm sure it was more to support their brother than me. No doubt, they all know about Easton and they are keen to meet him.

"It's fine, Audrey," Dillon says. "He's loyal to Reeve. I get it."

Dillon is wearing a black suit with a black shirt and tie to match his black soul. The usual rings and piercings adorn his hands and face. His hair flops in brown waves over his brow, and I'm grateful he didn't style it like Reeve usually did. I know I mistook him for Reeve at the hospital, but I'm chalking that up to stress and a drugged-up hallucination. Now when I look at him, I see glimpses of Reeve, but he's wholly Dillon.

"It's not fine," Ash says, working hard to rein her anger in. She walks right up to Alex. "I understand if you hate my brother, even if you don't know him and you're not privy to all the facts. We're all pretty pissed off with him right now too. But to say you wish he had died instead is horrible. Nobody should have to hear what you just said."

Two red spots appear on Alex's cheeks. "You're right," he grits out, lifting his head and eyeballing Dillon. "I don't like you. For a lot of reasons, but that was harsh and uncalled for. I apologize."

Dillon shrugs, eyeballing Alex in return. Cath glares at her son, and Dillon purses his lips before running a hand through his hair. "Apology accepted," he begrudgingly says.

It's fair to say there will never be any love lost between those two men.

Mom stands, ushering Mr. and Mrs. O'Donoghue over to the couches, making them sit down. She calls Charlotte via the intercom, asking her to bring some food and drinks to my office.

"We're sorry for barging in here like this," Cath says, narrowing her eyes at Dillon. "We know this is a very harrowing time, and we're so sorry for your loss, Vivien. So incredibly sorry." Tears well in her eyes as she leans across Mom to hug me. "We've missed you, and I hate we are meeting under these tragic circumstances, but we felt it best to speak when we are all in the one place. There are things we should discuss."

Dillon and Ronan move the chairs from the front of my desk over beside us for Audrey and Ash to sit down. Dillon, Alex, Ronan, and Jamie all stand to one side. Dillon's eyes drift to the window, instantly locking on Easton. Pain splinters through my chest, along with other indecipherable emotions.

"I'm not sure Vivien is up to discussing this right now." Mom drags me back into the conversation.

"It's fine," I say, my voice devoid of emotion again. "Might as well get all the breaking done in one day."

Dillon jerks his head around at my words, staring intensely at me, in the way he always does. I avert my eyes, knocking back a few mouthfuls of vodka, needing the liquid courage.

"We had no idea Reeve had a brother," Mom says, addressing Cath. "Felicia was my best friend, but she didn't know she was expecting twins, and Simon said nothing to us afterwards." Anger flares in her eyes. "I am curious though. How did Dillon end up being adopted by you?" Mom slides her arm around my back for support.

Charlotte enters the room, depositing sandwiches, cookies, cake, and tea and coffee on the table, along with plates and napkins. I thank her, and we wait for her to leave before the conversation resumes.

"My Eugene is adopted," Cath begins explaining, patting her husband's thigh. "And when we got married, we decided we would like to adopt too. But Shane and Ciarán came along quickly, and we shelved the idea while they were young. My sister Eileen was working with an international adoption agency based in London. She let us know they were looking for a family for an American baby and asked if we wanted to apply. We almost declined. Aisling was only a year old, but we both felt a calling in our hearts." She looks over at Dillon, smiling. "We just knew this was the child for us, so we processed the paperwork, met with representatives of the agency in Dublin, and a month later, we were waiting at the ferry in Dun Laoghaire to collect our beautiful baby boy."

Dillon rubs a hand along the back of his neck in a familiar gesture so much like Reeve it hurts. I close my eyes briefly, exhaling heavily. Mom gently squeezes my side, and I force my eyelids to open. Audrey exits the room discreetly as I set my empty glass down on the table. Dad hands me a plate with some sandwiches, and I accept it to be polite, even though I can't stomach the thought of food right now.

"Did you know he was a twin?" I ask Cath.

She shakes her head. "That was not disclosed to us, and Eileen died eleven years ago of cancer. God rest her soul." She blesses herself. "So I don't know if she was aware. The first we knew Dillon was a twin was when he phoned the other night to tell us."

"You didn't even tell your family?" Disbelief drips from my tone as I stare at him.

"No. He didn't." Ash thumps him in his stomach. "And he's getting hell for it."

"Love." Cath tilts her head to one side, peering into my face. "You remember our little chat in my kitchen that Sunday?" I nod because I haven't forgotten a single second of my time in Ireland. "Dillon kept all those demons locked up inside. He was always so guarded, no matter how hard we tried to break down his walls. You were the only one who got through to him."

"Ma." Dillon shakes his head.

"No, Dillon. You will not silence me. There have been too many secrets and lies. It ends now."

"Amen to that," Mom agrees.

"What Dillon has done has disappointed us as a family, but we love him, and we'll forgive him because we know the kind of man he is inside. I wouldn't blame you for thinking the worst of him, Lauren, and I'm not making excuses for my son, but he has struggled with abandonment issues his whole life. It has broken my heart." Her voice cracks, and Dillon looks down at his feet. Mr. O'Donoghue presses a kiss to Cath's temple, holding her close.

"Ma. Stop." Dillon lifts his head. "I'm fully responsible for my actions. It's not your place to apologize or make excuses for me."

"I couldn't agree more," Alex grits out.

"Could I talk to you alone?" Dillon asks, drilling me with piercing blue eyes I'm so accustomed to.

"No. Anything you want to say to me you can say here." If

we go somewhere alone, I'm liable to murder him in cold blood."

A muscle clenches in his jaw. "Fine. I know you hate me. With good reason. And I know I've fucked up. I—"

"Good speech. Mirrors my sentiments exactly," I say, glaring at him as I cut him off. "Was there anything else?"

"I lied, okay?" He claws a hand through his hair.

"About what?"

"Pretty much everything."

"So, you didn't really hate your twin and you didn't spend years plotting ways to take Reeve down? You must be thrilled you got your wish after all."

A strangled sound escapes Cath's mouth, and I instantly feel chastised. "I'm sorry you had to hear that," I quietly admit. "But Dillon has hated Reeve when there was no justification, and he used me to try to get back at my husband. Reeve was so happy when he discovered he had a twin, and he didn't deserve the way Dillon treated him." Just thinking about it enrages me all over again. I lift my eyes to Dillon's. "You never gave him a chance or an opportunity to speak to you. If you'd only talked to him, you would've realized Simon manipulated him too."

"You think I don't know that now, Viv? You think I don't know I fucked everything up with my twin? Simon spouted all that shit, and it made sense at the time. I was hurting, and confused, and there was other stuff going down. It was easier, in a way, to channel all that emotion into hating Reeve and Simon. Then I saw what he did to you, and I felt justified. He treated you like shit back then, proving he was a selfish prick so obsessed with his career he betrayed the one person he claimed to love more than anything."

"He was young and thrown into a world he was not prepared for!" I retort. "He trusted the wrong people, and he was manipulated and outmaneuvered. I don't need you to tell me how much he hurt me. I haven't forgotten how he made me feel. How heartbroken I was at that time."

"Until I pieced you back together, and then you ran straight back into his fucking arms."

I stand, glaring at Dillon. "You didn't piece me back together! I did that myself." He helped. Ash did too. The whole Irish experience helped me to heal and to grow. But I'm not admitting that now. "And I didn't get back with him until after Easton was born. Until he'd proven himself. And he did. He made up for his mistakes, which is more than can be said about you!"

"I'd like a chance to make up for mine, but you won't let me!" Frustration is evident on his face, and I'm glad to see it.

"Damn fucking straight, I won't!" I plant my hands on my hips. "The difference is Reeve was just a kid back then, but you're a grown man who should know better."

CHAPTER 16
VIVIEN

"YOU DON'T HAVE to explain yourself to him," Alex snarls as Audrey slips back into the room carrying a fresh vodka cranberry. "You owe him nothing." Alex rounds on Dillon, putting his face all up in his. "You don't get to come in here today, of all days, after the shit you've pulled, and the stress you put a pregnant woman under, and demand a second chance like you deserve one. Reeve was worth a million of you, and he loved Viv with his whole heart." Alex shoves Dillon in the chest, and I'm terrified things are about to go south.

Audrey places the vodka in my hand, fixing me with apologetic eyes. "Alex and I are going to look after your guests until you're done here." She levels her husband with a look. "Aren't we, honey?" She yanks on his arm, pulling him away from Dillon before he can retaliate with his words or his fists.

Alex mumbles under his breath but doesn't protest as she drags him out of the room. Air whooshes out of my mouth in grateful relief. As much as I'm thankful to Alex for standing up for me, I don't want a fight breaking out.

"Good riddance," Dillon mutters, and I level an evil eye in his direction.

"Immature much?" Sarcasm drips off my tone.

"Jesus Christ, Dil." Ash yanks him down, forcing him into Audrey's vacant seat. "You are your own worst enemy."

He sighs heavily, loosening his tie and unbuttoning the top button of his shirt. "For the record, I might have hated Reeve, but I never wished him dead. I'm willing to admit I was wrong. If you say Reeve didn't know and Simon was the one who manipulated me, then I believe you."

"Oh, *now* you believe me." I throw my hands in the air, almost dislodging the plate of uneaten sandwiches on my lap. Mom lunges for them, setting the plate down on the table. "Now he's dead, you're willing to accept the truth. I was blue in the face telling you it was all lies, and you refused to believe me!" I yell.

"Because I was upset and shocked and I'd believed what that asshole Simon said," he yells back.

"Don't you dare shout at my daughter. Act civilly or you can leave this house." Mom jabs her finger in the air at Dillon.

"Dillon. Please." Cath's teary eyes plead with her son.

Ignoring both moms, Dillon looks me straight in the eye. "I've spent years nurturing this hatred, Viv. How stupid do you think I feel knowing I was played completely? I believed Reeve knew about me. I thought he was a selfish prick who didn't give a shit about me. What I read about him on social media seemed to confirm it. Look at what he did to you! You were a mess when you first landed in Dublin."

"I know how I felt, thank you very much. I don't need a history lesson from you, and we've already covered this."

"He hurt you, but you forgave him. I'm just looking for the same opportunity. Please let me make amends. Please give me one more chance. I won't let you down. I promise." Desperation bleeds into the air, seeping from his words and the pleading expression on his face. "I know what I did was wrong. I see that now. I wish I could turn back the clock and do so many things differently." He thumps his chest. "I will have to live with that guilt for the rest of my life. I didn't know my brother, and now I never will. I know that's partly on me. If I could trade places with him, I would."

"Dillon, no!" Cath cries. "Don't say that."

Dillon's Adam's apple jumps in his throat, and I feel Cath's pain. "Sorry, Ma. I don't mean to upset you, but I've made a mess of things. Sometimes I think it would've been easier if Simon had just murdered me when I was born."

Fucking hell.

Cath's cries are louder, and Ash, Ro, and Jamie stare at Dillon in shock. I don't know what to think. Whether he's being sincere or if this is still a game he's playing. Mom and Dad look troubled, and I'm just so over this day and ready to draw a line under it.

"Don't say that, Dil." Ash shakes her head. "Yes, you're a dickhead. Yes, you've fucked up and hurt my best friend. But you've hurt yourself too." Her worried gaze meets mine. "We shouldn't have come here today. It wasn't fair on you. Emotions are still too raw. I know you distrust Dillon now, and I don't blame you. I really don't, Viv. I'm putting myself in your shoes, and I would feel the same way, but what you had in Ireland was real. Deep down, you know that too. One day, when you're not mourning your beloved husband and beautiful little girl, maybe you might be able to look at it differently. That day isn't today, and I think we should go." She looks at her parents, and Cath nods, swiping at the tears flowing down her face.

Ash slings her arms around her brother, squeezing him tight. Her apologetic gaze locks on mine, and there are so many unspoken words between us. I know I need to fix things with her. Especially now she will be in my life. She's Easton's auntie, and I can't continue to deny that fact, even if I'll be keeping contact with the O'Donoghues to a minimum until Easton has properly grieved Reeve and Lainey.

"Ash is right, and we will go, but I need to get this out first," Dillon says. "I know you're traumatized and heartbroken and you don't need any more of the heavy. But you need to know my biggest lie was what I told you about my feelings for you. I led you to believe I didn't care, but that's not the truth. *I care.* So fucking much." His eyes bore into my face. "I know you're not ready to hear this, but I need to say it. I still love you, Vivien Grace. I never stopped."

What a crock of shit, and I'm not buying it. Actions speak louder than words, and that is most definitely true in Dillon's case. I school my features into a neutral line, as he continues.

"I can see you don't believe it, and I can't force you to. But we need to try to find a way to get along, because Easton is my son, and—"

I interrupt his desperate word vomit because I refuse to listen to one more word of his bullshit. I see it now. I see what new game he's playing. Spewing all this shit, trying to win me over to his side, just so he can slide in and steal Easton away from me. Over my dead body will that happen!

"He's not yours!" I shout, rising abruptly. "He's Reeve's son! Reeve will *always* be his daddy, not you! You're just a sperm donor in the same way Simon Lancaster was."

Mom sucks in a breath, standing. "Vivien." I can tell I've shocked even her, and I know I'm being callous, but how dare Dillon show up here, thinking he can mouth some pretty words at me and all will be forgiven.

"We shouldn't have come," Dillon says, unfurling to his full height. Pain radiates from his eyes. "I'm sorry."

"Ya think?" I shout, shucking out of Mom's grasp. "My husband and my baby were only buried today, and you're over here already staking your claim on *my* son!" I stalk toward him, shoving his chest. "He's *my* son. He will never be yours! Never! Fuck you, Dillon! Fuck you! Fuck you! Fuck you!"

Ro's brows climb to his hairline, and concern is splayed across his face. Jamie's too. Neither of them has contributed to the conversation, and Ash has been quieter than normal.

"Princess." Dad wraps his arms around me from behind. "It's okay, sweetheart. Let it all out."

"He can't have Easton, Dad," I sob, curling into his warm chest. "He's not taking my son from me! E is all I've got left."

"Viv," Dillon's voice is deliberately soft. "I would never take him from you, and I would never do anything to hurt him or add to his pain. I was never going to share anything online. I just said that to make you do things my way, but I wouldn't have told the world about him or posted any of your pictures. I know you don't trust me, but you will see the truth in time." Hurt and longing shimmer in his blue eyes. "I just want to get to know my son. I understand it'll take time, but I'm begging you to let me develop a relationship with him as his uncle."

I sob into my Dad's shirt, unable to deal anymore. I'm physically and emotionally spent. The well is dry, and I just want them to leave.

"I know there are things to discuss, but this isn't the time or the place. You need to leave." Mom's stern tone leaves no confusion.

"I'm very sorry, Lauren," Cath says. "We shouldn't have come here today. I can see we've only added to Vivien's stress, and that wasn't our intent." She turns to me. "Honey, please forgive us for intruding on your grief in such a selfish way. My heart breaks for you and for Easton. Take care of yourselves."

"I'll give you my number," Mom says, compassion flaring behind her steely determination. "Call me, and we'll try to arrange something before you return home."

"I'm sorry, Viv. I'm sorry for everything," Dillon says, and I twist my head, staring at him through blurry eyes.

Ash approaches with tears streaming down her face. "I hate seeing you in so much pain, and I hate that our friendship was a casualty of all this. We always said we wouldn't let my brother come between us."

On instinct, I reach out, hugging her. "That one's on me. Not you," I sob, clinging to her. "I never wanted to cut you off. It hurt me to do it."

"I understand." She eases back. "And I understand some of what you're going through now. When you're ready, please call me. Let me be here for you now. If there is anything I can do to help, anything at all, just pick up the phone, and I'll do it." She presses a business card into my hand.

"Thanks, Ash. I've missed you."

"Missed you too. So fucking much."

Cath pulls me in for a hug. "We love you." She kisses both my cheeks.

"I love you too." It's true. I've always loved their family. They cared for me as if I was one of their own. I have no beef with Dillon's family, and I'm not surprised they turned up en masse today. It's who they are, and I haven't forgotten how they opened their house and their arms to me in Ireland.

It's not their fault their son is a lying, scheming bastard.

She kisses my brow. "You mind yourself, and hopefully, we'll see you soon."

"I'll give you space," Dillon says as his family walks toward the door. "But we do need to talk soon. I won't pressure you into anything. I just want a small window to get to know Easton."

And I just want to pound my fists into your self-centered face until you bleed. "Goodbye, Dillon," I snarl.

He glances out the window, his expression a mix of pain and longing, before casting one final look at me. "I meant what I said. I know you don't believe me, but I still love you. I always will. Even if you can never forgive me."

CHAPTER 17
VIVIEN

"ARE your parents flying in for the reading of the will?" Audrey asks, handing me some of Charlotte's delicious homemade lemonade.

"They can't take any more time off, so they're going to join us via video." My parents only returned to the set last week, and it took massive amounts of persuasion to get them to leave. The studio had run out of patience, and they were threatening to sue for breach of contract. I won't have my parents bankrupted or their reputations sullied because of me.

Easton threw a hissy fit when they left, and he had nightmares the first few nights. He's terrified they're not coming back, and I can relate. I'm clinging to my son, gluing him to my side, because I'm petrified something is going to happen to him.

"Reeve was so organized." Audrey drops down onto the lounger beside me. "We don't have a will. I guess it's something we should get around to."

"That's probably the only good bit of advice Simon Lancaster ever gave his son. When we got married and built this place, he told Reeve to ensure his affairs were in order."

I never imagined it would turn out to be prudent. Pain

licks at my insides, and I'm tempted to make some vodka cocktails, but that's a slippery slope I don't want to fall down. If it wasn't for my son, I think I'd be numbing my pain in a vat full of Grey Goose or a box of Valium.

Easton is splashing in the pool with Nash, and I'm glad he's presently happy. His moods are as fickle as mine lately. One minute, he's laughing, and the next, he's lashing out at something or someone. I know he's struggling to process his feelings, hence why I've hired a grief counselor to come to the house. She's going to do a session with Easton—with me present—and then do a one-on-one with me.

Mom forced me into it. It was the only way she would agree to return to the movie set. If it was up to me, I'd wallow in misery and grief because the thought of talking through everything with a shrink makes me want to puke.

"Did you speak to Easton's camp instructor today?" she asks, lathering sunscreen on her legs.

Easton has been attending summer camp since he was three years old. It's the same one Reeve and I attended as kids, and it's where his love of acting developed into his passion. There is a huge focus on the arts, and Easton loves the singing and drama classes, but they also do sports and outdoor activities too. I really didn't want to let him go this summer, as I panic any time he is away from me. But he wanted to go, and I know it's important to keep up his routine.

To help to give him some sense of normalcy, so I've been driving him there and back each day. I still can't get in a car with anyone else driving. I need to be in control. To know if anything happens, I control the outcome.

"Yes. She was sympathetic," I explain. "She understands he's grieving, but, at the same time, he can't go around hitting other kids." There was a situation yesterday where Easton got into a fight with another boy when they were outside playing football. I was terribly upset last night, because it's not like E at all. He's always been sensitive to other kids' distress, and he's usually the first kid to reach out a helping hand if anyone is hurt at Little League.

"Did Easton say anything else?"

I tried talking to Easton last night, but he was angry and sulking and he wouldn't talk about it. I didn't push, waiting until this morning to ask him again when he had calmed down. "The other boy told him his daddy was a drunk and he deserved to die," I say, through gritted teeth.

Unfortunately, the toxicology reports from the accident were made public and it's been reported in the media. I haven't watched any of the TV reports or read anything online, because I don't want to know how they are tearing my husband's reputation to shreds. Of course, Reeve's fans are defending him to the hilt, according to Edwin Chambers, Reeve's publicist. I have retained his services for the moment, as we deal with the aftermath of the accident and his death.

Audrey gasps. "What a little shit."

I nod my agreement. "It's no wonder Easton got angry and lashed out though I had to explain that he can't do that again. I told him he can defend his daddy with his words, but he can't use his fists. I said if anyone says anything nasty or mean it's best if he tells one of the instructors and lets them handle it."

It's hard to tell your kid not to retaliate when someone says something so horrible. I can't let violent behavior go, but I'm not punishing my child for protecting his daddy's memory either. I'm hoping by the time Easton returns to school in August things will have settled down and the press will have moved their focus to someone else. "I feel like I'm failing as a parent," I add. "Maybe I should remove him and just keep him home."

We haven't ventured outside our property, except for camp, because the paparazzi follow us every time we leave, hounding me for a quote and shouting shit at my son. I almost punched a photographer in the face last week when he asked Easton if he talks to his daddy's ghost. Some of these people are scum of the earth and they have no empathy or respect for our privacy."

"I know it's hard, Viv, but I think routine is important for Easton, and being around other kids is too."

"I just want to swaddle him in cotton wool and keep him safe here." I sip my lemonade through the straw while I share the truth with my bestie. "I've been having these nightmares." I swallow painfully. "I'm trapped in the car, but this time, Easton is there too. He's looking in the window, crying, and I can't reach him. He runs away, continuing to cry, and I watch as he races out onto the road and—" A sob bursts from my chest, and I set my drink down on the small glass table, turning to the side so Easton can't see me upset. "I can't even say it, but I'm scared, Rey. I'm scared of something happening to E too. He's all I have left."

A fluttering sensation builds momentum in my chest, spreading across my upper torso, and my heart feels like it's beating too fast, like it's trying to find a gap to erupt from my rib cage and escape. My breath oozes out in sputtered starts, and I'm struggling to pull enough oxygen into my lungs.

"Put your head between your legs and draw deep breaths, Viv. In and out, nice and slow. I'll do it with you."

I'm so busy concentrating on calming down I don't hear the little pitter-patter of feet. "Mommy!" Easton cries, and I whip my head up. "What's wrong?" he shrieks, racing toward me and flinging himself at me. Water droplets cover my skin as he clings to me, sobbing.

"It's okay, honey. I'm okay." I hold him close as tears stab my eyes. I meet Audrey's compassionate gaze over his shoulder. "I was just doing some exercises," I lie.

"You sure?" he asks, lifting his head to stare at me. His gorgeous blue eyes drill into mine, and I hate to see so much worry there. I need to do better. "I'm sure." I stand, taking his hand. "Who would like ice cream?" I ask as Nash hangs back nervously at the edge of the pool.

"Me!" they scream, and I take them inside, fixing a bowl

with vanilla and chocolate ice cream and strawberry sauce with sprinkles for each of them. The boys take their ice cream back outside, sitting side by side on one of the loungers, whispering and laughing as they devour their treat.

"You're not failing, Viv," Audrey says, continuing our previous conversation when I lie back down alongside her. "You are doing the best you can, and it's not easy. You're both trying to deal with this enormous loss. It's okay to admit you need more help."

I twist my head to the side. "I can't ask any more of you, Audrey, and I know you keep deflecting this conversation, but you need to return to Boston. I'm not letting you throw years of studying away because of me."

Alex had to leave, to return to Boston, a few days after the funeral because he got a huge opportunity to help coach at the New England Patriots summer youth camp. It's a once-in-a-lifetime opportunity to be around top coaches and players. It might open the door to a college job or an entry-level job in the pros. He was going to pull out so he could stay here with his wife and support me, but I can't expect my friends to give up their careers for me. I told him I'd never speak to him again if he passed on the chance, so he left a few weeks ago.

"I'm good for another week or two." She shrugs casually, as if it's not a big deal. I have no idea how she made it work, but she got extended leave on compassionate grounds. However, she can't stay here indefinitely, and I need to learn to cope on my own. She wets her lips and sits up a little straighter. "I will feel better about going once you talk to the therapist, and I think you should talk to your doctor about anti-anxiety and depression meds. They will help."

"It's not that bad," I lie. "I just need time."

"What the fuck is he doing here?" Audrey hisses the next morning as we get out of the car in the underground parking garage attached to the attorneys' offices.

"Who?" I spin around, and my mouth hangs open as Dillon and Ash walk toward us. He's wearing his signature black tee and ripped jeans with sneakers, and I wonder if he just buys the same clothing in multiple quantities.

"Hey." Ash steps forward, yanking me into a hug. "How are you holding up?"

"I rejoice when I can get out of bed in the morning," I truthfully admit, and she squeezes my hand. She looks very sophisticated in a gorgeous cream pants suit, looking like she's ready for a professional meeting. Unlike her rock star brother. "What's he doing here?" I ask, jerking my head in Dillon's direction.

"I'm right here, Hollywood. You don't have to keep pretending like I don't exist." I ignore that little dig and avoid looking at him, crossing my arms over my chest.

"Carson Park told us to be here," Ash explains after a few beats of awkward silence. "He said Dil is named in the will."

My eyes almost fly out of my eye sockets in shock. "What?" I splutter. Audrey and I exchange startled expressions.

"That's all we know." Ash tentatively smiles at Audrey. "Hey, Rey. Sorry I didn't get to speak to you at the funeral."

Tension lingers in the air. Ash and Audrey have a checkered history. They were bosom buddies at the start until they both took sides in the Dillon versus Reeve situation. I know Ash reached out to Audrey after I returned to L.A. from Dublin, when I was ghosting her, and Audrey ghosted her too, so I'm not surprised things are a little strained, even if Ash must know why by now.

Audrey surprises me, leaning in to hug my other bestie. "It's good to see you. The three of us need to catch up."

"I would really like that," Ash says, looking relieved.

"We should head inside," I say before Audrey sets a date

and Dillon decides to invite himself. He's been calling and texting, and I've been ignoring him. I know I can't continue to do it forever, but I cannot deal with him right now. I'm doing my best to put one foot in front of the other, and I'm trying to help Easton process his feelings. I don't have time to worry about Dillon's hurt ones.

"We need to talk," Dillon says when we're all trapped within the close confines of the elevator taking us up to Carson Park's office.

"Not now," I snap, staring straight ahead.

He repositions himself so he's directly in front of me, and I have no choice but to look at his face. "When then? You're ignoring my calls and texts."

"Because you're harassing me," I hiss, and Audrey and Ash turn around.

"I'm not harassing her," Dillon says, eyeballing both women. "I've messaged her and phoned her a handful of times in the past week because we need to talk about Easton."

"Not now we don't," Ash says, drilling her brother with a warning look. "You never learn," she adds, shaking her head.

The doors ping open, and I push past Dillon, walking into the reception area.

Carson's secretary escorts us to a small conference room where the Lancasters' attorney is already waiting for us. My parents' comforting faces greet me from the wall-mounted screen. Introductions are made, and then Carson gets down to business. "As I mentioned on the phone last week, Vivien, we had a small reading of a part of the will a couple of weeks ago. Reeve made several donations to charities, and I met with representatives of those bodies to explain the terms."

I nod because this isn't news or surprising. Reeve left a sizeable sum to Strong Together, as well as a number of other charities he had affiliations with.

"Today, I'd like to discuss the terms of the personal aspects of the will."

I listen dejectedly as Carson confirms Reeve left the bulk

of his estate to me. I have my first meltdown when he mentions Reeve has set up trust funds for the kids. Of course, I knew there was one for Easton, but I didn't know he'd created one for Lainey too. He also left them personal items. Lainey's will revert to me. I wish I had known before the funeral because I would have had them buried with her.

Carson stops talking while I sob against Audrey's shoulder, and Mom swipes at the tears streaming down her face. After a few minutes, I manage to compose myself, and the attorney continues. I purposely avoid looking at Dillon across the table, staring at the glossy walnut tabletop, wishing I could press the fast-forward button because I don't know if I can survive this.

Reeve left a few personal items to Easton too. The golf watch I've already gifted him is one of them, and I burst into tears again as another wave of grief washes over me. We knew each other inside and out, and our thoughts were often in sync. Our connection is so intimate it even transcends life and death, and I'm missing him so acutely right now. What I wouldn't give to feel his comforting arms around me or to hear his quietly uttered assurances.

I feel so lost without him. Like I'm wandering aimlessly through life, with no one to guide me along the right path. Reeve isn't here to hold my hand when I veer in the wrong direction, to help me to get back on track. Unlike the last time, there is no overcoming it because Reeve isn't merely on a different continent. He exists in a different realm. He's gone, and he's not coming back. He won't be waiting for me like last time. He can't ever be there for me again, and I want to die every time I remember that. It feels like I'm missing half my soul, half my heart, without him, and that's before I contemplate the gut-wrenching loss of the baby I had nurtured so lovingly in my womb.

The pain is never-ending, and I'm like a shell of the person I used to be.

Carson asks if I want to reschedule the meeting, but I struggle through my pain, shaking my head as I blot my tears with the tissues Audrey hands me from my purse. I've stashed tissues in all my purses and bags because I never know when grief will attack. Sometimes, the smallest things set me off. Something almost insignificant will happen to remind me of Reeve or the daughter I lost, and I'll fall apart, crying until my throat aches and my eyes sting. I tell Carson to continue, and he moves along to the next item.

Reeve bequeathed some personal belongings to my parents, along with the vacation house on the Italian Riviera. We hardly got to vacation there, with our busy schedules, while Mom and Dad spent several summers relaxing at the small Mediterranean-style villa. It makes sense Reeve would leave that to them, but it's odd in another way. It's almost as if my husband had a sixth sense about his passing. Why else would he leave my parents a house when they should have been gone before he was? My heart swells painfully as these thoughts flip-flop around my brain.

To Alex, he leaves a couple of his prized sports cars, a few of his expensive watches, and some mementos and framed photos from high school.

Audrey gasps when she discovers Reeve purchased a unit in a new modern office building being built in downtown L.A. in her name. Carson explains it is for her future medical practice and Reeve had initially planned on surprising her with it upon graduation.

Now it's Audrey's turn to dissolve into heartbreaking tears while I comfort her. She holds my shoulders, crying into my neck, and her pain speaks to mine. Reeve was her friend, and she's tried to be so strong for me, but she's entitled to her tears. She's allowed to mourn him too, and I feel selfish in this moment for not even considering her grief as I've been drowning in mine.

"Did you know?" she croaks, swiping at tears.

I smile softly, nodding at my best friend. "We were out for lunch one day, and we came across the development. The guy building it happened to be there, and he and Reeve got talking. He told me a week later he had purchased one of the larger units, thinking you might want to do something with it in the future. He made me promise not to tell you." Probably because he knew Audrey would not accept it easily. "You don't have to do it though," I add, not wanting my bestie to feel like she's forced into coming back to L.A. after she has graduated or that she even has to set up her planned practice here. "It's yours to do with as you please. Use it, or sell it, or whatever." I shrug casually as if I wouldn't be devastated if my bestie never returned home.

"Viv." Audrey kisses my cheek. "We were always coming back to L.A. after my graduation. Alex even has a potential job offer on the table."

Shock splays across my face—even if I'm thrilled—because this is the first I'm hearing of it. "Why didn't you say anything?"

"We were going to tell you on our Mexican vacation."

We had planned a trip to Mexico for September. It was going to be our first family vacation with our new daughter. I squeeze my eyes shut as brutal pain slaps me in the face. It is always like this. I might find a few minutes where I've forgotten the shitshow my life has turned into, and then something happens to remind me of everything I have lost.

"I'm sorry."

I blink my eyes open, brushing tears away. "It's fine," I whisper, deliberately not looking at Dillon or Ash. I'm clinging to my sanity by my fingernails at this point.

"I think it's wonderful you'll be permanently returning to L.A.," Mom says from the screen. "And now, thanks to Reeve, you have a location for your new practice."

"Yes, I do." Audrey hugs me quickly, and we manage to compose ourselves so Carson can finish the meeting.

"That brings us to the last item." Carson shuffles some papers on the table, pushing his glasses up the bridge of his nose as his gaze moves between me and Dillon. "Reeve came to see me one week before he died to make an alteration to his will." He wets his lips before reading from the papers in front of him. "In the event of my death, the inheritance I received from Simon Lancaster's Last Will and Testament, excluding the shares in Studio 27, will be split equally with one share going to my children, to be divided between them, and the remaining share will transfer to my twin brother, Dillon Thomas O'Donoghue."

CHAPTER 18

DILLON

"WHAT?" I almost fall off my chair in shock. Why the hell would Reeve add me to his will at the eleventh hour?

"It's a substantial inheritance," Carson Park continues as if he hasn't noticed the startled expressions on everyone's faces. "As well as the bank accounts, there are investment portfolios and several properties. The forty percent stake in Studio 27 now transfers to Vivien, as a caretaker, until her eldest child comes of age, and then it will pass to Easton."

"I don't want it," I blurt, gripping the edge of the table. "I don't want anything that once belonged to my asshole sperm donor."

Carson blinks at me through his glasses.

"What my brother means is, he needs time to digest this," Ash says, slipping into a practiced diplomatic role. She smiles that bullshit polite smile she usually rolls out at these rodeos. "You have my number. Please send me all the paperwork, and I'll handle it."

"Why would Reeve do that?" Viv asks, looking as confused and shocked as I feel. Her gaze bounces between the solicitor and me. "He suspected who you were. Yet he changed his will? I don't understand." She chews on the corner of her mouth, and the familiar gesture is like a punch in the gut.

Being around her hurts so much.

More so because I see how much pain she is in and I want to help glue back the broken pieces of her heart, but she won't let me. She won't let me in at all. She's still the same stubborn feisty girl I met in Dublin, buried under a bigger mountain of pain and grief.

And I'm still the same impatient determined fucker.

Viv can push me away until the cows come home. She can hurt me with her words and her anger and her indifference, but I'm going nowhere.

We're both still the same people we were, yet we're not. She's a mother now, and her protective instincts are strong. Her sense of self-preservation might be rocked in the aftermath of her loss, and she might feel like she's drowning, but she knows who she is and what she wants in a way she didn't understand when we first met. It's unlucky for me what she wants is my body transported to Mars where she never has to see me or deal with me ever again.

I know what I want too. I have clarity in a way I've never had it before. I want Vivien and Easton. I want a chance to prove I can be there for them. I don't know if Viv can ever love me again, but I will take her any way I can get her. Even if we are never more than friends and coparents.

I know I can never replace Reeve.

Nor would I want to.

My feelings for my twin are still a clusterfuck of epic proportions. I have accepted I got some of it wrong, but Reeve wasn't the perfect angel Viv seems to think he was. Those photos are still burning a hole in my pocket, and I'm fucking dying to know how they ended up in their car that night. I'm guessing Reeve hired a PI to spy on Viv when she was in Dublin. It's the only explanation that makes sense. I remember that guy I spotted creeping around a couple of times, and I'm convinced he was paid to watch us. My blood boils thinking about it. Every memory I have of our time together is singed around the edges now, knowing some fucking asshole was taking pictures of us and sending them back to Reeve.

No wonder he was lying in wait for her the instant she stepped off the plane that day. He knew we were in love, and he was determined to get her back and willing to play dirty to do it. Begrudging admiration wars with seething rage as I think of how he manipulated things. And, yes, I know I'm a fucking hypocrite.

The truth is, we both manipulated Vivien in different ways. Neither one of us was ever worthy of her.

"I don't know, Vivien," Carson says, dragging me out of my head. "Reeve didn't explain his decision. He just asked me to make the amendment to his will."

"You can have it all," I offer, locking eyes with her for the first time since we entered the room. "I'll reassign it back to you."

"I don't want it or need it," Vivien says. "I'm just shocked Reeve would do that. I know he spoke about giving you your share that day you were at the house, but that was before he suspected who you were."

"We won't ever know his motivations for sure," Ash says. "But I for one think this shows the kind of man your husband was. He was ensuring Dillon got the inheritance that was rightfully his. No matter what he thought of him, he didn't let it interfere with doing what he felt was right."

Vivien nods, and I glance at the blank screen on the wall, wondering when Viv's parents exited this conversation. I must have been lost in my thoughts when they said their goodbyes. "Perhaps your brother should dwell on that in light of his actions." Viv speaks to Ash as if I'm not even in the room, and it fucking infuriates me to no end.

"If I wanted to transfer the inheritance to Easton, is that possible?" I ask the solicitor.

He nods. "Of course. It's yours to do with as you please."

I expect Viv to object, but she says nothing, looking like she's checked out again.

Carson draws the meeting to a close, and I tune out his nasally voice, studying the woman who owns my heart. She stares at the wall, as if she's staring through it, while nibbling on her lower lip. I've noticed Viv zoning out, every so often, staring off into space with the most forlorn look on her face.

I never doubted she loved Reeve. She never tried to hide that from me, and I respected her for her integrity. But it's painfully obvious now how much he meant to her. He was her everything, in a way I've never been, and that's a bitter pill to swallow.

I know I shouldn't be envious of my dead brother. It's a pointless emotion. But I can't help how I feel. I have always been in his shadow, and I will continue to remain there, even though he is no longer here.

"Earth to dumbass," Ash says, tugging on my arm. "The meeting is over. Everyone is gone. I thought you wanted to talk to Viv."

"Shit." I jump up. "Yes. Come on. You need to hear this too." I drag my poor sister out of the room, telling her to take off her shoes so she can chase me down the stairs. The lift is already gone, taking Viv with it, and I need to stop her before she leaves.

Short of turning up on her doorstep—which I'm reluctant to do because a confrontation is the last thing Easton needs to witness—this is the only chance I may have to speak to her. Viv needs to know, so we can get ahead of this.

I burst through the doors of the car park just as Viv and Audrey reach their SUV. "Wait!" I holler, racing toward them. Viv, predictably, ignores me, climbing behind the wheel. I grab the door before she can close it. "Don't. Fucking. Ignore. Me."

"What do you want, Dillon?" Audrey asks, leaning across the console to stare at me.

"To get to know my son and the opportunity to make things up to the woman I love, but"—I raise one palm, keeping my other hand firmly on the car door, as I don't trust Viv not to slam it in my face—"I know what the reply would be, so that's not why we currently need to talk."

"Jesus Christ, Dillon," Ash says, materializing behind me. She's panting and a little red in the face. "I think I just ripped the seam of my trousers. If I did, you're buying me a new suit."

"I have nothing to say to you," Viv says, looking straight ahead.

"Look at me," I snap, getting sick of this crap. I know she's in mourning. I know I'm a piece-of-shit dumbass fuckface. But she can still look at me when she's talking to me.

"What, Dillon?" she hisses, turning to face me. "What do you want?"

"We have a mutual problem we need to discuss."

"What problem?" Ash straightens up, putting her serious face on.

"Don't freak," I tell my sister, knowing it's pointless. "I only found out about it this morning."

"Found out about what?" Audrey asks, looking troubled.

I blow air out of my mouth, hating I have to blurt it out like this, but if I don't, Viv will run off and she'll find out in the worst possible way. "The press know about me. They've found out I'm Reeve's twin brother."

"How?" Ash asks when it's clear Viv is in a state of numbed shock.

"A reporter noticed the resemblance as I was leaving the funeral, and she started digging. She got her hands on a copy of my naturalization application. It lists Reeve as my brother. She wants an exclusive interview with me. She's given me forty-eight hours to agree or she's running the story."

"Fuckity-fuck." Ash expels a breath heavily. Throwing a concerned look at a shell-shocked Viv, she addresses Audrey. "We need to strategize. We need to discuss our options and decide how best to minimize the impact so it doesn't bring any more heat down on Viv."

CHAPTER 19
DILLON

"I DON'T LIKE THIS," Viv says, traipsing moodily behind me as I enter the hallway of my L.A. pad.

"Don't worry, Hollywood. I won't kidnap you and tie you to my bed." I flash her a cheeky grin. "Unless you want me to."

She slaps me across the face, and it fucking stings. "I'm leaving." She turns on her heel but not before I see the tears glistening in her eyes. Shit. The last thing I want to do is hurt Viv, but I seem to have foot-in-mouth disease whenever I'm around her.

Ash levels me with a dark look that scares me. Outwardly, things might look perfect between us, but that couldn't be further from the truth.

After what transpired at Viv's house the day of the funeral, I had to come clean to my family about how I'd threatened her into keeping silent. Seeing the disappointed looks on my parents' faces made me feel horribly ashamed of my actions. My entire family are reeling from the revelations and feeling hurt I excluded them. Ma can't believe I've been harboring all this resentment and dealing with it alone. She doesn't understand why I didn't tell her and Da when Simon accosted me at seventeen. Why I chose to handle it myself.

It's going to take me some time to make it up to everyone.

As for Ash, to say my sister wants to murder me for the cruel way I treated her best friend is an understatement. She has blanked me for weeks, only speaking to me when it was official band business. Today is the first time since the funeral she has spoken directly to me, like we used to, and the first time I've felt we might be able to get through this without causing irreparable damage to our relationship.

I love all my siblings, but I'm closest to Ash. If I have permanently damaged our relationship, I won't come back from that. She is more than my sister. She's become my closest confidante and the person I trust most. I can't lose her without losing a part of myself.

It's the same for the broken woman standing before me, too lost to even steer her rightful anger in my direction. Instead, she's planning to flee, and I can't let her leave. "I'm sorry, Viv. Please don't go." I drag a hand through my hair. "You know this is my default setting, especially when I'm nervous. I'm not trying to be an ass on purpose."

"It just comes so naturally to you," Audrey drawls, scowling at me as she makes her feelings clear. She's never been a big fan of mine anyway.

"My husband—*your brother*—died a month ago, Dillon." Viv whirls around to face me with sad eyes and a trembling lower lip. "You cannot say those things to me. I didn't want to come here, and you're not making me want to stay."

I risk a step closer, gulping over my fear. "I'm sorry for upsetting you. That wasn't my intention. I know you don't want to be here, but we have little choice. To go out in public together right now is a disaster waiting to happen. I'm willing to go back to your place, but I didn't think you'd want me there with Easton."

I would happily chop off a limb for the chance to go to her

house and see my son. Not being able to see him is killing me. I'm trying to be sensitive to the situation, because I know how difficult this is for Viv, but I have already missed out on so much of his life, and I want to be there for him now. I know he's hurting. I know he's missing Reeve. I know I can't replace who he was to him, but I want an opportunity to form my own relationship with my son.

"We need to deal with this, Viv," Ash says. "If you don't feel up to talking about it, I can reach out to Edwin Chambers, and we can discuss a strategy for handling it together."

I glare at my sister, even though she's only trying to help. But I'm starved for Viv's company, and she's offering her a "get out of jail free" card.

"I want to know what's going on and how this will impact me and Easton." Viv straightens her shoulders, and a determined glint flashes in her eyes, reminding me of the woman I love. I know she's still in there, and I'm making it my mission in life to help her to rediscover herself. My shoulders relax a smidgeon now I know she's not going to leave. "We will definitely need to involve the PR people, but let's talk it through first now."

I lead them through the lobby, past the vast open-plan kitchen on one side and the games room on the other, and out to the patio. It's a glorious day. Sun shines brightly, illuminating my spacious back garden. Buttery beams glint off the inviting water of my large outdoor pool. Thanks to my expert gardener, the lawns and flowerbeds are pristine, colorful, and plentiful.

I show my guests to the seated area, pulling out one of the comfy wicker chairs for Viv. Ash opens the matching umbrella, providing much-needed shade. "Let me organize some drinks," I say when the ladies are seated. "I'll be back in a few."

I stride into my kitchen where Nancy, my full-time housekeeper, is busy at the cooker. I tell her what I need, and she rushes me back outside, assuring me she's on it.

The girls are talking when I return, their gazes fixed on the large wooden structure in the near distance.

"It's the band's main recording studio," Ash is explaining as I plop down on the chair across from Vivien.

"When we're not booked into Capitol Studios by the label," I add.

"Should we get the others?" Ash asks, her gaze darting to the soundproofed building where Conor, Jamie, and Ro are busy working on tracks for our next album.

"Nah." I scratch the stubble on my chin. "This isn't band related. We can fill them in later." After my revelations, things were a bit strained for a couple of weeks with the band. Conor exists in his own little bubble, so he said jack shit to me. Ro was quietly seething although he didn't bitch me out like Jamie did. Jamie was pissed because I'd upset and angered his fiancée.

"You'll have to grant that bitch of a reporter an exclusive interview," Ash says. "It's the only way to control the narrative."

"I agree," Viv says, drumming her fingers on the glass tabletop. "But what exactly are you going to say?" She stares at me across the table, but I can't see her eyes, thanks to the ginormous shades she's wearing. "No one else, apart from your family and us, knows you discovered the truth when you were seventeen, right?"

I nod. "Carson knows too, obviously, but he's not going to say anything." He's loyal to the Lancaster family.

"You can say you only found out after Simon Lancaster died," Ash says.

"Both of you only found out after he died," Viv corrects. "And you can say you had only just met Reeve and you hadn't had a chance to form a relationship with your twin. No one needs to know that was intentional. You can garner the sympathy vote by lying, and it's not like that will be a stretch for you."

Fuck. She really despises me.

"I'm going to land the blame squarely at that fucker sperm donor's door," I say through gritted teeth. "It will help to deflect the attention. Let them make it about the revered Studio 27 boss who loved his wife so much he banished the child he believed caused her death during childbirth and lied to his other son about being a twin. The world's media will lap that shit up."

Audrey looks at me with a glimmer of sympathy I fucking hate. I know in doing this I will be opening myself up to more of it, but I'll cope if it means they will focus on me and not Vivien and Easton.

"Are you comfortable with that?" Ash asks Viv. "We might attract some heat from Studio 27 if we paint Simon as the villain."

"Simon *is* the villain," Viv replies as Nancy appears carrying a tray with drinks. "I have no issue in tarnishing his reputation."

Nancy sets the tray down, and I distribute drinks, handing Viv a pink gin cocktail. "We don't have 7UP, but Sprite tastes almost the same." Her chin tilts up as she stares at me, and I wish I could see her beautiful hazel eyes. She audibly gulps, and I wonder if her mind has thrown her back to nostalgia lane like mine has. After a few beats of awkward silence, I set the drink down in front of her. "I can get iced tea or lemonade or a coffee if you prefer?" I offer as Nancy appears in my peripheral vision.

"This is fine," she croaks, wrapping her fingers around the stem of the glass. "I haven't drank one of these since Ireland."

I walk to meet Nancy, taking the second tray from her. "Thanks a mil."

"Will your guests be staying for lunch?" she inquires, tipping her head in Audrey's and Vivien's direction.

"Probably not, but make extra just in case."

"No problem, Dillon." When Nancy first came to work for me, she tried to call me Mr. O'Donoghue, which made me sound like an old fart. I told her Mr. O'Donoghue was my father and if she wanted to keep her job to call me Dillon. She hasn't messed up once since that day.

I carry the tray with crisps, biscuits, and fruit over to the table, depositing it in the middle before reclaiming my seat.

"What about your hair and your eyes," Viv says. "She is going to ask about that. How will you explain it?"

Kicking my sneakers off, I stretch my legs out under the table. "I'll tell her I experimented with my looks a lot when I was a teen. That I went through a rebellious phase and wanted to alter my appearance as a fuck you to the parents I never knew who had abandoned me. I'll say when I found out the truth and reconnected with my twin, I chose to change my look. I wanted to see how close the resemblance was and what our individual differences were." I'm sure the reporter will think it was a sweet gesture. A way of feeling closer to my long-lost twin, the brother she believes I hadn't known about my entire life.

There is no way she will know it was a premeditated attempt to mess with my twin's wife. Another way of driving the knife home to the love of my life, reminding Viv she picked the wrong brother.

No one needs to be privy to those disgusting truths.

Truths that make me want to lobotomize myself so I can never think of them again.

Awkward silence descends as the reality of my unspoken words resides in the space between us. We all know why I changed my look and why I changed it back. I'm only fooling myself if I think otherwise. There is no getting away from the full horror of my sins, and that is something I will have to live with for the rest of my life.

CHAPTER 20
DILLON

GRABBING A BEER, I guzzle it back as the usual blanket of guilt and remorse washes over me. So many times, I have wished I could go back to that last night together and do everything differently. If I had, everything might have turned out differently. Viv might be sitting here as my wife, and I might have been the only father Easton has ever known. Reeve would most likely be alive.

Or maybe nothing would've changed even if I had thrown myself at her feet a second time and begged her to stay. Offered to drop out of the band just to be with her. To this day, no one knows those were the thoughts floating through my mind back then. Even if I had told her what I was willing to sacrifice, it most likely wouldn't have been enough. The only way it would have worked is if I'd come clean and told her everything. I'm pretty sure she would still have walked.

I try not to look back at the what-ifs, but it's hard not to when I have so many regrets. If I had known at seventeen what I know now—how every action and reaction had a consequence with the most tragic fallout—I would have chosen differently. If my punishment is to have permanently lost the love of the only woman I will ever give my heart to, then so be it. I will have to accept that fate and try to find some way to make peace with it. But I refuse to lose my son in some form of twisted penance.

One thing I know for sure is I am going to fight for them to the bitter end. I won't stop trying to make amends for all the ways I have wronged Vivien, even if I haven't the foggiest notion where to start.

Viv drinks her cocktail like it's water, and I'm shocked to see it's almost half empty. She was never a big drinker. Even on special occasions, where everyone was knocking back drinks like they were going out of fashion, she always paced herself.

She stiffens, sitting up straighter and putting her drink down. "Wait. We're forgetting something." Air whooshes out of her mouth. "There are people in Ireland who knew about us. People like Cat and *Aoife*." Her mouth pulls into a hard line as she basically spits out Aoife's name. "That bitch won't hesitate to sell her story." She rubs at her temples. "Fuck. I can't have that coming out. They'll twist it and say I was cheating on Reeve with his twin brother and make it this whole sordid thing. It will all start up again. I'll be hated, and how can I protect Easton from that? It's already bad enough." The words tumble from her lush mouth in streams of liquid panic.

"Deep breaths, Viv." Audrey says, smoothing a hand up and down her back. Viv's chest heaves painfully as she draws exaggerated breaths, white-knuckling the table as she rides out her panic attack.

Ash and I trade concerned looks as we watch Audrey talk Viv off a ledge.

"You don't need to worry about anyone back in Ireland," I tell Viv when she's okay. "They won't say a word."

She barks out a harsh laugh. "I'm pretty sure your whore will have plenty to say on the subject. She's vindictive enough to cause trouble. Her gloating face that last day is something I've never forgotten." Hurt glides across her face, and I feel like a worthless piece of shit.

It's time to fess up.

"I'm sorry about that. What I did that night was shitty, but you should know I wasn't with her. Not that night and never again. It's like Ash said. I used her to hurt you because I was hurting so badly and I wanted you to feel what I felt."

Viv yanks her glasses off, almost crushing them in her hand as she leans forward, glaring at me. "You think I wasn't hurting?" she shouts. "I was hurting a whole lot before you did that and a whole lot more after. I cried nonstop the entire plane ride home. And don't make out like you cared. Everyone here knows it was a setup, and I was the gullible fool who fell for it."

"No." I vigorously shake my head. "It started out as a setup, but what I felt for you was real. I told you that. I told you, no matter what happened, to believe it was real."

"And then you told me a few weeks ago that you lied! You can't turn around now and say you meant it all along!"

"I was devastated, Viv." I hop up, grab my beer, and throw it at the side of the house as frustration does a number on me. I'm so pissed at myself for fucking everything up. It hits with a sharp thud, smashing into pieces, spraying beer over my cream-colored stone patio. "I loved you, and you left me for him." She might as well have taken an ax to my heart, because she left me a broken, shattered mess and I still haven't recovered.

Her hands are trembling as she puts her sunglasses back on. "There is no point rehashing old shit. I can't do this now. I won't do it." Ignoring me, she turns to face Ash. "How do we silence Aoife?"

And just like that, I've been relegated to the sidelines again.

"Dillon took care of it years ago," Ash explains, squeezing Viv's hand. "We thought he was stupid at the time, but it seems he was smarter than any of us gave him credit for."

I'm too angry and strung out to appreciate my sister's half-assed compliment.

"Took care of it how?" Viv asks, still ignoring me.

Grabbing another beer from the tray, I sit back down, staring neutrally at Audrey as she glares at me. "I gave her a hundred grand in exchange for signing an NDA," I explain, eyeballing Viv, even if she's not looking directly at me. "If she speaks out, she's breaking the terms, risking prosecution and a large financial penalty. No matter how vindictive she might be, she won't say anything. None of them will. I got everyone to sign it. All the groupies. Cat. That dickhead she was going out with and your other friends from Trinners." I smirk as I bring my beer to my lips. "At least that asshole's money came in handy."

"Why would you do that?" Audrey asks, staring at me like I'm a puzzle she needs to figure out.

"I didn't want anyone spouting shit about me to the press."

"You mean you didn't want anyone ruining your little revenge plan," Viv says. "If Aoife or any of the others had mentioned anything about me, you would've tipped Reeve off, but you wanted to wait to time that revelation when it would cause maximum exposure."

She's not entirely wrong, but that wasn't the main reason. "Simon's NDA was watertight. I was not to mention anything about Reeve or you or any children you may have. That's why I did it."

"Yet you had no qualms about coming forward after Simon's death," Audrey says.

I laugh. "It's not like he's going to arise from the dead and slap me with a lawsuit for breaching the terms, is it?"

"His estate could still come after you," she retorts, irritating me with her smug superiority.

"You think *my son* is going to sue me?" I snap.

"*I* could," Vivien says, slamming her empty glass down, almost shattering it. "But you knew I wouldn't. You knew Reeve wouldn't. You waited until the villain was dead before assuming his mantle."

I say nothing because I can't defend myself. While Simon was alive, my hands were tied. I knew the only way I could exact revenge was to manipulate the media into breaking the news, in a way that couldn't be linked back to me, or to wait for the bastard to kick the bucket. I had been working on Plan A when Plan B happened, but I will take that secret to my grave.

"Have your PR person draw up a press release and a contract," Vivien says, speaking to Ash. "Send it to me and copy Edwin on it. I want the details of what's to be said at the interview listed in bullet points and a commitment from Dillon that he will not deviate from the agenda."

"I won't say anything that will hurt you or Easton." I offer her what I hope is a sincere expression. "I will deflect the attention off you. I promise. I'll make it about Simon and the poor little abandoned Irish boy he gave away. I'll ensure the focus is all on me."

"Make sure you do." She grabs her bag, ready to leave.

"When can I see him?" I blurt.

Ash rolls her eyes and shakes her head. Audrey glares at me again, and Viv stares at me as if she's looking through me. "When he's ready."

"Can you give me a ballpark idea of when? I'm going out of my mind here, and we're leaving on a US tour in seven months. I—"

"Don't pressure me, Dillon," she snaps, cutting me off midsentence. "And there is no timeline for this situation. God, it's like you've never been around children. Like you don't have nieces and nephews."

Shit. She's right, and I know I'm being unfair. I'm just so desperate to spend time with my child, and believe it or not, I know I can help. I can help them if she'll just let me in. Even a little bit.

"Easton is going through a rough time, and I won't do anything to upset him. He's not ready to meet you yet. I will contact you when the time is right. Until then, stop fucking harassing me." She stalks off with Audrey, and Ash races after them.

I'm too heartsore to follow so I sit back down, sulking as I drink my beer.

"Dillon. What the hell?" Ash says, storming toward me a few minutes later. "How can someone so talented and so smart be so fucking dumb at the same time?"

"You'll have to enlighten me because I've no idea what you're talking about," I truthfully reply.

She sighs, kicking off her heels and rolling up the legs of her trousers. Carefully, she maneuvers down at the edge of the pool, dipping her feet and lower legs in the water. "Come over here, dumbass, and let me explain it to you."

I push the legs of my jeans up to my knees and join her, welcoming the tepid water as it laps at my bare flesh. I hand her a beer, and she readily accepts. We have no other appointments today, and I plan to vent my frustrations in the studio as soon as this little chinwag is done.

"I know you're dying to meet Easton. We all are, Dillon, but you've got to stop making this about you. This is about Easton and Vivien, and they've just been through hell."

"I know that, and I want to help. How is wanting to be there for them so wrong?"

She rubs my arm. "She's not ready to hear it or accept it, and, Dillon, you've got to at least consider the fact she may never want you like that again. You have hurt her, time and time again, and a lot of years have passed since you were together. People change. Feelings change."

"I love her, Ash." Pain bleeds into every corner of my being. "I love her so fucking much it kills me to see her in pain and not be able to do anything about it."

"You can't force your love on her, Dil. You can't force anything on her. Especially not when she's grieving."

"What do I do? I'm not walking away from her, and I'm sure as fuck not walking away from my son. I have missed out on so much of his life already, and he needs me now."

"You need to be patient." I scowl, and she chuckles. "I know it's about as natural as a colonoscopy, but you can't fuck this up, Dillon. You have one chance to make this right." She drills me with a warning look. "One last chance, Dil." She jabs me in the arm. "Don't blow it."

CHAPTER 21
VIVIEN

LAINEY'S pitiful cries wake me from sleep, and I crawl out of bed, careful not to disturb Easton as I head on autopilot toward the nursery. As I stumble from my bedroom, her cries grow louder and more insistent, and I'm overwhelmed with the need to erase my daughter's suffering.

The nursery door crashes against the wall, waking me from whatever quasi sleep-slash-comatose-slash-illusionary state I was trapped in. Pain slams into me like a freight train, knocking all the air from my lungs and taking my legs out from under me. I collapse on the floor in the doorway of the nursery, hacking up gut-wrenching sobs birthed straight from my splintered soul.

I don't know how long I cry for, but then Audrey is there, cradling me from behind, her cries mixing with mine. In between sobs, I tell her what happened. "Am I going crazy, Rey? Am I losing my mind?" I stare at the pretty pink and white nursery with the Tinkerbell mural on the wall with a new layer of horror. I can't lose my grasp on my sanity. I am all Easton has, and he needs me to get a grip. It's been six weeks since I lost Lainey and Reeve, and it doesn't feel like it's getting any better. Maybe I should try the meds Audrey and my therapist are suggesting.

"The brain is a complex organ." Audrey cradles me in her arms with my back to her chest. "One we will never fully understand. And you're not going crazy. You're traumatized, and grief manifests in different ways." I sniffle, nodding. "What are you going to do about the nursery?" she asks me, after a few beats of silence.

"I don't know. I can't even look at it without immense pain. It's why I never go in there. Reeve, Easton, and I picked every item for her nursery together. We even helped the artist paint parts of the mural. Everything is so personal I can't bear to throw it away, but I can't look at it either. It's the most painful reminder of my loss."

"I can't even imagine how difficult it must be for you, Viv. But I've seen enough grief and trauma in my medical journey to know it's not healthy to cling to the past. If looking at it prolongs your agony, I think you should consider clearing it out. There are plenty of charities you can donate the less personal items to. Maybe you can remodel the room for a different purpose?"

"Maybe," I murmur, knowing she's right but unable to contemplate even stepping foot in the room, let alone clearing it out.

"You should do the same with Reeve's things," she quietly adds. "I can help you pack up his stuff before I go." Audrey is leaving to return to Boston in two days, and I'm trying not to think about how broken I will be without her.

"I don't want to give his things away," I say, climbing to my feet. Audrey stands, and I close the nursery door, heading toward my bedroom. "I'm not ready."

"Okay." She tugs on my arm as I open my door. "But promise me you won't put it off indefinitely. It's not healthy to cling to him, Viv. I know it will hurt." Tears fill her eyes. "But it's got to be done." She glances over my head where my little boy is sleeping soundly in bed, occupying Reeve's vacant space. "And E needs to return to his own room. I know he comforts you and vice versa, but he can't replace Reeve, and you can't become his crutch. He needs to process his feelings, even if he can't put a name to them. You can't shield him from that."

"He's doing much better," I say, my tone more than a little defensive.

"All the more reason to get him to sleep in his own bed. Kids deal with things differently, and he takes a lot of his cues from you. I know you needed one another at the start, but it's time, Viv."

"Goodnight, Audrey." It takes mammoth willpower not to slam the door in my bestie's face. As I climb under the comforter and curl my body around my son's sleeping frame, I know she is right. Like I know she only has both of our best interests at heart, but having Easton sleep beside me helps to lessen the pain. Is it wrong to draw comfort from that?

"Can we talk when you get back?" Audrey asks the next morning as I'm getting ready to drive Easton to camp.

"Sure." My tone is a little cold, and I want to slap myself upside the head for being like this with my bestie, but my emotions appear to be ruling me, not the other way around.

"I don't want to fight with you, and the things I said last night weren't said to hurt you." Her sad eyes drill through my frosty outer layer, and I thaw instantly.

I pull her into a gentle hug. "I know, and I'm sorry. I don't want to be reacting like this, but it's so hard to think about moving on even though I want to and I need to." I ease back. "You're my best friend, Audrey. I could not have gotten through these last few weeks without you. Thank you for everything, and I'm going to try."

"You're strong, Viv. You know you can do this. As much as I hate leaving you, I think it's time. You need to fight to push through to the next level. You need to learn to start living again." Easton comes bounding into the room with his little backpack on his back. "For both your sakes."

She crouches down, doing a high-five with Easton before hugging him. "Have a great day, little man. I want to hear all about it when you come back."

"We're going hiking today," Easton confirms with an excited gleam in his eyes. "Mommy bought me hiking boots. Look." He lifts his leg, almost kicking her in the face.

Audrey chuckles, straightening up. "They are awesome boots. Have fun."

"Bye, Auntie Audrey." E waves as he clutches my hand with his other hand, dragging me out of the kitchen.

"Can Megan come over to my house after camp today?" Easton asks as I pull into the parking lot. He hasn't stopped talking the whole journey, and it's good to see him so excited. The familiar black SUV rolls into the space beside me. Leon and Bobby climb out of the car, wearing jeans and T-shirts, looking awkward as fuck. Turning up every day with our bodyguards looking like something from *Men in Black* was drawing way too much attention, so I asked the guys to dress casually so we can attempt to fit in. "Mommy? Can she?" he asks when I haven't replied.

"I don't know Megan's mommy, so I'll have to check. She can't come over today, but maybe one day next week."

"Mom!" My son fixes me with puppy-dog eyes through the mirror, and it's so hard to deny him, but I won't let anyone near my house until they've been carefully vetted. I don't trust any strangers who come into our lives. I hate I have to be like this, but I won't take chances with my son's safety. While there haven't been any other incidents of kids taunting Easton, I'm not naïve enough to believe it's gone away. I know people are gossiping and whispering behind my back. A couple of the moms say hello to me in the mornings, but most just stare, saying God knows what when I'm gone. I don't give a flying fuck as long as E is protected.

I overheard Audrey talking to Mom on the phone this week, and I know I've received some hate mail from that crazy element of Reeve's fanbase. They blame me for letting Reeve get behind the wheel when he'd been drinking, and they're mad he risked his life to save mine. Yet they are hailing him as a hero at the same time. Apparently, it's all my fault he's dead and I should have been the one to die with my baby daughter.

Stupid whores.

"When can she come over? I'm bored at home." E's pouty face pulls me away from the dark thoughts in my head.

"I said I'll talk to her mother. I can ask Nash's mom if he wants to come over for a playdate today?"

"He's got his cousin's party," he grumpily replies.

"Well, how about I call up some of your other friends from school and ask them to come over? I can get a bounce house and McDonald's, and you can have a spontaneous summer party?"

"Yay!" He jumps up, crawling through the gap in the front seat to hug me. "You're the best mommy ever. Thank you."

Crisis averted. For now. "Come on, buster. Let's get you into the hall before you're late for rollcall." I open my door, and Leon grabs Easton, while Bobby retrieves his backpack from the backseat.

Leon leads the way through the parking lot, heading toward the front entrance to the large redbrick building, as Bobby guards us from the rear. We have just reached the bottom of the steps when I'm jostled from behind. Screams ring out, and I almost take a tumble when Bobby staggers into me from behind. It all happens so fast, but I react immediately, thrusting Easton at Leon, aware there's some threat.

Blood rushes to my head, and adrenaline floods my veins as I spot someone tall in a hoodie racing toward me out of the corner of my eye. The next thing I know, I'm sprawled on top of Bobby on the ground with another body covering me. Piercing screams and shouts surround me, and whoever is on top of me jerks, grunting as if in pain.

"Are you okay?" Bobby asks, frowning as he eyes the stranger on top of me.

"I'm unhurt but struggling to breathe," I admit as the weight of the man covering me crushes me on top of my bodyguard. "Are you okay? Are you hurt?" I rasp.

"I might have a few bruises, but I'm fine. I'm sorry, Vivien. They caught me off guard, shoving me from behind."

Whoever is on top of me shifts a little, but they are making no move to get off me, which means the threat must still be present. I'm conscious of being pressed between two men, and there are various camera flashes going off.

There are always a few paps waiting at camp each day, hoping for something like this. Honestly, I wouldn't altogether rule out them setting this up just to get a story. Interest had grown in the initial aftermath of the interview Dillon gave confirming he was Reeve's long-lost twin. Reporters chased me for quotes, but I remained tight-lipped and the interest leveled off pretty quick. According to the text I received from Ash, the media is hounding Dillon for more information, so he has deflected some of the heat away from us.

"Shit, man," Leon says from above me. "Did that crazy bitch hurt you?"

The weight is lifted off me, and air whooshes out of my mouth as the sounds of a scuffle ring out in proximity.

"Let me go, asshole!" a woman with a high-pitched voice says. "I'm not the one you should be holding! Arrest *her*!"

Leon helps me to my feet while my mysterious rescuer bows his head, bending over at the waist and breathing heavily. I whip my head around, relieved to find Easton safe, with one of his instructors, at the top of the steps. He's crying, and I want to go to him, but I need to find out what's going on first. I need to ensure the threat has been neutralized. I blow him a kiss before turning around, hoping to reassure him with a smile.

Two camp security officers are restraining a skinny blonde with long stringy hair. She's thrashing about, trying to get free while snarling at me. "You fucking murdering bitch!" she shrieks. "Reeve should never have married you. You got him killed! He should've married Saffron, but you stole him away from her." Spittle lands on the asphalt beside me, and I fold my arms around my body, schooling my features into a neutral line, even though I want to take out her jugular.

Three photographers draw closer, taking pics, and I refuse to give them anything juicy to report.

"Fuck off," a man with a familiar Irish accent says from beside me, and I jerk my head around to Dillon, attempting to disguise my shock. The photographers are trigger-happy, snapping more pics as Dillon takes a step toward them. "I said fuck off," he snarls, yanking the camera from one of the men. He throws it to the ground and stomps on it.

Well, shit. I guess that's one way of dealing with it.

"I'll sue your ass!" the photographer yells, grabbing Dillon by the scruff of the neck. He must be a rookie because no experienced pap would lay hands on a celeb in this situation. He's just ruined any opportunity he might have had to take legal action against Dillon.

Good. We don't need any more freaking drama.

The hood of Dillon's gray hoodie falls, and I barely manage to stifle my shocked gasp. I didn't realize he had dyed his hair again, and it takes me back in time. Messy white-blond strands fall over Dillon's brow as he shoves the guy away.

"Dillon, look here!" the second photographer says as sirens blare in the background. These idiots clearly have no sense of self-preservation. Dillon stalks toward him, leaning a little awkwardly on his left side and I spot the tiny trail of blood he leaves in his wake.

Oh my God. He's injured.

Panic bites me in the face. "Get Easton," I tell Bobby. "We're leaving." I face Leon. "We need to get out of here before more paparazzi arrive. Can you handle the police? Tell them we want to press charges against her. Send them to the house, and we can give statements there. And can you talk to the camp coordinator too?"

He nods once. "I've got this. Don't worry," Leon adds before following Bobby back up the steps.

The woman is still hurling obscenities at me, but I tune her out as I advance on Dillon before he does something that will land us in even more hot water.

"You lot are fucking scumbags," he says to the second photographer. Dillon is in his face, pushing him back, but the photographer is still snapping away while retreating. His camera is on a strap around his neck that is fixed to the top of his shirt so Dillon can't rip it away as easily as the last one. "Can't you leave them alone? Give them some fucking privacy."

"Dil." I reach for his shoulder, and he winces, cursing out loud. My fingers are coated in blood, and I freeze, instantly taken back to the scene of our accident. I'm shaking all over as I stand rooted to the spot, the sounds of approaching sirens doing nothing to drown out the screaming in my head.

Dillon is saying something to me, but I can't hear him. I'm locked in my head, fighting an intense bout of panic as I'm trapped between the present and the past. Reeve's lifeless form resurfaces in my mind's eye, except this time it's Dillon's face staring at me.

Dillon is hurt.

He's bleeding.

He could be dying.

That crazy bitch did something to him.

I don't remember hearing any gunshots, but it all happened so fast.

Blood trickles from my fingers down my arm, and I stare in a horrified daze at it. No! Oh my God, no! My heart pounds painfully behind my rib cage at the thought of something happening to Dillon as well. I offer up silent prayers to a God I no longer believe in, begging him to let Dillon be okay.

The overriding thought ping-ponging around my frantic brain is I can't lose him too.

CHAPTER 22

VIVIEN

DILLON CARRIES me to my SUV, ignoring his pain, to get me away from the vultures. We arrive at my car as Bobby is strapping a sobbing Easton into his seat. "No!" I protest when Dillon places me in the back seat. "I need to drive."

"You are in no condition to drive, Mrs. Lancaster," Bobby says, sliding behind the wheel. "Climb in the back with Mr. O'Donoghue. You need to check his injury to see how bad it is. I can drop you and Easton at home before taking him to the hospital."

"I don't need a hospital," Dillon says, helping me into the car beside E. He climbs in after me and shuts the door, gritting his teeth as a glimmer of pain races across his face. "She stabbed me, but I don't think it's deep," he adds in a lower voice so Easton doesn't hear.

I want to run back and gut the bitch.

"Are you sure?" I ask, swallowing painfully.

He nods. "It's not serious." His eyes skate past me, to Easton, and his features soften as he drinks him in.

Bobby reverses the car out of the space and heads out of the parking lot.

"Are you okay, sweetie?" I ask my son, examining his face and his body to reassure myself he is unharmed.

He nods. "Are you?" His brow scrunches up as his worried eyes meet mine.

"I'm totally fine." Thanks to Dillon's quick thinking. Gratitude wraps around me, even if I would like to know what the hell he was doing here.

"Can I go back to camp?" he asks after giving me a quick once-over.

"Not today." My heart could not take that. "But if everything is okay, you can return tomorrow." I want reassurances from our security team and the camp officials before I'm letting Easton step anywhere near that place.

"But what about my hike?!" His lower lip wobbles as he pouts. He thrusts his leg out. "I want to try my new hiking boots."

"I'm sorry, sweetie." I rub my throbbing temples. "I know you're disappointed, but I'm sure there will be more hikes."

"It's not fair," he wails, balling his hands into fists. "I want to go back!" Tears well in his eyes, and I hate upsetting him, but this is nonnegotiable.

"It's not safe, and I'm not arguing with you about this. I'm the grown-up, and it's my decision."

Easton opens his mouth to protest some more, but Dillon cuts in, stopping whatever he was about to say. "Hey, Easton." Dillon leans forward, smiling at his son. "Do you like yo-yos?"

Easton's tears dry as Dillon produces a red, black, and gold yo-yo from his pocket. It has the Collateral Damage logo on the side, so it must be official band merch. Dillon's hopeful expression does something to me, and guilt mixes with panic, swooping down and pummeling me from all sides. After cleaning my hands with a tissue, I smooth the front of my summer dress as a familiar fluttery feeling invades my chest. E's brow puckers as he looks between me and Dillon, and I try to focus on my son and not the blossoming panic attack I'm fighting to keep under control. Easton gets real upset when I have an anxiety attack, and I try to avoid him seeing me like this.

"This is your Uncle Dillon," I say, almost choking on the words. "Remember you met him once before?"

"You look different," Easton says, still frowning.

"I like to change up my look." Dillon's Adam's apple bobs in his throat as he stares in amazement at his son. Tiny pinpricks stab me all over my chest. It's a bittersweet moment —watching Dillon engage with his son and feeling immense pain for all Reeve has lost.

Easton looks deep in thought as he reaches out, taking the yo-yo from Dillon's hand, effectively distracted. He traces the logo on the side with his finger. "What does this say?" he asks, the words too difficult for him to read.

"It says Collateral Damage," I explain.

"It's the name of my band," Dillon adds, leaning against the side of the door, while maintaining eye contact with E.

Bile swirls in my stomach as I spot the growing bloodstain on the upper left-hand side of his gray hoodie.

"You're in a band?! That's so cool." Easton's eyes are the size of saucers as he attempts to roll the yo-yo while staring at Dillon with newfound respect. "Do you play guitar or the drums?"

"Guitar," Dillon says, beaming at his son. "My brother Ronan is in the band too. He plays the drums."

I shoot daggers at Dillon. Opening this line of questioning will only lead to trouble. He needs to tread carefully.

"Is Ronan my daddy's brother too?" Easton asks, looking confused, and this is exactly what I hoped to avoid. Reeve had explained who Dillon is to Easton, telling him he grew up in Ireland with his adopted family, but I'm not sure he fully understands the implications.

Dillon shoots me an apologetic look that seems sincere. "No. Ronan is my adopted brother, and he's an awesome drummer. I bet he'd let you play his drum kit some time."

Easton drops the yo-yo in his excitement, bouncing in his booster seat. "Can I Mom? Puh-lease."

Wow, Dillon is pretty much a master of distraction techniques. Not that it should surprise me. This is what he does best. My lingering guilt poofs into thin air. "Sure thing, buddy. We can arrange something later in the summer, when camp is finished." That seems to appease him. I pull out my cell as I reach for the yo-yo, handing it back to Easton.

"I can show you how to roll it," Dillon says, watching Easton struggle with the toy. "It's all in the wrist action." I tap out a message to Audrey so she knows we are on the way and that Dillon needs medical attention.

"Cool." Easton eyes Dillon curiously as the yo-yo lands on the floor again. "What songs do you sing?" he asks, seemingly more interested in the band than the yo-yo.

"Mainly rock songs. You want to hear one?"

Acid crawls up my gut, and I draw a deep breath in preparation.

"Yes! Yes!"

Dillon's smile is so wide it threatens to split his face in two, and I hate how endearingly sweet it is. Then I feel like a bitch because I should be pleased they are bonding so naturally. Dillon hooks his cell up to Easton's iPad on the back of the seat, and a few seconds later, the opening notes of a familiar song start up. My eyes meet Dillon's green gaze as my heart dances wildly in my chest.

Of course, he'd pick this song—the very first one he wrote for me.

I suppose "Terrify Me" is a better choice than "Hollywood Ho" or "Fuck Love." I should probably be grateful for small mercies, but it's hard when it's resurrecting so many perfect moments. Moments I've refused to remember since Dillon reappeared in our lives because they all seemed so tarnished.

As we stare at one another, I'm transported back in time to Shane and Fiona's wedding, where Dillon serenaded me from the stage with so much love and longing on his face there was no mistaking the genuine emotion.

I'm so confused. So conflicted. I don't want to feel the things I'm feeling right now. I prefer to hold on to my hate and my anger because it's far easier than admitting the truth.

Dillon brushes an errant tear from my eye as his soulful voice floods the car. "It's still my favorite song to sing," he whispers in my ear, sending delicious shivers racing up and down my spine. "Every time I sing it, no matter what part of the world I'm in, I'm always singing it for you. I'm always remembering how you looked at the wedding when I sang it for the first time."

Tears clog the back of my throat as his husky voice wraps around me, offering comfort if I want to reach for it. Thankfully, my son comes to the rescue before I'm tempted.

"I know this song!" He jumps around in his seat. "My mommy has this song on her phone!"

My eyes swivel to my son's. How on earth does he know that? I was always careful to hide my semi-obsession with Collateral Damage from my husband and my son.

"She does, huh?" Dillon asks, and I hear the smile in his tone.

"I should check your wound!" I blurt, desperately needing to divert this conversation. "Audrey says she can tend to it provided it's not too deep."

"It's a flesh wound at most," he says, smirking that annoying smirk I've always loved to hate. Of course, he knows I'm deflecting.

"It seems to be bleeding a lot," I murmur, not wanting to alarm E.

"A knife in the back tends to do that."

"Don't make light of it. It freaked me out seeing it."

His humorous expression alters in a heartbeat. "I know." He tucks a piece of my hair behind my ear, brushing my cheekbone in the process, and I hate how my body yearns to lean into him. I can't forget all the ways Dillon has hurt me and Reeve. I don't know if I'll ever be able to forgive him for it. "Are you okay?"

"I should be asking you that." My eyes latch on to his familiar green gaze. I wonder why he's reverted to his previous look. Is it to divert attention from his resemblance to Reeve, or is there some part of him that hopes I might remember what we once shared if he looks the same? Or is he merely returning to what's more comfortable? The look his fans fell in love with?

"I'm fine. Nothing some stitches and a few painkillers won't cure, I'm sure."

"Thank you," I say as Easton sings along with the song, guessing the words. "Thank you for saving me back there."

"I would jump in front of a crazy bitch every day to save you if you'd give me the chance."

"Do I want to know why you were there?"

He shrugs, moving his mouth to my ear again. His warm breath wafts over my flesh, sending a fresh wave of shivers cascading over my skin. "You won't let me see him, so I've been showing up every morning at camp just to catch a glimpse."

That's borderline stalking, but I don't blame him. I have left him no choice. In this moment, I feel like I've been very unfair to Dillon. In my defense, I did it to protect Easton, but he's turned a corner these past two weeks, and I can't continue to refuse Dillon. Look how they've already bonded, and I can't deny my son the opportunity to get to know his father. That doesn't mean I'm going to let Dillon off the hook that easy. "You really don't understand the word no."

"That surprises you?" he asks, keeping his face close to mine.

"Not really." I sigh in relief as we turn into our driveway. I managed to survive a journey with someone else behind the wheel, and I successfully fought an anxiety attack. Perhaps there is hope for me after all.

"I'm the same irritating impatient asshole you hated to

love in Ireland." His eyes sparkle as he teases me, and it would be as easy as breathing to fall back into his arms. Except there are too many secrets and lies between us, too much hurt and pain, and I don't know if I'll ever be able to overcome them.

Besides, starting anything with Dillon again would be the ultimate betrayal to Reeve. Dillon needs to be back in my life, but his place in it is clearly defined. He is Easton's father, and we will be coparents.

That is all he will be to me.

"Things are different now," I say as Bobby pulls the car to a stop outside our front door. "I'm different, and no matter how much we both might want to turn back the clock, we don't have a time machine. You'd do well to remember that."

CHAPTER 23

VIVIEN

"FUCK, THAT STINGS," Dillon hisses as he lies on his stomach on the couch in our formal living room while Audrey tends to his injury.

"Stop being such a baby. I'm only cleaning the wound."

I've watched silently as Audrey helped him to remove his hoodie and shirt and lie down, saying nothing as my heart ached at the sight of the scorpion tattoo on his back. Dillon told me once it signified determination, rebirth, and resilience. Now I know the missing pieces of the puzzle, it makes so much sense.

Without thinking, my fingers trail over the edge of the design while Audrey threads the needle, ready to stitch him up. She doesn't have any local anesthetic and Dillon refused alcohol, so this will hurt like a bitch. Perhaps I can distract him. "Did you know if you are born under the totem of a scorpion in Native American spirituality, it means you are defensive? That you should be wary of threats and protect yourself from them with speed and stealth and always strike first. After I learned that about scorpions, I thought it interesting you would choose to ink yourself with one."

"You googled my tattoo?" he asks, in between clenching his jaw. "That sounds very stalkerish."

I roll my eyes as Audrey concentrates on his back, holding his skin together with one hand while she stitches with the other. "Don't get a big head. You know your tattoos intrigued me. Did you know what it represented when you chose it?"

"Of course, I did. Why else would I pick a scorpion? Ah, fuck." He squeezes his eyes closed and bites down on his lip.

"I'm almost done, and you're doing great," Audrey says.

"Yay! Do I get a lollipop when you're finished?"

"It's not advisable to tease the doctor when she's currently got a sharp needle pressed against your skin," I warn. "And stop deflecting. That ink is the physical manifestation of your vengeance plan. Isn't it?"

"Every time I'd look at it in the mirror," he pants, grinding his teeth to the molars. "It would remind me I needed to strike back. That no one else would protect me if I didn't protect myself."

Audrey and I exchange sad expressions as she sets the needle down. Dillon has been cruel and heartless and done a lot to hurt me. There is no excusing that. But there is no denying how he was grievously wronged and how much his life has been shaped by Simon's abandonment of him. No child deserves that. So much of the enigma that is Dillon makes more sense to me now I have all the facts.

"I just need to give you a tetanus shot, and then we're done," Audrey explains.

Outside in the hallway, I hear Easton arguing with Angela. I told his nanny to keep him out of here, because I don't want him seeing Dillon's injury. Thankfully, he didn't see him getting stabbed back at camp. That reminds me I promised him he could have some school friends over this afternoon. It will help to ease the disappointment of missing his hike. I make a call to the guy who usually supplies us with bounce houses, offering him double if he'll come over ASAP and set one up.

"You're throwing a party?" Dillon asks, wincing as he sits up straighter. Audrey is packing her supplies away in her medical bag.

I avoid looking at his broad chest and ripped abs because he hasn't lost an inch of his hotness and I don't need to be reminded of it right now. Audrey has no such qualms, staring at his body like he was chiseled from marble by Michelangelo.

"I promised Easton he could have some friends over this afternoon."

"Can I stay?" he asks, and I lift my eyes to his pleading ones. My chest inflates and deflates as I contemplate what to do. "Please," he whispers, and I can't deny him after he threw himself in front of a crazy Reeveron fan for me.

"Okay, but you're here as his uncle, and that's the way it's got to be for now."

"That's not a problem." He darts in, planting a kiss on my cheek. "Thank you. I promise you won't regret it." He flashes me a giddy smile, and my heart jumps.

"Famous last words, Dil. *Don't* make me regret it."

"So, have you decided to let him in?" Audrey asks a while later as we prepare snacks in the kitchen for Easton's incoming guests. The police have come and gone, confirming they have the crazy bitch in custody. I will sleep easier tonight knowing that. I glance out the window, needing eyes on Easton to reassure myself he's okay. I can see Dillon and E in the near distance from here. Dillon is showing him how to spin the yo-yo, demonstrating more patience than I thought he possessed, and Easton is hanging off his every word. It's fair to say my son has been enthralled by him from the second he climbed into our car.

"Yes, but it will be baby steps. I need to ensure Dillon understands that."

"I think you're making the right decision." She dumps chips into a bowl as I finish slicing the apples.

"You do? I thought you were anti-Dillon."

"I'm anti anything that hurts you or my godson." She pops a chip in her mouth while tossing the empty bags in the trash. I wash my hands in the sink while we both stare out the window at father and son. It brings a massive lump to my throat to see them together. "I'm not saying I've forgiven him, because he has pulled some terrible shit, but I believe he deserves a chance. If not for him, for Easton."

I pour two glasses of wine because I have a feeling I will need some alcoholic courage today. "I've been trying not to think about him," I admit, watching him race Easton toward the playground. Dillon is wearing one of Reeve's shirts because his own clothing is covered in blood. Giving it to him was awkward in the extreme, for both of us, but it's not like any of my shirts or E's would fit him. "Seeing him in Reeve's shirt even feels like a betrayal."

"Don't do that." She takes one of the wineglasses from me. "You aren't betraying Reeve's memory by having him here. It's a messy situation, but it was something none of you knew. Don't feel guilty for letting him into Easton's life. It's the right thing to do."

"There have been so many secrets and lies, and I'm tired of letting them dictate my life, but how do I forgive him, Rey? How can I ever trust him or believe a word that comes out of his mouth?"

She tilts her head to the side, sipping her wine as she surveys me. "There is no doubt he needs to earn back your trust, and you're right to be guarded, but answer me one thing. How much was keeping him away to do with Easton, and how much was it because you were terrified to be around him again?"

"Honestly, it was all Easton up until that meeting at his house two weeks ago. Before then, I was too consumed in grief and anger to even remember the other feelings I had for him."

"And now?" she prompts.

I glance out the window. His blond hair is blowing in the subtle breeze as he pushes Easton on one of the swings, and it makes me nostalgic. One of my favorite things to do was run my fingers through his hair. Seeing him like this reminds me of the Dillon I fell head over heels in love with. I stare out the window, hugely conflicted. They are both laughing, and pain spreads across my chest for a multitude of reasons. "I am terrified."

"You still love him." She says it as a statement, not a question.

"How can I after what he did?" I'm speaking to myself as much as to my friend.

"He loves you. You only have to see the way he looks at you to know what's in his heart, and you have loved him in silence for years."

"It was so wrong," I whisper, turning away, unable to look at Dillon any longer.

"You can't help how you feel. You loved Reeve, and you made each other happy. But he's not here, and Dillon is. It's okay to love him, Viv."

"Jesus, Rey." I swing angry eyes on my best friend. "Reeve is barely cold in his grave, and you're already pushing me at his twin?"

"You know I'm not saying that." She places her wine down and fixes me with a serious look. "I know you. I know what you're going to do. You're going to bury the feelings you have for that man"—she jabs her finger toward Dillon—"out of guilt and fear, and I don't want you to do that. It's a different matter entirely if you don't love him anymore, but the kind of feelings you had for him don't disappear overnight, no matter how much he might have wronged you."

I gulp my wine, wishing we had never started this conversation.

Audrey's shoulders relax a smidgeon. "Look, babe, I'm not arguing with you, and I'm not saying you should throw yourself back into something with Dillon. I know you're not ready to move on yet. I'm just saying don't close your mind to it and it's okay if that's where you end up. You have nothing to feel guilty or ashamed about. Reeve would want you happy."

I snort out a laugh. "I doubt he'd want me falling into his twin's arms."

"I wouldn't be so sure. Reeve knew you loved him. Yes, he didn't know it was Dillon or that Dillon was his twin, until more recently, but he knew you deeply loved your Irish boyfriend." She takes a sip of her drink. "I know Simon Lancaster was a bastard, and I hope he's rotting in hell, but you can't deny his twin sons share similar characteristics."

"In what way?" I prop my hip against the edge of the sink, waving through the window at Dave as he arrives to set up the bounce house.

"For starters, they share a manipulative streak." She drills me with a look. "You can't deny Reeve had his moments."

I nod because she's right. Reeve manipulated my feelings and used my fear and guilt against me during the time he filmed the *Rydeville Elite* movies and during our breakup. Now I know about the PI in Ireland and the photographer he spent years working with to stage photos, I can't help wondering how he might have manipulated me during our marriage in a bid to keep me sheltered from that side of his personality. I guess I'll never know because all his secrets have been taken to the grave with him.

"And all the Lancaster men are hardwired to only love once. It's an intense soul mate kind of love. Like swans. You're it for Dillon in the same way you were it for Reeve."

"You are assuming Dillon loves me because he loved me once, but we've been apart six years. A lot can happen in that time. You don't know he hasn't fallen in love with someone else."

She waves her hands in the air. "He's told you he still loves you on more than one occasion. He told your parents he loves you and regrets not fighting for you. He's not hiding his feelings. As for the other women he's been pictured with over the years? Come on. We both know they were nothing more than fuck buddies. He's never been pictured with the same woman more than once. If he was in love with anyone else, you'd know about it." Her tongue darts out, wetting her lips in an obvious tell. "You can always ask Ash. You know she'll give it to you straight."

"What did you do?"

"I invited her over. She's on her way. Don't be mad."

"I'm not. I want to repair my relationship with her, but I couldn't do that while I was keeping Dillon at arm's length because it would always be the elephant in the room."

"Good. I'm glad. I have spoken with her a few times. She wants to be here for you, and I would feel so much better knowing you have her back in your life. It will help me to not worry so much about you."

"I want Ash back in my life, but I'm scared too because it's going to dredge so many old memories and feelings to the surface, and I'm not sure I can handle it." Ash and I go way beyond her brother, and we have our memories separate from Dillon, but there's a lot of memories that are tangled too. It's hard to completely separate them, but I'm going to try because I need to make things right with my Irish bestie.

"Better out than in, babe, and Ash won't push you. She'll help to rein Dillon in."

"I'm not sure anyone is capable of reining that man in," I say, looking out the window again.

Easton is tugging on Dillon's hand as he talks to Dave while a couple of younger guys work on inflating the bounce house. Dillon swoops Easton up into his arms, which has got to hurt with his sore upper back, but the obvious joy on his face makes it clear any pain is worth it. Easton is animated in a way I haven't seen for weeks. I can't tell what he's saying, but his cute little mouth is working overtime as he tells Dillon something.

Memories resurface in my mind, and I remember how Dillon coaxed me back to life at one time. Dillon is a lot of things, but there's no denying he has this way of embracing life that is magical, and it's this part of his personality that really draws people in. "I'm not sure we should even try," I murmur.

Everything is about to change again, and I hope I'm making the right decision.

CHAPTER 24
DILLON

"MOMMY! Uncle Dillon has a surprise for me!" Easton yells the second we step foot into Viv's house on Friday afternoon. This past month has been heaven and hell. Heaven because I get to collect Easton from camp every Friday and spend the rest of the day with him and Viv. Hell because the six other days when I don't see them feels like six years.

East has instantly burrowed his way into my heart, earning a permanent place there. He is a breath of fresh air, and he has brightened up my world immensely. He takes so much joy in things, and I love that he loves the outdoors like me.

Not that he gets much of a chance to do stuff.

Viv is uberprotective, to the point I'm starting to worry. Apart from camp, she won't let East out of her sight, and they spend all their time cooped up at the house. I know it's not a chore. The place is frigging huge, and East doesn't want for a single thing. He has a pool, a treehouse, a massive playground and obstacle course, and an indoor playroom with every toy, activity, and game imaginable.

Viv fills his afternoons with playdates and activities so he's never bored, but I can tell he's feeling caged, and I'm wondering how to tackle it with his mum. I've considered calling Audrey to ask her if Viv is always this protective, but those two are thick as thieves, and I can't risk Audrey telling Viv. I'm treading on eggshells here, terrified if I do or say the wrong thing that Viv will change her mind and freeze me out again.

"He does, huh?" Viv says, appearing at the end of the hallway. Relief floods her features as her gaze roams her son, checking to ensure he's okay. Easton races toward her as she crouches down, opening her arms. He throws himself at her, hugging her close, and my heart does this twisty thing it always does every time I see them together.

She is such a good mother, always putting his needs before her own, spending hours playing with him or reading to him, and she ensures he eats well and he sticks to a daily routine that gives him comfort and structure. In a lot of ways, she reminds me of my ma, but in others, she is totally different.

Ma had a bunch of kids at home and a farm to run, so our routine was a lot less rigid, our house a lot more chaotic. I have always loved my parents, especially because they took me in and treated me as one of their own from the very start. But as I've grown older, I've developed a greater appreciation for them, especially Mum.

"Can I see it now?" East asks as I approach, bouncing from foot to foot. I chuckle, ruffling his hair. Intermittent blond strands lighten his brown hair, thanks to hours spent outdoors this summer. I can't believe it's the beginning of August already, and there is only five months left before we head out on tour. I have no clue how I am going to leave them behind. Even if Viv is still keeping me at a distance and there is no evidence of her thawing toward me at all.

Viv straightens up, smiling softly. "Everything was okay?" she asks, like usual.

"Everything was fine." I understand her concern, to a certain extent. After that crazy bitch came at her with a knife, the camp organizers asked Viv not to escort Easton anymore. They can't risk another incident, as it places all the kids in danger, so Viv had no choice but to reluctantly agree. Now, she drives Easton there and waits in the car while Leon or Bobby takes him inside.

Of course, the press went to town after the attack, and it dredged everything up again just as it had started settling down. Hate mail has doubled at the fan club, but Margaret Andre keeps it well away from Vivien. I have spoken to her and asked her to let me know if there are any serious threats made.

It seems crazy attracts crazy and that portion of Reeve's fanbase who never approved of Viv are more vocal online. It's ridiculous they are blaming her for the accident, and if I see one more post calling Vivien a murderer, I will lose my shit.

Ash changed the password on all my social media accounts after I started retaliating because fuck that crap. Does she really expect me to not say something when assholes are spewing poison at the woman I love? And don't even get me started on those lingering Saffhards.

Saffron Roberts is a junkie nobody these days, but she appears to have a core following who still think she's the bomb. They are loving a new opportunity to throw shit at Viv, and I couldn't not respond.

Until Ash put a stop to it, and now I'm banned from all my accounts. She has the band PA responding *appropriately*— her words, not mine—and I've just had to suck it up.

East tugs on my leg. "Uncle Dillon. Puh-leasssssee can I have my surprise now?"

I bend down, tweaking his nose. "I wonder where you got your impatience from, hmm?" I flash him a smile, pretending I don't see the troubled expression on Viv's face. I know this is hard for her, but it still upsets me to know she's conflicted over my growing relationship with our son.

Ignoring the painful ache in my chest, I tell East to wait

for me in the playroom while I run back out to my Land Rover to grab the small guitar case from the boot. I pull my weathered case out too and head back inside.

Easton is coloring at his desk in the playroom when I arrive. Viv is seated in the large high-backed velvet chair by the window, scribbling away in her journal. I have noticed her doing that a lot recently, and it brings a lump to my throat. She used to journal a lot in Ireland, at the outset of our relationship, and I know it was a suggestion from her therapist. I'm wondering if her current therapist suggested the same thing. If this is her way of coping. Of remembering Reeve and her little baby.

East swivels on his chair, and his eyes almost bug out of their sockets when he sees what I'm carrying. "Mommy!" he shouts, his chair screeching as he shoves it back. "Uncle Dillon got me a guitar!"

Vivien sets her journal down, lifting her head up. "I can see that." My shoulders relax at her genuine smile. I was a little worried how she might respond to this, but I didn't ask her in advance because I didn't want to give her an opportunity to say no.

"I thought you might like to learn how to play. I was five when I first started. I thought I could teach you."

"Yay!" He rushes me, clinging to my leg, and I stumble a little. "You're the best uncle in the whole wide world."

Fuck. This little fella kills me in the best possible way. He loves so freely and openly, and my heart is overjoyed at being included in his inner circle. I can't wait for the day when he will, hopefully, call me Dad.

Tears swim in Viv's eyes as she watches us, and I'm guessing it's as emotional for her but for different reasons.

"Come sit on the sofa," I say, handing him his case. "Careful with that little beauty."

We sit side by side on the leather couch, and I show Easton how to unpack his guitar and how to hold it. Viv watches silently, and her gaze is like a warm blanket spreading over every inch of my body.

"You still have it." Her gaze rakes over the Fender she gave me as a leaving present.

"It's my most prized possession," I say, peering deep into her beautiful hazel eyes. Today they look more green than brown, and I can see the little gold flecks in her irises that always mesmerized me.

Viv is still the most beautiful woman I've ever seen. And so effortlessly stunning. Her hair hangs in thick glossy sheets down her back, and there isn't a scrap of makeup on her tan skin. She is even more exquisite as she grows older, and my fingers twitch with a craving to touch her. Being around her again and not being able to touch her is one of the greatest challenges I've ever faced.

Snapping out of my melancholy, I run my fingers over the DOD engraving. "I purposely don't use this on stage, keeping it for recording and personal use. I even kept the Toxic Gods strap until it snapped and had to be replaced. Ash had a Collateral Damage strap made for me then."

"What's Toxic Gods?" East asks.

"It was the first name of our band. We changed it when we came to America."

"Why?" he asks, strumming his fingers along the guitar strings.

"Because our record label didn't like the name and they asked us to pick something else."

"I always assumed Ash was responsible for your name change," Viv says. "I know she didn't like Toxic Gods."

My lips pull into a smirk. "My sister is full of shit. Despite her very vocal protests, she loved that name and fought harder than anyone to keep it."

"Uh-oh. That's another dollar in the cuss jar." Easton waggles his finger in my face before thrusting his palm out for the money.

"I'll be bankrupt before the year is out," I deadpan,

removing a ten-dollar note from my wallet and slapping it into my son's little hand.

"It's one dollar per curse," Viv reminds me as Easton hops up to run to the shelf.

"I'm planning ahead. I'm sure my tally will be up to ten by the end of the day." I fight another smirk, and Viv rolls her eyes.

"The idea is to stop cursing, not to just hand over cash willy-nilly."

I snort. "Willy-nilly? Really."

"It's no joking matter, Dillon. E said fucking hell in front of my parents the other day. They were *not* impressed."

Well, shit. I don't need to give Viv's parents any more reasons to hate my guts. They returned home last week for a couple of months. Then they are off to Canada together to film another movie. To say Lauren Mills was cold towards me last Friday is an understatement. I'd receive warmer vibes from Jack Frost. Jonathon Mills was friendlier, but he's understandably still wary. "I'll try harder, but I really don't get why cursing is such a big deal. It's still part of the English language."

"It's uncouth," she says as I watch my son climb up on a chair to reach the shelf. He removes the lid from the jar, carefully placing my money inside.

"Wow, you're really throwing out some beauties today. You eat a dictionary for breakfast or something?"

She glances over my shoulder, to ensure East isn't looking, before flipping me the bird.

Laughter rumbles from my chest. "I think rude gestures should be counted as cursing too. I demand you place a dollar in the jar."

"Mommy." East reappears at my side, placing his hands on his hips. "Did you say a bad word?"

"I did nothing of the sort. Uncle Dillon is just stirring shit." She clamps a hand over her mouth, and her eyes pop wide as I chuckle.

East stomps over to his mum, thrusting his hand out. "Hand it over, Mom." He shakes his head, but his lips twitch at the corners. "Shocking behavior."

I burst out laughing. This kid. He's the fucking best.

"You are such a bad influence," Viv murmurs, giving me the evil eye as she hands her son a dollar from her purse.

I sit back on the couch, stretching my legs out as I place my Fender beside me. "Never pretended I wasn't, and there was a time you didn't mind being corrupted." Our last weekend together in Brittas Bay resurfaces in my mind, and I remember coaxing her into the freezing cold sea where I fucked her hard and fast before she climbed up my body and I ate her out with her legs hanging over my shoulders.

My dick *loves* that memory, hardening in record time. I adjust myself in my jeans before Easton returns and notices. Though it might be fun to see what kind of question he'd ask. He's an inquisitive little boy, curious about the world around him, and he's always asking questions.

Viv notices my boner, but she looks away, pretending she doesn't.

I spend an hour teaching East the basics of guitar playing while Viv writes in her journal. Every so often, she peers over at us with an emotional look on her face. After, I take him out to the playground for a couple of hours before dinner. We eat and then I give him a bath. It's one of my favorite things to do. I'm drying him with a fluffy towel that's about three times his size when he asks if I'll tuck him into bed and read him a story. "Sure, buddy." I kiss the top of his head as I help him into his pajamas. "Let's just okay it with your mom first."

"Mommy!" Easton races into the living room in his oversized slippers with semi-dry hair. He's so excited he barely let me blow-dry it. "I want Uncle Dillon to read me a story and put me to bed."

Viv's eyes fill up, but she composes herself fast, tentatively smiling at her son. "Okay. If that's what you want."

Easton jumps into my arms, and I hold him close as he wraps his little arms and legs around me.

A tear slips out of the corner of Viv's eye, and I hate she's upset. I can guess why, and I wish I could comfort her, but she'd never let me.

I wonder if she ever will.

CHAPTER 25

DILLON

"ARE YOU COMFY?" I ask, sliding under the covers beside my son in his bed.

"Yep." He grins up at me, and his obvious happiness at my presence does wonders for my self-esteem.

"Do you have a book you're reading, or you want me to tell you a story?" I wrap my arm around his shoulders as he snuggles into me.

"Mommy is reading me *The Enormous Crocodile* by Roald Dahl. You can read me that." He sits up against the headrest. "But first I need to tell my daddy about my day." Easton takes the framed photo of Reeve off his bedside locker, propping it on his lap. "Mommy says Daddy and Lainey are together in heaven and they hear me when I speak to them, so I talk to them every night before bed," he explains. Then he proceeds to mention everything that happened at camp and how we spent our afternoon.

I listen with a tight pain stretched across my chest, keeping my arm around my son as he tells Reeve all about his day. Staring at my brother's photo as Easton talks is a sobering experience. Ash says I need to process my feelings instead of burying them deep inside, and I know she's right. But I'm a chickenshit because I keep putting it off. Listening to Easton telling his daddy about his day opens the wound in my heart that little bit wider, and I know I'm going to have to face up to it, sooner rather than later.

"Night, Daddy." Easton leans in, kissing Reeve's picture. "I miss you." The saddest expression appears on his face as he reverently places the frame back on his locker. Grabbing a pink teddy, shaped like a bunny, he cuddles it, whispering, "Night, Lainey."

Aw, hell. A messy ball of emotion clogs the back of my throat, and I wish I could take my son's pain away. Wiping the moisture from my cheeks, I hug him closer. "Ready for your story, buddy?"

"I'm ready." His voice is smaller, quieter, and I wonder exactly what is going through his mind. He snuggles into my side, and I could quite happily never get out of this bed.

"Let's lie back down," I suggest, grabbing the book from the top of his locker, and we both snuggle under the covers. He turns a little in my arms so he's facing me. His big blue eyes are so innocent and trusting as he looks at me. My heart swells with love for him. I may have only known the truth for eleven weeks and I have only been involved in his life this past month, but my feelings kicked in immediately. I loved Easton from the instant I met him. It's hard not to. He's the most adorable little boy. Sweet, smart, caring with a fun sense of humor and a good heart, just like his mum.

He is everything I could ever wish for in a son, and there is still so much to discover.

I read some of the book, and it doesn't take him long to fall asleep against my shoulder. I stare at him for ages, noting every inch of his beautiful face, committing it to memory. He looks so young and innocent, and I silently rage at a world that would hurt him so much. Losing his father this young will always be a shadow on his soul. He might not understand until he is older, but it *will* leave its mark. He lost his sister too, but it isn't the same. Losing Reeve will always hurt him, even if he has me in his life.

As conflicted as I am about my twin, I can't deny the role he played in my son's life or how grateful I am to Reeve for the way he loved him. Easton adores his daddy, and I would never take that away from him.

With military precision, I inch out of the bed slowly so I don't wake him. My heart is both heavy and light, my head swimming with thoughts as I step out of his bedroom, slowly easing the door over. I don't know if Viv shuts it all the way over or not, so I leave it open a little.

Turning around, I find Viv sitting on the carpeted floor, with her back to the wall, silently crying. Tears cascade down her cheeks as she stares up at me. She looks so small, so lost, so broken, and there's a desperate pleading in her eyes that pains me to see. It's as if she's silently begging me to take her pain away even while another part of her is determined to push me away and never let me back in. I can tell from her blotchy skin that she's been out here for a while.

Without speaking, I bend down and scoop her up, cradling her against my chest. Her arms wind around my neck without hesitation, and she leans into me, quietly sobbing as I head downstairs.

She doesn't say anything as I step into her comfortable living room, and I don't push her. It's pretty obvious why she's upset. I scan the room as I walk toward the plush sofas positioned in front of the open fireplace.

I much prefer this space to the more formal living room they use for guests. There are family photos in both rooms, but the framed pictures on the mantelpiece and covering one entire wall in this room are the true history of their time as a family. Unlike the more formal portraits in the other room.

It hurts seeing them, but I'm glad Vivien and Easton had love in their lives. There is no way anyone looking at these pictures could ignore how much Reeve Lancaster loved his family.

When I was with Viv in Ireland, she would tell me some things about him, and he sounded like a possessive control freak. It made me wonder whether he truly loved her or if it was what she represented. Being around this house this past month has made me realize, once and for all, I was wrong. He did love her. Maybe in the same way I do. It's clear she was anything but a trophy wife.

The instant I sit down on the sofa, Viv crawls off my lap, scurrying to the corner and tucking herself in, as far away from me as possible. Hurt crawls up my throat, but I push it aside, focusing on her, like Ash suggested. "Are you okay?"

She shrugs, rubbing at her eyes. "Depends on your definition of okay."

"I'm not trying to replace him," I reassure her because I know I'm the trigger. "And I don't like upsetting you. I hate seeing you crying."

"It's not your fault, and you haven't done anything wrong. Easton already adores you, and I'm happy about that. I am." It sounds like she's trying to convince herself as much as me. "It's just hard seeing you doing things Reeve did."

I nod, understanding what she means. I wonder if it will always be this hard. Will I always feel like I'm in his shadow? Will my presence in their lives always remind Viv of Reeve?

"Can I get you something to drink?" I ask, handing her the box of tissues from the small end table.

"White wine," she rasps.

"Do you mind if I grab a beer?"

She frowns. "I thought you didn't drink anymore?"

I run a hand through my hair, loving that it's getting longer again. I feel more like myself. "Contrary to popular belief, I'm not an alcoholic. My stint in rehab was more about clearing my head and processing some shit than drying out." I stand. "Why don't I get the drinks, and we can talk?"

I'm half expecting her to kick me out, like she usually does after Easton goes to bed on Friday nights. But she nods, and I don't stop to question it, hightailing it out of there before she changes her mind.

The kitchen is empty, because Friday night is Charlotte's night off, so I rummage around, grabbing crisps and chocolate from the overhead press because I'm feeling peckish and Viv can easily handle the calorific treats. She's thinner than ever from a combination of stress and a lack of appetite. I pour her a chilled glass of wine and grab a bottle of beer before heading back to the living room with our drinks and treats.

Viv is staring off into space, looking deep in thought, and I wish I could read minds because I would give anything to know what she's thinking. I dump the goodies on the coffee table and hand her the glass of wine. Although I want to cozy up to her, I stay down my end of the sofa, giving her space.

"I used to drink far too much," I start telling her as I pop the cap on my beer. "But it was a conscious decision to blot out all the crap in my head. I wasn't addicted in the sense I physically couldn't stop myself from drinking although I know using it as a crutch is almost as bad. It's why I purposely don't drink as much now. That and I'm trying to be healthier." I have a son who needs me now. A son who has already lost one father, and I am determined to be there for him in every sense of the word.

"What crap is in your head?" She tucks her knees into her chest while sipping her wine.

"I wasn't in a good place after you left. Things happened pretty fast when the A&R scout came to see us in Dublin. I used the money I got from the NDA to relocate us to L.A. After we signed with the label, they booked us into Capitol Studios to work on our first album. I'd been writing furiously all year, and we had enough songs for two or three albums."

"Were they about me?" she blurts, and my heart melts when a familiar red stain blooms on both her cheeks. "'Hollywood Ho' and 'Fuck Love,'" she clarifies.

I nod. "I went through a lot of stages after I lost you. The first year I was heartbroken and drowning in pain and guilt and remorse, and that's when I wrote 'You are my Only Reason,' 'Queen of my Heart,' 'Broken Love,' and a whole load of other songs which went on to become bestsellers. By year two, I entered the next stage, and I was fucking pissed." I knock back a large mouthful of beer. "It started when I discovered you had gotten married and had a kid."

"Did you suspect he might be yours?"

"I was suspicious enough to google Easton's date of birth. I read a bunch of articles which all said his birthday was in June, so that was that." I stare off into space, remembering one of the hardest times of my life. "You and Reeve were plastered all over social media, and it seemed like he was in every fucking bestselling movie that year. I couldn't get away from either of you and it was killing me. I wrote 'Hollywood Ho' and 'Fuck Love' at the height of my rage and my depression when I hated you for what you did to me."

"I cried the first time I heard 'Hollywood Ho.' I knew it was about me, and I couldn't understand how you could hate me that much."

"There's a fine line between love and hate, Viv. I've heard that bandied about a lot, but it wasn't until I was in that situation that I could truly understand what it means." She opens her mouth to speak, but I shake my head to stall her. I'm not finished, and I need to get this all out. I lean forward, straining toward her. She drinks her wine, giving me her undivided attention, and while this stuff is tough to wade through, I wouldn't swap this moment for anything.

I have always loved just existing with her.

Vivien brings a sense of inner peace to my soul whenever I am around her, in a way no one else does.

CHAPTER 26

DILLON

"I NEED you to understand everything is about you," I explain. "Every lyric I have written from the moment I met you is all you. And there are far more love songs than hate songs, because even when I wanted to hate you, I couldn't. Writing songs was a way of bleeding my emotions, of venting my anger, but I never hated you. Not in the true sense of the word." I take another swig of my beer before I stare her straight in the eyes. "It was impossible when I was so completely in love with you. I didn't want to be, because you were with him, but my heart refused to be swayed."

"Why didn't you fight for me?" She pins me with glassy eyes. "I paced the terminal at Dublin Airport for hours, silently begging you to come and claim me. I waited until the very last minute to get on the plane, and you didn't come. You just let me go."

I shake my head, moving closer despite my earlier self-promise. I need to be closer to her when I admit this truth. "But I didn't, Viv. I came after you. I flew to L.A. to beg you to come back to Dublin with me."

Shock splays across her face, and her eyes pop wide. "What?" she splutters.

"I was going to get on my hands and knees and beg for forgiveness. I was going to lay it all out on the line. I was prepared to quit the band and stay with you in Dublin. I would have agreed to anything as long as you agreed to be mine."

Her brow creases in confusion. "I don't understand. How didn't I know this?"

I drink more beer, briefly squeezing my eyes shut. Even now, it hurts to relive this memory. "I arrived at my hotel in L.A. around two. You'd gotten in a few hours earlier. Ash gave me your US mobile number, and I tried it repeatedly, but it was either switched off or it had powered off."

"I'd forgotten to charge it," she explains. "I was too heartbroken on the plane to remember to do it. It died sometime after Reeve picked me up."

"I didn't want to leave a voice mail which might be misconstrued."

Confusion crosses her face. "It's so weird I never saw any missed calls."

I don't think it takes much to figure out what happened. "I'm guessing Reeve deleted them from the call log." He was determined to keep me away from her and obviously willing to do whatever it took to ensure she didn't come back to me.

"I can't believe he'd do that, but it's the only explanation that makes sense." She rubs at her temples. "If I had seen those calls, it might've changed everything."

I nod because there are so many things that could've ended up differently if we had all reacted differently. But there's no point dwelling on it now.

"What happened after that?" she asks.

"When I couldn't reach you, I turned on the TV to waste some time, and that's when I saw the coverage of you with him. I saw you together on the balcony. I knew you were naked. I knew what that meant. And I knew he was sending a message to me. It wasn't just the statement he gave to reporters. It was the way he used his arm to cover your tits, just like I'd done in the photo we sent him the day of your birthday. I know he was shielding you too, and maybe I'm reading too much into it, but I got the message loud and clear anyway."

Setting my bottle on the table, I bury my head in my hands. Pain slices across my chest, like it does every time I recall that image. It's forever imprinted on my brain, and I have wished so many times I could scrub it out. "How could you run straight back to him?" I lift my head, staring at her through stinging eyes. "You told me you didn't know where he was. Was that a lie?"

She vehemently shakes her head. "It was the truth. I had no idea he would show up to collect me from the airport. I'd had no contact with him since my birthday. All I knew, from Audrey and my parents, was he was working on stuff to make up for his mistakes. But no one told me what he was doing because Reeve wanted to explain it to me himself."

"But you slept with him." I scrub a hand over my prickly jawline as an invisible weight sits on my chest. "That fucking killed me. Especially when it was over a year before I could even kiss anyone else." I didn't understand how she could do it. That realization drove a lot of my anger. That had me believing she had outplayed me. That made me question every fucking moment we shared.

She worries her lower lip between her teeth and tucks her hair behind her ears. "It wasn't planned, but I was so heart-broken, and he was there. Reeve has always felt like my home. He was always the one comforting me when I was upset." A shuddering breath escapes her lips, and she's on the verge of tears again. "I didn't want to hurt you back then, and I don't want to hurt you now, Dillon."

"You don't?"

"I think we've hurt each other enough." That sentiment lingers in the air, and it carries so much weight. "But you've got to understand something about me," she continues. "It was never a competition between you and Reeve. I loved both of you in different ways. You shattered my heart into a million pieces, Dillon, and I was even more heartbroken flying home than I'd been fleeing L.A. When Reeve showed up, I was happy to see him because he's always been the air I breathe. He explained everything he'd done to rectify his mistakes. He said all the right things, and when he kissed me, I didn't fight him because his love meant I forgot the pain of losing you for a few moments in time, and I clung to that. I needed it because I was more broken and lost than ever before."

She takes a big gulp of her wine, averting her eyes. "I wasn't proud of myself after. I broke down in tears because it felt like the biggest betrayal." She rubs at her chest. "I felt so bad for doing that to you, but then I remembered how cruel you'd been and how you'd let me leave like I meant nothing to you. I believed you were thousands of miles away in bed with Aoife, and that helped to lessen my guilt."

"We really fucked up, didn't we?"

She exhales heavily. "I don't see it like that. I can't. That would be like admitting the life I shared with my husband and my son should never have happened. There are things I regret, but I won't regret that."

"I would never ask you to. And I don't begrudge you that time even though I was miserable as fucking sin without you for all of those years."

"Is that the truth?" She cocks her head to the side.

"It is. I didn't want to love you, but I did. I do."

"What about other women? I know you weren't celibate. Nor would I expect you to be," she rushes to add. "But I've seen pictures of you with tons of beautiful women. You never had feelings for any of them?"

I shake my head. "Nope. I couldn't be with anyone at first. Then, in the height of my anger, I set out to bang as many women as I could, hoping I could fuck you out of my system, but it didn't work. It made things worse because none of them were you. After, I'd feel even lonelier and the pain seemed sharper. It only served to make me angrier and miss you more.

It was a vicious cycle I couldn't break out of. And I was a prick, venting all my frustration at these random women because I couldn't bear to look at them, knowing they weren't you. No one ever came close, and I got sick of it. I turned to booze then."

"Are you saying I've been your only relationship?" Disbelief is clear in her tone.

"Yeah, Hollywood." I shoot her a lopsided grin. "It's only ever been you."

She nibbles on her lip as she stares at me with an assessing gaze. "You're different."

"I'm trying to work through my issues. Trying to be more open, more patient, and less angry. It's a work in progress." I rub the back of my neck. "I, ah, started seeing a therapist. I'd spoken with one in rehab, but Ash convinced me to see someone new to help me deal with everything that's happened recently."

"I've got a shrink too."

"Is that why you're journaling again?"

"Yes and no. I mentioned it was what Sheila had suggested when I was in therapy in Dublin, and Meryl said if it helped that I should try it again."

"Is it helping?" I grab a handful of crisps, stuffing them in my mouth.

"Yes," she quietly admits. "I'm documenting everything, and while it's sad, it's helping me to remember how fortunate I was to have known him. To have been loved like that." Tears brim in her eyes. "I miss him so much."

"I know you do."

Silence descends, but it's not awkward. It's the most comfortable silence I've shared with her since we have been back in contact.

"I missed you too," she whispers, pinning me with glassy eyes. "I thought about you a lot." She sniffles, gulping a mouthful of wine. "I harbored a lot of guilt during my marriage for still thinking about you."

"I went out of my way to avoid both of you at events, yet a part of me yearned to bump into you too. Even though I knew it would kill me to see you on his arm, I just wanted to see you again. To remind myself it had been real. That I hadn't imagined it all."

"You loved me?"

"Yes, Viv." I hate she still doubts it. I hate I was a prick to her and I've made her disbelieve everything I say. "I know you don't trust me, and I don't blame you for that. I did you wrong, and I hate myself for it, but I never stopped loving you. I've been stumbling through my life since you left, and it's been so lonely." I draw an exaggerated breath, gulping over the lump wedged in my throat. "I know I can't expect anything of you, but could we try to be friends?" We need to start somewhere, and I'm hoping she'll agree.

"I can't offer you anything more than that, Dillon," she warns.

"I know, and I'm cool with that." It's fucking bullshit. I'll be devastated if I'm permanently relegated to the friend zone, but I don't want to put her under pressure. I'm trying to prioritize her needs, and this is what she needs now.

"Okay. I'll try."

I flash her a blinding smile, and she looks momentarily dazed.

"Why did you dye your hair and start wearing the contacts again?" Her inquisitive eyes probe mine.

"Honestly?"

Her scowl is instant. "No, I want you to keep lying to me." Her eyes narrow.

Fuck. "I deserved that."

"You are going to be in our lives, Dillon. You'll be in Easton's life. We just agreed to be friends. The only way this will work is with complete honesty. Aren't you tired of all the secrets and lies?"

"I am, and it was all so pointless."

She nods. "We can continue to beat ourselves up for the

mistakes of the past or choose to move forward. To try to put it behind us." Air whistles out of her mouth. "I can't keep doing this. I want to wipe the slate clean and try to move on."

"Will you ever be able to forgive me?" I hold my breath as I wait for her to reply.

"I want to, but I don't know if I can. All I can promise is I will try."

"I can't ask for more than that." I clear my throat. "I thought it might be easier for you to be around me if I didn't look so much like Reeve," I admit though it's only half of the truth. I was stupidly hoping if I looked the way I used to look that she might fall back in love with me.

Viv nods like she was expecting this answer.

We were so good together, and we had so many good times. I don't want our relationship to be defined by those awful last moments. Especially not when we created someone so precious in Easton. In the future, I want our son to know his parents loved each other. That last night, I made love to Viv with my whole heart and soul. It felt magical at the time. Now I know it was because we were creating this incredible new life.

Her eyes lock on mine, and I wonder if my gaze is as emotional as hers. There is still so much that needs to be said, but I think both of us are done for the night. We stare at one another, and I want to kiss her so badly, but she is giving me no indication she wants the same thing. She's still mourning her husband, and the very last thing I should be doing is pushing her into doing something she would regret. It hasn't been long, and I have to respect that.

We just agreed to be friends, and it's a huge step forward.

So, I will learn to be patient.

I will become so patient they'll have to canonize me when I die.

If Ash was privy to my inner thoughts, she'd be so fucking proud of me.

Viv looks away first, and I sit back in the couch, bringing

my beer to my lips. I want to enjoy this. Just being with her. I hope someday my presence offers her comfort in the way being around her does for me.

We drink in silence, both lost in thought, though I notice the sneaky glances she sends my way when she thinks I'm not noticing. After a bit, she shifts on the sofa, swinging her legs around and planting her feet on the ground. "Could I ask you to do one thing?" she says, placing her empty glass on the coffee table.

"Anything." I pin her with earnest eyes.

She wipes her hands down the front of her dress in an obvious nervous tell. "Ditch the contacts, Dil. I want to see your gorgeous blue eyes."

CHAPTER 27
VIVIEN

"UNCLE DILLON'S HOUSE IS NICE," Easton remarks as I lift him out of his booster seat. His eyes scan the sprawling modern two-story property with enthusiasm. He was so excited for today I could hardly get him to sleep last night. I took Audrey's advice, and he's been sleeping in his own bedroom again, ever since the night Dillon put him to bed. I hate sleeping alone, but I know it's the right thing to do even if both of us are having issues adjusting.

The door opens, revealing Dillon and Ash, and I pretend I don't feel the quickening of my heart at the sight of him. Easton drops my hand like a hot potato and races toward his dad. My heart slams against my rib cage, like it does anytime they are together. I hang back, unsure if I can do this today. The urge to turn around, head home, and crawl into bed with a bottle of vodka is strong.

"Hey, you." Ash bounds over to me, hugging me without hesitation. "I'm so glad you agreed to come."

"I'm not sure about this." I watch Dillon throw Easton over his shoulder with a massive smile on his face. E shrieks in delight, and I'm glad he's not aware of the significance of today. "Maybe I should go home." I know it's bad if I'm considering leaving Easton here without me.

Ash loops her arm in mine as Dillon tosses Easton up into the air. Easton squeals and giggles, thoroughly enjoying himself. "You shouldn't be alone today. That would be a very bad idea."

I swing my eyes to hers. "You know what day it is?"

She nods, dragging me forward. "Audrey and I talk weekly. She told me."

I knew they were in touch, but I didn't realize it was a regular thing. However, I'm not angry. I know they are worried about me, and I like they are repairing their friendship. It's important to me that both my besties get along.

Ash has been coming over to my house weekly for lunch, and it's as if we were never apart. We still have plenty to catch up on, but I'm enjoying listening to her stories of life on the road with the band and hearing about all the amazing places she's traveled to. I'm glad she's back in my life and grateful she's forgiven me for the horrible way I treated her. "I'm sorry I didn't say anything," I admit. "It's just so hard to say it out loud. Every time I think I might be turning a corner, something happens and it feels like I'm back to square one again."

"It's barely been three months. I think you're doing amazing. Losing a baby is one of the most heartbreaking things you can endure. I can't imagine what it must be like to lose your husband as well." Tears prick her eyes. "I get upset just thinking about your pain."

We stop walking, stalling a few feet from the front door. "Last night, when I was lying in bed, all I could think about was how different today should have been. I hardly got any sleep, which would have been the case if my pregnancy had gone full term, but I had no little angel squirming and kicking inside my belly." I place a hand over my flat stomach. "I've never felt more hollow."

A sob erupts from Ash's mouth, causing Dillon to look over and frown.

"I don't mean to upset you."

"It's okay," she croaks, squeezing my hand. "I know today is going to be hard for you, and it's why I didn't want you to be alone. I think we should get shitfaced and toast to your little angel in heaven."

"Now that's a plan I can get behind." It sure beats crying my eyes out alone in bed.

"Hey, Hollywood." Dillon stops throwing our son in the air long enough to greet me. He flashes me that devilish grin I used to swoon over, and his entire face lights up when he smiles. Easton is good for Dillon. It's blatantly obvious how happy he is whenever he's around our son, and I don't remember ever seeing him so carefree. I'm glad he's in therapy, because he has a lot of deep-seated issues to work through. That's something else I have Ash to thank for.

"Hi, Dillon." I force a smile on my face.

Things have been better between us since we talked last week and came to an understanding of sorts. Meryl has helped me realize holding on to my anger, and clinging to the wrongs of the past, is holding me back from healing. I can't change what happened. I can only control what happens from now on. Fooling myself into believing I hate Dillon is exhausting, and I'm done pretending. He is going to be in our lives, and it will be much easier for everyone if things are amicable, so I'm determined to start anew. He came over for dinner on Tuesday night and he's been on FaceTime with E most every night before bed.

"Mommy." Easton sounds winded. "I'm trying to reach the clouds," he shrieks as Dillon throws him up into the air again.

Trying to give me heart failure, more like. "How about you come back down to earth for a while before you get a tummy ache?"

"How about you give your Auntie Ash a big sloppy kiss?" Ash reaches her hands out for her nephew. E practically jumps from Dillon's arms into Ash's, dropping a slew of sloppy kisses on her cheek. Ash lets him climb onto her back, and they race off down the hallway.

I trail after Ash and Easton while Dillon closes the door. He runs to catch up to me. "For you," he says, handing me a long-stemmed white rose. Our fingers graze as I take it from him, and little tingles spread up my arm, reminding me I am still very much alive. "I told you once white roses symbolize rebirth and new beginnings, but they also symbolize peace, innocence, and love. I thought we could plant some white rose bushes in honor of Lainey. I have everything outside, but if it's too much, we don't have to do it."

I stop walking, and my lower lip wobbles as emotion washes over me. I fight to regain control, smiling softly at him as I bury my nose in the silky petals, inhaling the familiar lemony scent. "That's a lovely idea and very thoughtful," I choke out. "Thank you."

"I also wanted to run an idea by you," he says, dragging a hand through his hair.

Blond strands tumble across his brow, and nostalgia slaps me in the face. Today is really doing a number on me. "What is it?"

"I want to build a memorial for Reeve and Lainey in your back garden. I thought Easton could help me with it. We can plant shrubs and roses and maybe erect a plaque against one of the trees and install a little stone bench. That way, East would have someplace he could go when he feels sad or he wants to talk to them."

"Dillon," I whisper as tears stream down my face. I clutch a hand to my chest. "That would be perfect," I sob.

Without hesitation, he pulls me into his arms, and I let him console me. I shut my eyes, letting his spicy scent wrap around me as he holds me close. I rest my head against his chest, and we stand there for an indeterminable time, just hugging one another.

Hugs are so underrated.

It feels so incredibly good to be held again.

To be held by *him*.

I jerk away from Dillon the second that thought lands in my mind, swiping the remaining moisture from my cheeks. "We should find the others."

He nods, looking sad as he shoves his hands in the pockets of his jean shorts. "I thought we could start the garden next week, if that's okay with you? I'd like to have it finished before East returns to school."

Easton starts kindergarten in ten days, but I'm having huge reservations. However, I don't want to think about that today. "Next week is good." I snap my gaze to his, instantly snared in his gorgeous blue eyes. I asked him not to wear the green contacts because I love him with blond hair and blue eyes. He's a beautiful man, and he shouldn't have to hide his eyes because he's afraid of upsetting me.

The truth is, I want to see his blue peepers. His eyes are the mirror image of my son's. Those eyes are familiar because I've looked into them most every day of my life, but looking at Dillon isn't like looking at Reeve. That would be wrong on so many levels. No, seeing Dillon with blue eyes helps me to see him in a different light, and it offers me comfort. "Thank you. It's a really nice gesture."

"I see how much he misses him. I want to help."

I nod, releasing a large breath as we resume walking.

"Before we get into the pool, I want to give you and East a tour of my studio."

"I'd like to see it."

"Cool. Come on." He lifts one shoulder. "We'll grab the little guy before he makes a beeline for the water."

Ash comes with us, but we leave Ro and Jamie lounging around Dillon's large outdoor pool. Dillon has a stone path that leads around the side of his house and all the way to the studio.

The studio is much larger on the inside than it appears from the outside and very stylish with high ceilings, asymmetric walls, and wooden floors. "This is the control room,"

Dillon explains to East as we step into a small rectangular room. A long console with tons of buttons rests under a glass window that looks into the studio beyond. A bunch of high-tech laptops and other gadgets fill the rest of the space in this room.

"What are these for?" East asks, gravitating toward the mixing console like a moth to a flame.

"That's for our sound engineers. They listen to the music and the songs as we record them, and they route the sound so it's balanced and adjusted."

"Awesome," East says, nodding as if he understands what that means. He sits in one of the large chairs, pushing buttons while Dillon gazes adoringly at him.

"He's an incredible little boy," Ash whispers, as we lean back against the wall, watching father and son. "Dillon never stops talking about him. The only other time I've seen him this happy was—"

"Yeah." I cut her off, unable to hear her vocalize it.

"It's okay to admit it, Viv. He's a part of your past, your present, and your future. I know your relationship isn't the same, but it's okay to admit you made each other happy."

"I can't think about that, Ash. Especially not today. It feels like too big of a betrayal to Reeve."

"I'll shut up, in a sec, because the last thing I want to do is upset you today." She steps in front of me as Dillon and East climb out of the chairs and exit the room. "I'm just going to say this, and there is no intent behind it. I know there is a lot of love between you and my brother. I know there are a lot of unresolved feelings. There is no pressure or expectation on you to feel a certain way, but I want you to know if you still have feelings for him, and if you ever want to act on them, that it's fine."

"Ash. It's three months next week since Reeve died. Only three months. It's too soon to even think about anyone else."

"There is no timeline for this kind of situation, and no one should tell you what's in your heart. I would never push you in

Dillon's direction. I would never force you to do anything you didn't want to do. I'm just saying it's okay to love him. Whether that's now, next week, next month, or next year, it's no one's business but your own. Don't close your heart out of guilt or fear."

She makes it sound so simple. But it's not. Can you just imagine what the world would think if I started something back up with Dillon? I can visualize the horrid headlines already.

"Mommy!" Easton's high-pitched shriek almost bursts my eardrums. "You gotta see this," he screams.

"Such impeccable timing," Ash murmurs, grinning as she loops her arm in mine. "I think that's enough of the heavy for today. Come on. I think I know why the little munchkin is so excited."

Ash leads me past the door to the recording studio, but I sneak a quick peek as we walk by. Various mic stands are dotted around the room, and a bunch of different guitars is propped against the walls. A few guitar cases lie flat on the floor. Ro's drum kit is situated at the back of the space. Framed pictures cover the wall, celebrating their various gold and platinum albums and the numerous accolades and awards the band has won.

"I think we have a budding rock star in the making," Ash says, dragging me past the room to the next door where East and Dillon are.

My jaw slackens as I take in the mini recording studio with child-sized guitars, a mounted keyboard, microphone on an adjustable stand, and a drum kit. Colorful bean bags are littered around the space. There's even a miniature refrigerator, loaded with drinks, and a small desk and chair. My eyes lift to Dillon's. "You did this for E?"

He nods as East strums a few chords on one of the guitars. Dillon has only begun teaching him, so he's still a complete novice. "I thought he might be able to come over on occasion, and I can give him lessons here. Maybe, sometime, he could come and watch us record or come over and hang out with some of his buddies. I had the desk installed so he could do his homework or color if he gets bored."

He has put so much thought into this, and my heart is a swollen mess behind my chest cavity.

Easton puts the guitar down and races to the drum kit. He plops down, grabs the drumsticks, and starts bashing away to his heart's content. His face is animated in a way I haven't seen in a long time. "Look at me, Uncle Dil. I'm a drummer like Uncle Ro!" Something loosens inside me, and I burst out crying. My emotions are all over the place today, and this is too much. I rush out of the room before E notices, not wanting to upset him when he's so happy.

CHAPTER 28
VIVIEN

I FLEE THE STUDIO, gasping for air as I struggle to breathe. Ash dashes out after me, pulling me into her arms as I break down. "It's okay, Viv. I've got you." She leads me away from the main house, over to the other side of the garden, to a stunning little seated area set amid copious colorful flowerbeds and shrubs. Lights are strung up over the open-fronted wooden gazebo as she leads me over to the homey wicker couch.

Ash wraps her arm around my shoulders, comforting me as I cry. "I'm so sick of crying," I rasp, sniffling and swatting my tears away with the hem of my summer dress. "I'm sick of being sad all the time." And I'm so freaking lonely. But I keep that thought to myself.

"It gets better."

I lift my head, fixing her with blurry eyes. "What happened?" This isn't the first time she's alluded to something.

She shakes her head and smiles, but it's off. "Not today. Today is about Lainey."

"Ash." I take her hands in mine. "It can still be about Lainey even if you tell me your story. I know there is one. Please tell me."

Tears instantly fill her eyes, and now it's my turn to comfort her. "Jamie and I… We lost a baby last year."

"Oh, Ash. I'm so sorry." I hug her tight.

"It was an ectopic pregnancy. We lost our baby at twelve weeks. I nearly died too. One of my fallopian tubes ruptured, and Jamie had to rush me to the hospital. We were at home in Ireland, so we managed to keep it out of the press."

I was wondering why I hadn't heard anything.

"We found out I was pregnant at six weeks, and we were overjoyed." Tears roll down her cheeks. "We told Dillon and Ronan straightaway. Ro's girlfriend Clodagh was pregnant with Emer at the time. I was so excited our baby would have an automatic best friend in his cousin. We had only just flown home to tell our parents when I collapsed."

"I'm so sorry, Ash." It's no wonder she's been so understanding. She knows exactly what I'm going through.

"I was in bits for months." She shucks out of my embrace, and we sit back on the couch. "I couldn't stop crying. Jamie was great, but he didn't know how to make it better."

"There is nothing anyone can say or do that takes away the pain. It's a process of surviving each day, and gradually you learn to live with it."

She nods. "But it never goes away, and you never forget."

"Never." I agree, placing a hand over my heart.

"They had to remove one of my fallopian tubes, but we should still be able to have kids. It might just be a little bit harder. We've decided to wait until after we are married before we attempt it. I need to build up the courage."

"I can relate. Even if Reeve were here, there is no way I could consider trying for another baby yet even if a part of me believes it's the very thing that will heal me."

"I didn't want to pry in case I upset you, but is everything okay after the accident? You'll be able to have more children in the future?"

I nod. "Yes. Thankfully, there was no permanent damage.

There should be no reason why I can't have more babies. Though that's the last thing on my mind right now."

She takes my hand, squeezing it. "No matter how long you mourn Lainey and Reeve, assholes are going to criticize you as soon as you move on. The timing really doesn't make any difference. So fuck what anyone else thinks. Life goes on, Viv. You have every right to look to the future and to think of having more kids. It doesn't dishonor them if you start living again. I'm sure it's what Reeve would want."

"I know he would, but I doubt he'd want me to move on with his twin."

"Wouldn't he?" Ash quirks a brow. "He knew there was love between you. A very special, rare kind of love, and Dillon is Easton's biological father. I didn't know Reeve, but the fact he included Dillon in his will speaks volumes. I think Reeve would be happy if you end up with Dillon. At least he knows his twin will love you as completely as he did."

I blow air out of my mouth. "Woah. This is a lot of heavy for a day like today."

"We're just talking." She smiles. "No one is pressuring you. Maybe Dillon and you will fall back into love, or maybe you won't. I'm just saying do things for you. Fuck what anyone else thinks."

I chew on the corner of my mouth, wondering if I should say this. But it's Ash, and I know I can tell her anything. "I have never stopped loving him, Ash. He has always owned a piece of my heart."

"I'm so happy to hear that."

"It doesn't mean anything will happen," I blurt because I can't even think of that without feeling enormous guilt.

"I know, but just promise me you won't dismiss your feelings because you are worrying about what others will think. If Dillon and you are meant to be together, it should happen naturally. Without any interference."

"How did me talking about being able to have kids in the future end up a conversation about Dillon and me?"

"There's a natural correlation with both those things."

I open my mouth to tell her that's the very definition of interference when she continues talking.

"You and I are always in sync in our lives. Back in Ireland, it was men. Now, it's this." She squeezes my hand again. "We have both endured the heartbreaking loss of our babies, but we will go on because we are strong and we can overcome the worst experiences to emerge even stronger."

"We *are* in sync, and I'm so glad you found it in your heart to forgive me."

"There was nothing to forgive, Viv." Her clear blue eyes stare earnestly at me. "I was so fucking pissed off at the time it happened, but after I discovered everything, I instantly forgave you. It wasn't your fault, and you did what you believed was the best for both Reeve and Dillon and for you and your baby. I would never, could never, hold that against you."

"I love you." I pull her into my arms. "You and Audrey are the sisters I never had."

"Right back at ya, Viv."

A crunching sound has us whipping our heads around. Dillon strides toward us, concern evident on his handsome face as he takes in our blotchy skin and our embrace.

"He worries about you," Ash whispers.

"Hey." Dillon steps inside the gazebo, his gaze immediately finding mine. "Are you okay?"

"I'm fine." I stand, pulling my Irish bestie with me. "I just got overwhelmed. Seeing you with E and seeing what you built for him…it was a lot. I'm extra emotional today."

"That's understandable." Dillon stares at me in that intense way of his, like he's drilling a hole into my chest in a bid to get to the heart of the matter.

"I'm fine too," Ash says, planting her hands on her hips and narrowing her eyes at her brother. "In case you were wondering why I was crying."

Dillon pulls his gaze from me, frowning as he takes note of his sister. "What's wrong? Why were you crying?"

"Why do you think, dumbass?" She rolls her eyes, and Dillon scratches the back of his head.

"I wouldn't ask if I knew."

Ash grabs my elbow, pulling me out past her brother. "Men are such idiots."

"I heard that," Dillon says from behind us.

"You were supposed to."

I giggle, and this is exactly what I need to get through the rest of this day.

That and pink gin cocktails, which are in plentiful supply throughout the afternoon. After we plant the white rose bushes in Lainey's memory, we all congregate by the pool. Dillon, Jamie, and Ro get in with Easton while Ash and I sunbathe around the pool, sipping our drinks. There isn't a cloud in the sky. The sun is beating down on us, and the sounds of my son laughing help to repair some of the cracks in my heart.

I will always remember Lainey, and I will always be sad I never got to meet her when she was alive. I got to hold her in the hospital for a few minutes, and she looked so peaceful, like a beautiful sleeping doll, bundled in her soft pink blanket with the white knit hat. Her eyes were closed, and she was unaware of her momma's pain as I sobbed and sobbed holding her.

I will never forget it, and my daughter will always be in my heart, but I've got to live in the present because my other child needs me.

I make a silent vow to only remember Lainey with happiness, not sadness, from now on. I owe it to myself and my son to try harder, and I will.

A subtle breeze gently lifts strands of my hair, and a serene sort of peace flows through me. Warmth infuses my insides, and the tightness in my chest is gone, as if a switch has been flipped. I stare up at the sky in silent awe, wondering what just happened.

"Is that you, my love? Are you watching over me today and helping to ease my pain?"

Tears prick my eyes, behind my sunglasses, but for once, they are happy tears. I am not a religious person, but something profound just happened, and I find enormous comfort and strength in the thought that Reeve is up there somewhere, still looking after me. Still loving and protecting me even after he's gone.

CHAPTER 29

VIVIEN

HOURS PASS PEACEFULLY, and I can't explain what happened. All I know is I feel more at peace within myself than I have felt in months. "Mommy! Come and swim with me," Easton pleads from his position on top of Dillon's shoulders. He's been taking turns diving off all his uncles' shoulders, and I'm sure his skin is wrinkled by this point—he's been in the water so long.

"I'm coming." I stand, removing my glasses and placing them on the lounger. I feel Dillon's eyes on me as I pull my hair into a messy bun on the top of my head. I'm wearing a one-piece black and gold bathing suit that is the most modest suit I own. Usually, I wear bikinis, but I didn't want to see my scar today and be reminded even more of my loss. By the way Dillon stares at me as I enter the pool, you'd swear I was naked. I'm uncomfortable with the intensity of his attention today, and I don't want to feel the way he makes me feel.

Desirable.

Horny.

Alive.

Like my skin is on fire in every spot where his gaze lands.

Like I might die if I don't feel his hands on me right now.

It feels wrong to feel like this, today of all days, and I wish he'd cut it out.

Water laps at my legs and thighs as I move farther into the pool, and the cool sensation is a welcome balm to my hot skin. "Yay, Mommy's here." Easton launches himself off Dillon's shoulders, plunging into the pool, drenching me all over. Dillon chuckles. Jamie grins, and Ro is rather expressionless as they wade by, exiting the pool to leave us alone.

I really wish they wouldn't.

"He's a little nutter," Dillon says as E bursts through the surface, splashing water droplets everywhere.

He throws himself at me, winding his little legs around my waist and his arms around my neck, as he plasters kisses to my face. "This is so fun." He fixes me with a toothy grin, and my heart melts. I live for these moments. I love seeing him happy and carefree without any lingering grief. Then he's gone again, diving under the water like a fish. We had an instructor come to the house when Easton was a baby, and by the time he was one, he was a bona fide expert in the pool.

"Yes. I wonder where he got that from?" I respond to Dillon's comment in a teasing tone, and it's good to be able to acknowledge the traits I see in E that belong to Dillon without feeling guilty or sad. "He's always been a little wild, but he's disciplined too, and he never gave Reeve or I any trouble."

"I have it on good faith that a certain Hollywood princess was a little wild when she was younger." Dillon waggles his brows.

"Lies. All lies," I protest, ducking down so my shoulders are fully submerged under the water.

Dillon mirrors my position as we watch Easton resurfacing. "I remember a story about someone climbing a tree and falling off and breaking her arm."

I smile at the memories. The original one, where Reeve caught me and injured himself. And the more recent one when I was sitting at the busy table in the O'Donoghues' house telling them who I was. "I guess I was a little wild," I say, treading water. "It's a miracle Easton isn't completely reckless."

"I think that must've been Reeve's calming influence."

I stare at him as if he's sprouted another head.

"You told me enough about him to know he wasn't a rule breaker," Dillon explains.

"If you had asked me in school, I would've agreed completely. But later, not so much." I'm still shocked Reeve turned to cocaine and other uppers during that awful period of our history.

"Do you have photo albums I could see?" he asks as we move around the water. East is swimming a few laps, babbling away to himself, seemingly content to be by himself while Dillon and I talk.

"You've already seen everything I have, and that reminds me. The prints I ordered for you are due to arrive next week." Dillon wanted to see every picture we had of Easton from the time he was born. We have hundreds of digital photos, which I gave him on a USB stick, but I always print out family photos and put them in albums. My parents did that for me, and I like to think I'm starting a tradition. One of my favorite things to do as a little girl was sit down with Mom and go through them.

"I meant albums of Reeve," Dillon clarifies.

I twist my head to look at him, frowning. "Why would you want those?"

"I want to get to know the real Reeve." He runs his tongue over his teeth. "My therapist thinks it will help."

"I have albums I can show you." I'm not sure I'll be able to look at them, but who knows, maybe they will help me too.

"Great."

"Mommy." Easton swims up to us. "Can I get on your back and you pretend you're a sea dragon?"

Dillon chuckles while Easton crawls onto my back. "Hold on tight," I say before swimming away with my son clinging to my back.

"I'm exhausted," Dillon says, an hour later, when we're seated around the table enjoying a few drinks. Easton is sprawled out on a blanket on the grass behind us, doing a jigsaw. "I don't know where he gets all his energy from."

"He's a livewire for sure. Wait until he's bouncing on your bed at six a.m. full of the joys of spring. It's especially awesome when you have a hangover."

"I can't wait," Dillon says, yearning clear on his face, and it's a strong reminder of how much he's missed out on and how badly he wants to experience everything with his son.

I know he's eager, but I'm not ready to let Easton have sleepovers with Dillon by himself yet.

Awkward silence descends until Ash breaks it as only she can.

"Aw, fuck it. Let's not do this. There have been enough secrets and lies. There is no point ignoring the elephant in the room. Shit happened." She eyeballs her brother. "You missed out on the first few years of his life, but you'll get to experience so much more going forward. And you, my friend"—she turns to me, squeezing my hand—"you have nothing to feel guilty about. It is what it is, and you both need to stop pussyfooting around it."

"I love the fuck out of you," Jamie says, leaning in to plant a hard kiss on her mouth.

"You owe one dollar to the jar, Uncle Jamie," East calls out without lifting his head from his jigsaw.

"Damn. He's one shrewd little hustler," Jamie says after dragging his lips from his fiancée.

"Make it two!" Easton adds, and Dillon's lips pull into a proud smile.

"We should be careful what we say," I murmur, not wanting E to overhear something he shouldn't.

"When are you going to tell him?" Jamie asks.

"Mate. Don't." Dillon shakes his head.

"It's too soon, but I won't leave it indefinitely." I look at

Dillon through my sunglasses. "I know you must be dying to tell him, and I'm glad you're not pressuring me."

"I am, but I would never do that. It's about what's best for him." Dillon is trying so hard. I cannot deny that, and it gives me hope we can make things work.

"Aw, this is too much." Ash hops up, rounding the table and hugging Dillon. "I'm proud of you, dumbass."

"Do you have any photos of your daughter?" I ask Ronan, needing to switch the direction of our group conversation. He's been extremely quiet with me, and I wonder if I've done something to offend him.

"I do." He squirms in his seat, looking uncomfortable.

"Have I done something to upset you?" I ask, my honesty spurred on by the liquid gin sloshing through my veins.

"Why would you ask that?" His piercing blue eyes lock on mine briefly before flitting away.

"Because you can hardly look at me."

"I'm just not sure what to say. I don't want to upset you."

My brow puckers. "You and I never had an issue talking to one another. I thought we were friends."

"We were. We are." He drags a hand through his messy brown curls. His hair is much longer now, curling around his ears and the nape of his neck, but it suits him. Ronan has grown up in the years we were apart, and he's lost that boyish look from his face. "I was trying to be sensitive. You've just lost a baby. I didn't want to be parading pictures of my daughter in your face."

The O'Donoghue men are really wowing me with their thoughtfulness today.

Ash crawls into Jamie's lap, wrapping her arms around him. "That's my fault." Her gaze bounces between Ro and me. "It was hard for me after we lost our baby. Clodagh was pregnant, and I had to avoid her because it hurt so much I usually ended up in tears." Jamie runs a hand up and down her back. "That made me feel so guilty because it wasn't poor Clodagh's fault."

"It wasn't your fault either," Jamie says, kissing her temple. "You couldn't help how you felt."

"Clo never held that against you, Ash." Ro lights a cigarette. "She was upset for you."

"I know." Ash reaches out, brushing Ro's arm. "Are you sure you two can't make a go of it?"

Ash had explained Ro was sullen because his fiancée—the mother of his daughter— broke their engagement off two months ago. She has been in Ireland for the past five months while Ro has largely been stuck here.

He shakes his head. "She doesn't want me anymore."

Visceral pain underscores his tone, and I feel for him. "I'm sorry to hear that. It must be so difficult being away from your daughter."

"It's killing me." He takes a long drag of his cigarette, blowing smoke circles into the air.

"Fuck, this conversation is depressing," Dillon says. "We all need cheering up. Jay, put on the music. Ro, come with me to get the meat for the barbecue."

Ro unlocks his cell, pulls up some photos, and hands his phone to me. "Those are the most recent ones Clo sent me."

Emer is sitting on a blanket on the ground, giggling at the camera, looking happy and content. She has a shock of thick dark curls and the biggest blue eyes. "She's beautiful, Ro."

His smile is sad, and my heart hurts for him.

Dillon slides his arm around his brother's shoulder, squeezing him. "We'll knock the rest of the album out in the next couple of weeks, and then you can go home to see her."

Ro nods, shoving Dillon's arm off before wandering into the house to get the meat for the grill.

"Can I help?"

"Nah. We've got this. Keep your pretty arse on that chair and have another cocktail." Dillon puts his fingers in his mouth and whistles. "East! You're on barbecue duty with me."

Easton hops up, wrecking the jigsaw he so painstakingly made. "Fiddlesticks."

Jamie snorts out a laugh. "Let me guess, that one's all you?"

I flip him the bird when I'm sure E isn't watching. "Damn straight it is, and I'm not apologizing. I'm not having my son go around cussing like a sailor."

"Girl, good luck with that plan," Ash says, swiping my empty glass. "You have zero chance of protecting those sensitive little ears around us lot."

CHAPTER 30

DILLON

"MY BELLY'S FAT," Easton proclaims, rubbing his hands over his slightly extended stomach.

"That's what happens when you eat *two* burgers and a mountain of chips," Jamie says, grinning.

"Chips?" Easton frowns.

"He means fries," Ash supplies. "In Ireland, we call them chips."

"Huh." His nose scrunches. "What's Ireland like?" he asks, climbing into my lap. He snuggles against me, and when his little warm hand lands on my bare chest, I practically melt into the chair. Today has been amazing, and I want a million more days like this.

"Very green," I tell him.

He pins me with wide trusting eyes. "Like the sky is green and all the roads and everything?"

I chuckle, tweaking his nose. "No, silly. The sky is still blue and the roads are the same color as here. It means that there is lots of green grass and lots of mountains and trees and bushes. There aren't as many cities or as many tall buildings as in America."

He curls his legs up, snuggling closer, and I could die from contentment right now. My fingers weave through his dark hair as he looks up at me. "Can I go to Ireland with you, and can we climb mountains?"

"Hopefully, someday." I glance over at Viv. "If it's okay with your mommy."

Viv has her shades on so I can't tell her reaction. After a bit of a shaky start earlier, she seems to be processing everything okay. I swear that woman has immeasurable strength. She never ceases to amaze me.

"We can visit Ireland. Maybe next year after the band has finished their tour."

She let me tell Easton about our impending tour because neither of us wants it to be a huge shock when I have to up and leave. I know it will be hard for my son. It'll be excruciating for me, and I honestly don't know how I'm going to do it. I don't want to leave him or Viv. I never want to be without either of them again.

"Yay." East fights a yawn.

"We should get going," Viv says.

"Not a snowball's chance in hell." Ash pushes the jug with the pink gin mix toward Viv. "It's not even seven. There's no way you're going home yet. East is fine here."

Ash has been amazing with Viv, and I'm happy to see them renew their friendship. Ash struggles to make friends with other women, especially within the industry we work in. Most of the women she has met are trying to use her as a way to get to the band, and she doesn't trust easily. She rarely talks to Cat anymore. It's been too difficult with them living on different continents. Besides, Cat was never the friend Viv was.

I expect Viv to protest because I know she's a stickler for routine with Easton, which I respect and admire. She always puts him first, and I only love her more for it. But I guess her desire to not return to her empty lonely home is stronger today because she doesn't mount any further arguments, happily accepting the gin Ash pours into her glass.

Twenty minutes later, East is sound asleep against my chest. I press my lips to his hair, closing my eyes and inhaling the familiar scent of my son.

Nothing compares to this.

Not even standing in front of thousands of screaming fans.

This little boy is already my entire world, and I would do anything to ensure his happiness. Lifting my head, I find Viv watching me. She's removed her glasses, and I see the emotion swimming in her eyes. "I can put him to bed," I whisper, "and just carry him out to the car when you're ready to leave." If I have my way, neither of them will be leaving tonight, but I don't want to admit that and freak the fuck out of Hollywood.

She thinks about it for a few beats before nodding.

I get up slowly and carefully, repositioning my sleeping son in my arms. He stirs a little, murmuring in his sleep as I walk off. Viv comes with me, and we don't talk as I carry Easton inside, walking the length of the hallway until I reach the stairs to the next level.

Emotion is heavy in the air as I push open the door to Easton's nature-themed bedroom. Viv sucks in a gasp as I stride across the wooden floor of the large room, toward the custom pine bed. I'm glad I decided against putting his bed in the little treehouse fixed against the right-hand side of the wall. While the ladder is large and sturdy, there is no way I would've been able to climb up to it without waking East.

Viv brushes past me, pulling back the green and blue duvet. Very gently, I place our son down, grateful Viv made him change out of his swimming trunks before we ate dinner. He's wearing light Nike training shorts that are comfortable to sleep in. Viv tucks the covers up over him, leaning down briefly to kiss his cheek. When it's my turn, I press a lingering kiss to his brow, attempting to calm my errant emotions.

We tiptoe to the door, both of us turning around at the same time to look at him. I have pictured Easton in this room many times since I designed it for him in the weeks after I discovered he was my child. Throwing myself into remodeling the bedrooms and adding the room for him in the studio helped to distract me from all the shit that was going down.

"Dillon, this is just…wow," Viv whispers, her face lighting up.

Pride swells my chest as I scan the room. It turned out better than I expected. "I know he loves nature and animals and the outdoors, so I wanted to incorporate that in the design. I had a guy come in to build the tree and the treehouse, and Ash found this super talented artist who drew the murals, but I did the rest myself. Jamie helped me to make the bed."

Her mouth hangs open. "You made that bed?"

A genuine smile ghosts over my lips. "Jamie and I did woodwork for our Leaving Cert. It was the only subject I enjoyed in school. I got a kick out of making it for him."

Her chest heaves, and she blinks back tears. "You did an amazing job. It's stunning, and he's going to love it."

Warmth spreads across my chest at her words. I was afraid she might go nuts at me for being so presumptuous. Truth is, I can't wait for Easton to have sleepovers.

Viv pulls the door over, not fully closing it. The dim glow from the lightning-bug lamp by East's bed ensures he's not in complete darkness should he wake up and be scared. I purposely put Viv's room beside his so she's close by if he stirs during the night.

"Thank you for today," she quietly says.

"It's been my pleasure. I've loved having both of you here." Before I can stop myself, I'm twirling a strand of her hair around my finger. "You know I'd do anything for you. If I could absorb your pain and take it away from you, I would."

"I'm at war with myself so much recently," she admits, staring deep into my eyes.

I'm immediately hypnotized in a way only Vivien has ever been able to do. Her face just calls to me. Everything about her does. I drown in her gorgeous hazel eyes, swimming in the goodness I always find there. It's like being sucker punched in the heart and the dick at the same time. God, I love her. I love her so much, and I want her so badly. "Why?" I croak, finally managing to find words.

"Because you make me feel things, Dillon. You always have."

I lean closer, winding my hands in her hair as I tilt her face up. "There is nothing wrong with that, Viv, and you know how I feel about you. How I've always felt about you."

"How can something feel so right yet so wrong too?" She almost chokes on the words, and I see the torment ravishing her beautiful face.

"There is no rule book for the things you've endured and no one-size-fits-all model for dealing with grief and moving forward." I rest my forehead against hers. "Just be true to yourself. Do what feels right for you."

"I'm scared, Dil," she whispers, staring into my eyes. "I'm scared if I move on I'll forget him."

"I won't let you." The irony of that promise isn't lost on me, but I mean it sincerely. I know how much she loved Reeve, and I would never ask her to forget the past she's shared with him. I realize how far I've come. How much Dr. Howard is helping me to process my feelings.

"Do you really mean that?" she asks, clutching my waist.

"I do." As much as I don't want to pull away from her, I need her to see my face, to believe this truth. I lift my head, putting a little distance between us as I cradle her cheek in my palm. "Reeve has been an enormous part of your life. You loved him, and no one can take that away from you. Least of all me. I'm just hoping there's room left for me. That you can get to a place where we can move forward, together. I want your future, Viv, but I will never let you forget your past. I will help you to remember him because him loving you has helped to shape the woman you are today. I happen to love that woman very much."

"So much for friends." She narrows her eyes, but the gesture is lighthearted.

"I'm still your friend, Viv, but let's be honest. Our connection is too explosive to ever let us be just friends."

"You have matured so much, Dillon."

"You aren't the only one impacted by his death. It has forced me to face things I've been ignoring for years."

"I want to move on, but it's too soon. If we ever get on the same page, I want it to be a fresh start, where there is no guilt or feelings of betrayal coming between us." She slides out from underneath me. "That day hasn't arrived yet."

"It's okay," I semi-lie, shoving my hands in the pockets of my shorts. "I understand. Take whatever time you need. I'm going nowhere."

We return to the others, staying outside chatting and drinking until it turns dark. When we move inside, Jamie and I get our guitars while the girls go to check on East. Ro leaves to go back to his house despite us asking him to stay. My brother isn't in a good place. He really loves Clo, and the breakup came completely out of the blue. He's devastated, and I know what that feels like, so I don't push him to stay.

We play a few songs, and I even coax Viv into singing.

"You should officially sing with the band someday," Ash tells her. "Not like permanently, but you should record a song with them. That voice is way too beautiful to deny the world."

"Yeah…no." Viv kicks off her sandals, pulling her legs up onto the sofa beside me. "I hate the spotlight." She shivers. "Even thinking about it gives me goose bumps."

"We could always record something that's just for us," I say, taking a swig of beer as I set my guitar aside. "It could be fun. Think about it."

She lies back, and I lift her feet onto my lap, massaging them without thinking about it. She used to love my foot rubs, and I was fond of bartering for sexual favors in return. Fun times. Slotting back into a regular pattern with Viv would be as easy as breathing for me.

Jamie and Ash watch with bated breath to see how she reacts.

She closes her eyes, settling down into the sofa, getting comfortable. "Hmmm. That feels good."

My gaze meets Jamie's as I knead Viv's feet, and I know he's rooting for us. He's been a rock for me these past couple of months. Honestly, I don't know what I'd do without Jamie and Ash. Jamie smiles, quietly pulling Ash to her feet. They leave the room, and silence descends, but it's not uncomfortable.

Viv sinks farther into the sofa as I move my fingers from her feet to her silky-smooth calves, kneading her supple flesh as I move higher. I have always loved her gorgeous long slim legs.

Especially when they were wrapped around my neck.

My cock surges to life as I remember all the times I ate her out while she was dangling off my shoulders. Her taste fills my mouth as if it hasn't been over six years since I last had my lips on any part of her.

"Dillon!" Her urgent tone yanks me out of my head. One of her hands is wrapped around one of my wrists, stalling my upward trajectory. I didn't realize my hands had moved so far up her thighs. My dick thickens to the point of pain, and if she looks down, there'll be no disguising my monster boner. I was oh so close to the promised land, but now the gates are being thrown up, shutting me out.

"You don't want this?" I ask, my gaze lowering to her mouth. "Let me make you feel good."

"We can't," she whispers.

"Why not?" I inch my free hand higher, brushing the tips of my fingers against her lace knickers.

"It's not right." She pushes me away, tumbling off the sofa onto the floor. I reach down to help her, but she swats my hands away. "Don't touch me. Please."

I raise my palms and back off. "I won't do anything you don't want, but I see the lust in your eyes, Viv. I know you want it. Need it." It's been three months since anyone has touched her. I know sex isn't the answer to our situation, but a few orgasms will do wonders for her state of mind.

"It's not about me not wanting you, Dillon." She stands, wobbling a little, but she's not drunk. She stopped the cocktails a few hours ago, switching to sparkling water. "It's about dishonoring Reeve's memory on the day our daughter was due to be born."

I instantly sober up. "You would never dishonor his memory, and taking something for yourself on a difficult day isn't wrong. But I understand why you feel that way, and I would never pressure you."

"Thanks." She looks around. "Where did Ash and Jamie go?"

"They've gone to bed."

She glances at the clock on the wall. "It's almost midnight. I lost track of time. I'd no idea it was so late."

"You should just stay here. I have tons of spare bedrooms. You can take the one beside Easton's room." I don't want to admit it's been remodeled specifically for her because that will probably send her running for the hills.

"I don't think that's a good idea." She chews anxiously on her lip.

"I'm not going to touch you, Viv. Not unless you ask me to." I stand, walking to her. "Stay. Easton is comfortable. It's late, and you're tired."

"Okay," she relents, and I nod, fighting a smile. Getting to wake up knowing East and Viv are in my house brings me enormous joy.

We head upstairs, and I show her to her room. "I thought you'd like to be beside Easton. That way, if he wakes, you will hear him."

"Thank you." She flips the light switch on the wall, and her eyes pop wide as she spins around to face me. "Did you do this for me?"

I nod. "I wanted you to have your own room here."

Tears prick her eyes as she drinks in the four-poster bed

with wispy white curtains. I had an interior designer come in to create this room because I wanted it perfect for Vivien. The walls are a purple-gray color. The furniture is dark wood, contrasting perfectly with the ash-gray wooden floors. A large patterned pink rug is soft underfoot, and the rest of the room is decorated in various shades of white, gray, pink, and purple. It's luxurious and comfortable, yet it has a cozy vibe too. Exactly what I wanted to achieve.

"God, Dillon." She clasps a hand to her chest. "I don't know what to say." Tears brim in her eyes as she stares up at me. "I appreciate your thoughtfulness so much and how you're not pressuring me or Easton. Thank you for understanding and for being so supportive."

"It's not a chore, Viv. I want to be here for you. If I can help to make things easier, I'll do it."

She sniffles, casting her gaze around the room again.

I don't want to leave, and physically pulling myself away from her is a wrench, but she needs her space. "I'm just down the hall." I point out through the door to the left where my master suite is. "If you need anything during the night, come get me."

She bobs her head. "I'm sure I'll be fine."

"There are towels and supplies in the en suite bathroom," I add, still reluctant to leave.

Her smile is shy. "I'll be fine, Dillon. Go to bed."

I lean in closer, pressing my mouth to her ear. I know I shouldn't say this, but hello, I'm me. "If you want me to make you feel good, my offer still stands. If you need to forget, I know just how to distract you."

She pushes my shoulders, forcing me back. "Goodnight, Dillon."

Her tone brooks no argument, but I don't give up that easily. I fix her with a cheeky grin, before blowing her a kiss. "Goodnight, Hollywood. You know where to find me if you can't sleep."

CHAPTER 31
DILLON

I CAN'T SLEEP KNOWING Vivien is down the hall, most likely tossing and turning in bed like I am. Today was a difficult day for her, but she surprised me, like she has a habit of doing. She handled it far better than I expected. I'd like to take some of the credit, but this is all on Viv. She is so strong. So brave. And I'm craving her worse than ever. For the first time since the accident, I feel a kernel of genuine hope kindling inside me.

She still has feelings for me.

Feelings she's fighting, but I can handle that.

Not feeling anything for me, or hating me, would be so much worse.

I slide my hand down over my stomach, wrapping it around my still-hard dick, deciding I might as well jerk off, right as the door opens, admitting a sliver of light from the hallway. My hand stalls on my cock, and I lift my head, spotting the shadowy figure in the doorway. "Viv?" She doesn't move, standing rooted to the spot, and I pull my boxers up and climb out of bed.

I walk toward her carefully, afraid to spook her. I stop a few feet from her. "Are you okay?" She shakes her head, stepping a little closer. "Can't sleep, sweetheart?" I brush my fingers across her cheek. She takes a step closer, and her chest brushes against mine. She's wearing the Collateral Damage T-Shirt I left on the bed for her earlier tonight, when I harbored hopes she'd stay, and she looks so fucking good in it.

"Dillon." My name is a whisper on her tongue, but it's enough. I hear the pleading in her tone. Planting one hand on my bare chest, she peers up at me, and I see it all in her eyes. She won't say it. That would be like admitting it to herself, and she's unable to do that right now. So I'll have to make the decision for her.

Taking her hand, I pull her into my semi-darkened room and close the door. "Are you sure?" I run my thumb along her lower lip, urging my cock to calm the fuck down because he's excited and presently trying to poke a hole through my Calvins.

She nods, and I back her up to the wall, caging her in on both sides with my arms. Her eyes dilate as we stare at one another, and electricity crackles in the tiny space between us. Tucking her hair behind her ears, I inspect every inch of her gorgeous face. She has no idea how stunning she is or how badly I want her. This is the culmination of every fantasy I've had since we broke up. I lean down, dying to kiss her, but she pushes my shoulders and shakes her head. "No kissing."

Disappointment crashes into me, and I could legit cry, but I force my frustration back down. This is about her. Not me. I don't turn the overhead light on, figuring it's easier for her like this with only a faint light illuminating us from the lamp on my bedside locker.

My eyes are glued to hers as I grip the hem of her shirt, slowly tugging it up her body. She lifts her arms without me asking, and I pull the shirt up, tossing it on the floor. Slowly, I drag my eyes down her gorgeous naked body, marveling at how truly exquisite she is, while precum leaks from my cock. It's quite possible I might come in my boxers like a horny teenager. It's been a while for me, and I've spent night upon night jerking off to thoughts of Viv, so it's no joke.

My hands are trembling as I sweep my fingers along her velvety-soft flesh. Rubbing my thumb and forefinger across her nipples, I feel like fist pumping the air when the rosy-pink buds harden under my touch. Bending my head, I lave my tongue along each nipple, gently drawing her tit into my mouth.

"Not gentle, Dil."

The unspoken end of that sentence is crystal clear. Viv likes it hard and rough. I was rarely gentle with her. Not until that last night when I made love to her with my very soul. But I know what she needs now, and I'll give it to her. Dragging her nipple between my teeth, I softly bite down, and she moans, throwing her head back to the wall and her gaze to the ceiling. "So beautiful," I whisper as I move my attention to her other breast. I spend a few minutes sucking, nipping, and kneading before I drop to my knees on the carpeted floor before her.

Pushing her legs apart, I take a few seconds to savor this moment. I never thought I'd get to taste her again, and my heart is beating so fast in my chest it feels like it might beat a path out of there. I rub my nose against her pussy, inhaling deeply, before I part her lips with my thumbs and trace my tongue along her slit from top to bottom.

A strangled sound escapes her lips as I lick her with a fervor that may well be the undoing of me. More precum leaks from my cock as I dive in, plunging my tongue inside her. I lift one of her legs over my shoulder so I can get better access as I feast on her tempting cunt.

She is magnificent, and I want this for the rest of my life.

She pivots her hips, grabbing fistfuls of my hair as she rides my face, needing more. I haven't forgotten how her body works, and I have no intention of dragging this out. Not tonight. She needs this release, and I will give it to her. I push two fingers inside her as my tongue swirls around her clit, and she rocks her hips against me, making all the sounds I love to hear as I devour her.

I add another digit, curling all three of my fingers in the right place just as I flatten my tongue against her clit, and she goes off, detonating like a firework on Halloween night. I pump my fingers harder while I suck her clit, keeping up my pace until I've milked every last drop of her sweet climax.

When I feel her sagging against me, I lift her up and place her on my bed, crawling over her. I want to kiss her mouth so badly, but I know it's too much for her, so I settle for worshiping every inch of her skin, kissing my way down her body, as I grind my hips against her.

Her legs part to accommodate me, and I'm losing control of myself as I lick and suck her hot skin, thrusting my boxer-covered dick against her pussy, wishing there was no barrier between us and I was slipping inside her. Fingers thread through my hair as I adore her body with my hands and my lips. I stop for a second when my lips touch the edge of the scar on her lower stomach. Planting a slew of soft kisses along her puckered skin, I feel her flinch under me, and that's all it takes to lose her from the moment.

"No!" she cries, scrambling off the bed.

"It's okay." I reach for her, but she crawls away, clambering awkwardly to her feet. "What have I done?" she sobs, ignoring me as she makes a grab for the door. I watch with a massive lump in my throat as she flies out the door, away from me, not knowing if I should chase after her or give her space.

Sitting on the edge of my bed, I bury my head in my hands. The urge to cry is strong, but I can't fall apart. Viv needs me, and I'm never failing her again. Decision made, I get up, swiping the shirt off the floor, and follow her to her room.

She's curled on top of the messy bed, in the fetal position, sobbing into her pillow in an attempt not to wake Easton. Pain stabs me all over, and remorse fills all the gaps. This was too much. I should have told her no. This is my fault, and I need to fix it.

I pad quietly across the floor, climbing onto the bed behind her. She continues to cry as I sit her up, sliding my shirt down over her body. She lies back down, still crying, and my arms go around her as I spoon her from behind, pulling her body into mine.

I hold her close as she tries to wriggle free, but I'm not letting her. I'm not leaving her to deal with this alone. "Don't fight this. I can't go back to my room and leave you here crying." I cover her upper leg with mine. "Don't feel guilty for accepting support when you need it."

"How can I not?" she wails, grabbing my arms.

"There is nothing wrong with seeking pleasure. You needed the release."

She twists in my arms, pinning me with the saddest eyes. "I'm so selfish. I was lying here in bed, thinking about you. Thinking about how you always made me feel so fucking good, and I went to you looking for that. How could I do that?"

"Shush, honey." I clasp her against my chest, running one hand over her hair and the other up and down her back. "Stop being so hard on yourself. You've been through hell, and it's okay to take this for yourself. Especially today."

"But that's it!" Tears stream down her face. "How could I let you do that to me today of all days? I should be in the delivery room right now with Reeve, holding Lainey. If the accident hadn't happened, that is where I would be."

I brush wispy strands of hair off her face. "I'm sorry you're not there, Viv. I know how much you wish you were. You're hurting, and there is nothing wrong with letting me comfort you."

She cries into my chest, and silent tears leak out of my eyes. I hate this. For her. For me. For us. "I'm so sad, Dillon," she mumbles against my skin. "So sad and lonely, and I feel like this pain will never end."

I hold her tighter. "It will get better, and I'm here for you. Whatever you need. You've got it."

I wake the following morning to an empty bed with only the scent of Viv lingering on the sheets beside me. "Uncle Dillon!" East charges into the room, wearing a T-shirt and shorts and the widest smile on his face. He jumps on top of me, hugging me to death. "Thank you for my room! It's awesome!"

Discreetly, I adjust my morning wood before sitting up with him draped all over me. "I'm happy you like it."

"I love my treehouse. Do you think my friend Nash could come over and see it?"

"Sure. But we'll have to check with your mom and his. Maybe we could arrange it one afternoon after you go back to school." That gives me a couple of weeks to work on Viv.

"Easton. Come on. We've got to go," Viv says, and I look up.

She's leaning against the door frame, wearing a blue summer dress I know belongs to my sister. It's way shorter on Viv's taller frame, and the hem hits mid-thigh, offering me a tantalizing glimpse of smooth toned skin I've been recently reacquainted with. From the strained look on Viv's face, I'm betting that's the last time I'll be getting close to any part of her body.

"Why don't you stay for breakfast? There's no need to rush off." I really want to talk to her about this in the cold light of day. I know Viv, and she's going to beat herself up for last night if I can't get through to her.

"I have things to do," she lies, avoiding eye contact with me.

East crawls off my lap, pouting as he says, "I want to stay."

"It's not possible." She jerks her chin up. "Now, come on. I have everything packed in the trunk. It's time to go home."

"I'm not going." Easton stands, folding his arms across his chest. "It's boring at home. I like it here."

"I'm your mother, and you don't get to make these decisions. Don't disobey me, Easton. Thank Dillon for having a nice time and let's go."

He shakes his head before turning pleading eyes on me. "Can I stay with you? Mommy can go home, and we can play."

I would love nothing more, but I know Viv wouldn't be okay with that, and I won't usurp her authority. "Come here." I call him over to me, looking into his eyes. "I will come to see you in a few days, but you've got to go home with your mommy now. She's the boss, buddy."

"She's mean. I don't want to go home to my boring house and my boring mommy. I want to stay here with you and Auntie Ash and Uncle Jamie."

I know he's sulking, and he doesn't mean it, but he can't speak to Vivien like that. "That's enough, Easton. You won't speak to or about your mother like that. Do you hear me?" I stand, hoping he doesn't notice my semi, and take his hand. "You need to do what your mommy says." I look down at him. "Always respect your mother. She loves you, and she knows what's best."

"You're mean too." He yanks his hand from mine, stomping past Vivien and out to the hallway.

"Do you want me to talk to him?"

She shakes her head. "I'll have a chat with him when we get home."

"We should talk before you go." I hold Viv's arm as she moves to go after him.

"There isn't anything left to say."

"C'mon, Viv. You know we need to hash this out."

She wrestles out of my hold, stabbing me with those beautiful hazel eyes. "Last night never happened. It was a mistake. A mistake I won't be making again."

Her words hurt, but I'm guessing that's the intent. My natural inclination is to argue, but I'm trying to put her needs above my own. It takes considerable effort to speak calmly, but I do it. For her. "Pretend it didn't happen if that helps, but I'll be here whenever you're ready to face up to it."

CHAPTER 32

DILLON

"PENNY FOR THEM," Ash says, walking into the kitchen with Jamie in tow, like the good little lapdog he is.

I grip the counter harder, warring with my emotions. It's been two weeks since the night Easton and Vivien stayed here, and she's barely giving me the time of day. I can't stand it, and I don't know how much longer I can do this without cracking. Slowly, I turn around, sighing. "Vivien is freezing me out again. It's like we take one step forward and then ten steps back."

"She's running scared since she let you go down on her." Ash casually throws it out there, like it's normal to just blurt that shit.

"What the fuck, babe?" Jamie stares at her.

"What?" Ash looks between us, jabbing her finger in the air. "It's not like you two don't talk about us."

"Hell no." I push off the counter. I won't be having that. "I get zero details of what you two get up to in the bedroom. Even knowing you have a sex life freaks me out."

Ash rolls her eyes. "You're being ridiculous. We're all adults. We all have sex."

"Except Dillon isn't getting any, and I think that's the

LET ME LOVE YOU

problem." Jamie smirks, and I'm tempted to punch him in the face.

I flip him the bird. "My hand is getting plenty of action."

Ash makes a face but refrains from commenting because that would make her a hypocrite.

I can't resist pushing her buttons. "I subscribed to a new porn channel. Damn, that shit is cheesy, but it does the job." I rub my hand up and down my crotch while I lie.

As if I need porn to get me off.

Just thinking about Viv gets me hard in seconds.

"Okay, enough." She holds up one palm. "You made your point, and *my point* is Viv moved too fast. I'm surprised she even confided in me, but she feels disloyal to Reeve, and she's too stuck in her head over what people would think if she starts anything with you."

"I don't give a flying fuck what anyone thinks."

"You don't, but she does. There is a lot of bad history there, as we all know, so I get why she's concerned."

"It's not just about us. She's regressing with Easton too. He got into a little trouble yesterday in kindergarten. Some fuckface said horrible shit about Reeve, and Easton shoved him. He fell over and hit his head off the side of a desk, and now his parents are threatening to sue the school and sue Vivien. She's talking about pulling him out and getting him a home tutor, which would not be good. The only time she lets him out of her sight is to go to school. She won't even let him go to Nash's house. Nash always has to go to them. It's not normal, and it's not helping Easton."

"Have you told her that?" Ash pulls a carton of orange juice out of the fridge.

"I've tried broaching the subject, but I'm largely still biting my tongue around her."

Ash frowns as Jamie pulls a glass out of the overhead cupboard for her. "Why are you doing that?"

"More to the point, how?" Jamie asks, watching Ash pour

herself a large glass of orange juice. "It's not like you are known for holding back."

"I'm doing what you told me to do," I tell Ash. "I'm putting her needs above my own."

"Oh my God." Ash dribbles juice down her chin. "Why are men so fucking dumb?" she mutters to herself as she swipes a blueberry muffin and heads outside to the patio table and chairs.

I'm not a massive fan of the warm California weather, but I've got to admit it's nice to spend so much time outdoors and not need a rain jacket. "Spit it out." I flop onto one of the chairs.

"I said put her needs above your own. That doesn't mean biting your tongue if things need to be said."

"If I tell her what I feel, it'll cause an argument, and that'll upset her. How is that being considerate of her needs?"

Ash rubs her temples. "I swear it's like dealing with children."

"Fuck you, Ash." Fire blazes from my eyes. "You are the one who told me to do this. Don't fucking turn around now and call me an imbecile and make out like this is all my fault. I'm doing the best I can." My voice cracks, and I feel like a pussy, but everyone seems to forget this has been hard on me too. Yes, I know some of it was my own doing, but I'm trying to make amends, and I'm only human.

Despite what people might think of me, I have feelings.

"This isn't easy on me," I admit. "You think I like holding back when I see the woman I love torturing herself because she believes she doesn't deserve to be happy? I know she has feelings for me, but she's going to bury them until she forgets they exist. And I have to hold back from telling my son he's my son because the timing needs to be right. Do you have any fucking idea how hard it is to be around that little boy and not tell him?" I lean my elbows on the table. "Do you know how badly I want him to call me daddy? And how badly I want to take care of both of them? How I lie in bed every night thinking of them over in that big sad lonely house wishing I could be there to help ease their pain?"

Pressure sits on my chest. "We built that memorial garden for Reeve. The three of us. And I thought it would help her to see that we can do this together. That she doesn't need to handle everything alone, but she's more withdrawn than ever." I rub at my stinging eyes. "I don't know what to do anymore. I constantly second-guess myself, and I don't know if I'm even helping."

"I'm sorry, Dil." Ash reaches across the table, taking my hand. "No one is dismissing your feelings, and we know it's difficult for you."

"You're doing amazing with both of them," Jamie supplies. "And Vivien may not want to see it or accept it, but she needs you, and you can't give up on her."

"I'm never giving up on her, Jay. Never again. No matter how tough it gets, I'm going nowhere." I exhale heavily, kicking my feet up on the table. "Fuck, I'd kill for a smoke." I gave the ciggies up last February, but I still crave them.

Ash squeezes my hand. "I love you, brother. And I truly believe Viv does too. I'm sorry for making fun of you. That wasn't fair." She wets her lips as Jamie sneakily grabs her drink, finishing off her juice. "I didn't mean for you to deny who you are or to bite your tongue around her. You can be cognizant of her needs and still be you. In fact, I think you need to be more you. That's what she needs now."

"What exactly are you saying, Ash, because you're confusing the hell outta me."

"You need to be your normal dickhead self. Viv needs Dickhead Dillon. You holding back from speaking your mind is the worst idea. Stop overthinking it, and just be you."

I look at my mate. "Women are batshit crazy. They say one thing but mean another. You deserve a fucking gold medal for putting up with that shite for all these years."

"*Fact.*" Jamie mouths behind Ash's back, but he doesn't say a word out loud, because he's so fucking pussy-whipped he's terrified to admit I speak the truth.

Ash pinches my cheek. "Way to piss me off when I was starting to feel sympathy for you."

"Aw, whatever." I stand. "I'm out of here."

She eyes me suspiciously. "Where are you going?"

"I'm going to talk to Viv about Easton."

"What are you doing back here?" Vivien asks when she opens her front door to me.

"I need to speak to you, and it can't wait until Friday." Viv lets me collect East from school every Monday, Wednesday, and Friday. I dropped him off earlier, but I didn't stay because I was in a foul mood. Ash's words have given me the permission I felt I needed, and I'm feeling invigorated. I don't want to argue with Viv, but she needs someone to talk sense into her, and that job has got my name written all over it.

I push past her, not waiting for an invite.

"Dillon, wait." Her sandals clack against the tiled floor as she chases after me. I duck into the formal dining room because the playground can't be seen from this room. I don't want Easton to see me. At least not until I have spoken to his mum.

Viv races into the room, scowling at me.

"Shut the door."

"This is my house." She folds her arms over her chest.

I glance at the large family portrait that hangs on the far wall. "I'm well aware. Now shut the fucking door, Vivien Grace. We don't want Easton to hear this conversation."

"I'm not telling him yet!" she shrieks, slamming the door shut. "It's too soon."

"Stop panicking, Viv. I'm not here about that. We need to talk about this crazy idea you have about taking East out of school."

She crosses her arms over her chest again. "It's not a crazy idea. It makes perfect sense, and I've already got tutor interviews lined up."

"He needs to be around other kids, Viv, and he loves school."

"I know he does, but this is in his best interest. You know what happened yesterday and we had a similar incident at camp. It's not going to stop, and I need to protect him."

"Mollycoddling him isn't the same as protecting him. You need to let him fight these battles himself. Trying to shield him from them will only do more harm than good. This is the world we live in. There will be more assholes to contend with. He needs to understand that and learn how to handle it himself."

"He's only five years old, Dillon! How the fuck is he expected to handle it himself?" She throws her hands in the air, pacing the room.

"The same way you did. You can't tell me you didn't get shit thrown at you over your parents growing up."

"Of course, I did, but—"

"Well, there you go." I pin her with a knowing look.

"Don't interrupt me before I am finished speaking." She glares at me, and I'm kicking myself that I didn't do this weeks ago. Viv needs to be challenged. I almost laugh at the irony. I've been mollycoddling her for months instead of forcing her to face the truth. I think it was right to do that at the start when her grief was so heavy there was no other way to manage it. But not now. Now, the gloves come off, and it's time to push her to face her new reality.

I smirk, and she growls. I laugh before reining it in when I see the murderous look on her face. This isn't a game. I came here with a purpose in mind. "Continue."

She bites on her lower lip, and my cock jumps in my jeans. "I've had my fair share of shit thrown at me over the years, but—"

"But what?"

She looks at her feet. "Reeve was there. He always defended me."

"That may be the case, but I'm betting he wasn't always there because you know how to defend yourself. I've seen you in action."

"It's not about me anyway. We're talking about Easton."

"Easton needs to learn to fight his own battles, and he's a smart little kid. I understand you want to protect him. I do too. But this isn't the way. He'll only come to resent you for it, and it'll make things harder. Hiding him away from the world doesn't make it go away. You need to let him be a child, Viv. You need to let him go to his friends' houses. You need to bring him bowling, or let me take him on a hike, or go to the movies. You need to let him resume his life. It's the best way of helping him to move on."

Her nostrils flare, and she bares her teeth at me. "Are you done telling me how to raise my child?"

"He's my child too."

She harrumphs. "Aw, here we go. I was waiting for this to happen."

"I'm not trying to question your authority or replace Reeve, but he is my flesh and blood, and I won't stand by and watch you make a mistake which you will live to regret and our son will pay the price for. This isn't the way to protect him, Vivien."

"Get out." She points at the door. "Get the fuck out of my house, Dillon, and stay out. You don't get to come in here and dictate to me. I make the choices for my child. I've been the one doing it for years when you weren't here."

"That's not fair, Viv, and you know it."

"Fairness doesn't come into this. The fact is, I have been the one raising my child. Not you. If anyone is qualified to make these decisions, it's me. Not you."

"Can you at least reconsider?"

"No." She opens the door. "You've outstayed your welcome, Dillon. Leave."

"This isn't the end of this conversation," I say as I move past her.

"Yes, it is."

We'll see about that.

I rock back on my heels, staring up at the impressive house with a healthy dose of trepidation as I wait for the door to open. I hope I'm not making a mistake coming here, but if anyone can get through to Viv, it's her parents. They arrived back in L.A. nine days ago, but I know they only have a few weeks at home before they are on the move again.

The door swings open, and I'm greeted by a tall thin woman in an austere white and gray uniform. Her cold gray eyes and the grim set of her mouth are as unattractive as the outfit she's wearing. "Can I help you?"

"It's okay, Renata. We've been expecting Mr. O'Donoghue. I'll take it from here," Jonathon Mills says, appearing beside the unfriendly woman.

She nods before walking off.

I quirk a brow. "Was being scary and unwelcoming a trait you sought when you were interviewing for her position or a surprise addition to her skill set?"

Jonathon chuckles. "Renata is an acquired taste. A bit like beer." He shudders, and now it's my turn to laugh.

"I like beer."

"I guess there's no accounting for taste." He is smiling as he stands aside. "Come in, Dillon."

I step into Vivien's childhood home, feeling like a trespasser. She is going to be so pissed when she finds out I did this. But it's a small price to pay if it means she changes her mind and lets East stay in school.

"When the gate security called and said you were here to see us, I'll admit I was intrigued," he says, jerking his head and urging me to follow him.

I was half expecting to be turned away. I think if Lauren Mills was home alone that's exactly what would've happened. "I wouldn't have come if it wasn't a serious matter."

A frown mars his tanned forehead, and he looks deep in thought as we walk. "How are things going with Easton?" he asks after a few silent beats.

"Great. He's a fantastic kid, and I'm mad about him."

"That's good, Dillon." He squeezes my shoulder. "I'm glad to hear it." I can tell he means that. He comes to a halt at the end of the hallway, opening double doors which lead to a large sunroom, where Lauren awaits.

She stands as I enter the room, offering me a tight smile. "Hello, Dillon."

"Mrs. Mills." I nod respectfully.

She rolls her eyes. "Please. You know better than to call me that. Sit down, and let's hear what this is about."

She doesn't beat around the bush, and I like that about her.

I sit across from her and her husband. "I'm here about Vivien. I'm a little worried."

"In what way?" Lauren asks.

I clear my throat. "She is talking about pulling Easton from school and hiring a tutor for him."

Lauren knots her hands in her lap. "I was afraid of that. She called me yesterday, and she had worked herself into a tizzy over the incident at school."

"I'm going to deal with that," I say. "It will be a non-issue in a few days." I have already spoken with the school and reached out to the parents of the other little boy. I'm just waiting for them to return my call, but I'm confident I can make it go away.

"There will likely be more incidents," Jonathon says.

"I know, but I believe Easton can handle them once we provide the right support. I don't think taking him out of school sends the right message, but it's more than just this. Are you aware Vivien hasn't taken him anywhere besides camp all summer long?"

Lauren frowns. "What do you mean?"

"I mean, he goes nowhere. She drives him to and from school because she doesn't trust anyone else to drive him. Nash comes over for playdates, and occasionally some other kids, but that's it." I feel so disloyal telling Viv's parents this behind her back, but they need to know how bad the situation has gotten. "She is terrified of something happening to him. She can hardly bear to let him out of her sight."

"Oh, princess." Jonathon shares a concerned look with Lauren.

"Why didn't Audrey tell us this?"

"I'm not sure how much Audrey is aware of. She's been gone for weeks."

"Does Vivien know you're here?" Lauren asks.

"No, and she's going to kick my ass for it, but I just tried talking to her, and she won't listen to me. I thought she might be more inclined to talk to you about it." I wet my dry lips. "I love her and Easton so much, but she's still keeping me at arm's length, which I understand. I've given her space, but this is something I believe she'll end up regretting. I'm going to work on getting both of them out of the house more, if you could talk to her about the tutor thing."

"We'll talk to her." Lauren bobs her head. "I understand why she wants to do this, but you are right; it's not a good idea for Easton. He's an extrovert, and he loves being around others."

"Thank you for bringing this to our attention," Jonathon says.

"I hate going behind her back, but I didn't feel like there was any other option. She's moving full steam ahead already, so there was no time to waste."

"We will try to make her understand that you had her best interests at heart," Lauren says, fighting a smile. "But you know our daughter."

"I do." I stand. "Thanks for listening. I can see myself out."

"Don't go just yet, Dillon." Lauren lifts her brows, pointing at the seat I've just vacated. "I have something I'd like to say."

"*We* have," Jonathon corrects her, as I sit back down.

She pats his hand, and they share an intimate look that only comes from years of loving and understanding one another. Her expression is more somber when she turns it on me again. "I'm not happy about certain things you have done, and it will take a lot more convincing for me to fully trust you, but I've had a lot of time to think in recent months. We both have, and the only way to truly let the past go is to wipe the slate clean. We believe you are sincere when you say you love our daughter and grandson, and everything Vivien has told us about how you have behaved these past couple of months confirms that."

"We also know you were responsible for her happiness in Ireland," Jonathon adds. "She was glowing when we visited her, and we know she was deeply in love with you. Vivien is a good judge of character, and you are Easton's father, so we are giving you the benefit of the doubt."

"We loved Reeve. He was our son, and we miss him a lot," Lauren says, her eyes growing glassy. Jonathon slides his arm around her shoulders. "For him to include you in his will tells us a lot about his intentions. Reeve wasn't perfect. None of us are, but he loved Vivien, and he loved Easton with his whole heart. I know, without a shadow of doubt, that he would want them to be happy. If their happiness lies with you, we want you to know we won't stand in your way."

"Provided you always put them first," Jonathan supplies, drilling me with a look that his wife usually reserves for me.

"That's a given." I run my hands through my hair. "Even if Vivien and I never reunite as a couple, I will always be there for both of them. I give you my solemn promise. There is nothing or no one who could tear me away from them now."

CHAPTER 33

VIVIEN

"SO, is Dillon still in the doghouse?" Audrey asks, smothering a grin as she peers at me through the screen of my laptop.

"You'd better believe it." It's been two weeks since Dillon went behind my back and spoke to my parents, and I'm still livid. "I can't believe he went to Mom and Dad or that they actually sided with him."

"Is that what you really think?" Audrey arches a brow while leaning back in her chair.

I sigh. "No." I drum my fingers on the top of my desk. "I know they were right, and I know Dillon acted out of concern for E." It's why I canceled all the tutor interviews and Easton is still in kindergarten. I can't let my insecurities mess up my son's life.

"And concern for you," she reminds me.

"I'm working through my fears with Meryl, but it's hard. East is all I have left and I'm terrified of anything happening to him."

"Easton isn't all you have left, babe." Audrey looks up, lifting one finger. Her head lowers again, and she moves in closer to the screen. "You have Alex and me. You have your parents. You have Ash and Jamie and Ro." She pauses for dramatic effect. "And you have Dillon."

"He's irritating the fuck out of me. He's always on my ass about something, and he's being…all flirty and shit. When I say stuff to annoy him, it only seems to amuse him." She grins, and I narrow my eyes at her. "Don't tell me you've moved to the dark side."

She barks out a laugh. "He's being typical Dillon. I wondered how long he could keep the nice guy routine up."

"Hey, he's still one of the good guys," I blurt, instantly feeling the need to defend him, even if I'm still seething at his interference.

Her grin expands, and I flip her the bird. "I know he's a good guy, Viv. He has far exceeded my expectations. From what you've said, he's great with Easton and pretty skilled with his tongue."

I roll my eyes. "I should never have told you or Ash about that."

"Aren't you tempted to go back for round two?" She waggles her brows.

"No," I lie. Truth is, I can't stop thinking about it or the way it felt to have Dillon's hands and mouth on me again. Now that he's on a mission to piss me the hell off, he's seriously getting under my skin and raising old memories to the surface.

"Liar." Rey calls me out on my bullshit.

I sigh again. "I can't stop thinking about him, but then I feel guilty. It's only been four months since Reeve died. How can I be thinking about another man already?"

"Babe, we've been over this. You've really got to stop doing this to yourself," she says as there's a knock on my office door. "And it's not like Dillon is just any other man. There is history there and a shit ton of love."

"It's the way I'm programmed," I tell my bestie, getting up to answer the door.

It's Charlotte. "Dillon is here to see you. He's waiting in the sunroom."

I glance at my watch, frowning. School hasn't let out yet, so I have no idea why he is here already. "Okay. I'll be there in a sec." I return to my desk. "Speak of the devil. Dillon is here early. He's probably come to torture me some more."

"I've got to go anyway. Tell Dillon I said hi, and call me this weekend, yeah?"

"I will. Love you."

"Right back at ya."

We disconnect, and I go out to see what he wants.

"Is something wrong?" I ask the second I step foot in my sunroom.

Dillon is standing, with his back to me, looking out at the garden. You can see the memorial we built from here. "Nothing is wrong," he says, turning around to face me.

Fuck me. How does he make a plain white T-shirt and normal jeans look so freaking hot? His hungry gaze roams the length of my body, making me feel self-conscious. I cross my arms over my chest in an instinctive protective gesture.

"Don't do that," he says.

"Well, don't look at me like that."

"Like what?" His lips curve up at the corners.

I drill him with a warning look. "You know what." I'm not playing this game with him.

He takes a step toward me, and I fight myself not to take a step back. He strides toward me like a hunter stalking his prey, and my heart slams against my rib cage in nervous anticipation. Dillon stops directly in front of me, leaving only a tiny gap between our bodies. Heat rolls off him in waves, crashing into me and almost taking my knees from under me. "Like I want to strip that pretty dress off your gorgeous body and worship every inch of your skin with my lips and my tongue?"

My cheeks sizzle as I stumble away from him. "Stop it. You can't say that to me."

Slowly, he drags one hand through his hair, grinning as he

maintains eye contact with me. "We both know you'd love me to do it, but we can keep pretending. You know how determined I am when I want something, and I want you. I can keep this shit up for months." He leans in close again, still grinning. "Years, if it comes down to it."

I'm calling bullshit on that. Dillon is not known for his patience even if he has surprised me a lot these past few months. Saliva pools in my mouth as liquid lust rushes to my core.

I like sex, and I miss it.

I know I could ask Dillon to fuck me, and he'd happily do it, but I just can't do that to Reeve. Which I know is ridiculous, because Reeve is gone and I'm going to have sex with someone else at some time, but I just can't go there yet.

"Why are you here, or did you just make a house call to annoy the shit out of me?"

He chuckles, rubbing a piece of my hair between his fingers. "I came to tell you I'm taking East for ice cream after school."

"Like hell you are," I hiss, swatting his hand away.

He narrows his eyes at me. "We talked about this, Vivien Grace. I've been telling you for two weeks, and I'm not listening to any more of your bullshit excuses." He lowers his face to mine. "Just so I'm clear, I'm not asking permission. I called here as a courtesy because I know you will freak the fuck out. I am taking our son out for ice cream. I will bring Leon with me. I will message you when we get to the ice cream parlor and message you when we are on the way home."

Acid crawls up my throat, and bile swims in my stomach.

"Or you could come too?" he asks, a hopeful tone to his voice.

I immediately shake my head. Being seen out with Dillon in public is a recipe for disaster.

"I thought as much," he says as he walks toward the corner of the room, bending down to retrieve a bag I hadn't noticed before. "You are not going to sit around this house, pacing and panicking while East and I do something perfectly fucking normal." Walking back over, he hands the bag to me. "I want you to work your magic. Create something amazing. Make a new dress so you have something to wear when I finally convince you to come out to dinner with me."

I open the bag, gasping at the pretty silk material. It's a gorgeous rich blue with purple and white floral prints all over it. "Where did you get this?"

"In a sewing shop," he deadpans. "Where else do you think I got it? I hardly magicked it out of my arse."

"There is no need to be rude or crude."

He smirks, opening his mouth to say something dirty, no doubt, but I clamp a hand over his lips to silence him. "Do not say whatever it is you're about to say. Thank you for the material, but Easton isn't going."

He nips at the skin on my palm, and I yank my hand back. Before I know what's happening, he's backing me up against the wall. "Sweetheart, I already told you this isn't a negotiation."

"But—"

Now it's his turn to silence me with his hand. I glare at him, and he chuckles. "Be grateful it's not my mouth." He winks, and I squeeze my thighs together. "Listen up, Hollywood. I love Easton. He's my son, and I know he's the most precious thing in the world to you because he's all that for me too. I will guard him with my life. Nothing is going to happen to him. I promise." He removes his hand, darting in to press a kiss to the corner of my mouth. "Trust me. Please."

I stare into his stunning blue eyes and nod. "Bring my baby home to me safely."

"Always." Without warning, he bundles me into his arms. "I know you're scared, but it's going to be fine. This needs to happen. You know it."

After Dillon leaves, I head into my sewing room for the first time since Reeve and Lainey passed.

I try.

I really do.

I work on some dress designs, but I can't concentrate. I can't stop thinking about Easton and Dillon out there in the big bad world. Surrounded by paparazzi and assholes who think it's okay to stick their noses into our business. Briefly, I contemplate hitting the vodka, but it's only four o'clock in the day, and it's a habit I don't want to start. Instead, I pace the floor and panic, exactly what Dillon suspected I would do.

I'm standing outside by the front door when they pull up an hour later, and I almost trip over my feet in my hurry to get to Easton. Opening his car door, I lean in and hug him, almost suffocating the poor child. "Mommy. You're squeezing me to death!" he says, and Dillon chuckles.

"Hollywood, let the little guy get out of his seat." Dillon tugs me back, wrapping an arm around my waist as Easton unbuckles his seat belt and jumps out of the car.

"I had the best time, Mommy, and Uncle Dillon got you some chocolate ice cream. He knew it was your favorite." Easton holds a small paper bag out to me as Dillon presses his warm mouth to my ear. "Remember that time we ate ice cream off one another? I even licked it out of your—"

"Dillon!" I shriek, twisting out of his hold. "Not in front of little ears." I don't care that he was whispering in my ear. Easton has razor-sharp hearing and an uncanny ability to hear things I don't want him to hear.

"Were you being naughty again, Uncle Dillon?" East asks, grinning up at his dad.

"I was just reminding Mommy of a game we used to play and asking her if she wanted to play it with me again." He flashes me a devilish grin I long to wipe off his face.

"I love games!" Easton jumps up and down. "Let's play the game!"

I glare at Dillon, and he discreetly swats my ass. "It's an adult game, buddy," he says, crouching down to E. "How about we play cops and robbers?"

That basically means they get to chase each other all over the house, screaming and shouting like lunatics. Dillon is the biggest kid, but I can't ever be mad about it. Easton loves his special brand of crazy.

"I wanna be the robber this time!" Easton screams.

"Well, what are you waiting for?" Dillon lifts a brow. "I'll give you ten seconds before I come looking for you." Easton races into the house, almost knocking Leon over in his haste to get away from Dillon. "Apologies, sweetheart." Dillon kisses my cheek, grinning. "We'll have to take a rain check on the naked ice cream party."

CHAPTER 34

VIVIEN

"WHY DOES my daddy look like a scaredy-cat in this picture?" E asks, pointing to a photo of Reeve I took when we were thirteen.

The three of us are seated on one of the couches in the living room, looking through another one of my childhood albums. Dillon said he wanted to know the real Reeve, and we usually spend an hour after dinner on the nights Dillon is here looking into my past. I thought it would hurt, but it's actually helping.

"Did you know your daddy was scared of spiders?" Reeve had a serious case of arachnophobia, something he managed to conceal from his son and his fanbase.

Easton's eyes pop wide. "What? How could he be scared of spiders? Spiders are awesome." I'm not scared of them like Reeve was, but there's no way I'm as enthusiastic as Easton.

Dillon chuckles. "He wouldn't have lasted pissing time on the farm. Our house was full of spiders."

"Hand it over," East says, thrusting out his palm, without even looking up.

"You must be loaded by now," Dillon retorts, handing over a dollar bill.

"I am. Mom said she's going to take me to the bank to 'posit it."

"I'm impressed, and I approve." He looks proudly at me like I've agreed to climb Mount Everest, not just go to the bank.

"It's only the bank," I murmur, feeling a mixture of embarrassment and shame.

"It's a step back into the real world. This is good, Hollywood."

My finger twitches with the desire to flip him off.

"Why do you call my mommy Hollywood?" East looks at Dillon with a perplexed expression.

"I first met your mom when she came to Dublin to study. We were *real* good friends," he says, shooting me a flirty look, and I swear I'm going to kill him if he doesn't quit it with the innuendos. "And I liked to tease her by calling her Hollywood because Hollywood is in L.A. where she was from."

"Oh." He looks satisfied with that explanation. Turning to me, he tugs on my arm. "Tell me the story, Mommy. Why was Daddy scared?"

"We were thirteen, and your grandpa and grandma had taken us up to a cabin at Big Sur. They had gone out to get food while Reeve and I were unpacking. I heard your daddy shout, and I rushed into his room. There was this massive spider on top of the pillow on his bed, and he was freaking out. The look on his face was priceless, and I couldn't resist taking a pic."

"What happened to the spider?" E asks.

"I got a cup, scooped him up, and put him outside." I don't tell him Reeve stood there like a statue, pale, sweating, and shaking, because Easton thinks his daddy is a superhero, and I never want to change that.

"Do you like spiders, Mommy?" East asks, moving the page to the next set of photos.

"I'm not sure *like* is the right word, but I'm not scared of them."

"I love spiders," Easton says. "When I'm older, I'm gonna let all the spiders live in my house." A shiver rolls over my spine, and I could almost swear Reeve is listening to this conversation and freaking out.

"That sounds fun," Dillon says, winking at me. "But I think it's time for someone's bath."

"Okay." Easton is always way more agreeable when Dillon is around. I think my little chat after his hurtful comments at Dillon's house has helped to settle him too. "Love you, Daddy." Easton kisses Reeve's picture before carefully closing the album.

A dart of pain glimmers in Dillon's eyes, and I know this is hard for him.

"Honey, why don't you go and get your pajamas and a towel ready. Uncle Dillon will be with you in a minute."

"Sure thing, Mom." Easton races out of the room, because that's the speed at which he lives his life, leaving me alone with Dillon.

Without second-guessing it, I reach out, linking my fingers in his. "He loves you too. He is always talking about you, and he misses you on the days he doesn't see you."

"I know Reeve will always be his daddy, but I want to be his daddy too."

"You are, Dillon. In all the ways that count, you are. And some day, we will explain it to him, and he'll realize how lucky he is to have two daddies."

Dillon folds his arms around me, holding me close. "I love him so much." When he eases back to look at me, I'm not surprised to see moisture in his eyes. "You too."

Reaching out, I brush strands of hair off his brow. "I know you do, and we're grateful to have you in our lives."

"Does that mean I'm forgiven?"

There's a double meaning there, and we both know it. I pause to consider my feelings, but it doesn't take long to confirm it. "It does."

"I want to kiss you so fucking badly right now." His eyes drop to my lips, and my heart starts running a marathon.

Blood rushes to my head, and I'm tingly all over as I place my hand on his chest and tip my chin up. We move closer, maintaining eye contact, and my heart is pounding like crazy as our mouths line up.

"I'm ready!" Easton shrieks, and we instantly jerk back from one another.

"Awesome timing, buddy," Dillon says, standing, and I lick my lips as I watch him discreetly adjust himself in his jeans.

"He's fast asleep," Dillon says, appearing in my kitchen forty minutes later.

"You're a miracle worker. Some nights he takes forever to fall asleep for me."

"I sing to him." He places his hands on the island unit. "My voice literally puts him to sleep."

I giggle, and it feels like forever since I've laughed. "Thank goodness it doesn't have the same effect on your fans!"

"Fuck, I've missed that sound. You need to laugh more, Viv. I'm making that my new mission."

I roll my eyes as I head to the refrigerator. "Do you want a beer?"

"I wish I could stay, but I can't. We're putting the finishing touches to the album tonight. Ro is desperate to get home to Ireland to see Emer."

Disappointment washes over me, but I disguise it behind a smile. "No problem." I remove the chilled bottle of white wine from the refrigerator, and Dillon strides to the cupboard, removing a glass for me. His fingers graze mine as he hands it over, shooting fiery tremors up my arm.

"I have something for you," he admits as I pour myself some wine. "I've had these for a while, but I wasn't sure if you wanted them back or when the right time was to hand them over." He pushes a plain, unmarked brown envelope toward me.

Opening it, I pull out a mountain of photos, and a rush of emotions slams into me. I grip the edge of the counter to steady myself.

"Shit." He's by my side in a second, wrapping his arms around me from behind. "I can take them back."

"No." I gather myself, staring down at the picture of Dillon and me. It's from one of our weekends away in Ireland. We were in Sligo in this old-fashioned restaurant that served the best fish. The picture is a little blurry, and you can tell it was taken through the window because of the angle, but it's clear enough to remind me of the memory.

Our arms are wrapped around one another, and we're both sporting the cheesiest grins as we stare at the stocky man with a protruding belly and shock of thick black hair holding Dillon's phone. We look so young and so in love. It practically radiates from the photo. "I remember the restaurant owner. He had this really loud booming voice and a bellowing laugh."

"I remember him too," Dillon supplies. "He insisted on taking that photo because he said we personified young love."

"We did," I quietly admit because there's no point denying the truth when it's staring us in the face. "How did you end up with these?"

"The cop investigating the accident gave them to me at the hospital. He found them in the car."

Pain glides up my throat, and I cling to Dillon's arms. "Reeve had only given them to me that night. That's how he confirmed who you were to me."

"I can't believe someone was following us the whole time you were in Ireland. I even spotted the fucker." Dillon's arms tighten around me. "I know he's not here to defend himself, but that was a total asshole move on Reeve's part."

"It was," I agree without hesitation. "And I told him that. I was disgusted someone was capturing our intimate moments on film. It makes me sick to think of someone watching us like that, but Reeve didn't know they had taken it that far. He told them not to send him the photos. He just wanted to know I was protected." Dillon is uncharacteristically quiet behind me, and I arch my head back, staring into his face. "You don't believe that?"

"Actually, I do." His eyes lock on mine. "Reeve was obsessive in the way he loved you. It stands to reason he'd have someone watching over you to ensure you were safe. Doesn't mean I approve or I'm pleased about it." Reaching down, he flicks through the photos, pulling up one that has me blushing furiously. "At least we got some incredible photos out of it."

I feel him hardening against my back as we stare at the photo of us in the sea at Brittas Bay. My legs are wrapped around Dillon's neck, and he's holding me up by my butt. My head is thrown back in the throes of passion as Dillon feasts on me. Intense heat creeps up my neck and onto my cheeks.

"I'm thinking of getting that one blown up and hanging it on the ceiling over my bed."

"No, you're not!" I twirl around in his arms, staring at him incredulously.

"Watch me." He flashes me his trademark smirk before kissing the tip of my nose and releasing me from his embrace.

I'm still staring in shock after him as he saunters out of my kitchen, whistling under his breath like he hasn't a care in the world.

He wasn't serious.

Right?

CHAPTER 35
DILLON

"YOU WANT A BEER?" Ro asks when we are settled in our booth in the VIP section of the bar. A waitress hovers at the edge of our table, trying to pretend she's not ogling me like I'm her meal ticket out of here. Ignoring her, I nod at my brother, and he places our order. Ro is returning to Ireland tomorrow, and I'm not going to see him now until Christmas.

"Thank fuck, we got the album wrapped in time." Jamie stretches his arms along the other side of the booth. "I am so ready for some sexy times with my woman under the hot Mexican sun."

"Do you want to kick him in the nuts or shall I?" Ro asks, leaning his elbows on the table.

"The honor is all yours. Go for it, little bro."

"You two need to get laid. Stat."

"I'm working on it," I say as the waitress returns with an ice bucket filled with cold beers. Her fingers brush mine as she hands me a bottle, batting her eyelashes and pretending to be demure. "You're wasting your time," I tell her. "I'm not interested." The only woman I have eyes for these days is a certain Hollywood princess who is determined to keep my current blue-balls status intact.

"I am." Ro leans back, leaving the ball in her court.

"Awesome. I'm on my break in thirty minutes."

"Looking forward to it, darling." Ro winks, but the instant she's gone, the smug smirk drops off his face.

"Getting back in the saddle?" Jamie asks, bringing his beer to his lips.

"More like forcing myself back in the saddle."

"Why force it if you're not feeling it?" I ask, instinctively knowing there's more to it.

Ro's Adam's apple bobs in his throat. "Clodagh is back with her ex." He drains half his beer in one go.

"Fuck. Are you sure?" I swallow a mouthful of beer, and the cold liquid is soothing going down my throat.

"She told me herself." He rests his face in his hands, looking glummer than the Grinch on Christmas morning. "I'm such an idiot. You all told me we were moving too fast. Now I've sent her running straight back into that dickhead's arms."

"You haven't done anything wrong, Ro."

"Except fall for the wrong girl," Jamie unhelpfully adds.

"If you hadn't met her, you wouldn't have Emer," I remind him because he adores his little girl.

"I know. It just hurts that she'd leave and go back to Colin so fast." A muscle clenches in his jaw. "I don't want that prick anywhere near my daughter."

My phone vibrates on the table, and I swipe it up, answering when I see it's my sister. "You all done?" I ask, wondering if she wrapped her meetings up quicker than planned so she could get here earlier.

"Not yet. I've still got two more meetings."

We have decided to hire a new publicist because we need someone who is completely on the ball to manage our publicity going forward. Dixie is competent enough, but things will get real when the news finally comes out about Easton, and I want the best person on our side. Which is why Ash spoke with Viv's mum and then lined up preliminary meetings with a few top publicists she put her in contact with. She'll pick someone suitable, and then we'll meet with him or her to ensure we can work with the person before we make an official hire.

"So, what's up?"

"I got a call from Charlotte."

I instantly straighten in my chair. "What's wrong?"

"She said someone needs to come over to be with Viv. She's worried about her state of mind."

"Did something happen?" I was over there yesterday, and everything was normal. As in, she's trying to pretend the sexual tension between us isn't close to combusting and still clinging to Easton like superglue.

"All she said was Vivien was upset and someone should be there for her. Easton is on a sleepover with Lauren and Jon, and my guess is she's lonely and getting lost in her head."

"Okay. I'll go to her."

"Ring or text me when you get there. I'm concerned."

"I'll take care of her."

We hang up, and I sheepishly face my brother.

"It's fine," Ro says before I can say a word. "If Vivien needs you, you should go to her. At least you still have a chance at salvaging your relationship. Mine is dead in the water, and I would give anything to have another chance."

"I'm not sure if I'll be able to come back. It sounds like she's not in a good place."

Ro stands to let me out of the booth. He pulls me into a hug. "Go take care of your woman, and I'll see you at Christmas."

"Give Emer a big hug and kiss from me," I tell him, slapping him on the back. "I know what it's like to lose the woman you love, so if you think Clodagh is the one and there's any chance of getting her back, fight for her. Don't do what I did." I'm not sure if I should be encouraging him because I happen to believe Clodagh *isn't* the right woman for my brother. He needs someone steadfast, not someone flighty. But I'm not going to be the one to tell him what he should or shouldn't feel.

Some indecipherable emotion flits briefly across his face. "I'm rooting for you guys," he chokes out. "I really hope it works out for you."

"Thanks, bro." I grab him into another hug. "Take care of yourself."

I salute Jamie. "Later, fucker."

"Dillon. Thanks for coming," Charlotte says, ushering me into the house.

"It's not a problem. Before I go home, let me give you my number so you can call me directly if you ever need to." I know Angela has my digits, but Charlotte really should have them too.

"That sounds like a good idea."

"Where is she?"

Sympathy splays across her face. "She's been in the nursery for hours."

Shit. She never goes in there, usually keeping the door locked. "Okay. I know my way."

I head upstairs with a heavy heart, wondering what I'm going to find. I slow my pace as I approach the door, not wanting to startle her. The door is ajar, and Viv is in the middle of the empty room, flat on her back, staring up at the ceiling as she sings. Two empty wine bottles litter the floor, along with a bunch of used tissues, and she's clutching a pink blanket to her chest.

She's singing "She Moved Through the Fair," and I'm instantly transported back in time. The haunting quality of her voice matches the sadness dripping from the lyrics as the words leave her lips. Listening to her sing this song is painful on several levels, but her grief adds an extra harrowing dimension. I prop my hip against the door frame, listening to the love of my life sing from her soul, wishing I could absorb her pain and erase the silent tears spilling down her cheeks.

Her chest heaves when she finishes, and she hiccups in between sobs. I rap softly on the door so as not to startle her. Sad bloodshot hazel eyes lock on my face as I step into the room. I don't speak as I walk over to her, dropping onto the floor and sitting cross-legged by her side. "Hey, beautiful." I brush the moisture off her cheeks as she stares at me with eyes drowning in deep emotion.

"Swans only have one partner for their entire life. Did you know that?" I shake my head, wondering if mention of the swan in the evening in the song has prompted her to share this. "They mate with the same partner until the bond is broken by death or they are preyed upon. They are the purest symbol of true love." She sits up, still clutching the pink blanket to her chest. "I think we're swans, Dillon." She hiccups, and the hint of a smile graces her lips. "Reeve, me, and you." Her lower lip wobbles, and tears pool in her eyes again. "And Lainey is an angel. They're both angels now."

"Was this hers?" I ask, gesturing toward the blanket.

She nods. "I kept it and the little hat she was wearing at the hospital. She was like a doll, Dillon. When I held her, she was like a beautiful sleeping doll. So tiny but so perfect." Her tortured cries bounce off the walls and stab me straight through the heart. "I don't want to give her things away. I know it's selfish. I know there are other babies out there who need her things, but I can't do it, Dillon. I can't."

I move a little closer, terrified to do anything that will spook her. "You don't have to do anything you don't want to."

"Audrey cleared out the room because I couldn't do it. Everything is in storage, and I'm gonna keep it. Lainey's little sister will wear her things and sleep in her crib. I think Lainey would like that, don't you?"

"I think that's a lovely idea."

"I have to have hope. Keeping her things gives me hope."

She glances around the room, and her eyes dart to the far wall. "We helped paint that. Me, Reeve, and Easton."

I spin around on my butt, marveling at the amazing mural on the wall.

"It's Tinkerbell," she explains. "This was going to be a room for my fairy princess, but God decided he needed an angel instead."

I want to say fuck God, but that won't offer her any comfort, so I clamp my mouth shut.

"I'm going to turn it into a reading room, because I can't bear to paint over that mural. Not when it's one of the last things Easton and Reeve did together."

"You should totally keep it, and I think this room would make a great reading room. It has a nice window, perfect for a window seat, and you could fill that back wall with floor-to-ceiling bookshelves. Jamie and I could build them if you want? Easton could help."

She bursts out crying, and I pull her into my arms, hoping it's the right move. She collapses against me, and I dot kisses in her hair as she cries against my chest, clutching my shirt. "I love you," she says, and hope swells inside me. "I shouldn't, but I do." She lifts her head, piercing me with tear-soaked eyes. "I have loved you all this time, Dillon. I never stopped. I was a terrible wife."

"That isn't even remotely possible. You were an amazing wife."

"But was I?" she whispers before hiccupping again. "I mean, I really loved Reeve. Truly, madly, deeply. He made me happy, but I loved you too. And I never compared you because you both held an equal share of my heart. It didn't stop me from feeling guilty though. It's hard loving two men at the same time. Some nights, when I couldn't sleep, I would sneak to the sunroom and listen to your songs. I have all your albums on my cell, in a hidden folder, so Reeve wouldn't find them. I love your music." A scowl mars her pretty face. "When you're not singing about hating me."

I open my mouth to remind her of our previous conversation on the topic, but she continues, and I shove the comment back down my throat, letting her get whatever she needs to off her chest. Her thoughts are veering all over the place, and I'm guessing her emotions are too.

"You're super talented. And I love listening to your voice. It lulled me to sleep on difficult nights. When I really wanted to torture myself, I would watch the wedding video clip of you singing 'Terrify Me.' That always made me cry." She bursts into floods of tears again, and I wonder if I should try to get her to her bedroom or let her continue purging her thoughts.

The egotistical part of my personality keeps my butt planted right where it is. I want to know what else she's going to say. They say the truth comes out when you're drunk, and I've been starved of Viv's truths for years, so sue me if I'm being selfish.

She cries into my shirt, plastering it to my skin, and I rock her gently in my arms, holding her close. "I spent years thinking you hated me and that I was the biggest fool for still loving you even though I loved Reeve too. But I couldn't stop it, Dil. I couldn't make it stop."

"I can relate to that. Not a single day went by where you weren't on my mind."

"We were good together. I didn't imagine that, right?"

"We're epic, sweetheart, and everything was real. Everything *is* real."

"I think I was always destined to love you, Dillon. Have you thought about how things might've been if that dickhead Simon hadn't given you away?"

"I've wondered what my life would've been like if he'd given Reeve away instead of me," I truthfully reply.

"Would we have loved each other from the time we were kids?"

"Of course, we would have. There is no measure of time or distance where I wouldn't be in love with you, Vivien. I was in love with you before I even met you. I know things got fucked up, but I truly believe I was waiting for you to walk into my life and make sense of the chaos in my head. It was always you. It will always be you. There will never be any other love for me. We *are* like swans." An idea pops into my head. "We should totally build a lake and get swans."

She bursts out laughing, and my chest swells with pride that I can make her laugh when she's so upset.

"You're crazy."

"Crazy about you."

"I like romantic Dillon," she murmurs, and I press a fierce kiss to her brow.

"You bring out the best in me, Viv. You always have. My family saw it way before I did."

"I love your family." A whimsical look materializes on her face. "They are awesome."

"They are pretty great." Even after everything I put them through and how much I disappointed them, they don't bear any grudges.

I've made more of an effort to speak to my parents and Shane and Ciarán, on a regular basis, letting them know how grateful I am for their forgiveness. Ma can't wait to meet Easton. I was going to fly them over for a visit, but I don't want to confuse my son by bringing more people into his life or invite questions I can't answer yet.

"You were the lucky one, Dil." She slurs her words a little and her vision looks unfocused. "Trust me, you were. You have an amazing family. I love them. Did I ever tell you that? I love your family like they're my own."

"That's because they are." Or they officially will be, if I have my way.

"I love them, and they love you sooooo much. Reeve constantly fought for Simon's affection, but he had none to give."

"He was a cold fucker." I grit my teeth, unwilling to go down that road right now. I have let go of the resentment I had toward my twin, but I will never forgive Simon Lancaster or forget what he did.

"If you'd come home with Reeve, we would all have been friends." She peers deep into my eyes. "Don't you see? I was always destined to love both of you."

I think I was always destined to battle my twin for Vivien's heart.

"My heart was always going to be torn in two," she continues, confirming she's given this much thought. "It's why fate led me to you in Dublin because how else do you explain it? Out of all the cities I could have escaped to, I chose the one you lived in. And out of all the people who live there, I befriended Ash and we met. I mean, it's crazy, right?" A little spark flickers in her eyes.

"It is, and I think you're right. I don't believe in coincidence, so it's got to be fate." I have thought about what might've happened if Reeve hadn't died. Would she still be with him, or would she have left him for me? We'll never know, and I don't mention it because what's the point? He's not here, and I am. Trying to second-guess what would happen if he was still alive will only hurt both of us. Instead, I choose to believe in fate. Fate brought us together, tore us apart, and then reunited us. I choose to believe that would have happened even if Reeve was still walking the planet.

"Yes, yes." She nods before resting her head on my chest and grasping my shirt. "Can I ask you something?"

I nod as she peers up at me.

"You said 'once a cheater always a cheater' about Reeve. Do you know something I don't?"

Shit. I really was a fucking prick when I first showed up. I shake my head. "I threw it out there to annoy you. I have no proof he cheated on you, and from what I know of him now, I think it's fair to say he didn't. I'm sorry if I made you doubt him."

"You didn't. Not really. I knew he would never cheat on me again. He was always so quiet and melancholy on

Christmas Day. I know he was remembering our breakup and how much it killed him to be separated from me. He loved our family and the life we shared. He wouldn't do anything to jeopardize that. I was sure of it, but I just needed to ask you about it."

"I was such an asshole to you. I'm sorry."

She waves her hand in the air. "It's water under the bridge now, Dillon, and I don't want to think about all that again."

Silence engulfs us for a few minutes, but it's the kind of comfortable silence I live for with Viv. There is such peace in sitting here holding her in my arms.

"I'm tired of feeling guilty, Dil," she admits, snuggling closer. "I'm tired of missing Reeve and Lainey, but most of all, I'm tired of not living. I want to be happy again. I just want to be happy." Her voice trails off, and she sounds dejected and sad.

"I want you to be happy too, sweetheart. Let me make you happy. Let me love you."

CHAPTER 36
VIVIEN

MY TONGUE IS STUCK to the roof of my mouth when I wake up in one of our spare bedrooms with Dillon draped around me from behind. Flashbacks of last night float across my mind, and I softly groan. I know I said a lot of stuff to him. As I examine my recollection and remember the things I said, I can't find it within me to regret any of it.

I forced myself to go into the nursery last night because it is time to remodel it. However, I wasn't prepared enough for the onslaught of emotions that hit me the instant I set foot in the room, and I came apart at the seams.

I think I needed to expel those emotions I was denying in order to turn a corner. Today, it feels like I have. As if a layer of pain has lifted from my body. I'm not saying I won't continue to grieve, because I know it's not as simple as that, but it's going to be different from now on.

Turning slowly around, I stare at the man sleeping beside me. When I fell asleep on him, he must have carried me in here. I'm glad he didn't take me to my bedroom because I couldn't sleep in my marital bed with Dillon without surrendering to enormous guilt. And I'm done feeling guilty for loving this man. Dillon is such an enigma, but he's really come through for me these past few months, and I can't deny my feelings for him any longer.

I love him.

I have loved him for years.

I don't know where we go from here, because I'm not ready to go full speed into a relationship, but he deserves honesty from me. I've kept him dangling from his fingertips, and it's not fair.

Reluctantly, I extract myself from his loving embrace, my heart melting when I find the pain meds and a bottle of water by the bed. He takes such good care of me. Just like Reeve did. I chug them down and get up, dragging my hungover ass into the shower.

After I'm dressed and feeling slightly more alive, I pad back to the bedroom to discover Dillon sitting up in bed. He's on his phone and he hasn't noticed me yet, so I take a moment to admire the fine sight of his semi-naked physique.

Broad tan shoulders give way to a toned chest and ripped abs. Ink covers both arms and one shoulder, and he truly is a work of art. With his messy white-blond hair and the stylish layer of stubble on his chin and cheeks, he could grace the cover of any magazine, and it would sell out in seconds.

"Done drooling yet?" he asks, not lifting his head from his phone, and I hear the smile in his tone.

"What has you so engrossed you can't even look at me?"

His head jerks up, and he pins me with that panty-melting smile of his. I have a hard time keeping upright. "I'm researching how to buy swans."

My mouth hangs open. "I thought you were joking!"

"Nah. I'm deadly serious. I'm getting us a lake and swans."

He's just stubborn enough to do it too. Dillon flashes me his famous grin again, the one that has his female fans fanning themselves, and his dimples come out to play.

That's it.

I'm a goner.

The dimples get me every time.

As if on autopilot, I walk across the room to the bed, climbing up beside him. "Hi." I smile shyly at him as a sudden bout of nerves attacks me.

"You're too cute for words." His fingers sweep across my cheeks. "I have missed this blush."

"Don't tease me right now. I have things I need to say."

His smile explodes across his face, and I lose all semblance of coherence. I stare at him in a daze. "You are too beautiful for words," I admit.

"If that's true, my beauty pales in comparison to yours. The instant you step into a room, I'm enchanted, Viv. You do the most amazing things to my heart." He fights a smirk. "My cock too." He winks, and I roll my eyes.

"You just can't help yourself, can you?"

"Not around you." He opens his arms. "Come here. I need to hold you."

I don't argue, snuggling against him and sighing contentedly. We fit perfectly, like we were crafted to seamlessly mold together as one.

"How much of last night do you remember?" he asks, tracing his fingers up and down my arm.

"All of it, I think."

"You said you loved me."

I tilt my head up, so I'm staring into his eyes. "I meant it. I love you, Dillon." I cup his cheek. "And I want to let you love me, but you'll have to continue to be patient."

"I can do that, but you have to set boundaries because my need for you is at an all-time high."

"Last night was a catharsis of sorts for me. My own 'come to Jesus' moment. I don't feel sad today. I feel more at peace than any other time since they died, and I want to move forward." My eyes penetrate his. "I want to move forward with you."

"Thank fuck." He bundles me in his arms, hugging me

tight. Warmth from his skin rolls over me, heating all the frozen parts.

"I can't promise I won't have bad days. Days where I miss Reeve are a given because I can't just forget about him or not remember how much we meant to each other."

"I get that, and it's fine. All I ask is that you don't shut me out. Tell me you're missing him. I would rather hear it from your lips than guess why you're upset or noncommunicative or distant."

"I'll be honest; even if I don't want to hurt you, I promise I'll always tell you the truth."

He lifts my hand to his mouth, kissing my fingers. "I promise you the same. We will never keep secrets from one another again."

"Agreed."

"What else?"

"We need to be discreet around Easton. It's not that I want to hide us from him, but it will confuse him. We can't tell him yet." I hate the thought of sneaking around behind my son's back, but it's only been four months since his daddy died. I don't know how he'll react if he sees me kissing another man. Especially his uncle. It could lead to other questions we can't answer yet.

"I hate having to agree, but it's the way it's got to be. For now."

"We can't go public for the same reasons."

He sighs. "I know you're right, but this is beginning to feel like a dirty secret, and I'm not loving that much."

"Nor me, but this is the way it has to be. It won't be forever." I need time to work up the courage to tell Easton and to go public, and I have no clue how long that will take me, but I'm hoping this more patient version of Dillon will last and he won't pressure me into doing something before I'm ready.

"I'll try not to be my usual needy, greedy self. To remember that having you back in my life, even if it's not quite the way I'd hoped, is enough."

I run my fingers through his hair, holding his head. "I love you, and you love me. That won't change, and that's what matters the most. The rest is stuff we can work through in time."

He rests his forehead against mine. "I have waited years to hear those words again. I love you, Vivien Grace Lancaster. I love you so much, and I would wait until the end of time for you."

My heart beats with a zest that is new, all because of this man. I am truly lucky to have found such amazing love in my life. Not once, but twice. And to be given a second chance with Dillon, after everything we have been through, is more than I dared to hope for. "Just be patient with me, Dil. Like you were the last time."

"You set the pace, Viv. You call the shots."

"Look at me."

He lifts his head, peering into my eyes as my fingers weave in and out of his hair. "I still love your hair." My hands move lower, touching his eyes, his nose, and his lips, brushing against his cheeks, and rubbing the bristles on his chiseled jawline. "I love every part of you but especially your heart." I place one hand over his bare chest, and his heart drums steadily against my palm. "Thank you for being here for me. Thank you for caring for me and Easton."

"There is nowhere else I would rather be."

I lean in, keeping my eyes on his as I brush my lips against his mouth. "Kiss me, Dillon. Kiss me like you'll die if you can't taste my lips." We both smile, remembering another first kiss that started with those words, and a serene sense of calm settles over me. All the tiny hairs on the back of my neck lift, and a very subtle breeze sweeps fleetingly across my face. It might freak others out, but I think Reeve is here, and it comforts me. I think that is his way of telling me it is okay.

Dillon's mouth descends, and I sink into his arms and the feel of his warm lips moving against mine. He angles his head to deepen the kiss, and I open my mouth, letting him push his tongue in. I sigh into his mouth, our minty breaths comingling, as he strokes my tongue in long leisurely strokes. Winding my arms around his neck, I climb onto his lap, pressing my chest against his.

His hands rest respectfully on my lower back, and he makes no move to push this to the next level, content to kiss me while holding me tight.

I get lost in him.

Drowning in the taste of his kisses that are both familiar and excitingly new.

Flames lick at my skin as he ignites a burning desire that covers me from head to toe. Every part of my body feels the effects of his kiss. There is no part that is immune, and I never want to stop feeling like this.

Dillon always lit a fire inside me, and now he's nurturing the flames, coaxing them to jump higher, enabling them to burn bright so they never die out.

So *we* never die out.

I feel that truth deep in my bones, and as I cling to him, I know there will be challenging times ahead, but I believe we can overcome anything together. We will emerge from the flames a single entity, ready to burn anyone who dares step in our way.

My heart beats to a new rhythm, and my soul dances to a new hope, as we kiss and kiss like we can't get enough of one another.

I don't know how I ever thought I could deny this man.

How I could ever live without him.

Because he is embedded in my heart and imprinted on my soul, and from this day forward, I know he is the only man I will ever want by my side.

CHAPTER 37
VIVIEN

SEPTEMBER TURNS INTO OCTOBER, and we settle into a new routine. I drop Easton at school each morning, and Dillon collects him every day. On Tuesdays and Thursdays, he drops East at his Krav Maga class, staying to watch because he gets a kick out of it. Other afternoons, they go out for ice cream or burgers or go hang out at his house, and we've even managed a few family outings without being spotted. We've gone bowling, to the movies, and on several hikes so Easton finally got to wear his new hiking boots.

I've been writing a lot, documenting my story in a more cohesive fashion, drawing from all my journals. I suppose it's a book, but it won't ever see the light of day. I'm doing this for me and for Easton so that, one day, when he's old enough, he might read it and understand how I came to love both his daddies.

I'm also sewing again, and Ash has given me a list of requirements of things she'd like to take on tour with her next year. Mom loved the gown I made her for her next premiere. They left a couple of weeks ago to go on location, in Canada, but not before they both pulled me aside to tell me they approve of Dillon and me being together. I was so nervous telling them, and hugely relieved when they didn't judge. Not that I ever thought they would. I know they worry about me, and they've been watching Dillon like a hawk to ensure he doesn't step out of line.

We eat dinner together every night, as a family, and slowly Dillon is finding little ways of injecting narrative into our conversations that hints at our friendship and how Reeve would be happy we are such good friends again.

He's easing Easton into the idea of us as a couple with small gestures like placing his hand on my lower back as we walk in the garden, tucking my hair behind my ears, or brushing his fingers against my cheek, and our son hasn't balked when he's occasionally wrapped his arm around my waist.

But I won't let him take it further than that, and we haven't progressed beyond kissing and heavy groping. On nights when Dillon stays over, I usually crawl into his bed, ensuring I set my alarm so I can sneak back to my room before Easton wakes up.

Dillon hasn't pressured me at all, seemingly happy with the pace, and it helps. Gradually, my grief is becoming less of a tangible thing. I still miss Reeve, and I still think of him every day, but it is getting easier. I'm laughing more, having fewer bad dreams, and waking up more regularly with a smile on my face.

Which is progress indeed.

"Mommy, you look awesome!" East says as I step into the transformed room in Dillon's house as Wonder Woman. The noise levels are through the roof, and my ears protest loudly.

The lady Dillon hired to create a Halloween-themed room did an awesome job. Fake cobwebs hang from the ceiling, and there are a few token spiders residing in larger webs, in an ode to Easton's obsession with all creepy-crawlies. The ceiling has been covered in an eerie nighttime sky, and sheets of red chiffon cover all the lights, bathing the room in a reddish glow. Entertainers dressed as skeletons and ghosts roam the room, while a man dressed as a magician performs tricks from a temporary stage mounted at the very back of the space.

Round tables and small chairs occupy the center of the room, and the kids from Easton's class are due to congregate there in a while for burgers and fries. After, we're doing a trunk-or-treat out in the driveway so the kids get the trick or treat experience without any danger. Staff from the catering company Dillon hired are presently filling our trunks, and the trunks of the class parents who are here, with tons of candy and chocolate treats. Easton is going to be beside himself with excitement when he discovers it.

"Thanks, buddy. You look pretty awesome yourself." Easton high-fives me before shoving the mask of his Iron Man costume down over his face and rushing off to play with his friends.

"Jesus, woman, are you trying to kill me?" Dillon asks, his hungry eyes taking in every inch of my exposed skin. We chose a superhero theme as a family, and I stupidly agreed to let the boys pick the costumes. "There's not exactly a lot of room in this costume." He points at his tight Captain America costume, and it's hard not to drool. He sure gives Chris Evans a run for his money, and I don't say that lightly because Chris is fucking hot with a capital H.

But he's got nothing on Dillon O'Donoghue.

"If you don't want our son or his friends to spot me with a giant boner, I suggest you go and get changed. What was wrong with the Black Widow costume I got you anyway?" He pouts, looking completely ridiculous.

"God, he's insufferable," Ash says, coming up beside me. She's Bonnie to Jamie's Clyde. "I should shoot him for suggesting you wear that boring all-in-one yoke he gave you." She jabs Captain America in the chest with her toy gun.

"It wasn't boring. I know Viv will look hot in it but hot in a way that won't have me showcasing my hard-on to a bunch of kindergarteners. You hear me." Dillon quirks a brow at his sister.

Ash pulls the shield off his back, thrusting it at him. "Use that, dumbass. If you had a brain, you'd be the full package." She barks out a laugh. "Ha, see what I did there." I giggle while Dillon rolls his eyes. Ash shoves the shield down over his privates. "There, problem solved, and now my sexy bestie doesn't need to get changed."

We got ready together in Dillon's master suite, and Ash went all out on my hair and makeup. I feel like a million dollars, and I'm looking forward to after the kids' party when the adults get to play.

"You have really outdone yourself," I say, checking to ensure no one is looking before I plant a quick kiss on his cheek. "Easton is going to be talking about this party for years." He was so excited this afternoon as he sat at the kitchen table carving pumpkins with his dad while Ash and I made pumpkin pie and chocolate apples.

"That was the intention." He smiles as he looks over to where Easton, Nash, and a couple of other little boys are intently watching the magician juggle a bunch of balls in the air. "I want to make lots of special memories with him."

I loop my arm through his, wishing I could kiss the shit out of him, but it's too risky. Parents of the kids in Easton's class are in the room as well as staff from the catering company. "Does that go for me too?" I ask, deliberately batting my eyelashes at him.

He swats my ass. "You know it does, and if you keep torturing me, you know I'll get you back."

I waggle my brows as I grin up at him. "Oh, I'm counting on it."

"Dillon," I scream, as he lifts me from behind, throwing me over his shoulder.

"We'll be back," he tells Ash and Jamie. "I just need to teach this little vixen a lesson or two."

Ash howls with laughter as Dillon swats my ass and races out of the room. It's just as well Easton is out cold—and tucked up snugly in his bed upstairs, exhausted after his crazy party—because my screams are enough to wake all the neighbors.

"Dillon, put me down!" I demand, but his answer is another stinging slap. "My ass is hanging out," I protest. This costume is tiny, and from the cool air trickling across my butt cheeks, I know I'm flashing plenty of flesh.

"So what?"

"It's not very ladylike."

His chest rumbles with laughter. "Oh, Hollywood, you really crack me up. Do I have to remind you of all the non-ladylike things you let me do to you in Ireland? Or outline the things you're going to let me do to you again?"

My core pulses with need at his words and the images they conjure in my horny mind.

"I thought so," he says, sounding pleased when I don't mount any protest.

He ducks in through a door, taking me into the laundry room, closing it behind him before putting my feet on the ground.

His mouth is on mine in a nanosecond, and I forget everything but the fruity taste of his tongue as it pushes past my lips. Grabbing a fistful of his costume, I pull him to me, kissing him with urgency, needing him closer. His arms band around my body, and he crushes me to him. Our costumes are flimsy, and the evidence of his arousal pushes against my stomach, trying to poke a hole in both our clothing. Liquid lust rushes through me, dampening my panties, and I moan into his mouth, thrusting my chest against his, needing more. If I could climb inside him right now, I would.

"Damn, Hollywood. If you keep kissing me like that, I'm going to come in my costume."

"Take it off," I demand, rubbing my palm up and down his hard length. "I want to taste you."

"Yeah?"

I could cry at the look of hopeful anticipation on his face. I know he's dying for me as much as I'm dying for him, and I've kept him waiting months, but advancing things sexually is a big deal for me, and I only want to make love to him when I'm fully ready to commit to him. I am almost there, and this will take us one step closer.

Dillon rips at the costume, tearing it in half in his eagerness to free himself.

I'm crying with laughter as I drop to my knees before him, but my laughter dies when he shoves his compression shorts down and his erect cock springs free, bobbing in front of my face like the most heavenly temptation. He still has his piercing, and my pussy throbs with need. I remember how good his cock felt stroking my insides with the little silver balls taking my pleasure to new dizzy heights. Sex with Dillon was always out of this world, and we had a very active sex life.

I want to have that with him again.

Gliding my hands up his legs, I run my fingers along the inside of his thighs before I cup his balls. Lifting my chin, I stare up at him, keeping my eyes locked on his as my tongue darts out, licking his crown, both sides of his piercing, and the bead of precum glistening there.

Dillon cusses, jerking his hips as his eyes burn with desire. "I've got to warn you. I won't last long. It's been more than a while."

His words comfort me. "Give me every drop. I want it all." Gripping the base of his cock, I stretch his velvety-soft skin before I kiss, suck, and nibble along his length, enjoying every stroke of my tongue against his hot flesh. He groans, thrusting his hips, and I take pity on him, drawing him slowly into my mouth. I pump his cock at the base while I suck and lick, stretching my mouth wide to take as much of him in as I can. Dillon is big, and I almost choke when his tip hits the back of my throat, but the look of lust on his face spurs me on.

He grabs my hair, holding my face steady while he fucks

my mouth, and I love it. I love that he doesn't treat me like I'm a porcelain doll. That he pushes me to my limits, always ensuring I'm enjoying it. Tears leak out of my eyes and saliva drips down my chin as I go to town, loving the taste of him on my tongue and the feel of him in my mouth.

"Viv," he grits out, a muscle clenching in his jaw. "I'm going to come."

With my eyes, I urge him to keep going, pumping and sucking him harder as he pivots his hips, thrusting into my mouth. I fondle his balls, moving one finger behind to rub his taint because I remember he liked that. A primal growl rips from his lips as he lets go, and ropes of hot salty cum splash my mouth, shooting down my throat. I stay with him, milking every last drop of his climax, until he pulls out.

Dropping to his knees, he reels me into his arms, plunging his tongue into my mouth and kissing me like I'm the air he needs to breathe. "Vivien, Vivien, Vivien." He dots kisses all over my face. "I must have done something right in this life to deserve you because you are a fucking goddess among women. I could live a hundred lifetimes and never be worthy of you." He presses his sticky brow to mine. "I fucking love you, Hollywood. I love you so much."

"That must have been some blowjob," I tease, but I'm secretly pleased. What woman doesn't want to bring her man to his knees? *Literally.*

"It was the fucking Oscar of blowjobs, sweetheart, and now it's my turn."

I shriek as he scoops me up, planting me on top of the washing machine. He flashes me a wicked smile, showcasing dimples and blinding-white teeth, as he turns the machine on.

"What the hell are you doing?"

"Giving you an Oscar-worthy experience." He winks while parting my thighs and shoving my skirt up to my waist. I'm not surprised when he rips my panties, tossing scraps of lace to the floor, because it's his signature. "Hello, pussy," he croons, leaning down so he's eye level with my vagina. "Miss me as much as I missed you?"

I snort. "Oh. My. God. You are seriously deranged," I say as laughter bubbles up my throat.

The second his hot tongue lands on my cunt, all laughter fades. He swipes his tongue up and down my slit while eye fucking me, and I'm already squirming when the machine picks up speed and the whole thing starts vibrating. "Oh!" I exclaim as sensation rockets through me. "Oh my."

"Hold on tight, Hollywood. I'm about to give you the best damn orgasm of your life."

I grip the edges of the machine, holding on for dear life as Dillon ravishes me with his fingers and his tongue while the vibrations from the machine send me into another realm. My booted legs wrap around his neck, and the sight of his blond head bobbing up and down wrecks me. It's been so long since I was touched it doesn't take much to have me shooting for the stars. When Dillon hooks his fingers inside me and gently bites my clit, I explode, screaming his name as I come apart on his face.

I melt against him as he lifts me off the machine. "Holy hell, Dil," I rasp. "That was definitely Oscar worthy."

"We're so fucking good together," he reminds me, kissing me hard as he plants my feet on the ground. "Here, put these on. Ash will throw a hissy fit if I don't get you back to her ASAP." He hands me a pair of my lace panties, and I narrow my eyes suspiciously.

"Where did you get these?"

Fake innocence drenches his handsome features. "From your bedroom. Where else?"

"You were rooting through my underwear drawer?" I shriek.

He holds up his hands. "What else was a guy to do? I've had the worst case of blueballitis this side of the Pacific. Sniffing your knickers never fails to get me off in record time," he admits, smirking, as he grabs a pair of sweats from the laundry basket and pulls them on.

I gawk at him. "You are a very disturbed individual." I grab the machine to steady myself as I pull on my stolen panties.

He shrugs. "Desperate times call for desperate measures."

"How many did you steal?" I inquire as he takes my hand, hauling me into his warm bare chest.

"A handful."

I shake my head, but I'm smiling. "What am I going to do with you?"

"I can think of lots of things." He bends down to kiss me. "All of them X-rated." He thrusts against me, demonstrating he's hard again. "See what you do to me? I'm so hot for you, sweetheart. I'm hard all the damn time."

My hands creep up his chest. "I know you are, and I promise I'll be ready soon."

His features soften, and he gazes adoringly at me as he brushes hair over my shoulder. "You set the pace, Viv, and I'm happy. So fucking happy. Never feel under pressure to have sex with me. I can wait. This is more than enough. More than I ever thought I'd have again. I just love existing with you."

Tears prick my eyes. "I didn't think I'd ever feel content again. You have given me so much, Dillon," I croak.

"You have given me everything, Viv." He circles his arms around me, holding me close. "You have given me Easton, and I have you. I don't need anything else. I'm the happiest man on the planet."

CHAPTER 38
DILLON

"REMEMBER, YOU CAN'T SAY ANYTHING," I tell Ma as I hold my mobile phone out in front of me. "Keep it casual."

"I just want to say hello to the little guy, Dillon. Not give him the Spanish Inquisition." She rolls her eyes, and I really miss the fuck out of her. "When do you think you'll tell him?"

"Soon, I hope." I have a plan, which I hope Viv will agree to. Finding the right time to raise it with her is the issue. I don't want to spring it on her at the last minute because that fucked everything up the last time in Ireland. But the timing has to be spot-on so she won't overreact and tell me to take a hike. Things are perfect right now, and I don't want to mess anything up.

"Will you be bringing him home for Christmas?"

I rub the back of my neck, hating to do this to her. "About that."

Her face falls, and I feel like shit.

"Lauren and Jon didn't make it back for Thanksgiving today, but they'll be back for Christmas, and they want us to go there for dinner. It's tradition for all of them to go to the Millses' house, and it will be hard enough for East as it is. I don't want to do anything to upset him."

"It's okay, love. I understand. We'll miss you, but there'll be other Christmases."

"I'm sorry, Ma. I hate to be missing it, but I can't leave Vivien alone at Christmas. It's going to be tough on her." I know Reeve's loss will hit her hard then, and I need to be with her to help her get through it.

"I'm very proud of you, Dillon."

I arch a brow because I've done a lot of bad shit in the past. Things they only discovered when Reeve died, so I think saying she's proud is a bit of a stretch.

"You made mistakes, but you're atoning for them," she adds, seeing the incredulous expression on my face.

I've finally realized what Viv has been saying is true. Instead of focusing on revenge, I'm grateful for the life I've had. For the life I'm living. I know how fortunate I am to have my family and to have grown up surrounded by love. I took that for granted before. I only thought about the life that had been taken from me, not the one I was gifted. I didn't believe I was the lucky one, but I was wrong all along. It took letting go of my anger for me to see the truth.

"Every night, I say a prayer for you and Vivien and Easton," Ma continues, dragging me out of my head. "I knew the instant I met that girl that she was the one for you. I knew she was the girl you'd end up marrying, and I'm glad I wasn't wrong."

"Steady on, Ma, and don't go saying that shit to Viv."

She sighs. "Dillon, do you think I was born yesterday? I know better than to put my foot in it." She rolls her eyes. "Now go and put my cute little grandson on the line so I can wish him a Happy Thanksgiving."

"How did she take the news?" Viv asks as Easton says hello to my parents and extended family in Ireland via FaceTime. It helps that Ro is there as he knows him, but I'm sure he's wondering who the hell the rest of the freaks are. Ash is beside East, introducing him to everyone, and he's delighted with all the attention.

"She was a little disappointed, but she understands."

Viv chews on the corner of her lip, and I sneak my hand under the table, squeezing her fingers. "Stop worrying."

"I feel bad that you'll be away from your family at Christmas."

"But I won't be." I peer into her eyes. "I'll be with you and Easton. You're my family now."

She gives me a wobbly smile, and I'm guessing today is as hard for her as Christmas will be. This time last year, she was pregnant and celebrating with her husband.

"I'm sorry. I didn't mean to—"

"Don't be sorry, Dillon. You've got nothing to be sorry for." She glances at Easton to ensure he's not looking before planting a quick kiss on my lips. "And you're right. We are your family, and I'm lucky to get to do this with you. It's just hard today. I'm feeling a little sad."

I slide my arm around her shoulders, holding her tight. "I know, sweetheart, and I'm here for you."

Thanksgiving was harder than I thought it would be. Easton threw a few temper tantrums, and Vivien wore a sad smile on her face half the time, but we got through it. I yanked them out of bed this morning to go hiking at Pelican Cove Park because I want to do something fun today to put a smile back on both their faces.

The weather is cooler at this time of year, and Viv and Easton wrap up warm. My Irish bones don't need as much insulation, so I take a light jacket, and we head out up the coastal road.

We hike one of the shorter trails before heading down to the park and along the cliffs. Leon and Bobby trail us from a distance, giving us some privacy. Waves crash against the jagged rocks, and the sounds of the ocean are relaxing as we walk hand in hand. I keep Easton tucked in on the inside because he's got the same reckless streak I have, and I don't want him running away and skydiving off the cliff. "How about some hot chocolate?" I ask him, spotting a silver van selling hot drinks and pastries.

"Oh, yay!" He tugs on my hand, hauling me forward.

"Do you want anything?" I call out to Viv.

She's smiling as she shakes her head, hanging back to admire the view as our son drags me along for the ride. There's a bit of a queue, so we get in line. Easton glances up at me before dropping his eyes to his feet. His brow puckers, and his nose scrunches up, the way it always does when he's thinking about something. "Spit it out, little dude. What's on your mind?"

He nibbles on his lips. "My daddy used to hold my mommy's hand like you did back there."

I gulp over the messy ball of emotion in my throat, sensing where this is going.

"Does that mean you're going to be my new daddy?"

Holy fuck. I look around for Vivien because I am so out of my depth here, but she's still staring out at the ocean, oblivious to my current panicked state. I run my hands through my hair, trying to think of the best thing to say.

"Does it, Uncle Dillon?" He looks up at me with so much hope and trust and innocence, and I would do anything for this kid. He means the world to me.

Taking his hand, I pull him out of the queue, off to the side where it's private. I bend down so I'm at his height. "Reeve will always be your daddy, buddy, but I'd like to be a permanent part of your life. If that's okay with you?"

He bobs his head, but he looks a little unsure. "I saw my mommy kissing you yesterday. Does that mean you're going to get married?"

Jesus, fuck. Where the hell is Vivien when I need her? I send juju vibes out to the universe, along with a silent plea, for her to come and rescue me. And someone must be listening because she appears beside me, and I release the breath I'd been holding.

"What's going on?" Her gaze bounces between East and me.

I scoop Easton up into my arms, grateful when he goes willingly. "I think we need to go back to the car and have a talk with East."

"I want my hot chocolate first."

"Okay. Come on. The line is gone now. Let's grab you a cookie and some hot chocolate."

After Easton gets his stuff, we walk back toward the parking lot in silence. I hand Vivien a coconut water, mouthing "He saw us kissing and holding hands. He has questions."

She nods, placing her hand on his shoulder and guiding him toward the car. The three of us climb in the back, and we keep Easton in the middle. I look to Viv, more than happy to let her take the lead on this.

She clears her throat. "I believe you have questions. What would you like to know?"

"Are you going to marry Uncle Dillon?" he asks, dribbling some hot chocolate down his chin. I dab the liquid with a napkin, cleaning it up before it can drop on his clothes.

"I don't know," she says, and it's as if she's thrust her hand into my chest and squeezed the life from my heart. "Maybe someday I will," she adds, and that helps a little. "Would that upset you?"

He thinks about it for a few seconds as he sips his drink. "Would it mean he'd come to live with us and I could play guitar every day?"

Vivien smiles adorably at him. "Yes, except for times when Dillon is working."

He considers this for another few beats, and the suspense is killing me. "I suppose that would be okay."

Vivien and I exchange looks over his head.

"That's good because Dillon makes me happy."

"He makes me happy too," he says, and two red spots appear on his cheeks.

"Me three," I quip, sidling up closer to him. "You and your mommy make me very, very happy."

"So, you're like my mommy's boyfriend now?" he asks, eyeballing me.

I look to Vivien, and she nods. "Yes. Is that okay?"

He shrugs, and concern spreads across Vivien's face. "You can tell me what you're feeling. Whatever you have to say, you won't upset me or Uncle Dillon."

His hands wrap around his cup as he stares at his mum. "You used to kiss my daddy, and now you kiss Uncle Dillon. Does that mean you don't love my daddy anymore?"

Fuck. The poor little kid. I wonder if this is why he was acting out yesterday, and I wish I knew what thoughts were troubling his mind so I could put him at ease.

"I will always love your daddy, Easton." Tears cling to her lashes, and her voice sounds choked up. "Always. I loved Reeve my whole life, and just because he's in heaven now, it doesn't mean I don't love him anymore. You still love him, right?"

He nods.

"And you love Uncle Dillon too," she prompts.

He nods again, and my heart soars.

"So, it's like that for me. I love your daddy, and I love Uncle Dillon. Does that make sense?"

"Yes." He's nodding again as he turns to me. Tears glisten in his eyes, and his lower lip wobbles. "Are you going to leave me too?"

Pain sits on my chest, making breathing difficult. Taking his half-empty cup, I hand it to Viv, pulling him up onto my lap. "You know I work in the band and that I have to go on tour in January, but I will come back. I will never willingly leave you or your mommy." East needs to be reassured, but I don't want to lie to him either. No one can give him a rock-solid guarantee. What happened to Reeve was tragic, and tragedies can't be predicted.

"Promise?" he whispers.

"I promise," I say, telling him straight from my heart, hoping I never have to break that promise.

"Pinky swear." He holds out his little finger, and I don't know if my heart can withstand this.

But his expectant little face tells me everything. He needs this, and I won't deny him this reassurance. I curl my little finger around his, almost choking on the words as I say them. "Pinky promise."

A sob cuts through the air, and when I look at Viv, she's crying. "Come here." Keeping Easton on my lap, I stretch my arm out for her, pulling her into my side. Viv's arms go around Easton and me, and I kiss both their brows, holding them close and silently vowing to do everything in my power to ensure I am always there for them. Even if it means severing ties with the band because right now there is no way in hell I can step on that plane in January and leave them behind.

"I want pizza!" Easton yells. "Pepperoni pizza and lots and lots of cheese!" We are on our way back after a fun-filled day, and we are all starving, so I suggested we head out for dinner. The three hours Easton spent racing around the indoor jungle gym, after our hike, hasn't dented his energy much, and he's bouncing in his seat, salivating at the prospect of pizza.

"Pizza it is," I say, knowing the perfect place. It's en route to my house and a little off the beaten track so we shouldn't be spotted. Viv is still paranoid about the media finding out about us, but we won't be able to evade them for long. Especially now she's going out and about again. Anyway, the band and I have eaten here a bunch of times, and nothing has ever appeared in the press, so it's a safe place.

I pull up to the curb in front of the family-run Italian restaurant and kill the car. Leon pulls up behind us, and I salute him through the mirror. They will wait outside and keep a lookout for paparazzi. After opening Vivien's door, I get Easton out of his seat and lift him onto the path. I grab both their hands, and we head inside.

Marco gives us my usual table at the back, and we have a lovely meal, filled with good food, good wine, and lots of laughter, and I wish every day could be like this.

"You look happy," Viv murmurs while we watch Easton shoveling ice cream into his mouth with one hand and coloring with the other.

"I am deliriously happy." I tuck her into my side and kiss her softly. "I love spending time with both of you, and Easton took the news better than I expected."

"He did. I'm pleased." She rubs her nose against mine, and her eyes are full of love as she props her chin on my shoulder. "Will you stay over tonight?" Her gaze glitters with unspoken promise, and my cock instantly hardens at the thought of what might be on the agenda.

I nip at her earlobe. "I will if you make it worth my while." I waggle my brows, and she shoves at me.

"Asshole," she mouths.

I reel her back into my side. "You know I'm joking." I press a lingering kiss to her temple. "Kind of."

Easton falls asleep in the car on the way back to Vivien's house. He's knackered after an action-packed day. We put him to bed together, carefully removing his clothes so as not to wake him. We stand silently by his bed, our fingers threaded together, both of us staring at this amazing little boy who is a piece of me and a piece of Vivien. My heart is so full it feels like it could burst.

Vivien leads me out of the room, softly closing the door. I

expect her to turn right, to head downstairs, but she turns left, toward the guest bedroom I've commandeered as my own. Viv even had it redecorated in more manly shades of gray and blue. "What's going on, Hollywood?" I ask as she pulls me into the room and closes the door.

Her eyes flare with need as she pushes me back against the wall. "I can't wait any longer. I need you."

Hallelujah starts playing in my head and ringing in my ears. "Are you sure, because once we make this move, I'll be all over you. I won't be able to keep my hands to myself if I'm inside you again. So, choose your next words very carefully, Hollywood." I'm like a starving man who's been wasting away on a diet and the second he drops the discipline he goes wild, eating everything in sight.

If Vivien gives me the green light, I'll devour her and make no apologies for it.

She leans in, grazing her teeth along the column of my neck. "I'm all in, Dillon. I want you so fucking bad it feels like I might explode." Her fingers trail through the stubble on my cheeks, and she pushes her thumb into my mouth. Rabid hunger blazes from her eyes as she stares at me. "Fuck me, Dillon. Make me yours forever."

CHAPTER 39

VIVIEN

DILLON PULLS my mouth to his, kissing me with months', no, years' worth of pent-up longing, and I'm drowning in him. In a skillful move, he repositions us, without breaking our kiss, so I'm against the wall and he's crushing his hard toned body against me. His tongue plunders my mouth as he pops the button on my jeans, and I moan when his tongue piercing strokes along the roof of my mouth. My hands slide up his shirt, finding warm skin, and I scrape my nails up and down his back as he lowers the zipper on my jeans and shoves his hand into my panties.

Two fingers slide into my slippery pussy, and I press against his hand as I bite down on his lower lip. "Fuck," he hisses against my mouth, pumping his fingers fast inside me. "I need in you right now. I can't wait."

We stumble around the room in our hurry to get undressed, only breaking our lip-lock when it's necessary to remove our clothing.

We fall back against the bed in only our underwear, and I climb on top of him, grinding down on his dick as he yanks my bra down, sitting up and burying his face in my breasts. He shoves them together with his hands as he sucks and bites my nipples and my tender flesh, and I think I could come just from this. "Love your tits," he murmurs, taking as much of one breast into his mouth as he can.

"Dillon, please," I beg, grinding my pelvis against his, my pussy pulsing with intense need.

"Please what?" He rips my panties at the side, and the material floats around us. "Tell me what you need, sweetheart. Tell me what you want."

I shove him back by his shoulders, remove my bra, and fling it aside as I slide down his body, tugging his boxers down his legs. "You." My tongue darts out, licking the top of his pierced crown. "I want all of you filling every part of me." Without giving him time to answer, I lower my mouth over his straining cock, moaning as I run my lips up and down his hot flesh.

"Fuck, Viv. I won't last long if you do that." He grabs my hips, yanking me off him and throwing me flat on my back on the bed. Dillon pounces on me, running his hands all over my body as his lips ravish my mouth. I spread my legs, rubbing my pussy against his cock, and he hisses between his teeth. "Goddamn it. The things you do to me. Don't move," he commands, straightening up and bending over to pull out the top drawer of his bedside table.

My chest heaves, and my body trembles in anticipation as I watch him remove a condom and carefully roll it down over his length. Electricity crackles in the air, and I'm dying for him, impatient to feel him moving inside me. I fondle my breasts, spreading my legs wider as I wait for him to hurry the fuck up.

"Look at you." A devilish glint appears in his eye as he moves his face in between my legs. "All spread out for me like the most decadent feast." He licks his lips before he launches himself at me, shoving his tongue into my cunt while his fingers furiously rub my clit. "Pinch your nipples," he growls, looking up at me as he pushes three fingers into my heat. "And keep your eyes on me." His tongue darts out, and he licks my clit as his fingers pump faster inside me. Every time his piercing hits the sensitive bundle of nerves, a jolt of intense desire shoots through my core, and I'm a writhing mess under his expert ministrations.

My climax is rising, and I'm getting close. Impatient to experience the ultimate high, I grind my pussy against his face. "That's it, sweetheart, fuck my face."

Grabbing handfuls of his gorgeous hair, I keep him pressed against my most private parts as I thrust against him and he works me with his fingers and tongue.

Sparks transform to flames inside me as I self-destruct in the most glorious fashion. I can't stifle my cries as the most earth-shattering orgasm rips through me, turning my limbs to mush, rendering me a pliable pile of limbs on the bed. "Fuck, Dillon. I want to do that every single day for the rest of my life."

Pulling up to his knees, he pins me with the sexiest evil grin. "That can definitely be arranged." Flinging my legs over his shoulders, he pulls me forward, lifting my ass off the bed a few inches as he lines his cock up at my entrance. "Hold on tight, Hollywood. This is going to be hard and fast."

"My favorite kind of ride," I quip, shivering in delicious anticipation.

Dillon thrusts into me in one powerful movement, and I slap a hand over my mouth to stifle my cries. "Fuck, yeah, Viv. God, how I've missed you." He pounds into me while leaning down to kiss me. "I love doing this with you."

Grabbing his head, I pull him closer as I cross my ankles behind his neck, lifting my hips, so the angle is deeper. "I love sex with you. I just love you," I pant before claiming his lips in a searing-hot kiss.

Dillon drives into me like a man on a mission, pushing his dick as far as it will go, and I see stars. Our kissing is as frantic as our fucking because we can't get enough. I drag my nails up his abs, and he hisses. Removing my legs from around his neck and shoulders, he situates me on his lap without breaking our connection. "Ride me, sweetheart. Fuck me until I come." His arms go around me as he plants a line of drugging kisses along my collarbone.

Keeping my hands on his shoulders to control my movements, I bounce up and down on his erection, throwing my head back and thrusting my chest in his face. Dillon sucks on my breasts, tugging on my nipples with his teeth, while his fingers slip down to my ass, tracing a teasing line along my ass crack. His mouth suctions on my neck, right in the place where I'm most sensitive, and I groan as I slam up and down on his dick, feeling my orgasm building again.

Dillon shoves his cock up inside me, his movements alternating with mine, and I cry out when he pushes one finger into my ass, falling over the ledge instantly. Pushing me flat on my back, he rocks into me with a new intensity as I come down from my high. A muscle clenches in his jaw, the veins in his neck pulse, and his entire body locks up as he roars out his release.

It's a miracle we didn't wake Easton with how loud we were. He really must be exhausted after such a busy day.

The blissful look on Dillon's face brings tears to my eyes, and I pull him to me as he collapses on the bed beside me.

His arms wind around me automatically, and he draws me in close, tipping my chin up. "Are you okay?" Concern is splayed across his face.

"These are happy tears," I rasp, cupping his gorgeous face. "I love you, Dillon. I love you with everything I am, and everything I have to offer is yours."

"You're mine. You're truly mine." His eyes fill up.

"I'm yours, Dillon." I kiss him softly, and he tightens his arms around me.

"This is right where you belong, Vivien Grace, and I am going to love you with everything I have every single day for the rest of our lives."

"You took your rings off," Dillon says the following morning as we are finishing breakfast. Easton is in the playroom watching cartoons on the TV. Dillon stares at my empty ring finger, as my hand gravitates to my neck.

"I did. It was time." I cried removing my wedding and engagement rings after I got out of the shower earlier, but it was the final cleansing I needed to do. "I've given you my commitment, Dillon. I've told you I'm yours. I can't continue to wear Reeve's rings on my finger when I've promised to give myself to you fully."

My hand curls around the two necklaces I'm wearing. "I'm hoping you don't mind if I wear them around my neck." I put the rings on a silver chain I had ordered for this day, and I took the claddagh necklace Dillon gave me for my birthday in Ireland out of the memento box I'd kept hidden from my husband.

Now I'm wearing both.

Side by side.

Existing in tandem like my love for both twins.

Dillon stares at the necklaces, looking a little dazed.

"If it bothers you, I can take it off."

Slowly, he lifts his gaze to mine, shaking his head. "I told you I'm fine with you remembering Reeve. I don't want you to erase him. Wear his rings around your neck. Keep your photos up. Whatever it is you need to do, I'm good. I've made my peace with everything."

"Thank you." I reach across the table, threading my fingers through his. "You don't know how much it means to me to hear you say that."

"You kept it," he whispers, his eyes lowering to my neck once again.

"Did you think I wouldn't?"

He shrugs. "I didn't really think about it, but I'm glad you did."

"I must be a glutton for punishment because I kept all the stuff I have of yours, and all the things that reminded me of

Ireland, in a box, hidden in my closet. I couldn't bear to part with any of it." I have photos, some of Dillon's T-shirts, some Toxic Gods merch, and tons of souvenirs from our many trips.

"Come here. You're too far away over there." He pushes back his chair, the legs squealing across the tile floor.

I get up and drop onto his lap, wrapping my arms around his neck. Our mouths move as one, meeting in a passionate kiss I feel all the way to the tips of my toes. Dillon hardens underneath my ass, and I break our kiss, quirking a brow. "I thought I exhausted you last night," I tease, squirming on his lap.

"Don't you know me? I'm insatiable." He nips at my earlobe. "Insatiable for you."

"Uncle Dillon!" Easton shouts, bounding into the room a few seconds later.

Dillon groans, burying his head in my shoulder. "He has the worst timing."

"Or impeccable timing."

"What's up, buddy?" Dillon says, keeping his arms around me.

"Will you play in the treehouse with me?"

"Absolutely." Dillon never refuses him anything.

"Awesome. I'll meet you outside!" he says, racing out of the room like a tornado.

"I see someone got laid," Ash says, grinning, a few hours later when she arrives for our lunch-slash-yoga date.

"Jesus, Ash. Tone it down, would ya?" Dillon points to where Easton is sitting at the kitchen table drawing pictures of Reeve and Lainey with the angels in heaven.

"Shit, sorry. I didn't see the little munchkin. All I saw was Viv's radiant glow." She waggles her brows.

"You know what you need to do, Auntie Ash," Easton says

in a singsong voice, sliding off his chair and walking toward us. He slaps out his palm. "Hand the goods over."

Dillon chuckles, beaming at his son as his sister removes a dollar bill from her wallet and hands it to E. "I'll be coming to you instead of the bank for a loan soon."

Easton grins before turning to his father. "Uncle Dil? What does got laid mean?"

I snort laugh, grabbing my gym bag and my purse, wiggling my fingers at my man. "And that's my cue to leave. Good luck handling that one."

"You're mean," he mouths. "And I'll make you pay."

"I look forward to it." Bending down, I kiss my son on the lips. "Be good for Uncle Dillon. I'll see you later."

Easton throws his arms around me. "We're going to practice with my guitar. Love you, Mommy."

I pull him up into my arms and hug him tight. "I love you too."

"Where's my loving?" Ash asks, fake pouting.

"You don't deserve one after the shit you've landed me in." Dillon sulks, and it's priceless.

Easton projects himself from my arms to Ash's, giving her a quick hug. "Love you too, Auntie Ash."

"Right back at ya, cutie." Pretending to whisper, she says, "Give Uncle Dil hell, and don't forget he hasn't answered your question yet."

Oh my God. Dillon is going to kill her if the thunderous look on his face is any indication.

We're still laughing when we step outside, climbing into Ash's car.

Leon gets behind the wheel of the security SUV, trailing us down the driveway.

"Don't you ever get sick of having bodyguards following you everywhere? We need security when the guys are on tour, and I hate it even if I know it's for our protection."

"It's all I've ever known, and I've gotten used to it. Besides, Leon and Bobby are like family now they've been with us so long, and they are discreet. Most times, I forget they're even there."

"Have you given much thought to going public with Dil?" she asks, pulling out of my driveway onto the road.

"It's been on my mind," I truthfully reply. "I know it's best to get in front of these things, and I know that means we'll need to put out a statement or give an interview."

"You will, and I know you're worried about what people will say, but fuck them. Seriously, it's none of their business."

"I'll talk to Dillon about it tonight, but I'm thinking maybe we could do it after Christmas." That gives us a month and a bit to plan it and enough time for me to recover my lady balls.

"So, you two finally bumped uglies," she says, taking the exit for the highway.

"We did." I can't contain my grin. "It was incredible. Even better than I remembered. We barely got any sleep, and I can't wait until tonight so I can jump his bones again."

"Blech." She makes a face. "TMI, sister."

I laugh, buoyed up by great sex and Dillon's love. "Your brother is a fucking beast in the bedroom. The things he does to me."

"Yeah, Viv. I know you're all loved up and sexed up, but you've got to quit that shit, or I'm seriously going to puke."

I giggle, and her expression softens as she reaches across the console to squeeze my hand. "All joking aside, I am made up for you. Seeing both of you so happy after everything makes me incredibly happy."

"I'm happy too. It's like it used to be, but better, if that makes sense."

She nods. "I get what you're saying."

"I still get moments where I feel the odd bout of guilt, and I still miss Reeve, but I'm done with being sad all the time. It's been almost seven months. It's time to live again."

CHAPTER 40

VIVIEN

"WE'VE GOT A BIT OF A SITUATION," Leon says as Ash and I emerge from the locker room, showered and changed after our yoga class.

"What situation?" Ash asks, thrusting her shoulders back and adopting her serious business face.

Sympathy splays across Leon's face as he looks at me. "The media knows about you and Dillon. There are a ton of paparazzi out front."

My face pales, and bile swims up my throat. Ash grips my hand. This is what I was afraid of.

Leon gestures behind him to where Bobby and another two bodyguards are waiting. "You were in the middle of your class when the news broke. I didn't want to interrupt you, so I called in reinforcements. There's no back door in this place, so we've got no choice but to go out the main entrance."

"How bad is it?" I ask.

"Bad."

"Right, fuck those assholes." Ash straightens up, eyeballing me. "Ignore them, and don't look at them. We'll figure out what to do when we get back to the house." She looks at Leon. "I assume my brother is aware?"

He nods. "It was Dillon who called to warn me. He wanted to come and get you himself, but I didn't think that was a good idea."

No shit, Sherlock. It would have been a complete clusterfuck if Dillon had shown up here, and I'm glad he listened to sense for once.

"Okay, let's do this." Ash grips my hand tighter. "You ready?"

I nod even though I'm never ready for this shit.

Leon and Bobby cover us from both sides while the other two bodyguards cover us front and rear as we make our way outside.

The second Leon opens the door, a ton of reporters and photographers rush toward us, shouting questions and sticking cameras in our faces. I keep my head down, ignoring them as we're jostled and pushed from all angles. The bodyguards are taking the brunt of the shoving, doing their best to protect us, but it's a total shitshow as we battle it to our car.

"Vivien, is it true you're having an affair with Reeve's twin brother?"

"Vivien, were you sleeping with Dillon when Reeve was still alive? Is that why you were arguing in the car the night of the accident?"

"Vivien, can you confirm reports you eloped with Dillon and got married?"

"Vivien, did you get married because you're expecting Dillon's child?"

"Vivien, were you planning to leave Reeve for his brother before the accident happened?"

On and on it goes until it feels like my head will explode. Eventually, we make it to the security car, and I bury my head in my hands as soon as the door is shut behind us.

"Motherfucking bloodsucking assholes!" Ash fumes, circling her arm around me from behind. "Don't let them get to you. I know it's easier said than done, but we'll put out a statement, and if they choose to believe that bullshit, they're idiots."

I lift my head, sighing. "I fucking jinxed myself earlier. How the hell did they find out?"

"Let's call Dillon." Ash is already dialing his number as Leon tries to pull out onto the road. Swarms of reporters and paparazzi surround our car, trapping us. "Mow them fucking down for all I care," Ash says as Leon keeps his hand on the horn, slowly inching away from the curb.

"Call the cops if you need to," I add. These assholes know they're not allowed to do this.

"I'm putting you on speaker," Ash says into the phone.

"Are you okay?" Dillon asks, worry evident in his tone.

"We're surrounded, but Leon is doing his best to get us away," I explain.

"Who reported it, and what's been said?" Ash asks.

"I'm so sorry, Viv," Dillon says. "One of the waitresses at the Italian restaurant gave an interview to *ET Live*. She must have been watching us the entire time, and she shared a video of us kissing and hugging. I've already talked to Marco, and she's been fired. She was new and on a trial. He's extremely upset and very apologetic."

"That makes little difference now," I say glumly. I rub a tense spot between my brows. "We need to call Edwin and your new publicist."

"Already done. Both will be here by the time you arrive home, and I've spoken to your mum too. Your parents phoned me when they couldn't reach you."

My parents are pros at handling this stuff, and I'm sure Mom will have suggestions we can consider. They are still on location, but I can call her back when we're discussing options if I need to. "Okay. We'll see you at the house soon."

"It's going to be okay," he says, and I wish I could believe him.

Ash ends the call as Leon finally makes it out onto the

road, picking up speed. Removing my cell from my purse, I log on to the internet.

"Are you sure you want to do that?" Ash asks. "It's all going to be bullshit."

"I need to know what I'm dealing with. Not just so we can respond appropriately but to understand what I need to tell Easton." There are a couple of nasty little shits in his class who seem to love rubbing Easton's nose in stuff that's said online. Thankfully, Dillon made that last incident disappear, but I hate he had to write a check to do it.

I pull up *ET Live*, and we watch the report and video. It's not too damning, but there is no doubting it's us in the recording even if it is a little blurry. The comments, however, are another matter entirely. Reeve's fans are out in full force, and I'm being called everything from a cheating slut to a murdering bitch.

Ash reads over my shoulder, and I can almost feel the anger rolling off her. "That is such horseshit," she snaps. "What kind of low-life scumbag would accuse you of fixing the accident and killing Reeve on purpose just so you could have your wicked way with his brother? These people are sick and twisted." She grabs the phone from me. "You've seen enough."

I have, and I'm sick to my stomach the rest of the ride home.

Dillon is waiting for me outside the house when we pull up, and I fall apart the second he pulls me into his arms. "Shush, sweetheart. It's going to be okay. I'm here, and I'm not letting anyone hurt you."

I cling to him as I cry, hating I'm back in this space again. It feels like all the progress I've made has just been undone. "They're accusing me of never loving Reeve. Of tainting his memory. Some are even saying I made the accident happen on purpose," I sob, looking up at him through clouded vision. "How could anyone accuse me of deliberately killing my husband and my daughter?" Pain punches me in the gut, and

I cling to Dillon as the sounds of a chopper resound over our heads.

"You have got to be fucking kidding me." Dillon bristles with rage as we look up, spotting the news helicopter in the sky. "Let's get inside. Ash, call the cops. This is a massive invasion of privacy and they can't do that. I already reported a drone earlier."

Drones are becoming a serious issue for celebrities. They are trying to introduce laws, but it's a tricky subject.

"I'm already on it," she says, handing me a tissue.

I dry my eyes and pull myself together. I can't let Easton see me upset. Taking Dillon's hand, we step inside the house after Ash. I fix my makeup in the mirror in the hall, making myself presentable, as Ash hurries off to meet with the publicists. Dillon confirms Easton is over at his house with Jamie. He felt it best to distract him while we figure out what to do.

Dillon slides his arm around my shoulders as we walk toward my office. I lean into him, siphoning some of his warmth and his support. He stops outside the door, turning me around in his arms. He kisses me softly. "I love you, and you love me. The three of us are a family now, and we haven't done anything wrong. Not back then, and not now. Keep remembering that. You are a good person, Vivien, and those idiots deserve to rot in hell for the horrible things they are saying. But that's on them. Not you." He tilts my chin with one finger. "Hold your head high, Hollywood, and never forget you are a goddess among women."

A small smile curls the corners of my lips. I fling my arms around him. "Thank you for reminding me of what's important."

We step into the room hand in hand, greeted by matching grim expressions.

Edwin rushes toward me, pulling me into a hug. "We'll get on top of this, Vivien. Don't worry."

Ash introduces me to Farrah Lewis, the band's new publicist. I'm glad Ash also mentioned she was openly gay because the tall thin redhead is absolutely stunning and I might have worried otherwise. Not about Dillon. I trust him completely, but I know the way some women throw themselves at rock stars. It's no different than actors, in that regard. She shakes my hand. "I wish we were meeting under better circumstances."

"Likewise."

"Don't worry. Between all of us, we'll get a handle on this and put our own spin on it."

We all know it's not as easy as that, but I appreciate her attempts to reassure me. "Please take a seat," I say, urging everyone to move over to the two couches as Charlotte steps into the room with a tray.

"Thank you, Charlotte." This woman is worth her weight in gold.

"Let me know if you need anything else." She leaves the room, discreetly closing the door.

I pour coffees for everyone as we settle down on the couches. Dillon leans back, with one leg crossed over the other, looking calm and unruffled. At least one of us is. He slides his arm behind my back. "How do you suggest we respond to this? Issue a statement or do an interview?"

"I think we need to issue a statement asap to stop some of the vitriol online," Edwin says.

"We can issue a joint statement from both camps along with a request for privacy," Farrah adds. "But I think a scheduled interview with Oprah would really put all the nasty rumors to rest."

"How quickly can you get that set up?" Ash asks, sipping her coffee.

"I'm confident if we pool our efforts we can have a contract on the table within forty-eight hours. Everyone will be clambering for this story, and it's right up Oprah's alley," Edwin says.

"What about Easton?" I ask because right now he's my

most pressing concern. I don't want our relationship to impact negatively on our son.

"I don't see any cause for concern." Edwin looks a little puzzled, and I know why. I turn to Dillon, and he nods.

"Easton is Dillon's biological child," I explain, and Edwin almost falls off his chair. To give Farrah her due, she looks completely unflappable, as if I haven't just dropped a bomb. I give them a quick summary of the background, and they both listen intently while I explain. Dillon holds my hand the entire time, offering me silent support.

"That changes things," Edwin says, when I've finished speaking, as Farrah's phone pings. "I know you don't want to be forced into telling him, but it's going to come out, Vivien. It's better that it's revealed from your mouth. I suggest you give that exclusive to Oprah, and we say nothing about Easton in the statement we'll issue today."

"Can you turn on *ET Live*," Farrah says, looking up from her phone with concerning frown lines. "And we will have to reconsider the entire strategy."

"Why?" Dillon asks, sitting up straighter as I turn the channel on.

My heart is in my mouth as the screen loads and I see the familiar face. Blood rushes to my head, and acid swirls in my gut. I think I might throw up. "That's why," I croak, pointing at Aoife's face on the TV.

CHAPTER 41
DILLON

I JUMP UP, glaring at the screen, wishing I could project myself into the TV and throttle the living daylights out of that conniving bitch. Everyone else stands, crowding around the TV. I tuck Viv into my side, hating how badly she's trembling and wishing I could make this go away, but I'm too late. The damage is done.

I'm seething as I watch Aoife talk to a Virgin One reporter in their Dublin studios. The news about Viv and me only broke three hours ago, so this must be live, which is crazy because it's after midnight there. I have no clue how she managed to set this up so fast, unless she was already in discussions with someone.

Despite reassuring Viv many months ago, I was worried Aoife might say something when the news came out about Reeve and me being twins. So, I contacted my Dublin solicitor and requested he send a reminder to all of those who had signed the NDA, reminding them of the considerable financial penalties if anyone spoke out.

Trying to ruin Viv and me must mean more to Aoife than money because she knows me well enough to know I'm going to go after her for this.

"Are you saying Vivien Lancaster and Dillon O'Donoghue had a relationship six years ago when Vivien studied at Trinity College Dublin?" the reporter asks her, in what is obviously a contrived interview.

"Yes. They were definitely a couple," the traitorous bitch says as old pictures of Vivien and me are shared on the screen. All the shots were taken in Whelans, which means the bitch was taking pictures of us on the sly.

"They look pretty infatuated with one another in these photos. Would you say their relationship continued after Vivien left Ireland and returned to America?"

"Most definitely," she lies. "I mean, why else would Dillon make me sign an NDA if not to protect his relationship with her?"

"That fucking whore." Ash clenches her hands into fists, seething as much as I am, when her phone rings. "Jay, I can't talk," she says, pausing for a few seconds. "We're watching it now. I'll call you back."

"Can you elaborate for the viewers? Are you saying you broke the terms of an NDA to talk to us today?"

Aoife nods, attempting, and failing, to look superior. "Censorship isn't right. Freedom of speech is a constitutional right, and I won't be bullied into keeping my mouth shut."

"What a dumbass," Ash says.

"Shut up. We're missing it," I say.

"Why did you speak out now? Why not when it was revealed earlier this year that Reeve and Dillon were twins?" the reporter asks.

"I wanted to, but Dillon's solicitor sent me a threatening letter, and I was afraid."

"Oh, please. You stupid bitch. You were waiting for the best moment to come forward." Ash grinds her teeth while Vivien is worryingly mute beside me. I hold her tighter, pressing a kiss to the top of her head.

"But it's not right, what they did, and someone needs to say something. That poor man died not knowing his wife was sleeping with his twin. For all we know, that little boy wasn't even his. I bet he's Dillon's. The timing is really suspect."

"You stupid fucking whore!" Vivien explodes, shucking out of my arms. She grabs a mug from the table, throwing it at the TV. Before I can stop her, she's grabbed another, throwing that one too. "That stupid fucking bitch!" She whirls around, fire dancing in her eyes, nostrils flaring, looking slightly scary. "I will kill her! I'm getting on a plane, and I'm going to strangle her with my bare hands." Viv grabs fistfuls of her hair and paces the floor. I stride toward her, attempting to pull her into my arms, but she swats me away.

"This is all your fault! You brought her into our lives. How could you have ever slept with that bitch?" Vivien asks, glaring at me. "I always knew she was poison."

"I tried to fix it. I—"

"I don't want to hear excuses, Dillon." She shoves my chest. "You were so confident you had it handled, but I've always known better when it comes to her. She always wanted to hurt me, and now she's found the perfect ammunition. I'm betting the next person who comes forward is that guy from the lab or one of his staff. This is going to be all over the news."

She breaks down, sobbing as she drops to her knees, all the fight fading. "We have to tell him now. It's only three weeks until Christmas, Dillon. His first Christmas without Reeve is already going to be hard enough. I didn't want to tell him until after."

We haven't actually discussed a timeline at all, so that's news to me. But I understand, and I share her concerns. The timing sucks, but we have no choice now. I sink to my knees too, wrapping my arms around her, but she pushes me away. Pain slices across my chest. "Don't touch me, Dillon. I don't want you to touch me." She climbs awkwardly to her feet. "I need some space," she adds before fleeing the room.

Ash extends her hand, helping me to stand. My shoulders slump with the weight of failure.

"She doesn't mean it," my sister says, giving me a hug.

"I promised I'd protect her. That I wouldn't let anything, or anyone, hurt her again, and I've failed already."

Ash grips my face hard. "Cut that shit out now, Dil. You haven't failed her. This isn't on you. It's on that stupid manipulative bitch."

Fury returns full throttle, and a muscle clenches in my jaw. "She's going to pay."

The two publicists hang back, afraid to intervene, I'm sure. Extracting my cell from my pocket, I punch the number for my Dublin solicitor. I don't care that he's probably sleeping. I pay the fucker enough he can take my call no matter how late it is. "Agree a statement with Edwin and Farrah," I tell Ash. "We need to get something out now. Viv's in no state to review it, so send it to Lauren and ensure she's okay with it before you issue it."

I look over at the two publicists as my call goes to voice mail. "Say nothing about Easton for now. We can't make that public until we have spoken to our son." I press redial as Farrah starts jotting notes on her phone. "Confirm we were in a relationship years ago before we knew Reeve and I were twins. Our relationship ended, and we didn't see one another again until just before Reeve died, when we discovered we were siblings. I've been helping Vivien during the grieving process, and we grew close again. We are now in a relationship. At no time did Vivien ever cheat on Reeve."

I growl as my call goes unanswered again. "You can add that Reeve was aware of my relationship with Vivien in Ireland." Everything I have said is true except for me not knowing about Reeve at the time. No one knows about that, so I'm comfortable telling that porky. I would gladly own up to the truth if I believed it would deflect the heat off Vivien, but I think revealing that will only make the whole story more salacious and ignite even more interest.

"Pick up the phone, you lazy fucker!" I shout as my call goes to voice mail again. I call him again, and I'm seriously considering chartering a private jet to fly me to Dublin when the prick answers. "About bleeding time!"

"Dillon, it's almost one a.m."

"Do I sound like I give a fucking shit what time it is?" I fill him in quickly, guessing he isn't aware of what's happened because he was in the land of Nod. "I want you to sue that fucking cunt. Take her to the cleaners! I want every fucking penny she got for that interview, and I'm sure that won't be enough to meet the financial obligations of the NDA, so take everything. When we're through, I want her left with nothing. I want her penniless and homeless with only the clothes on her back."

"That's the likely outcome," the solicitor says. "Are you sure you want to follow through? We could threaten to do it, lodge proceedings with the court, and scare her into shutting her mouth."

"Are you fucking deaf?" I roar down the phone. "She already opened her stupid gob. The damage is done, and she will pay the price. Start proceedings, and I want to see them carried through." I hang up before he can say anything else, tossing my phone on the couch as I drag my hands through my hair.

"I approve, and it will send a clear message to the others to keep their mouths shut," Ash says.

Not that they can do any more harm, so it really doesn't matter, but I get the point.

"She did this maliciously to hurt Vivien. She's always hated her, believing she stole you from her."

"Ha." I bark out a laugh. "Vivien couldn't steal something that never belonged to her. Aoife was nothing to me. She's even less now, and she's fucking lucky I live thousands of miles away because right now I actually believe I could commit murder. I want to fucking kill her for doing this to my family."

"Go and get Easton. It's getting late, and you should stick to his routine. I'll check on Vivien after we've finalized the statement."

"Thanks, sis. Love you." I bundle her into a hug, kissing the top of her head.

"I've got your back. Now go get your son."

I'm lying in bed, in Viv's house, unable to sleep, worried about her and Easton, obsessing over how he will take the news. Today has ruined everything. I just feel it in my bones. Vivien only emerged from her room to bathe Easton and put him to bed, but she was giving me the cold shoulder. She wouldn't even speak to Ash though she did talk to her mum on the phone, and Lauren called me after. She told me to give her some space to process it but not to let it go on too long.

I turn onto my side, pulling up photos on my phone, skimming through them with a heavy heart. I knew everything was too perfect. That something was going to happen to burst my happy bubble because that's the pattern of my life. Fuck it. I know I sound like a depressed head, but I can't help it.

Aoife is going to rue the day she crossed me. I fully expect some kind of pleading public message when she discovers I'm suing her, but there is nothing she can say or do that will get me to change my mind. She's a vindictive bitch, and it's time she learned there are consequences for her actions. Why couldn't she just be happy with the money I gave her? I know she used it to buy a house. Has she been stewing all these years, waiting for an opportunity to get back at Viv? All because I didn't fall in love with her?

I spoke to Ro earlier. He offered to go and torch her house. I was tempted to tell him to do it and to ensure she was inside when he set fire to it, but I won't have murder on my conscience. I'd much rather take everything from her—her house, her car, her money, her reputation, poor and all as it is. I've already emailed our label in Dublin and asked them to ensure she is banned from Whelans and other venues around Dublin we still sometimes play at.

I made my feelings known earlier when I posted on social media, and our fans are coming out in support. Aoife had to shut her accounts down after they attacked her in their thousands, and I hope she's gone into hiding, terrified for her life, because it's the least she deserves for what she's tried to do.

If she causes Viv to pull away from me, I don't know what I'll do. Time is running out. We leave in five weeks to go on tour, and I had finally plucked up the courage to ask Viv to come with me. East too. I was planning on asking her this weekend, but that's all shot to hell now.

The door creaks, and I lift my head, expecting to see Easton, but it's Vivien. I sit up, eyeing her carefully as she pads quietly across the room. I watch as she climbs onto the bed and wraps her arms around me.

"I'm sorry, Dillon." Tears pool in her eyes. "I'm so sorry for saying it was your fault. That was a terrible thing to say, and it's not true. It's not your fault. That's all on Aoife. I was just upset and scared and freaking out, but I shouldn't have taken it out on you."

Air whooshes out of my mouth in grateful relief as I pull her onto my lap, circling my arms around her. "I'm sorry I failed you and East, Viv, but I'm going to do my utmost to make it right."

She shakes her head, cupping my face. "You haven't failed us, Dillon. Not at all. And we'll get through this together."

I am so relieved to hear this. She was hysterical earlier, and I was really worried she was going to regress. "Stay with me." I plant a kiss on the top of her head.

"Yes," she says, "but not here. Come with me. I have something to show you."

I'm curious as she leads me out of my bedroom and along the hallway, opening the door to another one of her guest rooms. My eyes widen as I take in the large room with a giant four-poster bed, walk-in closet, seating area with a fire and wall-mounted TV, and an en suite bathroom.

"This is our new room," she explains. "I had renovators in

a month ago to work on it. I got them to come on days when you weren't here because I wanted it to be a surprise." She spins around, holding my hands and peering up at me. "I know you're worried this has made me have doubts. I won't deny I'm really upset over everything and very worried about Easton, but it hasn't changed how I feel about you. I meant it when I told you I was yours." She leans her head on my chest, snaking her arms around my waist. "I love you, and I need you, now more than ever."

"You have me. I'm going nowhere." I scoop her up, cradling her against my chest. After closing the door, I walk to the bed, gently placing her under the covers. I slide in beside her, pulling her back against my chest. My arms go around her automatically because it's as natural as breathing to me. "We have endured considerable challenges to get to this point, and it hasn't broken us or destroyed what we have. Today was a shitshow, and I know you're worried. I'm worried about telling Easton too. I'd rather the timing had been of our choosing, but he'll be okay. He's not losing anything. He's gaining, and if he struggles to understand it, we will be there to comfort him and answer his questions."

CHAPTER 42
DILLON

"I THINK I'm going to be sick." Vivien rubs her stomach, looking pale enough I believe it.

"I'm not feeling so great myself," I truthfully admit, rubbing a hand up and down her back. "But we've got to do this. We can't let him discover the truth any other way."

It hasn't even been twenty-four hours since that bitch of a waitress released her story, and things have escalated to scary levels. I've instructed my US attorney to slap her with a lawsuit too. California's privacy laws are pretty clear, and you can't record someone without their permission. I'll enjoy taking whatever payment she received for selling us out and teaching her a valuable lesson.

A horde of paparazzi, reporters, and TV crews has camped on the road outside the house, making us feel like virtual prisoners. They can't see anything from the road, so we're protected once we stay here. The second we have to leave, it's going to be crazy town. Our publicists are being inundated with requests for interviews. The only positive to come from that is we got agreement already from Oprah's team, and our interview is being lined up for next week.

Social media is exploding with all kinds of wild theories

and #Dillien is trending. Ash is gloating, *a lot*, over that, because she coined our ship name years ago in Dublin.

Reporters have even been bugging my parents, and I'm glad Ro is at home to handle it. He hired a couple of bodyguards to guard their house after a reporter drove right up to their front door, asking for a statement. These people have no morals and no shame.

I confiscated Vivien's phone earlier because she was looking at some of the more lurid headlines and I could see she was twisting herself into even greater knots. She's working hard to keep it together, but the strain is obvious. She had a FaceTime session with her therapist this morning, and I'm seeing that as a positive sign. Lauren and Jon are due home next week from Canada, and I know their presence will help too.

"We can do this." I bring her hand to my lips, kissing her soft skin. "And you said you were planning on telling him after Christmas."

"I was going to talk to you about that last night, before everything went down."

"He's as ready as he will ever be. I know you didn't want it to upset him before Christmas, but it might help him get through it."

"You're right. I just hate being forced to do it today because of that bitch." Her mouth pulls into a grimace, and her eyes burn with anger, like they do every time Aoife's name is mentioned.

"She will regret it. I will make damn sure of that."

"Good." She throws her arms around me, kissing me hard on the lips. "I thought about it after you told me your plans. Briefly, I wondered if we should take the moral high ground and not go after her."

I arch a brow, hoping she didn't decide that because I really want to make Aoife suffer. Her actions have hurt the woman who will one day be my wife, and she has hurt my son.

Neither of us ever wanted to air our private lives in public.

We knew there would come a time when we'd have to admit Easton's parentage, but that should have been at a time of our choosing and a narrative of our choosing. She took those options away from us, and I will never forgive her. I want to make her pay. Maybe I'm a bastard for wanting to go after her, guns blazing, but I don't care what anyone thinks of me.

You come after what's mine, and I'll fucking annihilate you.

"But I guess I'm not as magnanimous as I like to think I am because I want you to throw the book at her, Dillon. Make her pay."

I grab her ass, crushing her to me. "This is why we're so good together, and you can count on it, sweetheart."

We kiss for ages, and it soothes something in both of us. "I love kissing you," she says when we finally break apart.

"I love seeing your lips swollen with my kisses."

She takes my hand, pushing her shoulders back. "Come on. Let's go talk to our son. It's time he knows the truth."

We head out to the memorial garden with Easton because we thought this was the best way to keep Reeve's memory alive while we break the news to him. East is holding each of our hands, and we're swinging him between us. It's a nice day, warmer than usual at this time of year.

"Are we going to talk to Daddy?" Easton asks when we enter the little garden.

"We need to talk to you, and we wanted Daddy close by," Vivien says, looking like she's close to passing out.

I lean in, kissing her brow. "Breathe, Hollywood. We've got this."

I position Easton in between us on the bench, wrapping my arm around them.

"What's up, guys?" East says, and his sass helps to lighten the tension a little.

"We have something important to tell you," I say, "and it concerns your daddy and me."

"Okay." His nose scrunches.

"You remember I told you how babies were made," Vivien says, taking his hand in hers.

"Mommies and daddies kiss and hug, and they make the baby grow in mommy's tummy."

I cough to disguise my chuckle. I know he's only five, and it's the best way of explaining it, but it's fucking funny. Imagine how much the world would be overrun with babies if all it took was some kissing and hugging?

Viv nods. "And you remember how we told you Dillon and I were friends in Dublin?"

"Yup. I know all this." He shakes his head like we're wasting his time, and I ruffle his hair. This little kid slays me in the best ways.

"Your mommy wasn't married to your daddy then. They were just friends while Mommy was my girlfriend."

His brow creases, and he looks confused as his gaze bounces between us.

"Dillon was my boyfriend, and we only found out recently that it was Dillon who put the baby in my tummy."

Easton looks downright confused, and I don't blame him. This is virtually impossible to explain to a five-year-old. I try a different angle. "Reeve was the best daddy, right, buddy?"

"The best in the whole wide world." He stretches his arms out to prove his point, hitting both of us in the stomach.

"And he's still your daddy now even though he's in heaven," Vivien says, taking over when she sees I'm sweating bullets. "Reeve will always be your daddy, Easton." She takes his hands again. "But he didn't put you in my tummy. Dillon did." His brow creases, and the most heartbreaking, vulnerable look appears on his face. "Dillon is your daddy too, Easton."

He looks so lost when he looks up at me, and I tighten my arm around him, moving in closer the same time Vivien does. "You're my daddy?" he whispers, his eyes filling up, and my heart is rupturing behind my rib cage.

Tears pool in my eyes, and I don't try to hold them back

like I usually would. "Yes, buddy. I'm your daddy, and I love you very, very much."

"You are really lucky," Vivien adds, rubbing circles on the back of his hand with her thumb. "You have two amazing daddies. Daddy Reeve is watching over you from heaven, and Daddy Dillon is here to always look after you."

Tears spill down his cheeks, and he leans into Vivien, sobbing against her chest. "I miss my daddy," he says, in between sobs, and pain has a vise grip on my heart. Vivien warned me not to expect too much, and I know he's confused, but I can't help how I feel. Rejection has always been hard for me, and though I know that's not what Easton is doing, the feelings are the same.

Until I snap out of it.

I'm being a selfish prick.

The instant the thought lands in my mind, I wipe my eyes and focus on my son.

This isn't about me.

It's about him.

"It's okay to miss him," Viv says, reaching out to cup my face as our son clings to her. "I miss him too, but Daddy Reeve would want us to be happy, and Daddy Dillon makes us happy, right?"

Easton lifts his head, turning to look at me. Seeing his tearstained blotchy face kills me. He sniffles, staring at me, and it feels like my heart is about to disintegrate. "Uncle Dillon," he says.

"Yeah, buddy." My voice is hoarse, emotion clogging my words as well as my thoughts.

"Do I call you Daddy Dillon now?"

Viv sobs, holding on to me and Easton.

Tears prick the backs of my eyes, and I can scarcely speak over the messy ball of emotion in my throat. "You can call me whatever you want, East."

He thinks about it for a second, and then his hand reaches out, and he curls his fingers around mine. "Daddy Dillon?"

The trusting expression on his face knocks me for six, and I nod because I can't actually form words. This is the culmination of every fantasy I have had since I discovered he was mine. "Can we play on the slides now?"

Easton took it way better than any of us expected, and I'm delighted. There are still moments where I catch him looking a little lost, and I know he's still grappling to understand it all, but he seems to have accepted he has two daddies. I even heard him bragging to one of his little mates when I collected him from school on his last day before his Christmas break.

His mother is a different matter though. Although Vivien sleeps in my arms every night and we're together, in all the ways we can be together, she's emotionally distanced herself from me. From everyone.

The Oprah interview was a bit of a mixed bag. We gave a watered-down version of our story, not going into all the details but giving enough to try to explain the situation in a way that protects Viv. It fostered enormous online debate with camps split evenly down the middle. There are those who are sympathetic to the situation, who understand Viv's position, and wish us well. Most of my fans have been supportive, but there is an element who are jealous and lash out at Viv.

And don't get me started on Reeve's fanbase. They have all turned on Vivien, and the vitriol online is disgusting. I made Ash give me access to my accounts again so I could monitor things. But I had to shut them down before they banned me, because I was not holding back in my replies to the assholes calling my woman a slut, a cheat, and a murderer.

Someone started a petition to have Viv arrested for murdering Reeve, and it had over one hundred thousand signatures. Some of these people are legit lunatics who should be locked up in the nuthouse. How the fuck can anyone accuse a woman of deliberately killing her husband and baby in such a horrific way? They seem to forget she nearly died too.

Fucking assholes. I swear I want to punch the lot of them.

I have my US attorney working overtime, firing off threatening letters to publications and online sites and issuing legal proceedings. My Irish solicitor has begun the process with Aoife, and he's issued more reminders to the other NDA signatories.

The publicists are trying to put a positive spin on our official communications, and Lauren has her IT contact removing shit from the internet on a continuous basis. We have stepped up security and spoken to Easton's school and his friends' parents. There really isn't anything else we can do.

Understandably, it's gotten to Viv, and she's hibernating again. Refusing to leave the house. Going about her day on autopilot, and I can't get through to her. We're all worried, and I'm seriously contemplating quitting the band and pulling out of the tour. I can't leave her like this, and I haven't asked her to come with us either because I know she'll only say no.

Time is running out, and that calls for drastic measures.

On Christmas Eve morning, I decide it's time Dickhead Dillon came out to play. "Get dressed," I tell her when she emerges from our en suite bathroom surrounded by a steamy cloud. I'm fully dressed, sitting on the edge of the bed, waiting to battle her on this. "We're meeting Ash and Jamie and Audrey and Alex, downtown for lunch. Then we're taking Easton ice-skating at the outdoor rink at Santa Monica."

"No, Dillon." She shakes her head, beads of water dancing across her shoulders. "It will be crazy downtown, and I'm sure to get harassed."

"I'm not taking no for an answer, sweetheart." I pull her between my legs, ignoring the almost insurmountable urge to rip her towel off and fuck her until she agrees. "Today is no different than any other day in that regard." I pull her onto my lap and kiss her. "I know you're scared. I know some of the shit that's being said about you is awful. I hate how fucking sexist it is and how they're blaming you for everything. But it's not your fault. You didn't cause the accident. You didn't cheat on Reeve. And you couldn't help falling in love with me because I'm a fucking irresistible sexy bastard."

I flash her one of my trademark grins, encouraged when I see the hint of a smile on her beautiful mouth. "Remember what Meryl has told you. You can't control the media or jerks who post shit online. You can only control how you deal with it." I brush my fingers across her cheek. "I'm not being flippant when I say this. I know it's difficult to just shut it off, but they only have power over you if you let them. The people that matter know the truth. Fuck the rest of them."

I know this is difficult for her. She's been dealing with this kind of scrutiny since she was seventeen. I hate the attention that comes from being in a successful band, but what we endure pales in comparison to what Viv has to handle.

"You're right," she says, surprising the shit out of me. "I don't want this to be like the situation with Reeve. I don't want to end up broken or risk losing what we share." She snakes her hands around my neck. "But it is hard to forget it exists. People have been sending me death threats, Dillon. People actually wish I was dead." Her lower lip wobbles. "It's hard knowing that many people hate me."

"But they don't, sweetheart. They don't know you to hate you. They are projecting all their feelings of low self-worth on to you because it makes them feel better about themselves. This isn't about you. Everyone that knows you loves you. Easton loves you, and I fucking love you more than I ever thought it was possible to love another human being. Can't my love be enough?"

She inhales deeply. "You are so romantic, Dillon. You say the sweetest things."

"I write love songs for a living, Hollywood, and I'm damn fucking good at it. I live and breathe romance." I waggle my brows, grinning.

She rolls her eyes, and I count that as a victory. "I forgot about your ego," she says, standing. "God knows how when it's ever present."

I grab the hem of her towel, whipping it away. "Careful what you say when you're naked, sweetheart." I glance at the clock by the bed. "We have just enough time for me to punish you for daring to mock me." I wink at her, unbuttoning the top button of my jeans as she throws herself at me, wrapping her gorgeous legs around my waist.

Her eyes dilate, and she licks her lips. "Lock the door, and let the punishment begin."

CHAPTER 43

VIVIEN

WE ENJOY a casual lunch with our friends in a contemporary bar and grill in downtown L.A. Ash knows the owner, and he gave us a gorgeous circular table tucked away in a corner of the large stylish room. I'm surprised Alex agreed to come with Audrey, as he's made his feelings clear about Dillon, but he's been civil, and Dillon is behaving himself. Easton is in good spirits, chatting excitedly about Santa coming tonight, and he's looking forward to going ice-skating.

Easton is delighted Jamie and Ash chose to stay in L.A. for Christmas, and he's thrilled everyone is going to my parents' house for dinner tomorrow. I know they are all making the effort because they understand how tough it will be for both of us.

"Thank you for organizing this," I tell Dillon, wrapping my arms around him as he hands the waiter his platinum card to cover the check. "It's exactly what I needed." Yes, people have been gawking at us, but I'm feeling more confident surrounded by my closest friends, and I feel my bravado returning.

"That's my girl," he says, planting a passionate kiss on my lips. "How many fucks do we give, sweetheart?"

"Zero, babe." I rest my head on his shoulder, smiling at Ash across the way. "Zero fucks given."

Alex slides over to me when Dillon takes Easton to the bathroom. "You look happy," he says. "Are you?"

I nod. "I know you don't approve, but he makes me happy, Alex."

"It's not that I don't approve, Viv. I want you to be happy. Both of you. I'm just cautious."

"I get that, Alex, and you're a good friend, but you need to trust that I know what I'm doing. Dillon has been so patient and supportive, and I could not have gotten through this without him. We've chosen to leave the past in the past and concentrate on the present." I place my hands on my lap. "I can't force you to like him, but I hope in time you can learn to at least forgive and forget."

"As long as he does right by you and Easton, I'm sure I will."

I look into his eyes. "This might sound crazy, but I've sensed Reeve around." His eyes widen. "There have been a few occasions where I have felt his presence, and I chose to believe it's his way of approving and encouraging me to live my life. I will always love him, Alex. I will never forget him, and Dillon supports me. He's insisting we keep Reeve's memory alive for Easton, and he has gone out of his way to ensure we never forget what he meant to us."

"That's good to hear, Viv. And I know Reeve would want you to be happy."

Silence engulfs us for a few moments, and I see Dillon and Easton approaching from the corner of my eye.

"Easton loves him. That much is clear."

"They bonded instantly," I admit.

"Then I'm happy for you. Truly, I am." His smile is genuine. "Perhaps when we move back next year, we can try a regular couples' night out—get to know one another and try to let sleeping dogs lie."

"I would really like that." I lean in and kiss his cheek as my boys return to the table.

"Are we ready to go?" Dillon asks, quirking a brow at the sight of Alex sitting beside me. "Someone is super excited to get to the ice rink."

"Me! Me! Me!" Easton jumps up and down before hugging Dillon's legs. "Can we go now, puh-lease, Daddy Dillon."

Dillon chuckles, taking his hand. "Come on, Hollywood, before this little guy explodes."

I slide out of the booth, and Alex follows, high-fiving Easton. "Are you coming too, Uncle Alex?" he asks as Dillon threads his fingers in mine.

"I sure am."

"Awesome." Easton's smile is so wide it threatens to split his face.

"Hey, man. Thanks for inviting us today." Alex jerks his chin in acknowledgement at Dillon, and Audrey and I share a look.

"No problem. Easton wanted all his favorite people here, and Vivien needs to be surrounded by good friends right now."

I squeeze Dillon's arm, beaming up at him. I'm thrilled they are making an effort. I was a little worried things might be strained tomorrow at dinner, but those concerns have flittered away.

We head outside, and I do my best to ignore the finger-pointing, whispering, and the stares. We are walking up the sidewalk, heading toward where our cars are parked, when a woman steps out in front of me, appearing almost out of nowhere. "If it isn't the slut who murdered her husband so she could fuck his brother." Her eyes rake over me in a derisory fashion.

Dillon reacts fast, handing Easton to Jamie before turning around to glare at the woman. He puts his face all up in hers, and I would not like to be on the receiving end of that murderous expression. Camera flashes go off, and I spot a couple of paparazzi on the other side of the road, waiting to cross it. "Want to say that again to my face?" Dillon growls.

"I have no beef with you, and I can see the attraction." She blatantly eye fucks him with a smirk, and a red haze coats my retinas.

I pull Dillon back. "I've got this." I walk right up to the woman, loving the fact I tower over her by at least three or four inches. I enjoy looking down my nose at her. "How dare you approach me when I'm out with my family and hurl your hurtful accusations at me. You don't know me. You think you do, because you've seen comments online and reports on TV, but you know nothing about me. I loved my husband, and I miss him every single day."

She snorts, and I'm tempted to slap her stupid ignorant ass, but a crowd has formed now, and several people have their phones out, recording this. I won't lower myself to her standards, so I keep my shoulders back and my chin up as I ignore her derision and say what I need to say. "I honestly don't care whether you believe me or not, but you should take a long hard look at yourself." I glance over her shoulder to the young boy and girl, hanging back, clearly upset and scared. "What kind of a role model are you as a mother to accost an innocent woman in the street and level unfounded accusations at her? You don't care that your children are trembling with fright. You'd rather have your five seconds of fame. Well, shame on you."

She folds her arms and purses her lips, not paying her children any attention, and I feel for them.

"You're not fit to be a mother, and you have the nerve to throw shade at me? Get a life, you sad bitch. I'm done wasting my time on you." I grab Dillon's hand, pulling him in close. "And if you ever look at my boyfriend like that again, I will punch you in your self-righteous face. Go crawl back under that judgmental rock you came out of." I turn around, lifting one shoulder. "Come on, guys. We've got some ice-skating to do."

"Darling. Come in, come in," Mom says, almost blinding us with her dazzling smile as she steps aside, ushering us into the house. Dad is there too, and we exchange hugs.

"Merry Christmas, Easton." Mom bends down, pulling him into a hug. "Did Santa come?"

"He did, Grandma! And he even brought me a present from my daddy in heaven."

"Wow. That's amazing. I can't wait to hear about all your gifts."

Dad holds out his hand, smiling at his grandson. "I think I saw some under the tree with your name on them."

Easton rushes Dad, almost knocking him over. "Yay! More presents!" He starts tugging Dad down the hallway. "Let's go, Grandpa."

"Don't open them without me," Mom calls after him before reeling me in for another hug. "How are you holding up?"

"I'm okay." Dillon squeezes my hand, and I lean into his side. Truth is, I'm not sure exactly how I feel. I'm missing Reeve and sad he isn't here, but Dillon has gone out of his way to make this day so special already. He showered me with gifts that made me swoon, cry, and blush. I'm wearing some of the lingerie he bought me, having kept the racier stuff, as well as the sex toys, for our private time.

"Is this new?" Mom asks, fingering the pretty diamond bracelet on my wrist.

"It was one of my gifts from Dillon."

Mom smiles at him. "You have good taste. It's exquisite."

"I know." He wears a signature cocky grin, and Mom laughs.

"He also recorded an album of new songs, just for me, and

he gave me this gorgeous printed leather album with the lyrics to his sweetest songs." I smile up at him. "He has spoiled me rotten all morning."

Mom leans in, hugging him, and it brings a tear to my eye. "I have come to expect no less." Her smile is warm as she squeezes his hand, and I almost burst into tears. Knowing my parents have accepted him is honestly the best Christmas present I could receive.

"Merry Christmas, Lauren." Dillon hugs her.

"How is E?"

"He's good. It was Dillon's idea to leave a gift for him from Reeve, and we took him out to the memorial garden to open it after breakfast. He wished his daddy and Lainey a Merry Christmas, and he's been fine since." I was so worried he'd be upset today, but he's taking it in stride.

"Dillon and Jamie were up until four this morning setting up his train set, and we had to practically drag him out of the house to come here." Dillon had his old train set shipped here from Ireland, and he found a guy to spruce it up and another guy to build a wooden base for it. "Dillon designed the set himself, and it's a miniature replica of Ireland with cliffs, mountains, woods, quaint Irish shops, traditional housefronts, surrounded by the sea. There are even a few miniature people scattered around. The guys had to clear out the playroom to assemble it."

"That's wonderful. I can't wait to see it." She loops her arm in mine. "Come in and have a drink before the others get here."

I help Mom in the kitchen while Dillon joins Dad and Easton in the living room after he's opened his gifts from my parents. "I'll need to build an extension to the playroom at this rate," I joke as I sip my mimosa. "Easton has so many new toys."

"As long as he is happy."

"He is."

Mom leans back against the counter, facing me. "I can see

that. I'm glad it's working out for you, Vivien. God knows you deserve every happiness after the year you've endured."

"I'll be glad to ring in the new year," I admit. "And I'm looking forward to the future, but I miss him today."

"You'll miss him every Christmas, darling." She walks to me, giving me a hug. "But this one will be especially hard because it's the very first one you have spent without him. Don't be too hard on yourself, and from what I've seen, Dillon understands."

"He does. He's been amazing. He really has."

"I'm happy to have been proven wrong about him. I saw the video last night, and I'm so proud of you, Vivien. I know it's not easy putting yourself out there, but you can't let these people destroy your happiness. Watching you defend yourself and your family yesterday brought tears to my eyes. You were so dignified."

"Dillon encourages me to be brave, and I didn't hesitate to defend myself."

"He's good for you, and you're different with him. I see you coming to life again and that's all I want for you. It's what Reeve would want too."

Dinner is a lively affair, and Easton is the center of attention. We FaceTime the O'Donoghues, and it's an experience. It's nighttime there, and they have a houseful of family and friends over. Drink is flowing, and they are all in good spirits. Easton is already begging me to take him to Ireland, and if Dillon wasn't leaving to go on tour in ten days, I would suggest we book a trip.

But he is, and I don't want him to go.

"You look like you could use this," Dillon says, coming up alongside me as I stare out the window of my parents' sunroom, looking at the old oak tree that holds so many memories. The others are playing board games with Easton in the living room, and I broke away, needing a few minutes alone. I should have known it wouldn't take Dillon long to find me.

I take the champagne flute from his hand. "Thank you."

He circles his arms around me from behind, and I lean back against his solid chest. "You can talk to me. I know you're missing him."

"This is the very first Christmas I've spent without him. I have lived twenty-five Christmases with him by my side. I feel disconnected without him here." Tears spill down my cheeks because I don't have the energy to hide them anymore. "These last few years, Reeve was actually very quiet at Christmas, and I longed to remove the sad look I always saw on his face."

Dillon brushes my tears away with his thumb. "You mentioned that before. The night in the nursery."

I nod, remembering. "We broke up on Christmas Day, and I know it played on his mind every year." A sob rips from my throat as I think back to that horrible Christmas. No wonder Reeve got upset. "I'm sorry," I whisper, hating to do this to him.

"Don't be sorry, Viv. I always want to hear what you're feeling and thinking." He tightens his arms around me.

I lean back, angling my head to press a soft kiss to his lips. "You love me so well, Dillon, and I feel like you get nothing in return." He must be so sick of my mood swings and my tears. I know I am.

"Are you kidding me? You give me everything just by breathing, Viv." He kisses the tip of my nose. "You made today so special for me. The photo album of Easton with all of your memories and written notes will help me to feel close to both of you on the tour. I can't wait to hang the framed family photo of us over my mantelpiece, and don't get me started on that Bob Dylan Martin D-28. I can't believe you got that for me."

It cost me a small fortune at the charity auction, but it was worth it to see the look of shock and sheer awe on Dillon's face when he realized who it used to belong to.

"But best of all is the gift of my son and this second chance with you."

I spin around in his arms, drying my tears. "I feel so lucky to have you in my life. Thank you for loving me, Dillon."

"Thank you for letting me."

We return to the others, hand in hand, and like always, Dillon has managed to clear the cobwebs from my head and add a smile to my face.

Mention of the tour has my mind churning with ideas. I meant what I said back there. Dillon has given so much of himself, going out of his way to prove his love for me and Easton, and I feel I need to make some grand gesture to let him know how much I appreciate and love him. The perfect idea pops into my head, and a bubble of excitement bursts in my chest. I wish I'd thought of it before, because I'm not sure if I can pull it off on such short notice. I don't want to get Dillon's hopes up if I can't make it happen.

I need to talk to my Irish bestie. If anyone can help me to turn it into reality, it's Aisling O'Donoghue.

CHAPTER 44

VIVIEN

"SEX with you just gets better and better every time," I pant, later that night when we're home in bed, after a second round of fucking. "I'm going to go crazy when you have to leave." I turn on my side, facing him.

He pushes damp strands of hair off my brow. "Why do you think I bought all those sex toys?"

"I'm insisting on nightly video sex."

He cups my cheek. "I'd like to promise I can do that, but things will be fairly hectic on the road, and it might not always be possible."

Unspoken words linger in the space between us as tension bleeds into the air. We have both known this day was coming, but I had purposely put it out of my mind because I was dealing with so much other stuff. But now it's looming, it's all I can think of.

Ash is excited about my plan, and while the deadline is tight, she has agreed to help pull out all the stops to try to make it happen. She agrees we should keep it between us so I can hopefully surprise him with the mother of all surprises.

"You could come you know?" He twirls a strand of my hair around his finger.

"I can't," I blurt, panicked. "You know how important routine is for Easton. He has school, and I think I'm going to return to work in the new year."

"We could hire a tutor, and you're freelance, so you can work anywhere."

"I must be available to attend weekly team meetings in person, and I really don't think the rock and roll lifestyle is one Easton should be around." I avert my eyes because I know I'm a shit liar, and he can probably see right through me.

"I'll quit the band."

"What?" I shriek, sitting up and staring at him like he's just sprouted wings. "You can't quit the band. Especially not at the last minute like this."

He sits up, leaning against the headboard. "I don't want to leave the guys in the lurch, but you and Easton are more important." He threads his fingers through my hair. "I don't want to leave you. The thought of being apart from you makes me feel physically ill."

"You think I want to be separated from you either?"

He shrugs, and that pisses me off. "That was a fucking rhetorical question, Reeve."

He sucks in a sharp gasp, and pained eyes stare back at me. I don't understand what I've said until… "Oh my God." I crawl over to him. "I'm so sorry, Dillon. It was just a slip of the tongue. I didn't mean to upset you." I hope he's not remembering the hospital when I was confused and I thought he was Reeve.

"It's fine," he clips out, looking down at his lap.

"It's not fine. I'm really sorry, baby. Please forgive me." I squeeze his hands, willing him to look at me. I can't believe I slipped up like that. It's unforgivable, and I want to cry because I know I've just wounded him deeply, but he's not blameless either. "It wasn't intentional, Dillon. I was angry because you're discounting my commitment to you. You're acting like you're going to miss me more, but that's bullshit and totally unfair. I will miss you every bit as much as you'll miss me."

"I know. I'm sorry for insinuating you wouldn't. I just don't want to go without you. Please come with me, Viv. We'll find a way to make it work."

"Dillon, I want to, but I think it's best if we stay here," I lie. "Easton will have to get used to you being away for work. He needs to see you go and come back."

"Right." He removes his hand, and a muscle clenches in his jaw.

"We can come visit you on holidays and for weekends. I still have Ree—the private jet."

"Sounds great." He turns on his side, letting me know it's anything but great.

I chew on the inside of my mouth, wondering if I should just tell him. However, if I can't pull it off, he'll only be disappointed, so I decide to say nothing for now.

The next week is strained, and there's a distance between us caused by the elephant in the room. Dillon spends every spare minute when he's not rehearsing with Easton. He still sleeps here, in our bed, by my side, but he might as well be in outer space for all the attention he gives me. He's hurting, and I hate he is, but it will be worth it in the end to see the joy on his face when he realizes what I've done.

Dillon stays at his own house the night before the band is due to leave, and I don't protest as it gives me time to pack up our stuff without him noticing. Ash came through for me in the end, with some support from Mom, and it's happening. I'm so excited, and keeping this from Dillon now is virtually impossible, so it's just as well he hasn't been here much the last twenty-four hours. I haven't told Easton either because he'd never have been able to keep it a secret.

If I had known I could pull it off in time, I would've told Dillon last week and avoided hurting him. But it will all be forgotten in a few hours when Easton and I walk up the steps of the band's private jet and announce we are coming with them.

I bring Easton into my confidence just before Dillon arrives to say goodbye. He's bouncing off the walls with excitement, and I hope he doesn't let the cat out of the bag. At this late stage, I want to keep the surprise until the last moment. However, it backfires spectacularly when Easton says goodbye with a big smiley face and then runs off like it's no big deal that his daddy is leaving for seven months.

Dillon was already in a foul mood, but now he looks like he wants to burn the world down and then do it all over again.

"It seems like no one will miss me," he fumes, shoving his hands in his pockets. "And to think I considered quitting." He shakes his head.

"Dillon, that's not true. You know we're going to miss you."

He barks out a laugh. "Honestly, Vivien? This past week has me questioning everything I thought I knew."

Butterflies swoop into my stomach, but they're not the pleasant kind. "What do you mean?"

"Was I just the Band-Aid, Hollywood? You needed me to help you get over the true love of your life and now you're patched up, you don't need me anymore? Is that it?"

"Please tell me you are not serious right now." He cannot honestly believe that after everything we have been through. All because I said I wouldn't come with him, providing very valid reasons. It doesn't matter that it's not true because the fact he's even saying this shit to me now has me infuriated. How could he even suggest I used him as a temporary fix? He might as well have slapped me in the face. That's how much it stings.

He shrugs. "How else do you expect me to react when you are fucking rejecting me again?!"

"How else do you expect *me* to react when you spring it on me at the last second again?!"

"I was waiting for the right time to ask you, but it doesn't matter. You'll do what you always do. Run to Reeve, except he's not here anymore. He's dead, and I'm still living in his fucking shadow. I'm still second best, and that's all I'll ever be." His vitriol spews from his mouth like the worst sickness, and I stumble back, holding a hand over my mouth, disbelieving what I'm hearing.

"I'll call every night to speak to Easton, and we can make arrangements for the holidays," he says, opening the door of his Land Rover. "As for us, you're off the hook, Hollywood." Hurt is etched all over his face as he looks at me. "I guess I'll see you around."

I'm momentarily frozen in place. What the hell is happening right now? I snap out of it as Dillon fires up the engine, and I force my legs to move, racing toward his car as he takes off. To hell with the surprise. I need to tell him now. But I'm too late. He must see me in the rearview mirror, but he doesn't stop, and I give up chasing after him, standing in utter shock as I watch him leave.

Shock gives way to anger, pretty quickly, and I'm tempted to cancel our plans and tell him to take a hike.

But this is Dillon.

The man who has gone out on a limb for me, time and time again.

I know that was anger and pain talking, and a part of me understands even if I can't fathom how he could throw away what we've painstakingly rebuilt so easily. I know this is the past fucking with his head. How he's equating me telling him no to my rejection in Dublin. But it doesn't make sense because he has never been second best, and I told him that.

"I made a mistake," I tell Ash as Leon drives us to the airport. Easton has his AirPods in, listening to Collateral Damage's new album, because he wants to know all the songs so he can sing along at the side of the stage. I haven't had the heart to tell him yet he'll be wearing soundproof headphones to protect his little ears from damage.

The album released last night, and it shot straight to the

top of the charts. Something Dillon never even mentioned when he showed up.

"Please don't tell me you've changed your mind."

"I haven't. I meant I made a mistake not telling him what I was planning. We agreed there would be no secrets."

"This is different. You wanted to surprise him."

"Well, he's gonna be surprised all right. Especially when he just broke up with me."

"What?" she screeches in my ear.

I tell her how it all went down.

"He is such a dumbass. I'm going to kick him in the nuts when we get to the airport." I hear muffled talking in the background, and I'm assuming it's Jamie. Ro, Conor, and Dillon were making their own way to the private airfield where the band's private jet is waiting to take them to Texas to board their tour bus.

"I wanted to make a grand gesture, to show him how much he means to me, and I've ended up achieving the opposite result. And now I'm fucking pissed that he could say those things to me and dismiss what we have just like that, even if I know he's lashing out because he's hurt."

"I thought you guys had moved beyond this."

"So did I, but it appears your brother is still harboring doubts and comparing himself to Reeve. I didn't help the situation when I accidentally called him Reeve on Christmas night."

"You're only human, babe, and he knows you didn't mean it." There is more muffled conversation, and then she says, "We just arrived. I'll try not to punch the idiot before you get here."

"Traffic is shit, but we should still make it in time. I'll see you soon."

"But I wanna get on the plane now," East whines as we pull up alongside the band's jet.

"I need to talk to Daddy Dillon first, but I will come and get you as soon as we're ready. Watch a movie, or listen to your daddy's album again, or you could color," I add, pulling the box of coloring pencils and thick coloring book from the back of the seat where I keep an emergency supply.

He pouts but sits back in his booster seat, and I'm glad he's decided not to argue further. I'm in no mood to deal with *two* grumpy boys. "I shouldn't be too long," I tell Leon.

"I'll keep an eye on Easton. Go fix things with your man." He smothers a grin, and I narrow my eyes at him. Of course, Leon would have to be outside earlier when we had our fight.

I climb out, wiping my hands down the front of my skinny jeans, thrusting my shoulders back as I walk on high heels toward the plane. I'm wearing a white silk blouse under a formfitting black jacket, and a polka-dot chiffon scarf is artfully wrapped around my neck. My hair is pulled back off my face in a sleek ponytail, and I paid extra attention to my makeup.

I'm feeling confident and only slightly murderous when I walk up the steps and enter the plane.

The interior is luxurious, as I was expecting, with twelve leather seats, six on either side. Jamie and Ash are sitting side by side, facing Conor, while Ro and Dillon are sitting on the other side of the plane, facing each other. All eyes are on me. Ash and Jamie grin. Conor looks stoned already, and Ro looks confused.

Dillon smirks, leaning back in his chair with one leg crossed over his knee. "You're an asshole," I hiss, realizing this was all part of *his* plan. "I really want to slap you, but I don't condone violence." I walk closer to where he's sitting.

"Unless it's Aoife." Jamie throws it out there. "I bet you'd give her a few slaps."

I eyeball Jamie. "Truth," Ash and I say together.

"Put the dickhead out of his misery," she adds. "He's unbearable."

I don't doubt it because I know Dillon's hurt was real even if this was part of his game plan. His truths were mixed in with the bullshit, but he wanted me to chase him. "What if I hadn't come?"

"I would have quit the tour," he says, without hesitation, sitting upright and losing the grin.

Shocked faces and angry words litter the air.

I turn to his bandmates. "He's being an ass. Ignore him. I would not have let him quit." I face Dillon, crossing my arms over my chest. I'm still pissed at him. "You are the hardest person in the world to surprise."

Crease lines appear on his brow. "What do you mean?"

"I was planning to come all along, although the idea only came to me on Christmas Day. I didn't say anything because I didn't know if I could buy another tour bus and get it to Texas on time or if I could hire a tutor for Easton on such short notice."

I was less concerned about the latter. As long as the school was okay with me pulling Easton out, I knew I'd find a suitable tutor even if it was while we were on the road. And I can always homeschool him if I have to. "I wanted to surprise you. This was going to be my grand gesture of love, but you fucking ruined it all, and now, frankly, I'm pretty pissed."

"Sweetheart." He stands, moving over to me.

"Don't think your sweet talking will get you out of this hole you've dug."

"I was thinking my cock would do the trick." He waggles his brows as Ash makes a gagging sound behind us.

"Always lowering the tone." I shake my head, softening as his arms go around my waist. I let my arms drop to my sides.

"You bought us a bus?"

"Yes. There wasn't enough room on one bus for all of us, and I wanted us to be a family."

I also didn't want Easton around Conor and Ronan. They

are both single, and I know they'll be entertaining groupies on the bus. Easton does not need to see that, and I'm sure they don't want Dillon's girlfriend and son raining on their parade. Separate buses are the only way this will work.

"Leon is coming with us too." Ash assured me they have plenty of security on tour, but Easton is familiar with Leon, and I want to make this transition as easy as possible for our son. I know he's excited, but this is a big adjustment for both of us.

"You're really coming on tour?" His eyes are bursting with happiness. "The whole tour?"

"Yes, dumbass," Ash says.

"We are, even though you might not deserve it after the shit you said to me earlier."

"I didn't mean to say all of that. I got carried away in the moment." He grips my waist harder, pulling me in to his body. "I'm sorry."

"I'm not letting you off the hook that easily, and I have something I need to say." I cup his face in my hands. "How can you think you are second best? I have told you time and time again it wasn't a competition, but the truth is, I chose you, Dillon. I chose *you*." I let that truth settle for a second before continuing. "But you didn't choose me. All you had to do was come to the airport and stop me from getting on that plane. I told you that in my letter, but still you didn't come." Movement in my peripheral vision distracts me a little, but I stay focused on Dillon, watching the frown appear on his brow.

"What are you talking about? What letter?"

"The letter I wrote you the night I left Ireland. I put it through your mailbox."

He frowns. "I didn't see any letter. I didn't get it."

My eyes startle wide. "Oh my God. This explains so much. I couldn't understand how you could write those hateful lyrics about me when the ball had been in your court. I waited till the very last second to board the plane, praying you would show up, but you didn't." And of course, now I know he tried to come after me, but Reeve deleted his calls, leading me to believe Dillon never truly cared for me.

"That fucking bitch!" Ash jumps up, eyes burning. "Aoife was there that night. That bitch must have taken it."

"She didn't," Ronan says, and I swing my gaze on him as Dillon turns around. Ro wets his lips, looking nervous as he looks us straight in the eyes. "Aoife didn't take the letter. I did. I threw it in the bin before Dillon had a chance to see it."

CHAPTER 45
VIVIEN

SHOCKED SILENCE FILTERS through the cabin. Ronan drags his hands through his hair as he stands. "I'm really sorry I did it. I have felt enormous guilt for years, but it was worse when we found out about Easton. Especially now I'm a father."

"Why did you do it?" I ask, circling my arms around Dillon's waist because I can tell he's on the verge of doing something he'll regret.

Ro lifts his eyes to his brother's. "I knew you were in love with her, and I could see it on your face. I knew you were ready to quit the band for her."

Dillon sneers. "Pull the other one, brother. You always had the hots for her. Admit you were jealous."

He vigorously shakes his head. "I'll admit I was jealous when you first hooked up, but I got over it. That wasn't the reason." His Adam's apple jumps in his throat. "We were so close to making it, and the band would never have gotten signed without you. You're the star, Dillon. You always have been. I couldn't let you throw it all away."

"That wasn't your decision to make, Ro," Dillon grits out. His body is visibly shaking with rage.

"I was young and dumb. I knew you loved her, but I didn't know it was forever love. I thought you'd get over her, especially once we made it big and there were women throwing themselves at you. But I was wrong. I've had to watch you suffer and press the self-destruct button, knowing it was all my fault."

"Why didn't you fess up?" Ash asks.

Ronan rolls his neck from side to side. "I wanted to, but the longer it went on, the harder it got. Then Vivien married Reeve, and I knew there was no undoing the damage."

"You're a fucking asshole," Dillon snaps. "You should've told me when I told you Easton was my son. That was the time to come clean."

"I wanted to, but I couldn't. I was going through my own shit, and—"

"You're a fucking selfish prick!" Dillon lunges for Ronan, grabbing him by the shirt and shoving him against the side of the plane. "I lost five years with my son!" he yells. "Years I could've been around for if I had gotten Vivien's letter and stopped her from getting on that plane. I will never forgive you for this." He shoves him. "Never."

"Stop." I step in between them, pushing them apart. "What you did was selfish and manipulative," I tell Ronan, "but I understand your motivations, and you *were* young."

"That doesn't excuse him," Dillon snaps.

I turn to face my boyfriend. "No, it doesn't, but Ronan is the one who will have to live with that for the rest of his life." My features soften, and I let Ro go, sliding both hands up Dillon's chest. "I could just as easily say this is my fault for not giving the letter to Ash to deliver to you or handing it to you myself."

"Why didn't you?" Ash asks.

I glance between her and Dillon. "I mean no offense, Ash, but I wanted Dillon to make the decision free of interference and influence. If he came to stop me from getting on that plane, I needed to know it was solely his choice because I was prepared to completely change my life for him, and I needed to know he was all in."

She nods slowly. "That makes sense."

"Why did you put it through the letter box?" Dillon says. "Why not hand it to me personally?"

I arch a brow. "You honestly have to ask me that?" He looks confused. Typical man. "I thought Aoife was in there with you, and I couldn't handle another rejection. I told you I loved you in the bar, and you acted like it meant nothing. I was broken-hearted, Dillon, and I couldn't face seeing you with her again."

He bobs his head. "It was natural to assume that, except she wasn't with me."

"I know that now, but I didn't back then."

"God, it's all so tragic." Ash shakes her head. "All these little things conspired to keep you apart."

"I know, but what's the point in looking back? We can't change the past." I cup one side of Dillon's face. "The truth is, we don't know what would've happened if you'd gotten that letter. Maybe you would have come after me, or maybe you were too drunk and you still would've gotten on that plane the next day and everything would have played out as it did."

"Or maybe I would have fought harder for you, knowing you had chosen me."

"But would you?" I peer deep into his eyes. "I hurt you by running straight back to Reeve. That hurt would still have been there."

A muscle pops in his jaw. "I would've come after you and stopped you getting on the plane. That would have stopped everything from happening."

"I'm not so sure, Dil." Ash gets up, crossing to us. "You were stoned, drunk and incoherent, and so full of anger and bitterness. I would have encouraged you to go after her, but honestly, I think you're too stubborn to have made that call until you had sobered up."

"The point is, it doesn't matter now." I can't think like that because it would be like saying if things had happened differently then Reeve would still be alive and maybe Lainey would never have existed, and I can't think of alternative realities when I have battled so hard for this current one.

"How can you say that?" Dillon cries, pinning me with bloodshot eyes. "I lost years with East. Years I might not have lost if I'd been given your letter."

My heart aches for him, and I feel his pain. "We can't turn back the clock, and dwelling on all the what-ifs has gotten us nowhere in the past. We have all made mistakes, which contributed to the situation, but we are here now, in the right place, united as a family. That's what matters most. That's what we should focus on." I kiss him softly. "I know you're angry and you're hurt. I can't tell you how to react to it. I can't tell you to forgive your brother. I *can* tell you what I think, which is we've suffered enough from the mistakes of the past. We're dangerously close to undoing all the progress we've both made."

"What are you saying, Viv?"

"I'm asking you to look inside yourself and find it in your heart to forgive your brother. We need to look to the future, not the past. You're going on tour. You need to be united. Your family forgave you for the secrets you hid and the lies you told. It should end here." The situation is not the same. I know that. But we have to draw a line somewhere.

"I can't even look at him right now."

I hug him. "You need time to process and time to calm down."

"How are you so calm? So reasonable?"

"It's actually given me closure. I always thought you'd received that letter and didn't care. Plus, I'm tired of hating and hurting and feeling sad. This is a new year, and I want it to be a fresh start."

The pilot pops his head out then. "We'll be taking off in fifteen minutes."

"We need to get E." I turn to walk toward the exit, but Dillon reaches out his arm to stop me.

"Allow me." Some of the tension lifts from his shoulders and erases from his face.

I kiss him. "Go get our son. He's incredibly excited. He's been listening to your new album in the car. He wants to learn all the songs so he can sing along with you when you're on stage."

"Oh God." Ash gulps, slapping a hand over her chest. "I love that little human so fucking much. Thank fuck, he takes after you and not dumbass over there." I wouldn't be too sure about that, at all, but I smile anyway because Ash always brings a smile to my face.

Dillon flips her the bird as he stalks to the entrance and disappears outside.

"Thanks, Viv," Ronan says in a quiet voice.

I drop into the seat beside him. "Don't thank me yet. You know how stubborn your brother is, and he might not ever be able to forgive you." I feel I need to prepare Ronan for that possibility. "I know Dillon disappointed all of you when he concealed so much, but those secrets didn't hurt any of you. Mostly, he hurt himself."

"Whereas, what I did directly hurt my brother." He hangs his head. "I'm so ashamed."

"I can see that." I pat his arm.

"I'm unbelievably sorry for my actions, Vivien. If I could go back, I would never have destroyed the letter."

"I believe you, and I forgive you." At least it explains why he's had trouble looking me in the eye. He stares at me now.

"You do?"

I nod, and I'm proud of myself. I know forgiving him is the right thing to do, but I'm not saying it to keep the peace. I genuinely mean it, and it hasn't been difficult for me to reach this decision. It's completely different for Dillon though, and it will take him some time. I hope, for everyone's sake, they can find a way to move past this. "You were a great friend to me in

Ireland, Ronan. I know you didn't deliberately set out to hurt me."

He hugs me, and there are tears in his eyes.

"Hands off my woman," the caveman says as he reenters the plane carrying a little wriggly live wire in his arms.

Ro jerks back as if he's been electrocuted.

"Auntie Ash!" Easton exclaims, sliding down Dillon's body. "I'm coming on tour!"

"I heard, little munchkin." She high-fives him. "We are going to have so much fun."

"Mommy!" he jumps on my lap. "Daddy says I can play guitar on stage with him!"

I look at Dillon through hooded eyes. That is something we really should have discussed together, but I'll give him a free pass. "That is awesome."

"Not every night, buddy," Dillon says, scooping him up and putting him in the seat across from Ronan. "And we'll have to practice."

"Of course." East looks at him like he's being ridiculous.

"Swap with me," Ash says, looking over at Ronan, and he silently gets up, taking her seat. She drops down beside me while Dillon settles into the seat beside Easton. They are whispering with their heads huddled, plotting trouble, most likely.

"Do you ever feel like you live in a real-life soap opera?" she asks, as Leon climbs on board the plane.

"All the freaking time."

"The luggage is safely on board, Vivien," my bodyguard informs me.

"Thank you."

"Make yourself comfortable, Leon," Ash says, pointing at the spare seats behind Jamie and Conor.

The door shuts as the flight attendant appears, advising us to buckle our seat belts and prepare for takeoff.

Easton chatters nonstop until he falls asleep, lulled by the motion of the plane. Dillon reclines his seat and drapes a blanket over him, before offering me his hand. "Can we talk?"

he whispers, jerking his head toward the two empty seats behind us.

"I'll watch the treasure," Ash says, lifting her head from her book.

We resituate ourselves in the seats. Leon is across from us, napping, and the others all have their AirPods in.

"I'm sorry for being a jackass this morning," he says, threading his fingers through mine.

"It's okay. I'm well acquainted with your assholish gene."

He grabs my face, kissing me passionately. "In case you weren't aware, I'm over the fucking moon you're coming on tour with me."

"I'm excited."

"I love you."

"I love you too."

"I have a favor to ask," I say, twisting in the seat to face him. "I've decided I would like to get up on stage with you, once, and sing."

His eyes pop wide. "What's brought this on?"

"You. You've encouraged me to overcome my fears. I have always been the truest sense of myself with you. I want to do this. I want to prove to myself that I'm the only one who is in control of my life. I want to be brave and put myself out there knowing how some will perceive it."

"You should sing 'She Moved Through the Fair.' That will bring the most critical of cynics to their knees."

I very much doubt that. "That's an odd choice for a rock concert."

"It's our show, and if anyone dares to question me, I'll punch their lights out."

"Me too," Ash says from overhead. We both look up. "I'll square it with the label."

"Fuck off and mind your own business," Dillon says, but there's no heat in his words. "This is a private conversation."

"There is no such thing as privacy on tour," she retorts.

"Not for you." He grins smugly, sliding his arm around my shoulders. "We've got our own bus."

She flips him the bird before sliding back into her seat as Jamie comes over to join her.

"Are you mad I didn't tell you?" I ask, wanting to clear the air before we step foot on said bus.

"I understand why you didn't, but it raised old fears to the surface. And I reverted to default mode."

"You can't test the people you love, Dillon. What you did earlier was emotional manipulation, just like those early days in Ireland. We can't go there again. We're supposed to be older and wiser."

"You're right, and I've spoken about it in therapy. Maybe I need to do a few more sessions."

"I think that would be a good idea." I wet my lips. I'm slightly nervous to say this, but we've got to be honest with one another, and this needs to be said. "I still think you're triggered by Reeve, a little, and we need to discuss that and properly move past it. Would you be open to couples therapy? Meryl mentioned it to me before, and I'm sure she'd be open to some video sessions while we're on the road."

"I am willing to do whatever it takes to make this work and to make you happy. Line it up, and I'm there."

"Thank you." I peck his lips, resting my head on his shoulder.

He twists my ponytail around his fist. "We fucked up again, huh?"

"We're going to fuck up occasionally, Dillon. We're only human, and well, you're you." My lips twitch, but I fight the urge to laugh. "And I'm me. We're going to argue and not see eye to eye on things, and that's okay as long as we communicate. I was wrong not to tell you. I should've realized it would remind you of the past and cause you to doubt us." He loosens his hold on my hair, and I lift my head, resting my hands on his shoulders. "I just wanted to do something big. You have done so much for me, and I wanted to give something back. I wanted to see the shock and excitement on your face when we showed up."

"We'll do better next time we reach a stumbling block."

"We will because you're stuck with me, in a confined space, for the next seven months." In a way, I'm glad this happened. It has reminded us of what's important and shown us we are not infallible. We have worked hard to get to this point, but that doesn't mean it will be smooth sailing going forward. All relationships require effort and investment. What matters is that we love each other and we're committed to making this work, and that is half the battle.

CHAPTER 46

DILLON

THE PAST SEVEN MONTHS HAS, hands down, been the best seven months of my life. This tour has been the best touring experience of my career. And it's all thanks to Vivien and Easton. Living on the bus with them has been amazing, and we're as close as we can be.

Easton has taken to life on the road like a pro.

Seeing his obvious joy at being a part of my world has meant everything to me. During the day, when we're sleeping and later rehearsing, he does the tourist thing with Ash and Vivien after his schoolwork is done. They've managed to squeeze in tons of activities in the various cities we've visited, and we have mountains of photos for new albums when we get home.

Vivien rejoined social media, and she's amassed quite a loyal following who go crazy for the daily posts and pics she shares. Being on the road has done wonders for her anxiety. She no longer cares what people say about her, and the interest in us has eased off from the intrusive levels of the early days.

She conquered her fears and sang on stage with me in Ohio. It was just me on guitar and her singing to a packed stadium. There wasn't a peep from the audience as she delivered the haunting lyrics with so much emotion I know it came straight from her soul. They were as hypnotized as me, and at the end, they gave her a standing ovation.

I was so fucking proud of her.

Videos of her performing were all over social media the next day, and it garnered a lot of good will.

Tonight is our last night on the US tour, and it's extra special because Easton is joining us on stage. This will be his first time up here, and I'm stoked to be accompanied by my son on guitar. Originally, I had planned on letting him join us more often. Until Viv and I talked about it and she explained her concerns, which were all valid. She doesn't want him living under a media glare, and she's done her best to protect him over the years. Kidnapping is also a very real worry.

I thought East would throw a fit, but he's happy getting to jam with us on stage during rehearsal, and now he's getting his wish to play before a packed stadium. We've been practicing like crazy to get this performance right, and his perseverance, talent, and determination have impressed me to no end.

Vivien doesn't know I'm about to embarrass the shit out of her, but she's going to find out in a couple of minutes.

"Are you ready to hear our new single, Las Vegas?" I shout into the mic, grinning at the deafening roar of approval from the massive crowd. I pace across the front of the stage, wiping my sweaty brow with the back of my arm. "This is an extra special performance tonight because we have an extra special guitarist joining us."

I turn around, grinning when I spot East standing in the wings with Vivien. We planned this together because I need to get her out on this stage. I want to sing the words to her so she has no doubt how much I love her, and then later tonight, I'm going to propose. "Please welcome my son, Easton, to the stage," I shout, facing him as the crowd whoops and hollers.

Easton struts across the stage like he owns it, and Jamie

cracks up laughing at his swagger. He's holding Vivien's hand, beaming proudly at me for playing his part. "Thanks, buddy." I lean down, and we do our special handshake with our elbows and our arms. The crowd goes nuts because he's the cutest fucking kid. He turned six in May, and we threw a special party for him backstage at the venue in DC.

"What's going on?" Viv mouths, looking a little nervous.

"Stay put," I tell her, smirking.

Helping Easton up onto his stool, I fix his guitar around him, and then I reposition his mic so it's at the right level. "Hellooooo, Las Vegas," he booms into the mic, and Jamie almost pisses his pants. Ro nearly falls off his stool he's laughing so hard. Conor is as zoned out as ever. Vivien and I exchange smiles as the crowd screams for our little wannabe rock star.

"I asked my son to help me tonight because this is the first time I'm singing this song in public, and as it's about the love of my life, I wanted to make it personal by singing it to her."

Oohs and aahs echo around the giant stadium, as one of the crew rushes out with a high-backed stool for Vivien.

Vivien's eyes pop wide as I walk toward her. I pull her flush against me. "In case you're confused, that means you." She slaps my chest as laughter wafts around the large arena. I spin her around to the front of the stage, wrapping my arm around her waist. She's wearing a short, tight strapless black leather dress that has panels cut out at the waist and skyscraper heels that make her slim legs look even longer. I'm on a permanent horn looking at her. "How hot does my woman look tonight?" I ask the crowd. A chorus of catcalls and wolf whistles rings out, and I flash the audience a trademark grin.

"You are so dead," Vivien says, turning around to look at me.

Discreetly, I move the mic closer. "I can't hear you," I mouth.

"I said you are so dead." Her statement projects through the mic, bouncing around the venue, and everyone laughs.

LET ME LOVE YOU

"That means she wants me," I tell them, winking. "This is our version of foreplay."

"Jesus, Dillon!" she shrieks, gesturing toward Easton.

"Shit." I had almost forgotten he was there.

"A dollar for the cuss jar, Daddy Dillon!"

After the laughter has died down this time, I turn her around in my arms. "I love you." Before she has a chance to reply, I lower her back a little and kiss her hard.

"That is just gross, Daddy," Easton says into the mic.

I pull Vivien upright, both of us laughing along with the audience.

"He is such a carbon copy of you," Vivien says into my ear.

"I'll take that as a compliment," I reply into hers.

"I meant it as one." She smiles, and I'm relieved I'm not in the doghouse.

Tucking her under my arm, I maneuver us so we're facing the crowd again. "This woman is the love of my life and the only woman who has ever owned my heart. Every love song I've written from the time I've met her has been about her. She completes me in every way possible."

I hope someone records this and puts it online, and I hope Aoife sees it. Last I heard, she is back living with her folks after she lost everything in court. She had to liquidate all her assets, and she still fell short. She'll be paying us back every year for the rest of her life, and it will be a constant reminder of all she's lost thanks to her jealousy and her greed.

I stand in front of Vivien, taking her hand and bringing it to my mouth. My lips linger on her skin as I drink her in, my heart consumed with love for her. "I only ever want to exist with you, Vivien Grace. This song is for you."

The crowd swoons, and I know once we start the song I'll have them eating out of my hand.

I lift Vivien up onto her stool, planting another kiss on her lips before rejoining my son. East is sitting, so I've chosen to do the same. This song is a little different than most of our stuff, and it lends itself to this acoustic version. I put my lips to the mic, speaking to the crowd. "This is 'Exist with You.'"

I keep my eyes locked on Vivien as I sing the words that have come directly from my soul. A deathly hush has settled over the crowd as they listen. Easton messes up a couple of times, but he catches up, and I'm so freaking proud of him. To deliver a performance like he's just done at six years of age proves this little guy is destined to belong on stage. Whether it's a rock stage or a theater stage remains to be seen.

Vivien is crying by the time we finish to massive applause from the audience. Scooping Easton into my arms, I walk toward her as she rushes across the stage, throwing her arms around us. "Dillon," she croaks. "That was so beautiful." She kisses me before turning her attention to East. "I am so proud of you, Easton. You were awesome! You are every bit as talented as your daddy." She dots kisses all over his face, and he beams, delighted with her praise and high off his performance.

"We're going to wrap this up now," I say, placing Easton on his feet. "Go wait with Ash." I kiss her again because I can't get enough of her tonight. I crouch down to Easton, opening my arms, and he gives me a massive hug. "You did amazing, buddy. I couldn't be prouder of you."

"I loved it, Daddy! Can I do it again?"

I straighten up, chuckling. "The tour is over tonight, and we're going home soon, but there will be more tours and more opportunities to join us, I promise." I ruffle his hair. "Time to go with Mommy."

He steps around me and bows to the audience, and there's a giant collective swoon from all the female fans.

Jamie approaches, grinning. "You are going to be in so much trouble with this little dude when he gets older. He'd charm the knickers off a nun."

LET ME LOVE YOU

"Dillon." Vivien pushes my shoulders, looking up at the corner of the elevator. "There are cameras."

"Don't fucking care," I say, returning my lips to her neck and continuing my upward journey under her dress.

She slaps my hands away. "Have patience. We're almost at our suite."

"Have you seen yourself tonight?" I ask, wrapping my arms around her waist, burying my head in her shoulder. "You're sex on legs, sweetheart, and I've been dying to fuck you from the second you walked out on that stage."

"Is that why you arranged a sleepover for East in Jamie and Ash's suite?"

"It's our last night," I murmur, grazing my teeth along her neck as the elevator comes to a stop. "I want to make the most of it."

We crash into the penthouse, knocking over shit as we devour each other while tearing our clothes off. "Fuck, Hollywood. I need inside you right now."

"I'm ready for you, rock star," she pants, peeling her knickers off and standing before me in all her naked glory. "You're not the only one who's been horny all night." She flings herself at me as I kick my boxers away, grabbing a condom from the pocket of my jeans. "Seeing you on that stage turns me on like you wouldn't believe, and you definitely deserve a reward for that song." I lift her up, and her legs circle my waist as tears pool in her eyes. "It was beautiful, Dillon. I felt every word deep in my soul."

"Good," I growl, nipping at her earlobe as I walk us toward the floor-to-ceiling window. "Because every word was birthed from my soul." I kiss her hard as I slam her against the window, rocking my pelvis against her, moaning into her mouth at the feel of her hot flesh grazing my hard length.

"Fuck me, Dillon. Fuck me really hard. I want to walk around tomorrow feeling that burn for you."

I set her down to roll on a condom before lifting her again

and positioning her on my dick. Holding my shoulders, she lowers herself down my length, and we both hiss when she's fully seated. "Love you." I thrust into her, and her head goes back.

"Love you too, baby. So, so much."

She clings to me as I pound into her, holding her up with my arms as I brace her against the window, but I can't drive hard enough in this position, and I need to be balls deep in my woman tonight. Setting her down, I flip her around so her naked front is up against the window.

"What if someone sees?" she asks, jutting her ass up and spreading her legs.

"We're up high enough it's unlikely, but do you honestly care?" Vivien is more carefree and abandoned now, and she has moved past a lot of her fears, but I will never do anything to make her uncomfortable. If she doesn't like this, we'll move away from the window.

She glances over her shoulder at me, biting down on her lower lip. A grin graces her gorgeous mouth. "Nope." Her grin expands. "Zero fucks given." She wiggles her ass as I line my cock up at the entrance to her pussy. "Rock my world, babe."

I slam into her in one thrust and fuck the shit out of her, pressed up against the window, and the thrill of potential discovery only heightens our arousal.

After, we head to the hot tub, which is positioned on a balcony off the bedroom, and we drink champagne while we relax, talk, and kiss. It's blissful, but our night is only getting started, even if it's already past midnight.

"I have a surprise," I tell her when we've showered and dressed. She's wearing a gorgeous red silk negligee, and I'm in sweats with the ring box concealed in the pocket. I wrap my hand around hers, reeling her into my chest. I stare into her eyes before kissing her softly. "Want to sleep under the stars with me, Vivien Grace?"

Her eyes pop wide. "What have you done?"

"Come and see." I keep a hold of her hand as I guide her up to the rooftop terrace.

A gasp of delight escapes her lips, as bile travels up my throat. I haven't been nervous to do this until right now. What if she says no? What if it's too soon? What if she never wants to remarry? It's not like we've discussed it beyond the odd throwaway remark.

"Dillon, this is beautiful." Her gaze takes in the view. Softly flickering candles cover the perimeter of the terrace, but the pièce de résistance is the small marquee in the center of the space. Vivien walks toward it, gasping again when she sees the bed strewn with white rose petals and lavender rose petals. A side table houses a bucket with chilled champagne, two glasses, and a bowl of chocolate strawberries. She throws her arms around me, hugging me tight. "Have I told you how much I love romantic Dillon?"

"Maybe a time or two," I tease.

I step away from her and drop to one knee. My heart is pounding, and my palms are sweaty. I have never been more terrified than I am at this moment.

Vivien clasps a hand over her mouth, and her eyes well up.

"From the moment I met you, I knew you were the only woman for me. Even when I tried to deny you my heart, it was a hopeless endeavor because it was impossible not to fall in love with you. You are everything I never dared to dream of, and I loved you before I even knew you existed. It was always meant to be you and me, Vivien. I cannot exist in a world without you. I know what it's like to lose you, and I never want to experience that again. I love you, and I love Easton, and I want to spend the rest of my life proving that over and over."

Tears are streaming down her face, but she doesn't look like she's going to say no. Yet this woman has been unpredictable before. My hands are shaking as I remove the box and pop the lid holding the ring out to her. "Let me love you forever, Vivien." I'm fighting tears now too. "Marry me."

She sinks to her knees in front of me, laughing amid her

tears. "Yes, Dillon. A thousand times yes. I can't wait to marry you."

CHAPTER 47
DILLON

"I'M BETTING Viv didn't think accepting your proposal meant she'd be getting married five days later," Jamie jokes as we stand at the top of the small aisle in the chapel we booked for our wedding ceremony.

"She said she couldn't wait to marry me," I reply, smiling as my parents arrive the same time as Vivien's.

"I'm sure she didn't mean it literally."

I glare at Jamie. "You're the worst fucking best man in history. You're supposed to be calming my nerves not making out like I bullied my fiancée into a rush wedding."

Jamie chuckles. "You are so on edge."

"Don't tell me you weren't the same?"

After Vivien and I announced the good news to our friends and family the next morning, Jamie and Ash admitted they had gotten married last year when they were on vacation in Mexico. I couldn't believe Ash had kept that a secret or that my best mate hadn't told me. They explained they did it on the spur-of-the-moment, and they wanted to enjoy some time as a married couple before anyone knew and the press found out. I'm not mad, just gobsmacked my sister managed to keep it a secret for so long.

"Fact," Jamie agrees. "And I'm only yanking your chain. Vivien loves you. God knows why, but she'll be here."

I elbow my only groomsman in the ribs before I step away to welcome both sets of parents.

Vivien was more than happy when I suggested we stay in Vegas and tie the knot this week. Easton isn't back to school until next week, so there was no immediate rush to head back to L.A. She had a big wedding the last time she got married, and she told me she loved the idea of a small private affair with just our close friends and family. It was a bit of a tight timeline getting my family here from Ireland, but we pulled it off.

Ash, Vivien, and the hotel manager have been pulling long days organizing everything. Honestly, I would have eloped and married her in my jeans with just Easton, Ash, and the band there, but Vivien had a few requests, and I can never deny her anything.

She wanted her dad to give her away.

She wanted both families here.

And she wanted to wear a wedding dress and me to wear a monkey suit.

So, here I am, waiting in a chapel in Las Vegas in a black Prada suit with a black shirt and white tie, shitting bricks because my idiot best man has planted stupid doubts in my mind.

Jamie, Ash, and Audrey are the only other members of the bridal party, along with Easton, because we wanted to keep it low-key.

Before, I would probably have asked Ronan too, but things aren't the same between us. I managed to sidestep my feelings so we could get through the tour, and apart from that betrayal, he's been a good brother. But I can't forget the years I lost with Easton and the part he played. In time, I think I'll get to a place where I can forgive him, but I doubt our relationship will ever be how it once was.

"You look so handsome, Dillon." Ma yanks me down into her arms. "And I'm so happy for you."

"Thanks, Ma."

Dad slaps me on the back. "Looking dapper, son."

"Thanks for being here. Where is everyone else?"

"They are getting pictures outside, but they'll be in in a minute," Ma explains. "I'll be having more words with you and my daughter after the ceremony," she says over my head as Jamie approaches. She let rip at the two of them last night at dinner, but it seems she didn't get it all off her chest.

"You can't still be mad, Cath? You should be happy you got someone to take that wild woman off your hands."

Ma grabs him by the shirt, pulling him into a hug. "C'mere, you scoundrel, and don't be talking about my daughter like that."

"You know I love the fucking bones of her, and I'll take the best care of her."

"Suck-up," I mouth.

Jamie flips me the bird, and I spot Lauren smirking as she takes it all in. She was at dinner last night with the entire clan, so she knows what we're like by now. The two mums get on famously, and Viv's dad even managed to coax my dad into a discussion, which is a miracle in itself because Dad isn't known for his lively conversation. He's more of the stoic silent observer.

"The girls have agreed to a joint wedding reception in Ireland next summer," I remind her. "You can have your day out then."

"That's so far away. What about Christmas?" Her eyes light up.

I bark out a laugh. "Wild horses couldn't get Vivien on a plane to Ireland at Christmas. Are you mad? She'd probably get hypothermia." Ash had suggested a winter wedding to Viv, and the look on her face was fucking priceless. "You have no chance of convincing my Californian princess to get married in Ireland in the fucking dead of winter. No chance. Nada."

The noise level explodes as my brothers, their wives and children enter the chapel. Jamie and my parents move to go to them, but I pull Mum and Dad aside because there is something I need to say to them. "What's wrong?" Mum's brow instantly creases in a frown. "You're not having cold feet, are you?"

"Are you kidding?" My eyes almost bug out of my head. "My feet are about as toasty warm as you can get. I can't wait to marry Vivien. I have dreamed of this day for years."

Lauren's expression softens, and I'm glad I have a good relationship with Vivien's parents now. It's important to me. Not just because of Viv but Easton too. "This isn't about Vivien. There is something I need to say. Something I should have said a long time ago." I take both my parents' hands. "Thank you." Tears stab my eyes, and I swallow over the lump in my throat. "Thank you for taking me in, for loving me, and for always making me feel included. You never treated me any differently, and you never held it against me when I was in self-destruct mode." I hug Mum first. "I love you, Ma. I love you so much."

I rub at the tears leaking out of my eyes. Shit.

Dad comes at me, enveloping me in a hug before I've had the chance to hug him. "We love you, son, and we're very proud of the man you've become."

"Thanks, Da. Love you too." I'm all choked up.

"Who's the pussy now?" Jamie says, and I simultaneously want to punch him and thank him for helping to lighten the mood.

"Oh, I love weddings so much," Lauren says, wiping tears from her eyes. "They always bring out so much emotion. That was beautiful, Dillon."

"I'm not done," I say, improvising now. I had planned to talk to my parents before the ceremony, but I wasn't going to say anything to Viv's parents yet, waiting for my speech. But the perfect moment is now. I bundle Lauren in my arms. "Thank you for giving me another chance and for trusting me with Vivien and Easton. I promise I will love them and protect them for the rest of my life."

"Aw, Dillon, stop." She half laughs, easing out of my embrace. "You're ruining my makeup."

We all laugh, and then she takes my hand, squeezing it. "You have more than proven yourself to be a good man, Dillon. Jon and I know you're going to be as amazing a husband as you are a father. You have put smiles back on my daughter's and my grandson's faces, and that is something we worried would never happen." She tilts her head to the side. "But it's more than that. Vivien has come to life in a way I've never seen before. She literally glows with happiness, and we know that's due to you. Thank you for loving her and Easton, and welcome to the family."

"I am honored to be a part of your family."

"She's here," Ronan calls out, walking into the chapel with his daughter, Emer, in his arms.

The woman conducting the ceremony steps into the room from a side door, waving us forward. "Can everyone please take their seats. The bride will be with us shortly."

Lauren kisses my cheek. "Don't be nervous. She can't wait to marry you. I wouldn't be surprised if she runs up that aisle."

"I should've asked you to be my best man," I joke, shooting a dark look at Jamie. "This one sucks at motivational speeches."

"Just keeping it real, bro." Jamie nudges my shoulder, and I grin.

We take our places, and I try to control my nerves as the opening notes to "I Knew I Loved You" by Savage Garden starts playing. I turn to look when there is movement behind us, fighting emotion as Easton walks up the aisle, looking so fucking adorable in his little suit. He insisted on a miniature version of mine, complete with black shirt and white tie. He's carrying the ring cushion, looking proud as punch.

"Mommy was crying," he says when he gets to the top,

and I pull him into my side as Ash walks up the aisle next in a gorgeous green silk gown Vivien made. She's carrying a bunch of white roses which makes me smile.

"Is Mommy okay?" I ask East.

He nods. "She said they were happy tears because she's so happy to be marrying you."

A layer of stress lifts off my shoulders. "That's good, buddy."

"I'm happy you're marrying Mom too. Now I know you'll never leave."

I crouch down as Ash reaches the top of the aisle and Audrey starts walking. Easton still misses Reeve, but his life has gone on, and he doesn't get sad as often. This comment reminds me the impact of what he's lived through will always be there, and I hate he still feels insecure. That the tragedy means he probably always will. "I'm not going anywhere, Easton." I hug him. "I love you and your mom, and I'll always be there for you."

"I know, Daddy." He holds my hand as Vivien appears in the corner of my eye.

Everyone turns to look at her, and she's a vision in white as she walks up the aisle on her father's arm. Strong emotion is reflected upon her face, her smile is wide, and her eyes are bright, and I feel like running toward her because I need her in my arms stat.

We only have eyes for each other as she approaches, wearing a strapless knee-length white silk dress with a lace overlay she made herself. It's a pretty simple design but elegant and classy. Just like my bride. Her hair is pulled back in a bun, and her makeup is subtle. She clutches a larger bouquet of roses to her chest.

"You look stunning. I'm the luckiest man alive," I tell her when she reaches me, pulling her toward me before Jon can officially hand her to me.

Screw protocol.

My lips crash down on hers, and I kiss her with all the pent-up emotion racing through my veins.

"Ahem." Jonathon clears his throat. "You're supposed to wait until *after* you're married to kiss your bride." He's grinning when I reluctantly tear my lips from Vivien.

"My daddy is *always* kissing my mommy," Easton exclaims, and everyone cracks up laughing.

"That's 'cause your mom is the best kisser ever."

"Way to go, Mom." East raises his hand for a high-five, and everyone laughs again.

"Take care of my princess and my little prince," Jonathon says, his eyes looking suspiciously glassy.

"Always," I promise.

I take Vivien's hands, and we turn to face the minister as something on the inside of her wrist catches my eye. I flip her hand over, and my eyes widen. "When did you get this?" I ask, running my finger softly over the ink on her wrist. It's still raised and a little red, so it's recent enough.

"Last night," she confirms.

We had separated last night for our hen's and stag's nights. We hit the strip and lost a ton of money in the casinos before enjoying a few drinks in the hotel bar. The girls stayed in Ash's suite, drinking champagne, getting their nails done, and gossiping about us, no doubt.

"I love it." I peck her lips as my heart swells with love for her. "Now every fucker will definitely know you're mine." My name is etched on her skin forever, and damn, if that doesn't fill me with pride. I had a tattoo added to the top of my left arm with Easton's and Vivien's names on it, curled underneath a single rose. There is enough space around it to add more names when we decide to grow our family.

"Are we ready to begin?" the celebrant asks, and I'm sure she's getting fed up of my annoying ass, but feck it. It's my wedding day, and I'm not exactly known for following the rules.

"As ready as we'll ever be," I say, pulling Easton around so he's in front of us. I flash my beautiful bride one of my signature smiles. "Let's get married, Hollywood."

CHAPTER 48

VIVIEN

I GET off the phone with the real estate broker and squeal. "Someone sounds happy," Dillon says, entering my home office, carrying two mugs.

I stand, smiling. "We got it. We got the site."

Since we returned to L.A. from Vegas two months ago, we have been actively looking for suitable plots of land to build our new house. When we got home after our wedding, we talked about where we would live, deciding it was time we looked for our own place. It didn't feel right to start our new married life in the dream home Reeve built for me, yet I wasn't entirely comfortable living in Dillon's bachelor house either. Thankfully, we were on the same page, and we agreed to start looking immediately for a new family home.

We weren't planning on building from scratch, but we'd viewed tons of houses, and none of them were right. Our real estate broker told us about a site high up in the Hollywood Hills with amazing views, and we knew it was perfect the second we saw it.

"That is the best news." Dillon kisses me passionately before handing me a coffee.

"I have good news too," he says, taking my hand and

leading me over to the couch. "I spoke to the guys, and they're in agreement. We're delaying the European tour for a year."

"Are you sure, Dillon? You know we would come with you, and now I've decided I'm not going back to my freelance work, I have no commitments holding me back."

I take a sip of my coffee as I consider how fortunate I am that I don't have to work for a living. However, I do like keeping busy, and while, in the past, I enjoyed writing for TV shows and movies, my outlook on life has changed in a lot of ways, and my priorities are different.

I am still working on the book about my life, as well as a few works of fiction, and I'm more interested in dress designing right now. That and I want to be here for Dillon and Easton, and I want to focus on my family. Building the new place will be a mammoth project, even with a full-time project manager on board. I don't want to overstretch myself or make any huge commitments. I prefer to see where life takes me.

"I know, sweetheart, but I want to settle down here and enjoy life with you and East. I'm sick of touring, and I need a break." He drains the last of his coffee, setting his mug down on the table.

"And the guys are genuinely okay with it?"

He nods. "I think Jamie and Ash want to try for a baby, so he's happy to put down some roots for a change."

"She told me they're trying," I admit because I know she wouldn't expect me to keep it from Dillon.

"We should probably discuss that at some point," he says, looking a little anxious.

"Let's discuss it now."

"I know you've said you want more children, but the last time we talked about it, you said you didn't know when you'd be ready. I'm not pressuring you," he rushes to reassure me. "I'd just like to get an idea of when we can start trying."

"When would you like to start?" I ask, drinking a mouthful of my drink.

"Whenever you're ready. You set the pace, Hollywood.

You know that." He shoots me a lopsided grin, and I melt on the inside. I love this man so much, and I thank God every day for bringing him back to my life.

"Then I guess we're getting rid of the condoms."

"Yeah?" He sits upright, looking a little dazed. "You mean that?"

I nod, smiling. "I do. I want to have another baby with you, Dillon. I'm ready."

He puts my mug down and lifts me up, swinging me around.

I'm laughing when Charlotte sticks her head in the room. "Sorry for interrupting. I did knock, but—"

"My wife was squealing so loud we didn't hear you," Dillon continues for her.

I swat his chest. "Put me down."

Charlotte smiles, and her delight at my joy is obvious. She was the first to warmly congratulate us when we returned home. She adores Dillon, and he has her wrapped around his little finger.

We posted a selfie on our wedding day, confirming our marriage, wanting to break the news first. Dillien supporters went crazy, and there were the usual haters, but we ignored them.

One of the greatest gifts Dillon has given me is the ability to look at the media intrusion in a completely different light. I don't let it stress me out the way I used to, and I sure as fuck don't let it stop me from living my life.

"You have a visitor at the gate. She's not on the approved list."

I look at Dillon. "Were you expecting someone?"

He shakes his head.

"What is her name?"

"Lori Roberts." Charlotte wets her lips. "She said she's Saffron Roberts' older sister."

Bile churns in my gut. "What does she want?"

"She said she needs to speak to you urgently. She said Reeve told her to come to you if he wasn't around."

Dillon and I exchange looks.

"She gave the security guard this to give to you." Charlotte holds out an envelope with my name scrawled on the front.

My pulse picks up, and my heart beats crazy fast. "That's Reeve's handwriting." I take the envelope with trembling hands.

Dillon winds his arm around my back. "Open it."

I remove the single folded page as nausea swims up my throat. My inclination is to say to hell with this. Reeve is dead, and I want nothing to do with the Roberts family, but I'm stronger than I used to be, and I don't shy away from things as much anymore. So, I open the letter and read my dead husband's words. Dillon reads over my shoulder.

My darling Vivien,

If you are reading this letter, it's because something has happened to me and Lori needs your help. I know you're confused. She will explain, and then she has a second letter for you. Lori is nothing like Saffron, and you need to hear what she has to say.

Please do this for me. You're the only one I can count on.

All my love,
*   Reeve.*

"Oh God." I wobble a little as my knees buckle, but Dillon is there to keep me upright.

"You don't have to do this," he says.

"I do." I look up at him. "I have a really bad feeling about this, but ignoring it won't make it go away. I'll just drive myself demented trying to figure out what's going on." I turn to Charlotte. "Please tell the guard to let her through and send Leon to the gate to collect her."

She nods and leaves.

"What do you think this could be?" Dillon asks, steering me back to the couch.

"I'd rather not guess."

Dillon holds me as we wait for Lori to arrive and explain what the hell is going on. I rest my head against his chest, closing my eyes and breathing deeply, reminding myself I am strong. I'm glad Easton is at school so we can talk to her without disruption.

We move to our formal living room, and she arrives a few minutes later just as Charlotte brings in a tray with refreshments.

Dillon and I stand as Lori enters the room. She is not at all what I was expecting, and she looks nothing like Saffron with her short blonde hair, almond-shaped blue eyes, and pale skin. She is dressed in a navy pants suit with a cream blouse and flat pumps. The only thing they have in common is their short stature, but Lori is a lot thinner than Saffron, and she doesn't have her curves.

"We're half-sisters," she says, and I blush, feeling rude. "We had the same mom but different dads."

Remembering my manners, I step toward her, extending my hand. "Forgive me. I'm Vivien, and this is my husband, Dillon."

She shakes both our hands, and her palm is a little clammy. "Thank you for seeing me. I know you must be confused."

"Please take a seat," Dillon says, gesturing to the couch opposite us.

"Can I get you something to eat or drink?" I ask.

"Some water would be good. Thank you."

Dillon hands her a bottle of water and a glass from the tray.

"I don't want to take up too much of your time, and there is no easy way to launch this conversation, so I'm just going to be blunt."

"Okay. Reeve said in his letter to trust you, so I will give you the benefit of the doubt."

She removes a photo from her purse with shaking hands. I take a closer look at her, noticing the bruising shadows under her eyes, her cracked lips, and little beads of sweat forming on the pale skin of her brow. At this proximity, I can see her suit hangs off her frame, indicating she's lost weight. It's clear the woman is not well, and I wonder if that is part of the reason why she's here.

"I need to speak to you about my son. My husband and I adopted him as a baby." She hands the photo to me. "This is Bodhi."

My vision swims in and out as I stare at the photo in a mix of confusion, horror, and fear.

"He looks like Easton," Dillon says the same time I say, "He looks like Reeve."

"What is going on?" Dillon asks, tightening his hold around my shoulders, jumping into protective mode.

"Bodhi is Reeve's biological son. His and Saffron's."

CHAPTER 49
VIVIEN

WE STARE at her in complete shock, and it's a miracle I don't puke.

"What. The. Fuck?" Dillon says after a few silent beats, and I'm glad he has found his voice because I am still in a state of utter shock and unable to form any coherent thoughts, let alone words.

"Reeve discovered Saffron was pregnant a few months before you were due to return from Ireland," she begins explaining, looking at me.

I grip Dillon's arm as my body begins to shake.

"Saffron set the whole thing up."

That shakes me out of my daze. "Are you saying she got pregnant on purpose?"

She nods.

"How exactly?"

Lori takes a drink of her water. "Saffron has always been troubled, but things escalated after her father was killed in a botched robbery and our mother killed herself six months later. I had just turned eighteen, and Saffron was only fourteen. I dropped out of college and applied for guardianship because I couldn't let her be put in foster care. I switched to the local community college, and I tried to take care of her, but she went completely off the rails. Hanging out with a rough crowd, having sex with guys much older than her, drinking and doing drugs."

"If this is meant to garner sympathy, it's not working," I say. "Your sister did her best to ruin my life, and I will never forgive her for it."

"I know what she did to you, Vivien, and I'm sorry for how she interfered in your life and Reeve's. I'm trying to explain how this is more than just a woman out of control. Saffron has undiagnosed mental health issues. I cut her out of my life when she turned twenty and had that affair with the film director and his wife. She tried to coax him into leaving his wife and marrying her, and when he dumped her instead, she leaked those sex tapes on the internet to cash in on his notoriety."

I remember her discussing this when we were at Laguna Beach. "She told us it was a mutual decision and that it boosted all of their brands." I'm not surprised she told different versions of the story to different people. I wonder if she even remembers what is actually true anymore. The woman is a pathological liar.

"It catapulted her to instant fame, and she became insufferable. I had to cut ties with her because she was dragging me down. I was spending all my time stressing out about her, and Travis, my then fiancé, told me she was an adult responsible for her own actions. He saw how toxic she was and knew she'd only continue to wear on me, so I moved to San Jose to put some distance between us."

"How did you come to adopt Reeve's child?" I ask, almost choking over the words.

Dillon is quietly seething beside me but doing his best to hide it.

"Saffron showed up on my doorstep a few years later, drunk and rambling. We'd had very little contact since I'd moved away from L.A." She takes another sip of her water.

"I'm not sure if she meant to tell me everything, or if it was the alcohol in her system, but she told me she'd deliberately manipulated Reeve to break you two up and how she had planned to trap him into marriage by getting pregnant."

"Jesus Christ." Dillon shakes his head while running his hand up and down my back.

"Saffron was an opportunist, and she was essentially lazy. She knew she wasn't a great actress and that her fame was fleeting. She had no intention of working for the rest of her life. Her plan was to find a rich husband and become a trophy wife." Lori slants me an apologetic look. "She set her sights on Reeve. He was young, rich, and naïve. She knew he was going places too, but you were a stumbling block she had to eliminate. Reeve refused to have anything to do with her after she sabotaged your relationship, but Saffron is stubborn and determined, and she bided her time. She knew she'd find a window to make her move, and she did."

"In Mexico," I say, starting to slot the pieces into place.

Lori bobs her head. "She was planning to get him drunk and pounce on him when they were there, because she was ovulating, but he made it easier for her."

I look up at Dillon, not sure if I've ever told him this. "Reeve told me he found out I was dating you when he was in Mexico and he fell apart. He got drunk and took drugs and woke the next morning naked in bed with Saffron."

"She laughed telling me how easy it was to get him into her bed. She'd given him uppers, and well—" She clasps her hands nervously in front of her, not wanting to say it.

"It made him horny, and they fucked all night long," I surmise.

She nods. "Saffron couldn't believe it worked and she got pregnant, but her plan backfired, because when she went to Reeve, he went ballistic. He refused to marry her, so then she asked him for ten million dollars to have an abortion."

"There is no way Reeve would have let her abort his child." I know how he felt about abortion.

"You're right. He wouldn't entertain any notion of abortion. He told her he'd give her five million dollars if she went overseas to have the baby, stayed clean during the pregnancy, signed an NDA, gave the baby up for adoption, and stayed away from both of you."

"And he trusted her to not blab about that?" Dillon asks, disbelief clear in his tone. "Five mil couldn't have meant much to her back then. Surely, she could've sold her story for more?"

"Saffron didn't have good representation, and she was earning a fraction of what Reeve was earning for the *Rydeville* movies. Whatever money Saffron did have was snorted up her nose. She was pretty broke, but that wasn't the only incentive. Reeve played the ultimate card, and that's how she ended up on my doorstep that night."

"What card?" I ask, tucking my hair behind my ears.

"He found a couple of those girls who attacked you in that alley, and they confirmed Saffron had set it up. They also confirmed she'd paid them with drugs. One of them had a real smart mouth, Reeve said, but she was shrewd. She had video footage of Saffron asking them to attack you and a recording of her handing over the goods."

"She would've been sent to prison for selling to minors," Dillon says, pouring me a fresh coffee and placing the mug in my hand. "Drink that, sweetheart. You're shaking like a leaf."

I glance up at him. "Can you believe this?"

"No. I fucking can't," he grits out, and a muscle pops in his jaw.

"That's how Reeve ensured Saffron toed the line. He took out restraining orders in both your names and organized for her to go to a private rehab clinic in Switzerland. But Saff was always resourceful. She charmed one of the orderlies, and he was supplying her with drugs the last three months she was there."

"While she was heavily pregnant?" Horror and disgust wash over me. I knew Saffron was scum of the earth, but this proves it conclusively. What a reckless, selfish bitch.

Lori nods. "Reeve was furious when he found out. It's why she ended up going into premature labor. She wasn't due until the middle of January, but she ended up giving birth on Christmas Day."

"Oh my God." I look at Dillon. "That's why he was sad at Christmas. It wasn't anything to do with me."

"I'd say it was a combination." Dillon kisses my cheek. "Drink your coffee, love." He refocuses on Lori. "How did you end up adopting Bodhi?"

"I reached out to Reeve after Saffron left that night. I explained how my husband and I weren't able to have kids and we had been exploring adoption. Bodhi was my flesh and blood too. It made sense that we would take him in. We had a lot of love to give, and I wanted to take care of my nephew." She sits back, sighing, looking exhausted. "Reeve wasn't sure at first, but he did background checks on us, and we sat down and talked for hours, and gradually he agreed. He bought us a new house, sent a monthly allowance, and he set up a trust fund Bodhi gets when he is eighteen."

I cannot wrap my head around this. "How could Reeve abandon his child? That must have killed him! He suffered with self-esteem issues his whole life because his father was so neglectful. All Reeve wanted was a family of his own."

"With you," Dillon supplies, fighting to control his anger. "Reeve didn't want a family with her, and he knew if you found out you'd leave him for good." He fists his hands at his side. "He sacrificed his kid for the woman he loved. Exactly like someone else we knew." Dillon drills me with a look, and I'm sick to my stomach because he's right. Reeve turned his back on his child for me while Simon turned his back on Dillon because he blamed him for his wife's death.

This is so fucked up.

Lori nods. "That's exactly what Reeve said when I asked him why he was doing this. I knew he had the means to take care of his child, so I didn't understand it, at first."

"I still can't believe he'd give up his child." I bury my head in my hands. "How could he do that?"

"It wasn't easy on him, but he told me there was no choice. He said it was you or Bodhi. He was working to win you back at the time. He told me how lost he was without you, and he said his life was not worth living if you weren't by his side."

"What a fucking crock of shit!" Dillon hisses, losing the tenuous hold on his control.

Tears stream down my face, and stabbing pain settles on my chest. "This is so wrong!" I cry out. "How could both his parents abandon him?" I hate Saffron even more now, but I have no clue how I feel about Reeve. I'm shell-shocked and my head is a mess.

"Would you have left him if he'd told you?" she asks, removing a tissue from her pocket and wiping her brow.

I rub at my tears, leaning into Dillon for support. I don't need to think about it for long. "Yes. Your sister was a very sore subject for me. I was only twenty, and as much as I loved Reeve, I would never have forgiven him for getting my arch-enemy pregnant, no matter the circumstances. I know I would have walked away."

"If he hadn't been so fucking possessive with you, everything could've been different," Dillon says, standing and pacing the room.

"It wasn't a good situation, and I don't know how Reeve could make that decision because he seemed like a good man. I know he was a good man," she adds. "He wasn't like my sister. My sister would never have considered her baby for a single second, except as a means of extorting money or marriage from Reeve. She was absolutely furious when he went back to you and apoplectic when she discovered he'd married you and you had a child."

"Did Reeve visit Bodhi?" I ask, needing to know how deep the betrayal extends.

She shakes her head. "He held him as a baby when the

adoption paperwork went through, but he didn't visit again. At his request, I sent him a letter every year updating him, and he always sent gifts for him in December. One for his birthday, and one for Christmas."

"Does Bodhi know he's adopted?" Dillon asks. "Does he know who his bio parents are?"

"He knows he's adopted, and he knows the gifts he receives are from his bio dad, but he doesn't know their names."

"Has Saffron ever visited him?" I ask.

She shakes her head again, and it's becoming a familiar pattern.

"Never?" I wonder if she even looked at him or held him after she'd given birth. I fucking hate that bitch with every fiber of my being. I hate she gave Reeve a child when I didn't. I dig my nails into my thighs, feeling sympathy for Bodhi. He's an innocent child caught up in this mess.

"She has no interest in him, and he's the most adorable little boy. He has brought immense joy into my life, and I don't see how anyone could fail to love him."

"Does he have any health issues or problems because of the drugs she took during pregnancy?" I ask.

"He was underweight when he was born, and he didn't speak until he was three, and then he had a slight speech impediment. He attended speech therapy for a year, and his speech is fine now. Although, he's a quiet boy who doesn't talk a lot. He's been evaluated by child psychologists and mental health professionals, and there was no long-lasting damage, thank God." Tears well in her eyes. "He doesn't deserve any of this, and I'm so worried what it will do to him if this comes out."

"It seems Reeve and Saffron were well suited after all," Dillon growls, crossing his hands at the back of his head. "Both of them were selfish cunts."

His reaction is perfectly understandable to me, but I can't work out how I feel. "I don't know what to feel. What to think," I admit. "I had no idea Reeve did this or that he was carrying this secret all the years of our marriage." I wonder did I ever truly know him at all, because the man I loved would never give up his own flesh and blood. I feel sick thinking he did that for me.

"Why didn't Saffron say anything after Reeve died? She had a perfect opportunity to sell her story then, and it would have hurt Vivien the most." Dillon flops down on the couch beside me. "What don't we know?"

"Reeve's attorney sent her a reminder of the NDA, which is intact until she dies. Reeve left clear instructions that if she breached the terms his estate would sue her for the full financial penalty. He suspected she would do this, and he planned for every eventuality." She drinks the last of her water. "Her name isn't on Bodhi's birth certificate. Travis and I are listed as the bio parents. I'm not sure how Reeve made that happen, but I know he was worried about someone finding it at a future point and outing the truth."

"Wow. He really thought of fucking everything, didn't he?" Dillon fumes. "I wonder what else he was hiding, seeing as he was such a master at covering his tracks."

Acid crawls up my throat, and I wrap my arms around myself.

"I wouldn't know anything about that," she says.

"Are you sure?" Dillon eyes her warily. "He seems to have confided a lot in you."

"That was about Bodhi because we both had a vested interest."

"Saffron is going to be a problem," I say, knowing her silence will not last long, NDA or not. I might not know how I feel, but I know I don't want this coming out in the media. It will drag everything to the surface again, and I need to protect Easton.

Bodhi needs protection too.

"Saffron is an addict. All she cares about is her next fix. She showed up at my house a few months ago, saying she was going to sell her story because she needed the money. I panicked because I didn't want this coming out now." She hangs her head, exhaling heavily.

"How much did you give the junkie whore?" Dillon asks.

Shame is etched upon her face when she lifts her head. "Ten thousand, but I know she'll be back for more."

"Why didn't you go to Carson Park?" I ask.

"I did afterward when I calmed down. He told me if she comes back looking for more to call him and he'll deal with her."

I thought I had left Saffron Roberts in the past, but it seems she refuses to play dead. I still don't know why Lori is here, and I need to find out ASAP because I would like her to go so I can talk to Dillon about this. I need to talk to Alex too. If he knew about this and said nothing, there will be hell to pay. That will be the end of our friendship, awkward and all as it would be.

"Do you need money?" I ask. "Is that why you're here?"

She balks, and I think I've offended her.

"I continue to receive the generous monthly child allowance from Reeve's estate, and my ex is still paying alimony under the terms of our divorce. This isn't about money."

I make a mental note to rip Carson Park's head off his shoulders for hiding this from me. I'm sure he'll pull the "client-attorney confidentiality" line, but how the fuck could he have kept quiet about this?

"You're not well," I surmise.

She shifts uneasily on the couch. "I have terminal cancer. It was only diagnosed a month ago, but my condition is deteriorating rapidly, and I've only been given a few months to live."

"I'm so sorry to hear that," I say.

She knots her hands in an anxious trait. "I have no one else to turn to. Travis lives in the UK with his new wife, and he refuses to take him. I don't really want to send him overseas anyway. He's a sensitive little boy, and this is going to devastate him."

"What exactly are you asking us to do?" Dillon asks, sitting forward, placing his arm on my lower back.

"Bodhi is your son's cousin, and he's your nephew," she says, turning pleading eyes on Dillon and then me. "I know your feelings toward Saffron, and I know this is hard for you, Vivien, but he's your husband's flesh and blood, and he's an amazing kid. So intelligent and compassionate and caring." She sits up, taking my hands. "Please, Vivien. I'm begging you. Please agree to take Bodhi."

CHAPTER 50
VIVIEN

DILLON BREATHES fire as he reads Reeve's second letter over my shoulder. Lori has just left. We promised her we would talk about it and reach out to her in due course, but we need time to process everything. It's a lot to take in. I lower my eyes to the letter, leaning in closer to Dillon, siphoning some of his warmth and his ever-present support.

My darling Vivien,

I know you are in shock and your mind is reeling at the news I have another son. A son I gave up because I knew there was no way I could keep you both. Giving Bodhi up for adoption was the hardest thing I have ever done. The hardest decision I've ever had to make, but I knew it was a choice between you and him, and I can't lose you without losing myself.

Choosing him would have meant turning into my dad because I would've pined for you, the same way he pined for my mom. I didn't want my child to grow up in that kind of situation. To experience the childhood I had. Letting him go, giving him to good parents who will love him and give him a good life, is the best way I could demonstrate my love for my child.

"That is the biggest sack of shit I have ever heard in my life," Dillon hisses, dragging his hands through his hair. "He didn't even give you a chance to consider it, for fuck's sake. He just made that decision for you too."

"He knew me well enough to know I could never have accepted Saffron's child."

Dillon holds my face in his large, callused palms. "I think you're selling yourself short, Viv. I know you would've been upset, at first, but I think, in time, you would have done the right thing. You have a big heart, and you're a natural mother. I don't think you would've turned an innocent child away."

"You have a much higher opinion of me than I deserve," I admit, not wanting to say this out loud, but we have promised each other complete honesty. "Because even now, I'm wondering how I could consider doing this knowing that bitch's DNA flows through his veins." Shame crashes into me. "What if I look at him and all I see is her?" I squeeze my eyes shut for a moment. Soft lips land in my hair as my husband pulls me close. "You're in shock right now. We both are, and we might feel differently once we've had time to digest the news."

I rest my head on his chest. "I don't know what to do."

"Read the rest of the letter."

I have tried to move on and forget about my eldest son, but it hasn't been easy, no matter how wonderful our life together is. Lori has sent me pictures of Bodhi, and it's hard sometimes not to look at Easton and see my other son. It's hard not to feel guilty when I consider how I've denied Easton his brother.

My chest heaves painfully because that's one of my greatest fears now. I underline that part in the letter with the tip of my finger. "That is very true." I look up at Dillon. "If we don't take Bodhi in, how do we tell Easton we turned him away? We would be no different than Simon."

"Don't talk bullshit," Dillon snaps. "This *is* different. Simon made a conscious decision to give me away and split us up. He either gave no consideration to our feelings or he realized the full extent of his actions and he couldn't care less. You and I haven't made the decisions which have led to this point."

"No, but the decisions we make now will impact Bodhi and Easton. We may not have asked for the responsibility, but it's ours whether we like it or not."

"Is it really though, Viv?" His troubled blue eyes penetrate mine. "Lori is his mother. It's her responsibility. Her and Travis." He scoffs, looking disgusted. "Reeve sure did a great job picking the right parents. Bodhi is only six, and he's already lost his dad due to divorce, and now he's going to lose his mother."

"That's not fair, Dillon. I'm sure Reeve thought he was making the best choice giving him to family. Lori is nothing like Saffron. It was obvious she's a decent parent and a good mother who loves her son. It's not her fault her marriage didn't work out or that she got cancer."

Dillon blows air out of his mouth. "I know it's not her fault, but this is what happens when you give your kid away. You're gambling with their future."

"It turned out okay for you," I remind him.

"I was lucky. So fucking lucky."

I smile, caressing his face. "I love hearing you acknowledge that now."

He presses a kiss to my palm. "I was an idiot for taking it for granted." A dark expression washes over his face. "Finish the letter before I burn the damn thing."

I haven't regretted my decision, no matter how callous that makes me sound.

"I'm glad he realizes what a selfish prick he was," Dillon grumbles. I ignore his little outburst, wanting to finish this so I can call Alex.

*But I **have** suffered huge remorse. My only salvation is knowing Bodhi is loved and well cared for and he's happy.*

I don't know the circumstances under which Lori has come to you. I send her an updated letter every December so she has a way of contacting you if she needs help and I'm not there to support her. If you are reading this, it means she has nowhere to turn and she needs you. I know this is a lot to ask, especially if something has happened to me, but there is no one else I trust more than you.

Please help her. Do what you can for her and Bodhi.

If you can find it in your heart, please forgive me for making this choice and for keeping it a secret from you. Everything I have done was for you, for us, for Easton. I have tried to do right by Bodhi too, but I'm well aware of how it must look. I could never have asked you to take in her son. I know how much I hurt you back then, and I never want to be the cause of your pain ever again.

I love you, Vivien. I have loved you my whole life, and I know I will love you in the afterlife too. You have given me more joy than you know, and I will love you for eternity. Kiss Easton for me, and tell him I'm proud of him.

Until we meet again.

All my love,
Reeve.

I fold the letter and put it in the envelope, flopping back on the couch and sighing. Dillon is quiet beside me. Too quiet. I twist my head, eyeballing the side of my husband's handsome face. "Spit it out, Dil."

He leans forward on his elbows, and I sit up straighter, linking my fingers in his.

"I always thought the way he loved you was obsessive bordering on psychotic, and this confirms it." He turns to me. "That kind of love is not healthy. He was obsessed with you and had to have you at any cost."

"I can't reconcile that Reeve with the Reeve I knew and loved. I just can't believe he abandoned his child so he wouldn't lose me. I feel so guilty. Like it's my fault that child was deprived of his father."

Dillon glares at me. "Don't you fucking dare take that on. That is not on you."

I'm contemplative as I try to organize my thoughts so this comes out right. "Perhaps you are right and the way he loved me wasn't healthy, but it grew from the best foundation. Reeve was my best friend growing up. He was always there for me. It was the two of us against the world, and when we became lovers, it seemed like the most natural progression. I don't remember at what point we acknowledged we were always going to be with one another, but whether we were right or wrong for each other, doesn't take away from the fact he did his best to love me the only way he knew how. I don't condone what he did. He should have told me and accepted the responsibility that came with his actions, but I know he did it because he believed he was protecting me and protecting our future."

Dillon twists around to face me, and his knee brushes mine. "That sounds scarily like some form of Stockholm syndrome."

"You don't get to do this!" I shout. "You don't get to take every single memory I have of him and twist it into something nasty." Tears spill down my cheeks. "This doesn't redefine everything we were to one another or change the happy marriage we had or alter how good of a father and husband he was." I break down, sobbing, covering my face in my hands.

"Come here." He pulls me into his arms, and I cry into his shirt, hating I'm back to this.

"I'm scared, Dillon." I brush the tears from my eyes and look up at him while clinging to him. "I'm scared that this news will do all of that, and I don't want to look back on my memories and feel like they were lies."

"I'm not going to lie to you, Vivien, but the truth is, you have to accept there were things about him you didn't know. How can that not influence the things you did? You say he was protecting you? Well, why the fuck didn't he turn that evidence into the police? Those bitches assaulted you and left you bleeding and unconscious in an alley. They should've been brought to justice. Instead, he used it to bargain with that cow."

"Why did you do any of the hurtful things you did? You showed up here, prepared to ruin my marriage and shatter my heart again." He moves to pull away from me, but I won't let him. "I'm not saying that to hurt you, and I know it in no way compares to what Reeve has done. What he has done is unforgivable."

I let that thought settle in my mind for a minute, and I realize behind my confusion is a lot of anger. "I'm mad at him for using me to shirk his responsibility to his son, and I am questioning everything. But I'm trying to get you to see it's not as black-and-white as you think it is. I know this is personal for you because of your experiences, and I hate that Reeve did this. This revelation has definitely shaken my belief in him, and I don't know how to process all of my emotions."

"I don't want us fighting about this. I don't want him coming between us again."

"We won't, and he isn't."

"We may not see eye to eye on this, Vivien." He stares deep into my eyes. "I know we're not in a position to make any decisions yet, but what if we want different things?"

"You want to do this," I quietly admit.

Dillon stands, pacing. "I'm not sure yet, but how can I abandon my flesh and blood? As much as I am disgusted with my twin, I can't deny the facts. Bodhi is my nephew, and I don't see how I can turn my back on him. The thought of him going into the foster care system breaks my heart." He drills me with a look. "Or worse, ending up with Saffron."

All the blood drains from my face. "She doesn't want him."

"Lori is desperate. If we don't do this, she may go to Saffron. Leave her everything if she agrees to take him in."

A full-body shudder takes control of me. "We can't let that happen, but we can't let it drive our decision either. If we decide to do this, it has to be for the right reasons. That we want to care for him, offer him a loving home, and the same attention and care we give to Easton or any other children we may have in the future."

"I know." He flops back down, burying his head in my shoulder for a few seconds. "We should talk to my parents. They know a bit about this."

"Definitely," I agree. "But let's talk with Alex first. I want to know if he knew about this."

CHAPTER 51

VIVIEN

"I SWEAR TO YOU, Vivien. Reeve never mentioned a word to me. I'm as shocked as you are," Alex says, looking as pale as a ghost.

Audrey and Alex moved back to L.A. in July, and he's coaching football at a local private school while Audrey is getting her new practice off the ground. Renovations are underway on the space Reeve bought for her medical practice, and she's hoping to open for business in a few weeks. I love having my bestie close again, and it meant they were able to come over after Alex finished work for the day.

"I just can't believe he would do that. It goes against everything I thought I knew about him," Audrey says, sipping her glass of white wine.

I was tempted to hit the vino immediately after Lori left, but I abstained until my friend and her husband showed up. My parents were here earlier, and they have taken Easton for a sleepover.

"What did your parents say?" she asks.

"They are shell-shocked too." I cross my feet at the ankles. "Mom thinks we have to accept there were parts of him we didn't know. She believes this is a direct result of the damage

Simon caused. This is what abandonment, neglect, and abuse can do to a person."

"I can't believe he had a kid with that whore and he told no one." Audrey's mouth pulls into a thin line. "I remember how stressed he was that summer you were in Ireland, but I put it down to his anxiety over getting you back." She slants a sympathetic look at Dillon. My husband is sipping a beer, perched on the arm of the couch, looking drained. And I get it. It's been an exhausting emotional day.

"I knew she was harassing him," Alex admits, and we all swing our gazes in his direction.

"Sit down and tell us everything you know," Audrey demands, leveling her husband with a look that warns him not to refuse.

"I don't know much." Alex drops onto the couch beside Audrey. "But he did confide that Saffron was hounding him, constantly calling and showing up at his house, and he told me Carson Park was working on obtaining restraining orders for you and him. It had to be done discreetly so the press wouldn't find out, and he didn't want you knowing either." He has the decency to look ashamed.

"Was he having an affair with her the whole time, Alex?" I eyeball Reeve's best friend. "Did he sleep with her on more than one occasion?" It's not that I'm doubting what Lori believes or that Saffron could've gotten pregnant from one night. If she was ovulating and they used no protection, it's totally possible. What I am doubting is whether Saffron told her the truth. And whether Bodhi's existence is the only thing Reeve was concealing.

"No." He vigorously shakes his head. "Absolutely not. He hated her, Vivien. He hated how he let her come between you." He takes a mouthful of beer while I gulp my wine. "She played him perfectly from the start. She was friendly, wanting to know about you, gushing about how amazing it was you two were so close and had such big plans. She stroked his ego, telling him how talented he was and how he was going places."

"And he fell for that bullshit?" Dillon looks and sounds incredulous.

"He was out of his depth, Dillon. He was struggling without Viv. She always grounded him, and he had never been away from her before. He was drowning under the weight of responsibility. He was always trying to prove himself to that prick, Simon, and he wanted to prove to Vivien that he could go it alone and he could take care of her." Alex looks at me. "That's why he refused your mom's help. He wanted to be able to say he'd done it all on his own."

"But it backfired because that bitch stuck her claws in him," Audrey adds.

"She had been acting all sisterly, speaking about her boyfriend, showing no sexual interest in Reeve, but she was gradually planting seeds of doubt, gradually getting more flirty and touchy-feely. By this point, things were strained with you, Viv, and he was seriously stressed and depressed. That's when she started properly manipulating him. He was surrounded by older actors who all made it seem like doing drugs and fucking each other was the norm on sets."

"And you expect me to believe he only kissed her at Christmas and had sex with her that time in Mexico?"

"I can only tell you what he told me, and that was it." He scrubs a hand over his jaw. "By the way, he only told me all this after the fact. If you remember, I didn't see much of him when I first moved to Boston."

"I remember."

"I wish he'd confided in me at the time. I might have been able to decipher the signs and warn him about her."

"And you're sure he was only with her on those occasions?" I ask because I need to know for my sanity.

"One hundred percent, Viv. Oh, she tried to seduce him many times, but he knocked her back."

"I don't know if I believe that anymore," I admit. "And I

don't want to focus on that. It will only make me all ragey." I reach out, squeezing Alex's hand. "I just needed to know you weren't keeping it a secret too."

"I'm hurt you'd think I would, but I understand."

"What are you going to do?" Audrey asks, her gaze bouncing between us.

"That's the million-dollar question," Dillon says, and we exchange a look.

"I don't know if I can take him in, knowing he is hers. But he's Reeve's flesh and blood." Tears fill my eyes. "At the funeral, I remember thinking how sad it was that there was no physical part of Reeve left behind. No son or daughter who carried his DNA. Now there is, and I don't know what to do about it." I scoot down on the couch, taking Dillon's hand in mine. "And it's not just my decision. This is something we have to decide together, and it's got to be what's best for our family."

A week passes, and it's hard to think about anything else but the situation we find ourselves in. Lori has called, asking if we want to come and visit. She thinks it might help if we meet him. I agree it makes sense, but how do we meet the child and then let him go if we decide we can't do this? Having met him will make it all the more real.

"We need to make a decision," Dillon tells me when he arrives back at the house after dropping Easton at school. "We are torturing ourselves and going around in circles."

I turn away from the window, clasping my hands around my mug of peppermint tea. I've been staring out the window since I got off my call with Audrey. "I know." Time is something Lori doesn't have, and if we can't do this, she deserves to know so she can make alternate arrangements.

"Let's talk outside." Dillon approaches, and I drink the

rest of my tea, setting the cup down on the counter. Bending down, he kisses me. "I love you."

I wrap my arms around his neck. "I love you too." I kiss him softly, and we rest our brows together, just holding one another for a few minutes, both of us understanding the magnitude of our impending conversation—the culmination of many, many conversations we've had this past week. We have spoken among ourselves and talked with Jamie and Ash and both sets of parents. My in-laws spoke about the rewards and the challenges of adopting, and they offered a different perspective.

Dillon takes my hand and leads me out to the memorial garden. My heart is swollen with conflicting emotions as we sit down on the bench.

"You're a prick," Dillon barks, glaring at the wooden plaque he nailed to the tree. It has Reeve's and Lainey's names on it. "How could you do this to your son? To Vivien and Easton? To us?" He clutches my hand. "Now, we're the ones left picking up the pieces." He flips his middle finger up at the sky. "I hope you see that, you selfish jerk."

I shouldn't laugh, because there is nothing humorous about this, but I can't help giggling. I rub his back. "Feel better?"

"A little." He grins.

"I remembered something last night," I tell him. "When we were arguing that last night in the car, Reeve mentioned how he had made sacrifices for me. I didn't understand it at the time, but I know this is what he meant. He must have regretted his decision in that moment, Dillon." I lift my hand, brushing waves of blond hair off his brow. "He must have felt so betrayed. I hate to think he died feeling like that."

"He died protecting you, Vivien. That was his sole purpose in life. Keeping you safe was the last thing on his mind. He died loving you. You can be sure of that."

"I never thought I'd wish for a boring life, but I really

fucking do." I stare into his gorgeous blue eyes. "Is it too much to ask for?"

"Life is never dull, that's for sure." He tweaks my nose, grinning when I slap his hand away.

"What do you want to do?" I ask, and his grin fades.

He lifts my hand to his mouth, and delicious tremors whip up my arm when he plants his lips on my skin. "I want to adopt him, Vivien. I want to give him a chance at a normal life. I want the boys to be brothers."

My smile expands. "I want that too."

Shock splays across his face. "Are you sure?"

I nod. "I'm terrified to do this, but I can't say no either." I chew on the inside of my mouth. "I spoke to Audrey before you came home. She and Alex offered to take him."

His eyes pop wide. "Wow. That's a big commitment to make."

"They loved Reeve, and neither of them want to see Bodhi going into the system or being adopted by strangers."

He is silent for several minutes, processing, no doubt, like I was when my bestie made her kind suggestion.

"That is very generous of them, but we can't let them do it."

"I agree." I rest my head on his shoulder. "Bodhi belongs with us. He's Reeve's flesh and blood. I can't turn my back on him, and it's not just because I know this is what Reeve would want. It's what I want." I lift my head, looking my husband in the eyes. "Reeve lives on in this little boy. If I can have a little piece of Reeve with me, then I'm going to grab Bodhi and hold him close." I examine his eyes carefully, to ensure he understands what I mean and that I'm not hurting him.

He stands, pulling me to my feet. "I'm glad we're on the same page, and it's like that for me. I missed out on getting to know Reeve, but now I get to care for and love his son." He bundles me into his arms, and I go willingly. "When should we tell East?"

I lift my chin up. "I think we should tell him when he gets home from school."

"Should we wait and visit Bodhi by ourselves first?"

"I don't think so. We're either all in or we're not. Visiting him should just be a formality because the decision is made. It's not like we get to say no if he doesn't warm to us immediately or it looks like he might have behavioral issues or problems adjusting. All of those things are probably par for the course, and in agreeing to accept him into our family, we are agreeing to love him through the good and the bad."

"I love the fuck out of you, Mrs. O'Donoghue."

"Right back at ya, babe." I plant a loud kiss on his cheek as a trickle of nervous excitement bubbles up my throat. "We're doing this. We're really doing this."

"Yeah. We are." He hugs me tight. "This already feels right." He rests his chin on the top of my head.

"It does. It really does."

"Come on then. Let's call Lori and give her the good news."

CHAPTER 52
DILLON

"DO you think he'll like his gift?" Easton asks as Vivien helps him out of the back seat. I parked directly outside Lori and Bodhi's comfortable two-story family home. At first glance, the large garden at the front is a little overgrown, and all the flowerbeds need tidying. Upon closer inspection, it's obvious someone has been lovingly tending to the garden until recently.

"I'm sure he'll love it," she reassures him. "Who doesn't love superheroes, am I right?" She waggles her brows, keeping the tone lighthearted for Easton's sake, even if she's a bag of nerves underneath.

I'm not exactly Mr. Cool, Calm, and Collected myself.

Since we spoke to Lori a few days ago, I've been dying to meet Bodhi, but we all agreed to tell the boys the truth and give them a few days to process it. We feel it's important to go into this as openly and honestly as possible. So, Bodhi now knows who his bio parents are and who we are. Easton is aware Bodhi is his cousin and he's going to be his brother.

He had tons of questions, as I'm sure Bodhi did, and we did our best to answer them truthfully while protecting him from the harsher aspects of reality. I'm not sure how much of it he understood, because he is so freaking excited over the news he has a new brother. Lately, Easton has been praying to God, and Reeve, and Lainey, to give him a sister or brother, so the timing is kind of perfect.

"Remember what we told you about Bodhi's mommy, Lori," Vivien says, straightening up Easton's shirt.

He blinks profusely as he looks up at his mom. "It's sad she's sick, but I'm glad she will be coming to live with us so I can help my brother to take care of her."

With Lori's agreement, we have decided to transform one of our spare rooms downstairs into a hospice room, and we're in the process of hiring a full medical team to care for her. It's not ideal that we have to speed through this process, but her health is failing rapidly, and we need to get this done as soon as possible.

Vivien and I have already met with Carson Park, and he's getting the paperwork completed. We need to get the adoption paperwork finalized before Lori dies to prohibit Saffron from making a play for him. I have no doubt that bitch would try for custody, if she knew what we were planning, purely to spite Viv.

Vivien places a hand over her chest, audibly gulping as she looks up at me. I lock the car and walk to her side. "That is very kind of you, East." I place my hand on top of his hair, careful not to mess it up and incur my wife's wrath. She has put him in one of his best outfits and styled his hair. She even made me change his socks because they weren't color coordinated. You'd swear we were meeting the queen.

"Can we go in now?" He bounces from foot to foot, and he's practically bristling with excitement.

I slide my arm around Vivien and rest my hand on East's shoulder. "We sure can. Let's go."

"Relax, sweetheart." I press a kiss to Vivien's temple as we stand at the door, waiting for Lori to open it. I can feel my wife trembling with nerves. "It's going to be okay."

The door swings open, revealing a frailer Lori and a little dark-haired boy clinging to her leg from behind.

"Hi. I'm Easton Lancaster, and this is my mommy and my daddy Dillon." East thrusts out his hand, giving her a big grin.

Lori smiles, shaking his hand. "It's a pleasure to meet you, Easton. We've been very excited waiting for you to arrive."

"Are you my brother?" Easton asks, peeking around Lori to where Bodhi is hiding.

Slowly, he emerges from the protection of his mother. Vivien barely stifles her gasp, and I tighten my arm around her waist. I know this is like looking at a ghost. I've seen enough pictures of Reeve as a kid to know Bodhi is the fucking spitting image of him. He has the same brown hair with little blond highlights and the same shape blue eyes. I see none of Saffron in him, and relief is instantaneous. I was a little concerned Vivien might struggle if he bore any resemblance to his tramp of a mother, but he is all Reeve.

"Why don't you come inside?" Lori steps aside with Bodhi still clinging to her side. "We have cupcakes and lemonade."

"Do you have chocolate cupcakes?" Easton walks into the hallway. "Those are my favorite."

Lori beams. "Chocolate cupcakes are Bodhi's favorite too. Isn't that right, love?" She pats his head, and he nods shyly.

"Who's your favorite superhero?" East asks, stepping in front of his soon-to-be brother and thrusting the gift at him. "Mine is Iron Man. I dressed up as him last Halloween, and my daddy had this massive party at his house, and all my friends from school came, and it was awesome. Daddy dressed as Captain America, and Mommy was Wonder Woman, but Daddy wanted her to be Black Widow because the costume wasn't as schmexy and it meant no other men would be cov'ting his woman."

"Oh my God." Vivien looks at me like she wants to murder me in cold blood.

"Buddy, that was supposed to be our little secret." I smile as Bodhi peers up at me.

"But Bodhi is my brother. I can't keep secrets from my brother." Easton loops his arm through Bodhi's. "Open your present. It's Avengers Assemble. Wanna play superheroes?"

"Cupcakes and superheroes. That sounds like a good plan," Vivien says, crouching down a little. She smiles at Bodhi, and I can tell she's fighting her emotions. "Hello, Bodhi. I'm Vivien. I'm Easton's mommy. It's really nice to meet you."

"Hi." His cheeks flush red as he looks at her. "Thank you for the gift."

"You're welcome. I hope you like it."

"This is my daddy Dillon," the little motormouth says, reaching back to grab my hand.

"Hey, Bodhi," I lean down, holding up my hand for a high-five.

His mouth hangs open, and his eyes widen as he stares at me. "You're in a band!" he exclaims in an excited voice. He looks up at Lori. "I saw him on TV! Remember!"

"My daddy is the best singer and the best guitarist in the whole wide world," East says. "And our daddy Reeve is the best actor ever. I've got his movies at home. We can watch them when you live with us."

Poor Bodhi looks a little overwhelmed.

"Let's move out of the hallway," Vivien says, lifting her shoulder in Lori's direction. Lori is clutching the door frame, looking a little wobbly on her feet.

I offer Lori my arm, as Vivien closes the door behind me. "Lean on me."

We make our way into the main living area, and it's a large open space that looks well lived in with comfortable sofas, a colorful worn patterned rug, and tons of pictures of Bodhi on the wall. A packed toy box is open in the middle of the room, and the boys gravitate there after helping themselves to a cupcake. I help Lori to sit in a recliner chair while Vivien pours lemonade into two plastic glasses for the boys. "I should make coffee." Lori moves to stand.

"Don't get up," Vivien says. "I'll make some."

"The kitchen is through there." Lori winces as she points through an archway. Pain lances across her face as she tries to get comfortable in the chair.

"Have the doctors not given you anything for the pain?" I ask when Vivien has left the room.

"I have pain meds, but they make me groggy, and I kept falling asleep. It's only the two of us here, and I need to be alert to take care of Bodhi."

"I know we were going to wait a couple of weeks until we had the room set up for you, but I think you should move in with us ASAP."

"I don't know." She looks over to where Bodhi and Easton are playing with their superhero figures on the floor. "This has all been a big shock for Bodhi. He's been quieter than usual."

"It's only delaying the inevitable. At least at our place, you can take your meds and grab some sleep knowing he's being cared for. Our housekeeper, Charlotte, is an amazing cook, and she'll make all your meals. It will remove the burden from you and give you more time to spend with your son."

"What about school?"

"They have a place for Bodhi at Easton's school," Vivien says, coming into the room carrying a tray with some mugs and a coffee pot, milk, and sugar.

"You have that lined up already?" Lori looks shocked.

"Once we made the decision, we started putting plans in place," my wife confirms, pouring coffee into a mug for Lori and handing it to her. "Dillon made a bed like Easton's for Bodhi, and we added it to his room. We thought it might help if the boys roomed together? Although, we have plenty of space, and he can have his own room or stay with you, if you prefer."

Viv hands me a coffee, taking a seat on the couch next to me.

"Mommy, look what Bodhi got me!" Easton comes bounding over, holding out a Hot Wheels set.

"Awesome. Did you say thank you to Lori?"

"Thank you, Lori." Easton leans down, kissing her cheek. "I love it so much."

"Bodhi picked it out for you."

"My brother made a good choice." He runs back to Bodhi, sinking onto the floor.

"He's a very confident little boy," Lori remarks. "I think he'll help to bring Bodhi out of his shell."

"Reeve was very quiet as a kid," Vivien remarks, sipping her coffee. "Then he got to eight or nine, and it was like he suddenly found his voice."

"How did he take the news?" I ask Lori, watching Bodhi smile at something Easton says.

"He was happy to hear he has a cousin but sad he never got to meet his daddy."

"What did you tell him about Saffron?" Vivien asks.

"I told him she was sick and couldn't take care of him and I was desperate to love him so I adopted him and he came to live with me and Travis."

"Travis signed the paperwork," Vivien confirms. "Carson called this morning to confirm he has legally relinquished all of his parental rights."

"I'm so disgusted with him. It was one thing to abandon me but quite another to walk out on Bodhi. He was only three, so he barely even remembers him now." She purses her lips. "I'm glad he didn't challenge it. At least it makes it a little easier."

"Vivien." Bodhi clears his throat, standing in front of Viv with two red spots on his cheeks and his hands behind his back. He looks to Lori and she smiles, nodding in encouragement. "This is for you." He whips a rose from behind his back —a lavender rose—and hands it to Vivien.

Her hand shakes as she takes it from him, but she keeps her composure as she smiles at him. "Thank you so much, Bodhi. It's beautiful." He flushes, looking at his mum before racing back to join Easton.

Vivien stares at the flower in shock, and I slide my arm around her shoulder. Viv glances at Lori. "How did he know Reeve used to give me lavender roses?"

Lori's eyes widen. "He did?"

Viv nods.

"Well, I'll be damned." A smile graces Lori's mouth. "I'm a keen gardener, and I have a few red rose bushes out in the backyard. Bodhi was playing out there just before you arrived, and it was the strangest thing, but that rose was in the middle of one of the bushes. He stared at it for ages, and then he asked me if he could give it to you." She wipes a tear from her eye. "I think Reeve is looking out for him. Looking out for all of us, and that's his way of saying he approves."

"How much longer is this going to take?" I ask Carson Park, leaning back in my chair, having a hard time not snarling at the guy. I've never been overly fond of the dick, but since we discovered he knew about Bodhi and continued to keep it a secret after Reeve died, I have zero time for him. The only reason we're using him to manage the adoption is because he's been involved from the very start and he has paperwork which was supposed to help speed up the process.

"I'm pushing it through as fast as I can, Dillon, but there is a lot of red tape and a lot of procedures to comply with. These measures are in place to protect children, and we can't cut corners."

"We're running out of time," Vivien says. "Lori may not last the week. I'm concerned about Saffron making a play for Bodhi if we don't get it finalized before Lori passes."

It's been four weeks since Lori and Bodhi moved into our place, and her health has been steadily declining. She can't get out of bed anymore, and we have a medical team watching her twenty-four-seven. Bodhi is getting more and more withdrawn. It's been tough for the little guy.

Easton is helping. A lot. They formed an instant bond, and when Bodhi is feeling sad, Easton always knows how to cheer him up. Bodhi is cautious around Vivien and me, but he's never rude or disrespectful. He's a very well-mannered kid.

"Try not to worry. Dillon is Bodhi's uncle, and Easton is his cousin. You are Reeve's widow. You have the means to take care of him and the support of his adoptive mother. You have passed the family assessment process. Saffron Roberts has had no contact with her son, and she relinquished her rights at the time of the birth. Even if she does try something, I doubt she would get custody. She works in the porn industry, and she's a known drug addict."

"You don't know how manipulative and cunning she is," I say, kicking one heel up onto the table 'cause I know it will piss the dickhead off.

"Or how much she hates me," Vivien adds.

Carson narrows his eyes on my foot as the phone on his desk rings. He gets up from the meeting table and answers the call, listening to whoever is on the other end, nodding. He looks up, his gaze darting between me and Viv as shock registers on his face. I drop my foot to the ground and sit up straighter in my chair as he ends the call and returns to the table.

"Well, we've just gotten one piece of good news." He rests his palms on the table in front of us. "That was a police contact friend of mine. This isn't public knowledge yet, but Saffron Roberts OD'd last night. She was officially pronounced dead two hours ago."

Lori passed away three days before Thanksgiving and two days after we became Bodhi's legal adoptive parents. Bodhi was inconsolable, and it was hard to bear witness to his grief. Watching him go through what Vivien and Easton had endured was hard, but we got him through it.

The four of us built an additional bench in the memorial garden for Lori, and I nailed a plaque up beside the one for Lainey and Reeve. Our project manager has been given strict instructions to ensure it's taken with us to the new house. I've no idea how they'll uproot and replant the tree, but we're paying him enough fucking money to make it happen. He burst out laughing when I told him we want a lake with swans —until he realized I was serious, and then he nearly passed out.

The work on our new family home is progressing well, and we're hoping to be in by the end of the summer because we have a new addition to the family on the way. Vivien surprised me on Valentine's Day with the news she was pregnant, and we're expecting a daughter in early November.

We were concerned about telling Bodhi, worried it would make him more unsettled, but if anything, it has helped. He's seeing a therapist too. The same woman who helped Easton deal with his grief, and gradually he is opening up to her. Vivien or I sit in on the sessions so he has someone familiar to support him as he deals with his emotions.

Easton is very excited for the new baby, and his enthusiasm spread to his older brother, and it helped to distract him from his grief. Every night, the three of us sing to Vivien's expanding belly, much to her obvious delight. Her pregnancy is moving fast, and I can't wait to meet our little girl in four months' time.

"Where are the little monsters?" I ask, stepping into the kitchen when I arrive home from work. We've delayed our European tour indefinitely now, choosing to focus on new music instead. We're still using the recording studio at my house, but I'm having it extended once we get this album wrapped. We have decided to set up our own label when our contract expires next year, and we're going to use my house as the base. We have an architect drawing up plans to remodel it so it's fit for purpose.

"Out in the treehouse," Vivien says, sniffling. She's

standing at the window, staring out at the garden with her back to me.

I slide up behind her, circling my arms around her swollen belly. "What's wrong, sweetheart?" She has had some emotional moments recently, and I know she's remembering Lainey and worrying everything will be okay. I'm trying my best to assure her, but I know she won't fully relax until she's holding our beautiful little girl in her arms.

"Nothing," she says, almost choking on a sob. She whirls around in my arms, smiling at me through blurry eyes. "These are happy tears," she adds, seeing my concern.

"Are you sure?" I kiss her softly.

"Bodhi called me Mommy Vivien." More tears fall down her cheeks. "It was the most amazing feeling in the world. I'm so happy."

"He loves you, Hollywood. Just like we all do." I press another sweet kiss to her lips, which is hugely at odds with how I've been devouring her mouth lately. Pregnant Vivien is horny as fuck, and we're going at it like rabbits any chance we can get. I have sex on the brain permanently, and I couldn't be more in love with my wife, or my life, if I tried.

"I love him so much," she says. "I can't believe I was ever worried that I wouldn't. He's the missing piece we didn't realize we needed."

"And our daughter will be the cherry on top." I tilt her gorgeous face up, staring at her in awe, amazed that with every passing day I love her more and more. "Thank you for making my world complete, Vivien. Thank you for letting me love you."

EPILOGUE

VIVIEN - NOW

THE AFTER-PARTY IS in full swing at the plush five-star hotel the label rented for the occasion, and the room is packed with well-wishers, family and friends, and industry heads. I'm proud of our movie even if it was painful to sit in the theater knowing everyone was dissecting some of the most heartbreaking and intimate moments of our lives.

But it feels cathartic too. Everyone knows the truth now. The good, the bad, and the ugly, and they can decide what they want to do with that themselves.

"For the woman of the hour," Ash says, materializing at my side, offering me a glass of champagne.

I shake my head and hold up a hand. "I'm abstaining. That glass I had earlier went straight to my head. That's what I get for hardly eating all week."

"I need to live vicariously through someone," she pouts, running a hand over her growing belly. "Hurry up and get here, little monster, so your mummy can have an alcoholic drink!"

I smile at my sister-in-law because I know she's joking. Ash adores being pregnant, and she is positively glowing. It took them some time to conceive, but her pregnancy has been smooth sailing so far. They are both very excited, and I'm thrilled for them. I can't wait to meet my new niece or nephew.

"I'm happy to help," Audrey cuts in. She drains the dregs of her current glass of champagne, sets it down on the high table behind us, and plucks the fresh glass from Ash's hand.

"I thought you were still breastfeeding," Ash says.

"Nope. Emily is taking formula now, and as it's Alex's turn to do the night feed tonight, this mommy is partying to the max!" Audrey gave birth to their first child four months ago, and Ash is due in three months' time. Our daughter, Fleur Belle Lancaster-O'Donoghue, is twenty-one months old now and the apple of her daddy's eye. I love that my daughter will have a ready-made friend in Emily and her new little cousin, and she has two older brothers who dote on her.

"You must be relieved the movie was so well received," Ash says.

"I am, and I love that it was a true family affair." I wrote the screenplay. Studio 27 made the movie. Dillon and I were executive producers, Mom played herself, Dad directed, and Collateral Damage recorded a number of new songs specifically for the movie soundtrack.

Easton played Reeve in a couple of scenes, and I couldn't stop the tears from flowing during those parts of the movie. We had asked Bodhi if he wanted to share the role of young Reeve, but he is more of an introvert than Easton, and he turned pale at the thought.

"It makes it more special," Ash agrees, glancing over her shoulder to where the guys are chatting.

I look over, and Dillon's bright blue eyes lock on mine. He mouths, "I love you."

I blow him a kiss, admiring how hot he looks in his suit. Waves of white-blond hair tumble over his brow, and nobody would ever believe he turned thirty in January. He is so unbelievably gorgeous, and every time I look at him, I'm reminded of the young guy I met in Dublin who showed me how to let go of my reservations and truly live.

"Earth to Vivien." Ash waves her hands in front of my face before poking her tongue at her brother. "You two are always sending googly eyes at one another. It's disgustingly adorable."

"We have fought hard for our love. I never want to take it, or him, for granted." I'm feeling especially emotional after watching my life with both my loves play out on the screen. "I'm relieved I got through tonight without puking," I truthfully admit. "Dillon will tell you I've been a hot mess all week. I could barely sleep or eat, worrying if I'd done the right thing."

"That's understandable." Audrey knocks back her champagne like it's water. "You have serious lady balls, my friend. I'm not sure I could have opened my heart and my life for the entire world to see."

"It hasn't been easy, and I've been panicking all week that I made the wrong call. I have a responsibility to both my loves and my children to do right by them, and I was plagued with last-minute doubts."

Dillon has been repeatedly talking me off a ledge all week long. He is my rock, and I know I couldn't have done this without his support and his permission. He wasn't sure when I first broached the subject, until he read my book, and then he told me I had to do it.

"That's completely natural. I would've been the same." Ash gives me a quick hug.

"I was shaking like a leaf on the red carpet, and when those women hurled their accusations, it sent me reeling back in time. It was like Reeve had only just died, and I felt the pressure sitting on my chest again."

"I can't believe the nerve of those bitches. I thought that was all behind us," Ash says.

"I knew what I was getting into when I chose to make this movie. I knew it would dredge up good memories as well as bad, and I knew it would bring the crazies crawling out of the woodwork. This is only the beginning too."

"Do you regret it?" Audrey asks.

I don't have to think about it. "No. So much has been said over the years that is incorrect, and I wanted, *needed*, to set the record straight. I know there will be people who won't ever understand, people who will probably hate me more after this, but I didn't do it for them. I did it for me. For Dillon. For Reeve. But most of all, I did it for the kids. I hope when Easton and Bodhi are older they will understand how I came to love both their dads. I want them to know the true story, not the twisted version that will forever remain on the internet."

After we adopted Bodhi, we filed the relevant paperwork to have his birth certificate changed. While Lori will always be Bodhi's mom, and we do what we can to nurture her memory and ensure he never forgets her, his biological parents were Reeve and Saffron, and that needed to be officially documented, for a number of reasons. One of them is so Dillon could transfer his half of the Lancaster inheritance to Bodhi.

At the same time, we got Easton's birth certificate altered to list Dillon as his father.

We had a dilemma then in terms of our family name. The changes we made meant Bodhi became a Lancaster and Easton became an O'Donoghue. But Reeve is still Easton's other daddy, and we promised we would never take that from him. Bodhi and Easton are brothers, in every way that counts, and we didn't want them having different last names. Also, Dillon's US citizenship was proclaimed around the same time, and his birth certificate now confirms Felicia Lancaster and Simon Lancaster as his bio parents. Technically, in the eyes of the law, Dillon is a Lancaster. Which means I'm still a Lancaster too.

For me, the solution was simple: Lancaster-O'Donoghue. But I knew it wouldn't be as easy for Dillon because of what Simon Lancaster had done to him. However, my husband surprised me when he readily agreed. For him, the decision was simple too. He loves our sons enough to put aside his own feelings to do what we both felt was right. Plus, the Lancaster name is a way to remember Reeve and Felicia, and none of us want to forget them.

So, now we are all Lancaster-O'Donoghues, and it feels right. The press and the haters had a field day when that news broke, but they can all kiss my ass.

"Uh-oh." Ash looks over her shoulder, and I turn around.

Dillon is jabbing his finger in Deke Rawlings' face, looking like he's seconds away from punching him in the nose. Deke is the head of security for Studio 27, and he was in charge of security for tonight's premiere. Ultimately, it's his fault those women slipped through the net and were able to harass me on a night that was already going to be difficult enough. I'm not surprised Dillon is tearing strips off him. I'm only surprised my dad isn't joining in.

My parents are around here somewhere, along with all our Irish family. Conor even graced us with his presence, and he brought a date too. He's the only remaining single member of Collateral Damage now that Ro tied the knot.

Ronan shocked the whole family when he returned from a weekend in Las Vegas married to Shania Webster—an up-and-coming name on the country music scene. Apparently, it was love at first sight. The guys had bets on how long it would be before they broke up, but it's been seven months, and they seem more in love than ever.

I'm happy for Ronan.

He deserves love in his life after the ordeal he's been through with his ex, Clodagh, over access to his daughter Emer. Things are good between him and Dillon again, but they're not quite as close as they once were, which makes me a little sad.

"I think you should get over there," Audrey says, pulling me out of my inner monologue. "Dillon looks like he's about to commit murder."

My husband has fistfuls of Deke's jacket now, and he's shoving him up against the wall. I spot several security guards getting ready to move in, so I walk toward them to defuse the situation.

As the temporary caretaker of the Lancaster shares in Studio 27, I need to ensure amicable relations continue. From the way Reeve's will was constructed, the forty percent stake in Studio 27 will now pass to Bodhi when he turns eighteen. It's why it made sense to have the company produce our movie. If it's as profitable as the analysts expect it to be, it will significantly enhance the value of Bodhi's investment.

So, it's a win-win all around.

"Dillon." I place my hand on my husband's arm. "This isn't the time or the place." I fully intend to request an investigation into how this happened, but I don't want anything to put a stain on tonight.

"Learn to own up and accept responsibility," Dillon growls, glaring at the man as he releases him. "And if you ever put my wife in that kind of position again, I will punch first and ask questions later."

"I'll find out how it happened and ensure it doesn't happen again." Deke smooths a hand down the front of his tuxedo jacket as he turns to me. "I apologize for any upset, Vivien."

"We'll discuss it next week," I curtly reply.

I don't have a controlling interest in the studio, and I'm not on the board of management, but I will be strongly advising James—the current head of Studio 27—to let the incompetent Rawlings go. James listens to me, and I was thrilled when he agreed to let me adopt a special child ambassador role. It's something I'm working on pitching in a more official capacity within the industry.

Having seen what Reeve went through, and becoming more familiar with the stresses and pressures placed on child and teen actors, I want to help to create a better working environment for kids who act. I also want to ensure that when the Studio 27 shares pass to Bodhi he is inheriting a production company that is not only profitable but one that sets and maintains high standards extolling family values and a nurturing environment where child actors thrive without unnecessary responsibility, stress, or peer pressure.

Safeguarding children within the movie industry is something I am very passionate about, and I've spoken to Dillon about creating a company in Reeve's name. Some kind of governance or regulatory body with a set of guidelines every studio would have to adhere to. It's only an idea right now, but it's something I'm invested in exploring and developing at some point.

Rawlings walks off, feeling the daggers Dillon is embedding in his back, no doubt.

"I can't stand that prick," Dillon seethes.

"I think everyone in the room can see that, and I think the feeling is mutual." My lips twitch. Dillon has been breathing down Rawlings' neck for the past week, wanting to know all the security measures in place. Deke isn't the kind of man who appreciates being put on the spot or being challenged, so they've been butting heads nonstop. "Come dance with me." I take his hand, leading him out onto the dance floor as the song changes, and a slow number begins to play.

I wrap my arms around my husband's neck as he pulls me in close, placing his palms on my hips.

"Are the kids okay?"

I nod. "I just spoke to Charlotte. They are all sound asleep. The boys are in East's room."

Dillon chuckles as we move in sync to each other and the soft, sultry beat. "I don't know why we bothered giving them separate bedrooms when they always sleep together."

"It was important they each had their own space, but I love they're so close. It warms my heart to see them together." When we moved into our new home in the Hollywood Hills, we had adjoining rooms built for the boys, but we put twin beds in both rooms because they love rooming together. Now, they alternate between the rooms, making them happy, and that's the main thing.

"Yeah. Me too." Dillon smiles. "Sometimes, when I look at them, I imagine that's what it would've been like if Reeve and I had grown up together." There are only six months between Bodhi and Easton, and they look so alike they could easily pass for twins.

A veil of sadness shrouds his face, and I feel it deep in my heart too. "I think the same way on occasion." I cup his face. "Are you okay?" This is the first opportunity I've had to speak to my husband alone since we left the theater. Everyone has wanted a piece of us, and it's been exhausting. I'm just about ready to call it a night and go home to my kids.

"I should be asking you that." He leans down, kissing me softly. "I know watching it, with an audience, can't have been easy."

"It wasn't, but I'm glad we did it. I just hope the people who turned on Reeve, after they discovered the truth about Bodhi, understand him a little better now. I want people to see he wasn't a bad person. I want people to know his actions were driven by love. It may have been misguided and wrong, but he was tragically flawed, like we all are in some way. I hope people see the damage that abandonment and neglect can cause. He craved love and acceptance his whole life, and it twisted his reality of things."

"It twisted mine too." Dillon moves us around the dance floor, swaying us in time to the music.

"It did, but you overcame it because you had a loving family to help keep you on the right path and you were more self-aware. When the chips were down, you did what you had to do to be there for me and Easton. You accepted your responsibilities and fully owned them in a way Reeve didn't do."

"Seeing your childhood play out on the screen helped me to put the last few things into perspective."

"In what way?"

"I see what you've been saying all along. He was a part of you the same way you were a part of him. Watching those scenes, rather than just reading about them, really made it come alive. I understand it better now. I understand how it was you came to love each other and how it was he came to rely on you so much."

"I love it out here in the moonlight," I say, nestling into Dillon's side on the stone bench. I tilt my head up. "Look at all the stars."

"It would be so much more romantic with a lake and swans." I hear the pout in his tone and see it on his face under the illumination of the moon and the dim nightlights dotted around the memorial garden.

"We'll have our swans when the kids are older," I reassure him, resting my chin on his shoulder. We decided to forgo our plans for a lake with swans because it's not really advisable to have either when you have young kids. Dillon was really hung up on the idea, so it's a bit of a sore point.

He peers deep into my eyes as he links our hands. "Do you still feel him around?"

I told Dillon how I feel Reeve is still with me, explaining the instances where I've felt his presence. We're both still shocked over Bodhi and the rose that day we first met. I know some people don't believe in an afterlife or spirits or that our loved ones look after us when they are gone, but there is nothing anyone could say that would convince me that wasn't Reeve's work. "Not in a long time." I snuggle in closer to him. "I like to think it's because he sees how happy I am and he knows I don't need that reassurance or comfort anymore."

"I bet it makes him happy too. To know his two boys are with the love of his life, like he always wanted."

"And with you." I clasp his face in my hands, kissing him passionately. "If there was anyone Reeve would have trusted me with, it's you." I lower my hands to my lap, threading my fingers through Dillon's.

"I will always be sad that I never got to know him."

"And I will always miss him, but this is the way it was supposed to be, Dillon. I truly believe that now." I've given it a lot of thought these past few weeks as we prepared to premiere the movie. I don't understand why I had to lose Reeve and Lainey, but I do believe it was preordained. In a lot of ways, that makes me so freaking angry, but in other ways it helps me to accept it. "I think I was destined to love Reeve because his fate was already decided. I'm glad he got to experience my love for the short time he was with us. That he got to experience fatherhood and the kind of family he always craved."

"I'm glad he had you too." He laughs softly. "Man, I never thought I'd ever say those words, but I can't be selfish. Not when I get to spend the rest of my life loving you, Easton, Bodhi, and Fleur."

"Do you think you have room in your heart for one more?" I run my fingers through his hair.

He straightens up, his eyes popping wide. "Do you mean?"

"I'm pregnant again," I blurt, unable to keep the news in any longer. "I did a test this morning and then another one just to be sure."

He places his hands on my belly and tears glisten in his eyes. "You have no idea how happy this makes me. Another kid. Yes!" His eyes light up with sheer happiness. "Thank you, sweetheart." He examines my face carefully. "Are you feeling okay?"

"I'm fine, apart from being tired, but that's more than likely down to not sleeping well all week."

"We should go to bed, but I just need to hold you first." He reels me into his arms, pressing fierce kisses into my hair as he hugs me close. I melt against him, loving the security and familiarity of being in his embrace. If I'm having a bad day, all I need is a hug from Dillon to make everything all right again. "Thank you, Vivien Grace. Thank you for this life we lead. I never take it for granted. I hope you know that."

"I know," I say, fighting a yawn. "And I don't either. I cherish every day with you and our children."

Dillon stands, pulling me with him. "Time for bed. It's been an exhausting day."

"You can say that again." I lean my head against his shoulder as his arm slides around my back.

As we walk away, a subtle breeze appears out of nowhere, swirling around me, moving wispy strands of my hair. The strong, sweet fragrance of lavender roses tickles my nostrils even though there are none in this part of our garden. Invisible fingers sweep across my cheek, and I know he's here. Tears pool in my eyes, but they are happy tears because I know, in my heart and soul, this is Reeve's way of telling me he will always be with me.

It was never a competition between my loves.

I have loved Reeve and Dillon with my whole heart, and it will forever belong to both of them.

They were always destined to be mine, and I will live out the rest of my days safe in the knowledge they are both with me.

My first love.

And my forever love.

Would you like to read another emotional, angsty new adult romance from me? Check out *When Forever Changes, Inseparable,*

Surviving Amber Springs or *Only Ever You*. Available in e-book, paperback, and audiobook format.

Subscribe to my newsletter to claim a free e-book and be the first to hear about new releases and sales. Type this link into your browser: http://eepurl.com/dl4l5v

WHEN FOREVER CHANGES
#1 NEW ADULT & COLLEGE ROMANCE BESTSELLER

Gabby

Looking back, I should have seen the signs. Perhaps I did, but I subconsciously chose to ignore them.

From the time I was ten, when I first met Dylan, I knew he was my forever guy. Back then, I couldn't put words to what I was feeling, but, as the years progressed, I came to recognize it for what it was—soul-deep love. The kind only very few people ever get to experience.

Dylan was more than just my best friend, my childhood sweetheart, my lover. He was my soul mate. We were carved from the same whole—destined to be together forever.

Until he changed.

And I believed I was no longer good enough.

Until he shattered me so completely, it felt like I ceased to exist.

And I'd never experienced such heart-crushing pain.

Until he leveled me a second time, and I truly wanted to die.

But I had to stay strong because I wasn't alone in this cruel twist of fate.

I look to the sky, pleading with the stars, begging someone to tell me what I should do because I don't know how to deal with this. I don't know how to cope when my forever has changed, and I can't help wondering if I had seen the signs earlier, if I'd pushed him, would it have been enough to save us?

Or had fate already decided to alter our forever?

Available in e-book, paperback and audiobook format.

ABOUT THE AUTHOR

USA Today bestselling author **Siobhan Davis** writes emotionally intense young adult and new adult fiction with swoonworthy romance, complex characters, and tons of unexpected plot twists and turns that will have you flipping the pages beyond bedtime!

Siobhan's family will tell you she's a little bit obsessive when it comes to reading and writing, and they aren't wrong. She can rarely be found without her trusty Kindle, a paperback book, or her laptop somewhere close at hand.

Prior to becoming a full-time writer, Siobhan forged a successful corporate career in human resource management.

She resides in the Garden County of Ireland with her husband and two sons.

You can connect with Siobhan in the following ways:
Author Website: www.siobhandavis.com
Facebook: AuthorSiobhanDavis
Twitter: @siobhandavis
Instagram: @siobhandavisauthor
Email: siobhan@siobhandavis.com

NEVER MISS A NEW RELEASE:
Follow Siobhan on Amazon
Follow Siobhan on BookBub

BOOKS BY SIOBHAN DAVIS

KENNEDY BOYS SERIES

Upper Young Adult/New Adult Contemporary Romance

Finding Kyler

Losing Kyler

Keeping Kyler

The Irish Getaway

Loving Kalvin

Saving Brad

Seducing Kaden

Forgiving Keven

Summer in Nantucket

Releasing Keanu

Adoring Keaton

Reforming Kent

STANDALONES

New Adult Contemporary Romance

Inseparable

Incognito

When Forever Changes

No Feelings Involved

Only Ever You

Second Chances Box Set

Reverse Harem Contemporary Romance

Surviving Amber Springs

Dark Mafia Romance

Condemned to Love

RYDEVILLE ELITE SERIES
Dark High School Romance

Cruel Intentions
Twisted Betrayal
Sweet Retribution
Charlie
Jackson
Sawyer*
*Drew^*

THE SAINTHOOD (BOYS OF LOWELL HIGH)
Dark HS Reverse Harem Romance

Resurrection
Rebellion
Reign
The Sainthood: The Complete Series

ALL OF ME DUET
Angsty New Adult Romance

Say I'm The One
Let Me Love You

ALINTHIA SERIES

Upper YA/NA Paranormal Romance/Reverse Harem

The Lost Savior

The Secret Heir

The Warrior Princess

The Chosen One

*The Rightful Queen**

TRUE CALLING SERIES

Young Adult Science Fiction/Dystopian Romance

True Calling

Lovestruck

Beyond Reach

Light of a Thousand Stars

Destiny Rising

Short Story Collection

True Calling Series Collection

SAVEN SERIES

Young Adult Science Fiction/Paranormal Romance

Saven Deception

Logan

Saven Disclosure

Saven Denial

Saven Defiance

Axton

Saven Deliverance

Saven: The Complete Series

*Coming 2021

^Release date to be confirmed

Visit www.siobhandavis.com for all future release dates. Please note release dates are subject to change based on reader demand and the author's schedule. Subscribing to the author's newsletter or following her on Facebook is the best way to stay updated with planned new releases.

Printed in Great Britain
by Amazon